IN PLAIN SIGHT

By the same author in the Lincolnshire Murder Mystery Series

Dead Spit
Seaside Snatch
Once Bitten
Dead Jealous
Or Not To Be
Twelve Days
Sacrificial Lamb

You can contact the author by e-mail at:
carysmithwriter@yahoo.co.uk

AN INGA LARSSON NOVEL

IN PLAIN SIGHT

Lincolnshire Murder Mystery No 8

Cary Smith

IN PLAIN SIGHT
Copyright © 2018 Cary Smith

All rights reserved, including the right to reproduce this book, or portions thereof in any form. No part of this text may be reproduced, transmitted, downloaded, decompiled, reverse engineered, or stored, in any form or introduced into any information storage and retrieval system, in any form or by any means, whether electronic or mechanical without the express written permission of the author.

This is a work of fiction. Names and characters are the product of the author's imagination and any resemblance to actual persons, living or dead, is entirely coincidental.

The views expressed in this work are solely those of the author and do not necessarily reflect the views of the publisher, and the publisher hereby disclaims any responsibility for them.

ISBN: 978-0-244-99615-4

PublishNation, London
www.publishnation.co.uk

There is more stupidity
than hydrogen in the universe,
and it has a longer shelf life.

Frank Zappa

August 2006

The early morning silky sunlight had begun to filter through the kitchen window highlighting views out to the lawn, flowers and vegetables in the moderately well-tended back garden of the post-war semi.

As white fluffy clouds in a cluster drifted slowly by, pasty faced Kathleen Streeter was sat slumped on her green kitchen chair at the wooden table, of no mind to notice or savour whatever the weatherman had in store. Were it to snow the self-absorbed woman would just never have noticed, all wrapped up in morbid thoughts had she so quickly become preoccupied by.

The poor woman was in no mood to spot the myriad of tiny insects scampering up and down invisible threads of gossamer outdoors.

Hands clasped tightly together in her lap just looking at but not truly seeing the partly burnt toast she had spread badly with what her mother had still called margarine long after new names became all the rage.

The half empty jar of Somerfield own label thick-cut marmalade was stood in front of her waiting to be useful. When she was young Kathleen used to lather her toast at weekends with Sandwich Spread and her mother would make her sandwiches with it on. How long was it since she'd bought a jar?

In truth Kathleen was in no mood for thoughts of yesteryear, or what she might spread on her over-toasted wholemeal she'd made more through decades of habit than any real desire.

A glance at the old clock on the wall in need of a dust, told her it was eight twenty five after she'd taken off the five minutes she always set clocks forward in her house. How long had she been going through such a rigmarole? Be back when she worked at the mini-market and missed her bus once or twice.

Been a good hour or more now since that ghastly Thomasz had phoned. Why could her Christine not see what he was like? How on earth had she allowed herself be taken in by the likes of him? The merest thought of just being within touching distance of the hideous creature filled Kathleen with absolute shivers of horror.

"Is Chrissie with you by any chance?" he'd asked in the deep gruff accented way of his, as if it was ever likely to happen. Christine had more sense than to visit her mother for she knew what she'd have to say about the lazy sod and the despicable shoddy life the pair were leading.

Why wasn't he there at home looking after her Christine, is what Kathleen wanted to know? What on earth did a grown man find in the least bit attractive or even interesting in the slightest about sitting on a damp river bank all night in the dark trying to catch a tiddler he'd no doubt toss back anyway?

She knew whoever it was who had first said fishing is a hook at one end and a fool at the other certainly got it spot on with this Thomasz.

But then having said that, what about her Bill? How had he ever get mixed up with all his stupid war games nonsense now controlling his whole life? What happens in men's brains Kathleen wanted to know to turn somebody like her Bill for whom she had been so proud of once upon a time, into a lazy useless great boring lump?

Likewise, what had Christine ever hoped to gain by getting herself mixed up with the waste of space which was Thomasz Borowiak? Like father, like daughter.

And another thing. What a stupid way to spell an ordinary simple name.

Such high hopes Kathleen had for her only daughter at one time with her good grades, then as if she was absolutely determined to let herself down it all just went to pot. She'd seemed so happy at the Forest School, had a whole bunch of good friends apparently and thoroughly enjoyed such firm relationships with so many of the teachers. Kathleen had often wondered how it had all gone so wrong, so badly wrong to result in her only daughter entering lengthy periods of surly moods when she had no real desire to go to school.

A bright caring and loving young lady she was so proud of for so long. Now what?

Kathleen's musings and worrying came to a sudden halt when the back door suddenly opened and in strolled husband Bill in filthy baggy jeans without a care in the world. The man she had unashamedly once truly loved with an absolute passion, a man who could so effortlessly at one time stir the innermost naughty feelings and cause her to erupt out of character with absolute total satisfaction.

Where had her true happiness and contentment wandered off to?

Now Kathleen felt herself flinch just at the sight and increasingly the smell of him.

Bill the man, if she were really honest with herself, she could not now stand to even touch her. To be fair the touching, the intimate touching was thank God a very much now and again event she'd avoid at all costs if she could. Just the thought of this dirty old man in need of a shower groping about would make her shudder with revulsion.

Whether he made a right hash of stroking her or a clumsy effort at what he thought was foreplay, she'd do all she could to steer clear if she spied the merest of hints somewhere down the line. The longer the sexual drought continued so much the better.

'Nothing so far,' she said to him as he was shutting the door. Bill Streeter had been to the local Co-op store as he did most Saturday mornings to buy a paper. Bit of a stroll up there and back always took him going on for twenty minutes or so, providing of course he didn't meet someone he could bore the pants off.

How typical she had thought. Concern over their daughter's whereabouts and he just shoves it all to one side as if it is utterly inconsequential to take a leisurely walk to buy a damn paper.

'Sorry?' he grimaced with his mind no doubt off somewhere else engaged in sporting trivia or some other political nonsense from the rag in his hand.

'Christine,' she had to remind him. 'He hasn't phoned back of course.'

'You know what her's like.'

'Exactly. And that's what worries me.'

'She'll no tie this one to her apron strings I've told you before, pet,' said Bill and she wondered if it was a snide remark about her. Kathleen was not at all sure which was worse. A fish wife or Owls widow like her friend Amanda. Both were certainly better than the nonsense she was stuck with.

At least Amanda knew where her husband was. Not real owls of course; hers were the Sheffield Wednesday kind, who hell or high water, rain or shine there was Ian Chambers. He'd no doubt be shouting at Hillsborough later on or any other place infested with football fans once a week now the season had begun.

Kathleen also knew boozy Chambers would be amongst those desperate for a pint or two before and after the match in some dragged-down pub.

'Look at the time,' Kathleen suggested but only she bothered to glance.

'Prob'ly gone to do classes by now should imagine and I bet she were out with those pals of hers. You know what some o'them are like on a Friday night these days. Getting themselves bloody hammered as fast as they can, then off tottering about with those clones I bet she mixes with. What's the chance of a coffee?' useless lump Bill said as he just plonked his big arse down on the other chair and began to scan the back page of the *Daily Express*.

Kathleen looked at him just sat there in his grubby Battle of Waterloo sweatshirt as she struggled to her feet, leaving the toast just sat there looking all forlorn and unwanted still waiting for sight of the thick-cut. Bill she knew was just talking hogwash as was frequently the case. Their Christine had never been one to go gallivanting about to the likes of pubs and clubs or any of those ghastly places. Not be a fat cow waddling home stuffed full of cheap kebab. Just shows how much he knew about his own daughter. Typical.

One thing amongst Kathleen's thoughts still awash with Christine, was how this was Saturday morning, one of the good days for her. She'd be alone, on her own on a non work day to do exactly what she wished to do without a shadow of complaint from the lump of lard sat there.

He'd be off to his stupid war games, be gone in an hour or two, then when he'd had his fill of fighting some ridiculous battle, home he'd trudge and if luck was against her this week he'd think he had a divine right get her out of her pyjama bottoms. At the end of the day for Kathleen these wars he fought only ever had bad results if he'd won some stupid battle.

She'd never been a joiner and had certainly never signed up for exercise classes, not even those her daughter ran tirelessly. With him out of sight and out of mind for hours it would be Kathleen who would normally enjoy her own form of escapism, but on this occasion just wished she could break free of the gnawing pain about her daughter Christine.

'Not like her not to get home,' she said to the wall as she flicked down the switch on the green kettle. She'd have to bung that sweatshirt in with the washing if he'd ever take it off.

'It were Friday,' he sniggered. 'Clue's in the day. Who on earth started this getting pissed up on a Friday I wonder?'

'When were the last time Christine went out drinking?'

'How should I know?'

'I'm gonna call him,' said Kathleen and turned.

'Coffee?' he shot at her.

Kathleen lifted the cream handset from the wall mounted phone, tapped numbers, phone to ear, elbow resting in the cup of her other hand.

'Thomasz?'

'Y'awright?'

'Any news?'

'Nothun.'

'Where was she going?'

'Dunno. Didn't tell me like, but then what else is new eh?' he sniggered.

'You've checked everybody?'

'Far as I know.'

'What about her lessons this morning?'

'Not be there yet will they?'

'Hospital. What about the Hospital?'

'Why?' he sniggered.

'Just in case…you never know.'

'Just in case what?'

'Something's happened. Thomasz, you need to phone the County. You got their number?'

'Be at her mates I bet, go straight from there reckon.'

'You tried them?'

'One or two.'

'Was she with 'em?' she almost demanded.

'Said not,' was no surprise to Kathleen.

'What now?'

'She'll turn up. Could've fell asleep in the loo, heard it's happened like.'

'What are you on about?' she wanted to scream as the anger deep inside increased.

'Heard 'bout this fella what fell asleep sat on the lav in some place, finished up there all night. How daft was that eh?'

'What place?'

'How the hell should I know you stupid cow?'

Kathleen Streeter just looked at the receiver in her hand for a moment and slammed it back onto the rest, it fell off and was left dangling on the coiled curly cable. She lifted it back up and plopped it into place. 'Please…no!' she shouted as she gasped in a breath.

'Coffee? Or have you forgotten already?'

'Just shut up you stupid man!' she screamed to produce a visual sneer in return.

June 2017

There was always music. All who knew Charlotte Elliott were aware they'd have to contend with her choice whenever they visited. Eclectic and certainly loud, raucous and indeed quite often far too much bass of the depth to keep neighbours awake at night.

Changed over the years of course, and frequently in tune with her moods. From her youthful enthusiasm for the likes of Beyonce now she had matured in a place of her very own to Skepta and Joy Division or Free and pleased not have some farting bloke moaning all the while.

Charlotte had all Kanye West's albums lined up in release order on her completely full rack she'd pick and choose from, with the very latest fave just sitting on the top.

No music tonight with other thoughts in control of her mind. Lottie just felt so absolutely crap and the problem she'd had since leaving the pub was not something even the tonal quality of Adele's phrasing could cure. Just had to be what she'd eaten, but for the life of her couldn't fathom what it might have been, with the last thing she remembered through the haze scoffing down was a blueberry muffin before she'd hurried off to the bar.

The chicken and stuffing sarnie she'd had for lunch and the crisps perhaps? Can't be surely, that was hours ago, although she knew chicken can often be a bit funny. If it was, she'd sue bloody Asda.

Her plan had been to grab a bucket of KFC or a kebab from the fat foreign guy on the corner on her way home. Her mistake. Just one bloody muffin had not been enough to soak the alcohol she guessed and now she felt absolutely wretched.

Charlotte knew something was seriously wrong with her guts despite the state she was in. Please no, not A&E at night, not joining all the punch drunks and old folk, the tarts with broken nails, blisters on their feet and kids spreading measles the poor medics hate clogging up their system.

She'd wait a bit Charlotte decided; the rotten guts ache's sure to ease soon. Worse thing you can do is get a nasty look from the triage nurse for wasting their precious time.

Her next thought was, had the wine in the bar been off? Had it gone bad, can wines do that? Can you get rotten wine, not being French might make it dodgy to drink, be more likely to rot your guts? Charlotte remembered she'd just asked for white wine like normal, but what if it was some cheap-jack stuff from one of those odd places. Be Uzbekistan, maybe what they call it…Kyrgy…whatever.

Felt so sorry for Steph having to remove herself post haste from the lass's leaving do before she spewed vomit all down her blouse. She'd buy her good friend flowers to say sorry once this bloody pain was gone, with her saying she'd look out for any jobs going once she's settled in at Morgan's new place. Knew doing it on line'll be easiest.

If it's not one of these virus things, she wondered through the pain, can you really get this bloody sick from two glasses of bloody plonk?

Charlotte switched on the TV and when she turned to head for the settee her legs just buckled beneath her and she tumbled down nose first to her wooden floor.

She peered up from her ungainly position as she tried to scramble with her hands suffering with pins and needles to her knees to spot somebody stood in the doorway she vaguely recognized grinning at her like a Cheshire cat.

'Hello Lottie.'

'Who…?' she gasped as her vague mind tried hard to cope with what was happening to her and around her. 'Just need a hand,' she gasped and lifted one shakily.

'Relax, won't be long now,' Charlotte heard as she peered up still on all fours desperate to place the face. 'Just lie back, soon be over.'

'You're…?' was gasped as she desperately tried to recall. 'Oh for God's sake!'

'Don't worry, you're almost there,' was sneered above her.

'What's going on, I mean what are…?' just talking was now more difficult as she dragged words through her confusion and increasing agony.

'I remember as clear as day, but you being the nasty bitch you've always been, can't even remember my name.'

Charlotte just slumped back down onto the floor and wasn't really listening as she realized her forefingers had gone numb when she grasped at her stomach and a shiver ran right through her all of a sudden. Better get off the floor.

'What...?' she was going nowhere.

'What have I done do I hear you ask?'

'Yeh, yeh, please.' Charlotte gasped as saliva built in her mouth and the slime just dribbled out and down her chin. Now her legs had gone as she tried hard to move, there was nothing there. 'Please! Help me...bloody...God.'

'Hemlock,' she heard but could only see trainers in front of her now.

The pain had become quickly unendurable with concentration difficult beyond her reasoning.

'What?' she gasped. Who, where from? Surely not.

'Guts ache's what you've got,' she was told as the blue trainers moved closer. 'You really should take stuff with your drink, dear. Just a spot of water with a good scotch next time remember...oh, sorry there'll not be a next time will there,' sniggered close by above her.

'I...didn't...jeez...'

'No. But I did,' was close and loud and Charlotte Elliott was absolutely desperate to move. 'And what's coming next? Like a naughty nasty little girl who can't quite make it to the loo, very soon you'll mess your pants. Hope mummy told you to wear clean ones!' was chortled close by.

'Please,' a frightened Lottie only just managed before she heaved and the blueberry muffin came back up to race through her mouth and slither across the floor. Her cheek was laid in it before she puked up more to spew and slither out. She tried to speak, clear her throat, spit it out, to plead with...God what was her name? 'Please...' was desperate.

'Let's play a game you and me,' and there held in front of her face was a thin knife. She blinked to improve her sight, a scalpel. 'Wouldn't allow these in school, remember? Nasty sharp things aren't they?'

'Just help me, please,' was forlorn, more desolate than before with that ghastly taste still slithering around in her gob. 'What's…' she gasped for air. 'What's going on?'

'Time to play a little game me thinks.'

'Please no,' she sucked in a breath and panted.

'Lottie. Surely you remember. Pleading with you never worked for me did it?'

1

Saturday 7th October 2017

DI Inga Larsson had struggled to remove the very fetching protective white Tyvek suit, slip off the blue overshoes and pull off her matching gloves with a snap after a quick personal scan of the inside of the house.

The inner and outer cordons had been set before she'd arrived, and now she had left the Crime Scene team members to deal with the gruesome scene. She knew an interview as soon as possible was absolutely critical and the only place at such an hour had to be in the first on the scene Response Officers' Volvo.

Anyway, prioritizing the interview with this guy Kempshall was top of her list. Cliff the CSI photographer had shown her his scene shots already, with video to come later so she had a real understanding of the grim situation indoors and combined with the verbal briefing from Scott it would all be sufficient for now.

Golden hour was long gone and so far there were no corroborating witnesses, and she knew CSI would fast track forensic tests she'd requested all of which would take time.

The house this Kempshall and the dead Mindi Brookes rented was a common or garden 1930s red-brick tidy semi with downstairs bay window like the rest of the uphill street in Lincoln. The garden had been given over to lawn and if any flowers were still offering blooms they were not visible in the dark.

'I appreciate this is not a good time...'

'Is any?' this Kempshall spat out as he peered out of the back seat window intent on watching all the comings and goings. Just up the road he could see through the windscreen the white CSI vans parked on the pavement in front of where he lived.

'But as I'm sure you will appreciate any information you can come up with right now will certainly help with our enquiries.'

'This like sticking a mic under players' noses soon as they come off?' He smirked. 'This *the moment* is it?'

'No Mr Kempshall it is not.'

'Clever, I'll give you that. Guess it gives me no time to come up with a half-cocked pack of lies, what you reckon eh?'

Inga Larsson responded with just a slight curl of the sides of her mouth as she sat half turned to see him. What an odd reaction from somebody to the fact his girlfriend, partner or whoever had been found dead in their house. 'Can we start with where you were and with whom?'

'Can I just ask?' Aaron Kempshall was going to anyway. 'Am I right in thinking you're not letting me indoors?' There was a hint of booze in his breath.

'I'm afraid not.'

'And I'm in the back here so I can't get out. Right?'

'Sorry?'

'Seen 'em on the tele, people like you lot. Miscreants get put in the back so they can't open the door.' What a strange word to use Inga thought from this guy with a hard cocksure expression. Fortunately he'd not decided to go in for a gelled quiff to make him look like a candidate for Year 8.

'Thought there'd be more room where you are and if any of my colleagues need to speak to me they can come in here,' she tapped the front passenger seat.

'Huh,' he responded somewhat dismissively. 'Go to see him play live couple of times a season on average. Picked tonight because I knew it'd be a cracker of a match what with the Sharks struggling to win at The Stoop in the past.'

'I think you need to explain,' said Larsson. She'd not seen a tear yet, but guessed this was all the ubiquitous British stiff upper lip coming out to play. That or a ridiculous man thing about being unwilling to be seen crying by his peers or a mere woman. Keep your emotions in check whatever happens because you're scared stiff your mates just might see you. Inga knew the sort. Not good form to display any weakness, stay away from a doctor as long as you can. "Don't go worrying the doctor," his old man no doubt had drummed into him. "They're important people with better things to do than listen to your nonsense."

'Sorry?' was the word from a confused man with his concentration understandably elsewhere.

'You'll need to explain who it is you're talking about.'

'Really?' Kempshall looked at her as if it was all so bloody obvious. 'Quins' Owen Edwards,' he said as if it answered her question in full. Inga's face said it didn't. 'Welsh Rugby international, British Lions Number Eight.' Inga nodded at the improvement in her knowledge. 'Went to school with him, played with him actually,' had a hint of a boast. 'Only at school mind,' he then added to drag down any kudos he had built up.

'And Quins?' she asked.

'Harlequins.'

'And they are who you went to see, why you've been to London?' He nodded. 'The match was tonight?' Inga said, glanced at her watch and corrected herself. 'Last night now.'

'Yeh, just got back, like I said. Had a good first half and we won well in the end.'

This dork with the omnipresent heavy stubble excuse for a beard to cover his weak chin had said more about the damn rugby than his dead woman. Sight of his scruffy look told Inga about this Brookes women, as she understood beards are generally preferred by the lower incomes.

'And your relationship with Miss Brookes?'

'Live together.'

'Permanent?'

Kempshall grimaced. 'As much as any these days I guess.'

'You were not planning for the future then, putting down roots?'

'Need more water under the bridge first,' had just a hint of a chortle she noticed.

'Any reason?' She really wanted to ask if she was boring him.

'Not ready to settle down. Things I need to do first, don't want to look back full of regrets like loads of me mates 'ave done.' He pushed a breath down his nose. 'Got too long a bucket list on top of activity holidays, I'm not giving them up for nobody. No way.' Inga decided this was the eternal teenager lacking in the maturity to accept responsibility. 'Not just for some woman anyway.'

That course she'd been on recently had told Inga people are these days maturing much later than was the norm decades ago, and lads were the worst. Inga guessed this could well be one lacking in life experiences to hold him back.

'You say regrets? What do you mean by that?'

'Just things, you know.'

Inga glanced at her notebook. 'You're twenty nine.'

'And?' he shrugged. Was this guy ever going to show any feelings? Was this his problem, the reason why he hadn't seen it as an enduring relationship? Would her Adam refer to her as 'some woman' she wondered?

'Enemies,' she said to move on. 'Can we talk about who might have done this?'

'These do all the ANPR business?' he ignored her question and asked pointing towards the dashboard.

'I believe it does,' was to the point. 'Now can we talk about who might have done this do you think?'

'Don't have a clue,' was said without a moment's hesitation to allow time for thought.

'Somebody she'd fallen out with, had smart phone fisticuffs on Facebook with maybe?'

'D'you have enemies?' he threw back.

'No,' said Inga with the slightest of head shakes. 'Except for those I've put away probably.'

'Why should we then?'

'There's no getting away from the fact somebody was upset enough tonight.'

'To do what?'

Inga looked hard at him sat there staring morosely out of the windscreen. 'As has already been explained to you, Mindi Brookes is the victim in an unexplained death situation. What did you think I meant?'

'Now look, I don't know what's bloody going on.' he said and turned his head. 'Reckon I've been hung out to dry with this, like nobody's had the decency to tell me what's going on. What happened, was she shot, poisoned, stabbed to bloody death eh? What? Come on, out with it.'

'Calm down please Mr Kempshall.'

'Why should I calm down, you've treated me like a piece of shit from the moment I got back here? You play straight with me I'll play ball with you. I've not been here I've been in bloody London for crissakes. Mindi sent me a text before the match and called me at half time when I assume she was here. I'm bloody sure you've got somebody bright enough to check all that out.' He sighed. 'Or maybe not, looking at those PCSO planks with acne you see about.' Kempshall just folded his arms and went back to peering down the avenue to his home fifty yards away.

At last a touch of emotion. Only trouble was, it was all about himself, no concern whatsoever for Brookes.

'We felt it was in your interests not to go into the house,' she said calmly. 'It's a crime scene and I'm sorry but we can't have the situation compromised.'

'Treating me like a bloody kid now eh?'

'No Mr Kempshall,' was the annoyed Larsson. 'How would you have liked it if I'd told you about the mayhem in there, how the whole place has been ransacked, there's blood all over the place, up the walls and half her guts have spewed out onto the carpet?'

'Oh my god!' he screeched, closed his eyes and looked as though he might retch.

Inga knew blood spatter is in essence a general over-arching term as the red stuff leaves the body by dripping, spurting and flowing to name but a few, and every spatter patterns is by nature different.

'Calm down. It's nothing like that,' she assured him, although it was very bad. 'Just listen to me for five minutes,' was loud. 'We're here doing our very best to help you all we can, and trying to protect you from the worst elements. So how about you come on side with this.' She pointed at the house. 'There are teams in there combing every inch of the place, there's a doctor, pathologist, CSI and forensic experts. People from the Scene Evaluation Branch have just arrived and there's coppers with their hands down drains all trying to work out what went off here tonight. We don't need the likes of you having a go. It's unnecessary and disrespectful. Do I make myself clear?' was close to being shouted.

'Yeh,' he sighed. 'But she is dead, like?'

'I'm afraid so, we told you as gently as we could when you first arrived. What we need from you now is everything you can think of to help us find whoever did this.' Inga hesitated a moment. 'We're on your side, I have team members in there,' she said pointing. 'Who've left their warm homes and their families to race up here, walked out of meals with friends or a glass or two in the pub to get here. For God's sake just give them a break!'

'Sorry.'

Inga is of the opinion too many people these days spend more than a reasonable amount of time watching the vast array of CSI programmes on the hundred and one channels now available. She was quite sure word had gone out the moment some goon just happened to spot the CSI van turning up and within minutes they'd all spilled out onto the street like flies around a honey pot.

Everyone with the latest must-have camera phone and Twitter account.

Her team knew how she'd react to them all gawping, so had told them they were all too late, the show was a sell-out, all the tickets had long gone and they'd been successfully corralled further along the road with PCSO's keeping watch.

Why she had asked herself yet again at an incident like this is it always the living and breathing waste of space nosey parker scruffbags of this world? Another question she'd never had an answer to was why some members of the public are so selfish and bloody minded about the obvious need to protect a crime scene from contamination.

They'd taken the inescapable bad photos of course when this Kempshall had been let through the barrier and now lies, lies and more damn lies would be littering social media with a nascent whiff of odd ball protest in the air.

They'd saved Aaron Kempshall from the horror of walking in to find Mindi in their open plan living and dining room. What she could not save him from will be the utter garbage spewing all across the internet as she talked to him.

His alibi appeared to eliminate him from suspicion. A check of his phone and ANPR would probably suffice, unless somebody else was driving and using his phone. Something Inga had fallen foul of before. One unexplained iota was the wiff of alcohol about him.

2

City Yoga Death

A yoga instructor found murdered in her own home is thought to have been attacked by somebody known to her.

Mindi Brookes, 33, was stabbed several times at the three-bedroomed house north of the city, she shared with her partner, but the motive remains a mystery.

Detective Inspector Inga Larsson, who is leading the investigation, said the attack appeared motiveless as there was no forced entry and nothing appeared to have been stolen.

Her partner Aaron Kempshall, 29, had travelled back to Lincoln after attending a rugby match in Twickenham that evening and it is thought he may well have discovered the body on his return.

Police said Ms Brookes was found with no defensive wounds meaning her attacker had caught her very much by surprise.

This thoroughly decent and popular Ms Brookes who organizes Yoga and Pilates classes throughout the city was last seen alive when she left a local fitness club to the west of the city just before 6pm.

Police enquiries into the circumstances surrounding the incident are continuing.

Why do people think it can't happen to them, why do they not heed the warnings staring them in the face?

Just one of a multitude of questions DI Inga Larsson was trying her best to fathom stood in the very front to back living/dining room where this Brookes woman had been found.

The rapid first twenty-four hours of any such murder enquiry or what appeared to be is always just that. Rapid, and in this case the immediacy of the situation was long gone. From thereon it slowed to a run, a jog followed and if she were not careful it would ends up at walking pace.

Inga knew no matter how respectful and careful they were they would none the less inevitably run roughshod all over people and their lives. It would be all invasive as they strip away any remnants of dignity and respectability.

The pre-war street particularly in the morning drizzle, was like most from the era in that each house was roughly the same apart from the add-ons, or take-aways. The subtle differences of opinion by the owners. Those with a porch stuck on, the one who had gone for cladding for some reason. The paved gardens, the scruffy unkempt ones, the wall, a hedge or two and those who'd done nothing much and these days it seemed to be all about solar panels.

It was daylight and activity in the street had returned to what Inga assumed passed for normal around there. Crowds of nosey goons on their phones, rubberneckers, TV camera crews and reporters away now chasing down the next juicy story. One police car, her own and a white CSI van.

The house was too hell bent on being funky for her taste. Television plonked on the top of a stack of three orange boxes in one corner painted deep orange as some ludicrous witticism. Two last century bean bags covered in a garish green and purple material with objectionable nasty swear words printed in yellow and red. A scratty wooden crate as a coffee table and a black corduroy sofa which appeared to be all sag and no substance.

Look at us we're all young and in-vogue was probably the idea, Larsson thought to herself. In reality it was surely a case of look at us we're immature, stupid and have no taste. We don't have curtains so any passing didicoy can just gawp at us.

There was the sound of a clock ticking somewhere. Not the sort of annoyance she and Adam would tolerate at home. Do people still purchase ticking wind-up clocks she wondered as the tick, tick, tick, tick began to annoy?

Larsson guessed somewhere down the line there'd been a job lot of magnolia paint on special offer, when these days the likes of Elderflower Tea and Honey Beam are all the rage. She always had in the back of her mind colours she and Adam had come across at one time. Elephant's Breath was a grey.

The kitchen was quite basic, quite uninspiring ice cream colour and two of the three bedrooms which were doubles appeared adequate, but with CSI still at work up there it had only been a cursory glance.

So this was where Ms Brookes had sort of lived with her bloke.

He looked a pretty decent sort of fellow, Inga considered. This Aaron Kempshall even though the interview had not gone too smoothly, she put down to his reaction to the news. Boyfriend, lover, friend, mate, casual sleep-over when he felt like a bit. Whatever his role in life, did he not have enough gumption when they arrived home two weeks previous to find somebody had broken into their home to do something about it?

To be fair Inga Larsson told herself and to his credit, according to their records he had phoned the police, and these days of course there are not the feet on the ground there once were to be able to send a copper to every caller. Change the locks he'd been told apparently by Control when this Kempshall admitted they'd left a key in the lock inside the back door which was now missing.

A passageway led from the front through to the back garden laid almost exclusively to lawn like the front.

Was this in effect the pair of them having another stab at being funky, groovy and snazzy by doing nothing about the damage to the back door? Deliberately going against convention for some obscure in-vogue idiocy.

Had Kempshall been responsible, had he changed the locks? No of course not, got more important things on his mind like rugby, booze and sex. Had Brookes done anything, apart from sticking a piece of cardboard over the broken pane in the door with sellotape? Not the sort, by the sound of her this unfortunate Mindi Brookes, to do anything which just might hint at being practical or sensible. How about something simple like phoning a locksmith if you think changing a lock is beyond you?

The moment such a thought came to mind Inga knew exactly what the answer might well be. *"Have you seen how much the call out charge is?"* was the nonsense you get too often. Such attitudes meant in the end she had paid the price with her life. Why she wondered do people not understand there is always a price to pay?

Larsson had known all weekend as head of the Major Incident Team how she had been lumbered with clearing up this mess and finding out who killed her.

Keeping the breathalyzer out of the scenario was a decision she had made on the spur of the moment in the early hours of Saturday. He was clearly suffering and under the influence but would stuffing a tube in his mouth and making a trip all the way to the cop shop have produced the information she was desperate for? Not likely.

Mindi Brookes was dead and no doubt this Kempshall'd be looking for someone else to lay his head beside.

No need to ask how the perpetrator got in to carry out the deed? Didn't even need to push in the cardboard as he or she most probably used the key he or she had nicked.

Detective Inspector Inga Larsson just stood there stock still in the centre of the open plan lounge/dining room, hands thrust deep into her charcoal grey coat pockets, eyes closed, head down. This was now Operation Lancaster so the computer had decided. Based on the place she had never visited and not on an old aircraft which she recognized and had seen flying. Nothing as simple as the name Lancaster being chosen appropriately for Lincolnshire. Names of beetles, those of Egyptian kings and types of antelope were ones she had never got her head round in the past.

Knew CSI would have done it already but Inga just had to press the answerphone button with a finger encased in blue rubber.

'Hello Ms Brookes, just a quick call. My name's Evie and I'm just calling from Lexi-con about a quote I thought you might like, Mindi, for a new conservatory. I'll call back again as you appear to be busy right now.'

Inga just stood there peering down at the machine which had uttered the rude and intrusive message and for a few moments considered the idea of phoning whoever this Lexi-con were and put the wind up them by explaining they were now part and parcel of a suspicious death enquiry.

Women were so easily taken in by her. For as she talks Inga has this unaffected friendly air that seemingly all Swedes enjoy. Her jaw length pulled-back blonde hairdo is as severe as it is glamorous.

The male species such as this Aaron Kempshall fare less well, as despite her captivating image she is most certainly not always the nicest person to deal with.

She guessed Mindi Brookes had no idea who this Evie and her Lexi-con were. Trying to sell her a conservatory barnacle to stick on the back of the house she didn't own. To use Mindi's name was unnecessary and creepy and to Inga it could very well have reeked of the outset of a stalking scenario which didn't bear thinking about.

The Swede had just never understood why society tolerates such behavior or any other form of intrusion into people's lives. She could also not fathom why such calls apparently work. Would anybody, she asked herself for the umpteenth time like this Mindi, wait around for goodness knows how long for some bozo to phone up on the off chance from this Lexi-con to offer a deal rather than calling three reputable companies friends had used and asking for a quote?

In truth she knew why. Chances were people are forever on the lookout for something cheap, and anything this Lexi-con shower had would certainly be that by the sound of it. Probably manky and as their name implies, more than likely a con.

One of Adam's clients had a phrase which came to mind as she stood there. *"If something is cheap as chips, it might very well be made of them."*

There was only so much the police and society can do to help and protect Joe Bloggs and their loved ones. There are some things they really have to do for themselves was her main thought.

'Penny for them,' brought Inga to life as chestnut haired DC with clean clear bright eyes new to the team strolled into the room behind her.

As well as the task set before her, Inga was also extremely concerned how planning for her wedding just weeks away in Stockholm was more work than she had ever imagined and nowhere near as much pleasure.

'Hi,' she responded to her Detective Constable Ruth Buchan as Inga turned and blew out a sigh. 'Only a couple of specialist CSI lads upstairs, just running around with Bluestar forensics seeing what blood it'll pick up. All done in here on Saturday.'

'Know what you think of coincidences,' Ruth suggested. 'But surely CSI were round the corner in Longdales only last week with all that mustard gas business they found in Woodhall Spa.'

'Just for once think that's all it is. Pure coincidence.'

'Burner phone I hear?'

'Looks that way but why? Why warn us at all?'

Fairly new Ruth Buchan was stood there just inside the door half a metre in front of an offensive bean bag. Navy blue suit, sensible tie-up shoes looked rather like quality trainers, hint of a cream blouse or shirt hidden in the most part by a pale blue silky scarf.

At work her hair was pulled over to the side and plaited before being drawn back across her head and pinned in place.

'What you thinking ma'am?' Buchan posed. She really wanted to know what on earth her boss was doing stood in the lounge of the rented semi where this Mindi Brookes had allegedly been murdered back on Friday evening. Signs the CSI lads had been over the place were clearly evident.

'Apart from asking what idiot gave her the name Mindi?' Inga sniggered.

'Think it must be from Mork and Mindy and her mother couldn't spell,' meant nothing to blonde Inga. 'American comedy starring Robin Williams before he was big,' was an explanation of sorts Ruth guessed was required.

'Was this woman to woman or just the killer's piece of skirt carrying out his orders when she phoned it in? This a case of this Mindi falling out with a pal over something bloody trivial. This a social media stramash turned nasty?'

'Think it's time we had a word in the ear of whoever invented the internet.'

'You and me both. We didn't used to have all this business.'

'Kempshall's not permanent remember, bit ships passing in the night for a quick how's your father.' Inga looked at her young officer. If she asked her team to explain every single phrase as a

Swede she did not begin to understand, they'd be translating all day long sometimes.

'But to be fair, she did phone him at what would have been half time, so we know she was still alive at eight thirty six Friday evening.'

'Couldn't have could he?' nervous Ruth knew her boss had interviewed the boyfriend. 'CCTV at Peterborough Services on his way home Friday night. Take how long from there?'

'We know how long, not including the stop, be an hour and a half around that time of night and I was here when he turned up. If he's still in the frame we could do ANPR on him.' She released a breath. 'But he's not is he?' she grimaced. 'Except.' Ruth waited. 'When he turned up here he was wearing a Harlequins sweat shirt in pale blue, red and navy. On the CCTV at Peterborough he's wearing a jacket. Looks very much like an expensive Hugo Boss grey one Adam took a shine to recently.'

'Easy for travelling?'

'Sweatshirt has to be the look at the rugby, I'm guessing.' Inga sighed with frustration. 'Changed into it after he left the services and still wearing it when I spoke to him.'

'So, what's with the jacket?' Ruth asked.

'And looks like a black shirt.'

'And Sandy has just established Kempshall did go to school with Owen Edwards.'

'Told me he goes to watch him play two or three times a season,' was purely confirming what they all already knew. 'Just out of interest. Why are they so bothered by his number?' Ruth grimaced without actually answering. 'Lads keep saying the Quins number eight.'

'Rugby term,' arrived with a slight smile. 'Fly Half, Hooker, Number Eight, what they call a position in rugby.'

'Hooker?'

'Don't go there!' Chestnut haired Ruth chuckled and looked all about, and knew she'd have hell on explaining such rugby talk to her Stockholm born boss even though people like Sandy and Jake would watch the Six Nations avidly. 'And being here achieves what exactly?' Not actually her mentor, but understanding the reasoning was all part of on the job training.

'Is there a female to female atmosphere, are there clues to this one being a one denomination attack? No pint glass with his DNA, no dirty pants in the bin, no socks walking out on their own. No crafty fag smell.'

'Tell me, ma'am,' Ruth dared. 'If I walked into your home right now what would I find would link it to your Adam? What is there says he was involved if it had happened to you?'

'Empty coffee mug. Tele stuck on BT Sport,' Inga said and grinned after a moment's thought. 'And yes, CSI always check. Turn on the TV see what they've been watching.'

'And here?' Ruth asked looking at a big screen in the corner.

'BBC One,' heralded another sigh of frustration.

'No *Undateables, Gogglebox* or *Impact Wrestling* then?'

'No thank goodness,' the DI shook her head. 'Why are we so stereotypical I wonder? Why do we assume if this Mindi had a pal or pals over they'd watch what Adam calls DTV. Dregs television?'

'Because they do,' said the Detective Constable. 'People stereotype themselves remember, like the dimwits who dress themselves and young girls in pink. They also spend their benefit money drinking crap fizzy wine at fifty pence a bottle and think they're sophisticated. I once knew women who had a party every week to watch some reality utter garbage. What likeminded people will think of them on social media is the only reason they do any of it.'

'You ever done yoga?'

'No,' Ruth responded and grimaced a little.

'What Mindi Brookes did. Ran classes.'

Friends and family so far could shed no light on reasons why and are not aware of any threats this Mindi might have received. Knew of nobody she might have fallen out with. Employers were stunned when they heard the news and could offer no explanation whatsoever.

Inga could well remember how Kempshall had reacted when she'd asked about enemies. Not in their world.

On Sunday DS Raza Latif had even interviewed lazy dog owners this Mindi walked dogs for. No great dog lover herself according to this Kempshall, but an easy bit of exercise with a few hounds to provide extra income at times to suit her.

Parents absolutely devastated, mother in a haze provided by her GP to help her through the worst. Mindi's phone and laptop were being gone through by the CAT (Computer Anaysis Team) guys, known by all except the chinless wonders at the top as the eTeam, but so far nothing untoward whatsoever.

Aaron the boyfriend or whatever he was, had been in London at the rugby and visiting the house was a darn sight better for Inga than twiddling her thumbs waiting for DNA and toxicology. Something somewhere had to click into place, offer her a clue.

Ruth in need of clarification, asked nervously, 'Why's the big boss taken on this Critical Incident Manager role?'

DC Nicky Scoley who'd been with the team at one time would always refer to him as the Darke boss. Big boss was different.

'Supposed to be for ops beyond the scope of say MIT, but we all know it's not so complex and I can't imagine this is linked to the twelve days of Christmas nonsense we had. Think this is just him using it as an excuse to keep his hand in rather than spending all day attending yet another strategy meeting with the Police Commissioner, listening to more self-important tirades from councillors or sorting through a hundred emails.'

'Rather him than me.'

'Tomorrow apparently he's off to MAPPS,' Inga advised without an explanation just to annoy. 'Multi Agency Public Protection Symposium,' she popped in with a wry smile.

Ruth sighed and looked all about her. 'You don't think this Kempshall didn't bother to get the back door fixed or locks changed on purpose do you?'

Before blonde Inga could respond her phone played a little ditty. 'Sir,' she said and raised her eyebrows to Ruth Buchan.

'And where might you be right now Inspector?' she was asked in a tone suggesting if she didn't know better, he was hinting she might just be skiving off somewhere.

'Monday morning priority, I'm at the house,' she said. 'Mindi Brookes' place,' and listened.

'Back here soon as you can, there's an issue with DNA,' was an unusually bluff Craig Darke.

'How do you mean?' Larsson queried, looking at her detective colleague and mouthed 'boss' to her.

'If I tell you, you'll not believe me.'

'Try me.'

'DNA at the scene they've found belongs to a woman who's been dead around eleven years. More than just plain old fashioned dead,' Darke sniggered, then hesitated to annoy. 'She was murdered.'

'You're kidding me!' Inga exclaimed. 'Where'd they find it?' showed to Ruth a surprised look.

'Up in the bed apparently so Jack from CSI reckons.'

'On our way,' Inga said quickly to snap the mobile shut move towards the door as she pocketed her phone. 'Issue with DNA,' she told Ruth who reacted facially. 'Thought the good news was too good to last.'

'What good news?'

'Loads of blood and stab wounds, cause of death was pretty obvious even to me. So we've not had to wait for toxicology and all the rest before we start work.' Inga knew it was the pathology and DNA lab these days where investigations are solved.

'What DNA?' Ruth responded honestly.

'Found here,' she pointed at the ceiling. 'But that's not the best bit. Belongs to a woman who was murdered ages ago!'

'Be serious!' a frowning Ruth Buchan just stood there looking at her boss.

'You coming or not?'

3

'I've insisted they double check, told them to send it to Leicester if they have to, but according to the interim report there was DNA but more to the point according to CSI it was as if somebody made sure we'd find it.'

'Lab'll not be happy with you.'

'I didn't know they can do that,' she suggested to her boss.

'Apparently it's not always a guaranteed source,' he told her and looked down at the pad on his desk. 'Usually because there are not enough...' Darke read. 'What they call nucleated cells. Difference in this case is it's not diluted as it would be in a toilet. Worked though, which is a real bonus. What they knew straight away, which they've told me you can pretty much get every time, it is definitely female.'

By the time Inga'd got back to Lincoln Central, Darke had issued an all forces alert to tell the police world how it was with Christine Streeter. No new photograph of course, just the at least a dozen year old one. What were the chances? New hairstyle, new hair colour, fatter in the face, wearing glasses now, more make-up, tattoos, stud in her nose maybe? Could be thinner. Whatever, it still had to be tried, they had to gamble and then hope.

'So be it. Too damn important to cock up.' Det Super Craig Darke scrunched up his face as if he didn't believe what he was about to say. 'Came back as this Chrissie Streeter or Christine Laura Streeter to be precise.' Inga looked at him, the name meant nothing whatsoever and sounded rather odd. 'Murdered a few weeks less than eleven years ago, body never discovered, but the boyfriend was sent down for it.' He just glanced at his notes. 'Tomasz Borowiak, and he's still inside, basically because he's still not admitted it or said what he did with her body.'

Larsson had her hands up. The names Chrissie Streeter and Tomasz Borowiak meant absolutely little to her, although in the back of her mind was the thought she'd heard the name before somewhere. Probably on the news at the time, but she'd been at university back then. 'Can we go back a bit? This DNA boss. Where was this exactly did you say?'

'In the bed,' said Darke as if it was obvious.

'At the house?'

'Of course.'

'And Forensics say they've found this…Chrissie Streeter's DNA there.'

'In the bed,' Darke sucked in a breath as a cautionary measure. 'Fresh urine and a couple of strands of hair as well.'

'In the bed?' Made her sound as she was, flabbergasted. 'How old is she?'

'If she really is still alive, be about thirty two or three.'

'Still wetting the bed?' she almost shouted in disbelief.

'Deliberately they think. Either that or she's got a problem,' he smirked.

Inga was all too aware how killers in particular the serial kind, love to leave messages. A sort of signature at the bottom of their work to say clearly *Hello This Is Me Again.*

She was not aware of any unusual treatment of the body, no message as such they could look out for next time if there was to be a next time. Was wetting the bed in fact the message in this case and was this something else to investigate?

'There are adverts on the tele about having such problems,' made Darke smile. 'I'm tempted to ask how they know,' she smiled. 'Be the reason why two from CSI were still working upstairs this morning?'

'Probably.'

'Are you saying this Christine Streeter has risen from the dead all of a sudden?'

'Not me saying it,' Darke responded confidently and smirked. 'Forensics say she has, which is the reason why I've asked them to double check.' Darke leant forward and rested his arms on his desk. 'If she is still alive, where has she been for eleven years? If she's not, how on earth did her fresh DNA get into this Mindi Brookes's two up two down house?'

These days such was the progress of forensic science they only needed one single skin cell smaller than you can hope to see with or without your glasses to know they have a trace.

'Could be a cold case,' Inga enthused which pleased Darke to see.

'And it could be a very hot one. Remember he's still in nick,' he blew out a breath. 'Be a hell of a lot of compensation if she really is still alive and kicking.'

'And still pleading his innocence?'

'Apparently. Wouldn't you if she's still alive?'

'If I'd not killed her I would.'

'Waiting on more from the Intel Cell.'

'Was it her who called us?' Darke raised his eyes and grinned. 'This...Streeter killed Brookes then phoned us.'

'Who else would know?'

'Cheeky bitch,' Inga scoffed with her eyes closed. 'She must have ignored all the publicity there would have been at the time. Why would you do that?'

'Getting her own back,' Darke suggested.

'How?'

'Got him jailed by pretending to be dead possibly?'

'Be serious,' and by the look on her boss's face she could see he was. 'Beggars belief! There's no guarantee they'd find him guilty without a body, surely. Be a heck of a thing to achieve.'

'To save time I've asked PR to look up press reports on the case and they're emailing anything they discover. Find out what went on without trudging through the whole case files. I was still in Staffordshire at the time, so I'm not au fait with it either. We need to know why they were so sure it was Borowiak.'

'I'll need to read them too, remember I was just out of uni at the time. Took six months out back home before I started work.' Inga was still struggling to get her head round it all. 'We saying rather than her being murdered, this Chrissie Streeter is now the murderer?'

'About the size of it. You got a better idea?' Inga knew Craig Darke would not let go of this one very easily. A man with his reputation would never go back to shuffling papers and listening to bad speeches when he'd got this to get his teeth into

'D'you think this Borowiak knows she's still alive and is the reason why he's holding out?'

'All I've got so far Inga, is him saying he never killed her. He claims and always has done when he left their flat this Christine was fine. Had a real rumpus before he left according to him, said their relationship was very much a love hate thing with constant rows.'

'Could just be a coincidence. Maybe our Mindi and this... woman were just pals, this Chrissie just stopped over one time and has nothing to do with what happened to Mindi.'

'Bit of a tall order,' Darke sniggered. 'It's one thing us all having a good laugh when traffic pull over some numpty for not wearing his seat belt and hey ho they smell cannabis, then discover the ned's banned and has no insurance. Different kettle of fish suddenly finding a woman who's been dead eleven years linked to a suspicious death. Which is a whole different ball game.' He smiled. 'You saying she's just a friend who stayed over and wet the bed?' Before Inga could react he went on. 'And this Mindi hadn't bothered to change the bedding since then?' he sniggered.

'Bedding was still damp apparently according to the report from Jack.'

Darke sniggered. 'I was going to say.'

'Murdered turned murderer?' Inga smiled at her boss. 'You don't get many of them on a shift, it's usually the other way round.'

'And if it was her who phoned it in. Why?' he asked. 'Why not wait for the boyfriend to get back and find her?'

'Could link her to Kempshall, but made sure he was not involved at all. Phoned it in when she knew he was still on the road.' Inga sucked in her breath. 'This her being kind to Kempshall maybe? She know him d'you think?' Darke just pulled a face.

'Another thing to ponder,' the Darke boss went on. 'This Chrissie's been missing for eleven years, and she's still missing now so it's not a case of just knocking on her door.'

'She'll be easy to find, then. Not.'

'Back then it'd not be like it is when a child goes missing, this was an adult with lower priority. They'd have been searching for some bit of information, a clue as to why just a crumb of evidence.'

'We have to assume they didn't find anything back then.'

'What about her social circle back when she disappeared, assume they were all tried.'

'Not like it is now with social media. '

Inga Larsson was never entirely happy with holding press conferences although she was well aware of the supposed advantages.

Ignore the media and they'd just publish any tripe they could attach to a trumped-up headline to sell papers or get housewives to stop ironing grimy underpants and listen for a minute. Giving them a press conference didn't mean they'd get closer to reality but it did mean they were less likely to have their moaning hat on later as the story developed.

At least what she was about to announce even Donald Trump could not regard as fake news.

She'd noticed Craig Darke was conspicuous by his absence, so it was just her and some dolly piece from the press office to do the spouting. One lone girl with a mic in hand and tape machine slung over her shoulder with a link to some obscure on-line nonsense looked bored to tears. Inga who had to spell her name for the silly bitch was sure she was only there for the coffee and Nice biscuits and wondered how many of them there would try to fiddle their expenses by claiming for the free refreshments they'd say they'd been forced to buy from a machine with no receipt.

Their disinterest was patently obvious when not one of the hacks young or old asked any really pertinent sensible questions. Just wanted to know the stuff all duly covered by the three-page press release handed to all had they bothered to read it.

Inga was well aware how those such as the drip with the mic would when left to their own devices never listen to local radio or read such as the *Lincoln Leader*. She and many of those in the room had their precious phones and tablets and thought that'd be enough.

Inga guessed by the look of them two others thumbing their phones looked like they were part of the ridiculous demographic cohort Millenial generation. With their stereotypical look and demeanor they would more than likely make the news rather than report on it. Chances are they'd be the latest to be shamed or blackmailed or both by an old lover in revenge for being dumped by sending sexually explicit images to the whole world.

Back in the incident room, once Inga had recovered from the ordeal, she had her whole team sat at work stations waiting on her every word.

She scanned the faces of her team carefully before starting, because in her inimitable style she had already done something off the wall as she tended to from time to time. Those waiting for her had got used to it. "She's Swedish", seemed to be the stock answer if anybody queries what she was up to as if this was a sensible excuse for her.

'Let's be sexist for a change,' she said speaking briskly with a wicked smile aimed at them all, in particular the add-ons peering over monitors. 'It seems to me we need to look into the old case which in the end got Borowiak sent down for the murder of Streeter and then Streeter herself, who we're now told has been leaving her DNA about last Friday. Then we have this Mindi Brookes who has just been killed.' She scanned the room. 'Scott. I want you to head up a team with Sam and Kenny,' who had been brought in from PCT to lend a hand. 'Julie,' was another sent up to MIT courtesy of DCI Stevens, 'you will work on Ruth's team with Gillian.' Jake who looked concerned at his omission. What a surprise, he had not been forgotten. 'DS Goodwin, Please take an overview we don't want both teams chasing the same people.'

'Doing what exactly?' Jake Goodwin queried. At a good six foot, Jacques 'Jake' Goodwin with grey-green eyes was a fully fit good looking man. Not bulked up like some but he could most certainly look after himself.

'Scott's team look at the male situation as it is now. Firstly this Borowiak. Check the old files and come up with a précis of what according to the prosecution is supposed to have happened to get him convicted without a body.' Feeling engaged with this train of thought Inga repeated it. 'Without a body.' She then continued. 'Then having done that take a close look at our rugby fan Kempshall, as he's the only likely candidate we have so far. Where does he fit into this whole scenario? May not have done the deed but was he involved somehow, does he know Streeter? Then take it on from there like any other murder enquiry.'

'But ma'am, we already know he was down in Twickenham and she sent him a text and phoned him at half time.'

'But can you be sure it was Mindi Brookes texting and phoning? What if somebody else had control of her phone by then?' Inga knew from experience some crims could make your phone suggest calls had come from someone else entirely as the eTeam had demonstrated to her at one time by sending her a message purporting to be from Adam, except it was not.

'Excuse me,' said Jake when Inga wanted to move on. 'Are we suggesting this Kempshall was involved back with Borowiak? Surely that'd make him not much more than seventeen or eighteen at the time.'

'No I'm not, but who else do we have right now? Brookes is dead and they have her body in the mortuary, Borowiak's still in nick and the only other major DNA belongs to Streeter and Kempshall.' She then turned her head to smile at the women as a warning they were next in line. 'During my briefing with the boss it was even intimated Kempshall may well be linked to Streeter somehow.' She looked at Jake.

'Thanks boss,' got him a grin from Inga.

'Julie, Gillian first up for you, I'd like you to look at this from the standpoint of how this Christine Streeter really is still alive. Look at the situation from a female's perspective. Want you to tell me how come. Where she's been and how?' More than one person went to speak but a hand from Inga stopped them in their tracks. 'Christine or Chrissie Streeter which makes life easier with her not being Smith or Jones.' She looked down at her tablet. 'Apparently it is almost exclusively a Sussex name. Derived from the pre 6th century straet,' she spelt for them all. 'Or stroet', she repeated the process. 'Means somebody, believe it or not who works or lives near a street or as it was then, a Roman road. Where places such as Stane Street in Sussex and Essex got their name.' She looked up. 'Probably if the truth be known where all streets get their name too.' The smile she gave Jake stopped him from asking. 'Stane, in case you're wondering is an old word for stone.'

'Street made of stone,' he nodded and pouted.

'Exactly. Unusual name I appreciate but it seems to be where it comes from.'

'This Kempshall I take it is on Scott's list?' Jake Goodwin checked when he was sure the boss had finished with the name lesson.

'Very much so. I know we have his alibi, but the background is nothing like we've had before to say the least, not often we have people coming back from the dead.' Inga looked at her senior sergeant. 'Jake. Can you take an overview to stop the lines being crossed? Cut out the possibility we're interviewing the same person twice which could happen,' she sniggered. 'Don't think you've got away lightly. You need to head up the Mindi Brookes death. Stevens is letting us have a couple more of his PCT lads to help out over these initial stages and right now we need to know all about her while we wait for the PM.'

'Old case files heading our way by any chance?' Brown-Reid asked.

Inga nodded. 'Ruth. Take what you've learned today away with you and keep giving thought to the idea of her changing her identity. Based on what you already know, come up with all the things you'd need to do if you were her. Put yourself in her position eleven years ago, what would she need to achieve? Simple things like getting a driving licence in another name; would she need to sit the test again? Registering at the doctor as somebody else for example, how hard would it be? I want a master plan just like she would have had in her mind if she had been thinking about this all for a while.'

'Any connection?' Ruth asked. 'We know of between this missing Streeter woman and our dead Mindi Brookes?'

'Not as yet,' Inga responded. 'Lizzie,' she said glancing at her long term pal. 'You will continue to look after the HOLMES system but ladies please feel free to use her expertise and knowledge on this conundrum'

Inga wondered why she had felt embarrassed to a degree when she had asked Lizzie to put bed wetting, urine, deliberate urination and incontinence into the system just to see what might pop up.

It would have been better if the killer had left a pink ribbon around her neck, or *Catch Me If You Can* scribbled on a Post It note and stuffed in her hand.

The bed wetting of course had immediately been listed as Not For Media Eyes, as an unusual fact would more than likely be what real genuine callers would want to brag about.

'Can't see Streeter doing this on the spur of the moment,' said Ruth. 'Might be the case if in the end she finished up on the streets,' she stopped to snigger. 'No pun intended. But I can't see how likely it is Streeter is on the streets and has been all this time. Year or two at the outside which I doubt, but not eleven.'

'And you don't choose that sort of life deliberately, surely.'

'Need to get inside her mind set,' Inga continued to brief Ruth. 'We're talking 2006. Remember, it was World Cup year, then there was George Bush and Tony Blair and at the end of the year Saddam Hussein being executed, so Iraq is big news.'

'Damn good reason for anybody to run away!'

'We're also talking Beyonce, *Life On Mars* and *The Apprentice*.'

'Some of that Beyonce's stuff was murder, I know that!' Jake quipped.

'Think what you were doing back then if you can,' said Inga ignoring the remarks. 'Was this all planned, was it her releasing the bad news when the world is distracted like politicians do? Whole world focused on what's going on in Germany with the football and all the trouble in Iraq. If she wasn't murdered, could be she chose precisely then to do a runner.'

'When the world is looking the other way.'

'Exactly.' Inga's office phone rang and she walked across to answer it. 'Bugger, bugger, bugger!' was all she said before she walked back out. 'Bad news from the eTeam. The phone used to call it in just happens to be a pay as you go in the name of a Helen Nevins registered to an address in Leeds.' Inga closed her eyes in frustration before she spoke again, doing her best to keep her voice free from irritation. 'Which apparently doesn't exist.'

'How soon are stories like this Streeter forgotten by the public, by us even,' said Jake scanning the room. 'Used to be yesterday's paper had chips in it next lunchtime. Now it's all this breaking news bobbling along the bottom of our screens. News feeds come in faster and faster and then before you can turn round it's gone and replaced by fake news.'

'What happened to her parents who must have endured an absolute horror?' Inga posed.

'The bloke who killed her, what about him?' Jake asked. 'Open prison by now maybe. The internet will never allow you to forget your misdemeanors, but it never issues updates. What happened to the Streeters?

'News flash!' said Ruth suddenly. 'And suddenly they're gone and forgotten.'

'Exactly. Right this minute it's somebody else's turn to go through their fifteen minutes of fame. Lives turned into a nightmare like the Streeters but will they recover, did the Streeters recover?'

4

When she had briefed Detective Super Craig Darke on what little progress had been made he'd suggested this Kempshall may not be as innocent as he was painted. Inga was surprised super sleuth DCI Stevens had not wanted to poke his nose into what had all the makings of a high profile case.

'Jake. Your boys are looking after this Aaron Kempshall, how far have we got with him?'

'Twenty nine year old Aaron Edward Kempshall, known to his friends as Ned. We've checked with…'

'Hang on. What's Ned all about?' the Swede asked.

'What people called Edward are sometimes known by.'

She looked slightly confused by yet another British oddity. 'I just thought Ned was a name.'

'Anyway, what was I saying?' DS Goodwin went on. 'Yes, Collyer's College is where he and this Owen Edwards the rugby player were at school together. We also checked with Edwards' agent and he confirms the player went to the school at the time we already have it confirmed Kempshall was there. We've checked with Harlequins Rugby and their records show he did buy a ticket for the Sale Sharks match. Claims he finished work at lunchtime to drive down. We have also seen CCTV of Kempshall at Peterborough Services after the match, with about the right amount of time to reach the house when he did for you to speak to him.'

'Conclusive?' Inga asked the gathered forum and was paid in nods.

'As near as watertight as you're likely to get,' Jake responded.

'Except,' Sandy MacLachlan stopped to give the boss a cautionary look. 'Could have got the score off Radio 5 Live and it was live on BT Sport remember.'

Larsson sucked in a breath. 'PM said she died somewhere between eight and eleven and if push comes to shove between nine and ten. We have the 999 call somebody made timed by Control at 22.17 ages before we've got him at Peterborough.'

'We had sight of the case notes from 2006 yet?' Sandy MacLachlan checked.

'Just briefing notes so far. But when they do Sandy, I want you to concentrate on the people who were interviewed before. Go back to them, see if time has made a difference, do they look upon the whole episode from a different standpoint now?'

Sandy looked all about. 'Am I a team of one?'

'Is there a problem?'

'No,' said the chunky Scot. 'Enjoy being the high heid yin,' he remarked with his twang and sniggered.

'Thomasz Borowiak,' Inga went on without commenting on Sandy's remark. 'Was banged up for the murder of Christine Streeter his girlfriend, but her body was not discovered then and never has been. Been a few sightings over time apparently but nothing really positive.' She lifted a hand to stop anybody butting in. 'Back then her DNA was all over the flat understandably but more importantly an amount of blood was found on the duvet cover and inside in the kitchenette with a splash or two on the wall. Borowiak claimed and still does apparently how she was fine when he last saw her, but Borowiak had no alibi for the time pathology say she was done for.'

'And he was where?'

'All night fishing.'

'Alone?'

'Alone.' Inga spun round to give her Detective Constable a fixed stare.

'Is night fishing allowed?'

'Not now I don't think, but maybe back then it was,' Sandy offered.

'Ruth. Talk me through not being dead,' was one hell of a curved ball of the sort she used from time to time. Truth was it was just her way. 'Back in 2006 in the summer a little after the World Cup the story is this Tomasz Borowiak murdered this Christine Streeter, for which he is still serving time. What if he is telling the truth and this Chrissie was never murdered? Talk me through what issues she had to deal with to still be alive and well today. Well enough to leave DNA and hairs at our murder scene on Friday having wet the bed.'

What a question Ruth struggled to cope with. 'Not only, er would we... want to know how, er we'd also need to know why.'

'Being seen would be an issue. Dead people don't walk down the street.' Inga offered straight away. 'Family, friends, workmates could spot her. First and foremost she'd need a job, somewhere to live away.'

'I've been giving this some thought. Ask yourself this question,' was Gillian Brown-Reid. 'When was the last time any of us bumped into each other in town out of work?' She looked at the others in turn. 'Think of friends away from work, do they ever just pop up when you're out and about?'

'You can be in the same town even, probably in the same street at times and never see anybody you know.'

'Truth is,' said Inga. 'A course I went on a while back about witnesses says how we don't look at people. Most you see just walk along looking down and of course these days they have the phone to look at in case god forbid they miss a message.'

'Did this Chrissie move away, did she have to?'

'Abroad?'

'You wanted to know about not being dead,' a disgruntled Ruth piped up. 'You can't be surely if you just move two streets away. Head for London or some other big city you have no previous contact with. Abroad would be best.'

'Passport,' Gillian offered to annoy Ruth. 'In a new name?'

'Bank account.'

'Doc...'

'Enough,' said smiling Inga to stop the list. 'I've got a list as long as your arm,' the DI said waving a sheet of paper. 'Everything and anything which can be used to trace you, think about it.'

'National Insurance Number.'

'Let's just take what you've got for starters.' Inga then allocated each subject matter to an officer and in Ruth's case left her with family and friends and spread the others out. 'On top of what you're already doing, take it on board and come up with how you would have handled all this if you were her. Put yourself in her position, it's a Friday evening in August when she walks out of their flat with

Borowiak off fishing, be ready to talk me through what she does and how she does it.'

'Social media,' was a late contribution.

'You can take that one as well then Gillian.'

'What I'm saying is, back then it wasn't like it is now on people's phones and not everybody was into it.'

'Not everybody's into it now. Most people I know have never been on Twitter in their lives.'

Morning briefing the following day started after several had snapped shut Tupperware boxes and wiped the backs of their hands across their crumbed lips.

Been through her daily ritual. Emails and a quick check through the overnights, the log of all reported crime mostly alcohol or drug related. Occasionally she's spy a mugging, mispers, RTCs of course, fights in and out of pubs and clubs, drink driving and break-ins. That Tuesday morning nothing to concern Inga Larsson or her Major Incident Team, therefore she could just bat on.

'Team briefing. I know its early days, but let's just see where we are.'

Drafted-in on a temporary basis DC Michelle Cooper from the Prisoner Handling Unit had taken on what turned out to be an easy task and Inga was already aware she'd discovered Chrissie Streeter had no criminal convictions. When the name Christine Laura Streeter was plopped into the system it had produced two in the UK with driving licences, and this Michelle had advised everybody how when they changed to the shortened Chrissie it had been reduced down to just one, and then in both cases when they had included date of birth the numbers dropped to zero.

They were all aware they had discovered her driving a Seat Ibiza Mk2 from early 2005, then nothing. As far as records went the car just no longer existed, it had not been taxed or insured beyond 2006 or given an MOT. Not officially anyway with backstreet cowboys not included in the data.

'After she died, if which is what happened, did nobody deal with her car? How did it just vanish?' Inga turned. 'Ruth, can you ask the family what happened to her car? Was she in cahoots with somebody who dealt with things like the car? Got a friend who just took it to the scrappy, no questions asked?'

'No convictions,' Michelle said when Inga's attention returned as if it was all she was going to offer. 'Nothing anywhere, nothing on PNC, went through all the normal channels, did Open Source and even got onto DVLA as we've already put on the board. Nothing for a Chrissie or Christine Laura Streeter after 2006.' The good grin she received from her boss had her wonder what she had missed.

'Julie?' was next on Inga's list.

'Her bank account has never been touched since she disappeared,' the auburn haired DC offered. 'Her solicitor put a stop on it after two months as there were Direct Debits including rent and she was running out of money or would do pretty soon without any income. Remember freelance aerobics means no classes, no pay. Nat West have another four accounts in the name Christine Streeter but so far the ones I've tracked down are not her. Still a way to go, and all the other banks and building societies as well of course.'

'Thanks Julie keep at it.' She glanced at Kenny Ford when he was smiled at by Inga as if she knew something he didn't. 'Gillian,' was next up. 'Social media you were also looking at.'

'Been through as much social media as I can so far, but the other work has been a priority so I've not really got too far into it. There's a complete lack of people called Christine Streeter on Facebook, but remember you don't have to use your real name. I still need to go through Instagram and all the rest.'

DC Michelle Cooper dragged in a breath. 'Boss, wasn't this all done before at the time? Surely they hunted high and low for her?'

'Of course, but what we have now they didn't back then was her DNA found some place it shouldn't be. Plus of course all the technology we now take for granted.' Inga looked around to check they'd all got the message. 'Suggest you speak to the techie boys in the eTeam upstairs, understand they have a siphoning system save you going laboriously through all social media sites. Remember some of them didn't even exist back then.'

'Yes ma'am,' had a sigh of reluctance running right through it but knew she had to trudge on. 'There's a place called Streeter in North Dakota,' she read from her screen. 'Lots of Americans have Streeter as a surname, but apparently there are more than three thousand more popular surnames in the UK than hers.' When slim and attractive Gillian glanced up the look from her boss was encouraging. 'Sandy tells me Streeter is a name associated with a poker hand, particularly in Texas Hold'em. Nothing of any great interest except low life in Queensland who try to lure young girls into their cars are called Queen Streeters.' She grinned. 'Usually the sort who are a couple of lace holes short of a shoe.'

'Called hoons ma'am,' DS Raza Latif popped up with. 'In Australia I was once told, hoons are blokes in cars up to no good.' Got the pair of them a clapping motion and a grimace from boss Larsson.

'Thanks for that,' she said with a wry smile to their British Asian. 'Good but no good. Ruth, how have you got on with your specifics?'

The look on Ruth's face told its own story. 'To register with a GP you need your name and address, date of birth and National Health Service number if you know it.' She looked around and could see her colleagues had no idea what theirs might be. 'They may ask for details of your previous GP, some ask for a passport or driving licence and silly ones ask for proof of address, with a utility bill. Of course we all know they are next to pointless as we all do it on line these days if you've got any sense, and it proves nothing anyway. Most people need a new GP when they move house any distance and the one thing they don't have in such a situation of course is a utility bill.'

'What dollops decided we didn't need ID cards?' was inevitably handsome Jake Goodwin.

'Crooks.'

'Exactly. Half-baked dopes only interested in their liberty nonsense but not ours, and MPs as daft as a brush as ever,' the DS just sat there shaking his head with an exasperated look on his face.

'What else have we come up with of major importance?' their DI asked.

'We've looked at banning orders, unpaid bills, county court judgments and even delinquent Child Support Agency payments,' Michelle popped in. 'Nothing's been flagged up.'

'Left the country do we think?'

'Tell them Jake,' sighed Inga.

'No passport.'

'For who?' she asked. Nobody answered for fear it was a trap they'd not want to fall into in front of the team. 'That's the crux of the matter and our problem surely. If you were her when she walked away if it's what she did, would you still be Chrissie Streeter? Would you be the person easily traceable with a rare name if you were trying to hide? Useful exercise which has answered a lot of questions, but the big one is, in my considered opinion, who did she become, and just as important. Why?'

'The very reason why eleven years ago they didn't find her, why she is still missing or was until her DNA just popped up with all this Mindi Brookes business.'

'Think on this, when people change their name for criminal purposes they usually choose the same initials.'

'Why?' was Ruth.

'People give you things,' she said to Ruth. 'With say RM on them. A necklace, a bracelet, key ring or a pen, all sorts. If today you want to be Andrea Sompting say, you have to remember not to have anything on you or with you with your RM initials to give the game away. If you choose Rosalind Munnery as your false name you're safe.'

'What did they check back then do we know?' Gillian asked. 'Bail hostels, homeless centres, charities even food...' the DC looked at her colleagues. 'Not be food banks then was there?' shaking heads confirmed. 'Just a thought as some keep records.'

'Not be like it is now with all these millions of immigrants either we don't know even exist.'

'She planned it, is that what we're saying?' Ruth posed 'She had a new identity up and running, had somewhere and possibly someone to run to and keep her head down, lie low...'

'Kept her head down for eleven years?'

'Maybe,' Ruth continued. 'She had a job even and because she never used her Chrissie Streeter bank or credit cards ever again, quite probably a bank account.'

'Not wishing to throw oil on your water,' said a self-satisfied looking Inga Larsson. 'We don't even know for sure whether she is dead or alive although fresh DNA has surely to be a bit of a clue. But if she is alive and just walked out, just think about doing such a thing with no money and no sightings.'

'Here's another,' said Gillian. 'She'd need something like a passport to open a bank account.'

'No passport so no bank account, unless she got a false one. Could you pay for everything in cash in those days? Yes, very easily.'

'It was only a couple of years ago when those thirty odd illegal workers were rounded up for deportation,' Inga reminded them all. 'They were working for a high-end burger joint and they all had counterfeit documents the company'd been hoodwinked by.'

'Remember it,' said bulky Brown-Reid. 'Big fuss on social media if I recall.'

'If it is so very simple for so-called migrants turning up in a rubber dinghy to get their hands on false papers how easy must it have been for a Brit like her?'

'Her poor family have spent every waking hour for nearly eleven years trying to find her,' said Ruth. 'I'll get back on to her brother see what he knows about her car. Poor sods have tried all these missing persons' websites and anything else they can think of. Torn their lives apart for more than a decade and her mother's still in a right state about it all.'

'Not the only ones,' slim dark haired Gillian piped up.

'When I spoke to him,' said Ruth quickly. 'He admitted he's got a file of all the places they've looked into. What we're doing now he did all that time ago I bet.'

Inga still missed a lot of the good work DC Nicola Scoley had done within the team when she was there, but this Ruth had good assets too. Time spent with Family Liaison was proving useful, especially dealing with as family on the edge of grief for so long.

In time Inga was hoping she would be able to rely on Ruth in much the same way as she had done with Nicky. Whenever there was a major incident Craig Darke would loan Inga a few younger less experienced DCs like Julie and Gillian from the PHU. Ruth she hoped would help to balance their naivety and lack of experience.

'There's still the case of Claudia Lawrence the chef who went missing.'

'I've been reading, a lot of the case,' said Ruth. 'Apparently the investigation up there has been hampered by being compromised by some idiots refusing to co-operate.'

'Beggars belief.'

'Why would you?'

'Got an idiotic grudge about coppers for some ridiculous reason so they take it out on her.'

'How did we get onto that?' Inga wanted to know from Ruth.

'Decided to have a look at POLKA and she popped up.' Police OnLine Knowledge Area, is an opportunity for officers to share knowledge and ideas.

'I'd normally be looking where the evidence chain had got us, but we're still stuck in the past,' hinted at a degree of frustration. 'Stick her name into the electoral register please somebody. You never know we might get lucky.'

An hour later they were no further forward on the subject. Ruth Buchan had talked to Chrissie's brother who said Christine had always kept her Seat in a lock up round the back of the terraced houses where she shared a flat with Borowiak. He claimed the police had told him when they checked, the place was empty apart from a pile of rubbish at the back. They'd not seen hide nor hair of the green Seat since.

Brother Daniel Streeter had been checked all those years ago and he was on holiday in a caravan just outside Mevagissey at the time of his sister's disappearance with his wife and two kids.

'You also asked me to go through the old stuff on the Borowiak trial,' said Ruth. 'She was all over the papers at the time, even some social media though it wasn't as strong as it is now of course,' she looked at her monitor to remind herself. 'We're talking 2006 when she disappeared. Twitter had just been launched so wasn't widespread amongst those with nothing better to do with their lives as is the case now. Became mainstream when the smart phones came in.'

'Must have been...'

'Ma'am,' said auburn Julie Rhoades. 'The iPhone came out around 2007 and Android a year later but popularity was slow to take off and was never in the big time much before 2010.'

'By which time the world had moved on and Christine Streeter was very much yesterday's news.'

'Think it was the *News of the World*,' said Ruth. 'Who offered a fifty thousand reward in return for positive news on Christine's whereabouts?'

'Back in the bad old days.'

'Watch out,' said Jake Goodwin with his head down. 'Be phone tapping next,' was his usual sardonic humour.

'And mega bucks for a photo I bet.'

'Another thing of course,' civvie Lizzie joined in. 'Back then we didn't have every Tom Dick and Harry Houdini thinking they're David Bailey with cameras in their phones and there was no mileage in a selfie in those days.'

'I still wish there wasn't!' was cynical Jake naturally.

'It was all on *Crimewatch* of course and has been back on again since. Posters went up, you know the sort of thing. Missing. Have you seen Christine? Phone Crime Stoppers.'

'Sounds as though she'd not be able to move without somebody wanting to claim fifty grand.'

'Has to be why some of the media still suggest she's dead.'

'Only thing they didn't do was drag Hartsholme lake where Borowiak still claims he was fishing all night.'

'Haven't you got to ask why?'

'Here's a thought for you,' said Inga with a wry smile to make one or two show visual concern over what was coming next. 'There are still over a thousand people reported as missing from 9/11. One theory about some of them is they took the opportunity to disappear, to run away from the life they'd been leading and set up some place else as another person.'

'What sort of mind thinks in such a way?' Gillian chirped in. 'Oh gee, look what's happened,' she imitated in a bad American accent. 'Been waiting for something like this, what a stroke of luck gotta be my chance to get away from the missus.'

'This is all good stuff,' said Inga. 'Everything you've investigated has been thorough, but think on this. If she simply changed her name, so what?' Inga shrugged and watched the facial expressions change. 'In my time I've come across plenty of women who have done just that. Know of three who did it because they'd been stalked. Several who were raped or were victims of serious assault and even one woman just didn't like her name.' She hesitated again. 'Topliss she was, by name but not by nature,' she said and grinned. 'One guy I knew at uni was even worse. Tony Willey known as Tiny.' She had to wait for the chuckling to stop. 'Remember, changing your name is not a criminal offence.'

'Could have been attacked by Borowiak.'

'You're right and some just want to get the hell out of it. People who their relatives and friends still think were in the twin towers when the planes struck but by sheer chance weren't,' Inga went on. 'There were those bombs in Brussels remember? Read somewhere how one man is still missing.'

'But is he?'

'What about Grenfell? People fraudulently claimed to have been living there and were looking for compensation. That'd be an opportunity to disappear. Just suppose you're in serious trouble, up to your ears in debt with heavies knocking on the door. Big fire in Grenfell so you change your name and claim to have been made homeless. Easy finish up living in a new place, take on the new identity saying your passport was in the fire.'

'If you remember,' Inga joined in. 'There were hundreds of messages people desperately looking for friends wrote on walls and hoardings. Surely if you made a note of a name or two and headed off down the Council you could be someone new in no time.'

'With a council finding it difficult to cope.'

'Wonder if that's what the fraudulent ones were trying to do?' Gillian again mimicked. 'Hello, I'm Joe Bloggs, you bin looking for me?'

'Bet somebody tried it on.'

'We all know now that story about a baby being thrown from a burning window and caught by someone never actually happened.'

'Streeter could have pulled a stroke like some of these.'

'Except she didn't have a fire.'

'Hmm, there is that.'

'Exactly,' Inga confirmed then smiled. 'Don't want you to find the man in Brussels, any of those missing from Grenfell or the Trade Center, but what I would like you to do is go back to when Streeter went missing. What happened on that day?' she emphasized. 'Was there something, not necessarily a bomb or a massive fire, but just something which would take people's eye off the ball while she did a runner?'

'Christine Streeter could well have been on her bike and away when the world was looking the other way.'

'People just go missing all the time, especially men...'

'But we're looking for a woman.'

'Well observed,' was Jake's sarcasm. 'Relationship breakdown and these days no marriage contract to hold them back. Mid-life crisis hits about the same time.' He looked across at Gillian. 'Remember it affects women and men. Mental breakdown is now more recognized, so is depression than it was when she cleared off. If she did do a runner, maybe she was just pissed off with her lot.'

'Isn't embarrassment one you've forgotten?' Ruth suggested. 'Have a blazing row over next to nothing. Lose control, tell yourself when you're in such a mood anything's better than this and off you go. Then when you've calmed down you feel a complete prat but are then too embarrassed and too proud to creep back.'

'It's a man thing!'

'Go cap in hand,' Ruth carried on. 'To somebody who probably hates your guts anyway and worse still will laugh at you. So its sod it, this is not worth the hassle, don't need any more of this. Off you trot, goodnight Vienna.'

'Here's an interesting fact,' said Inga to cut the inevitable chatter breaking out. 'Every year two hundred unidentified bodies turn up. Right this minute just over a thousand bodies are lying in morgues none of which have ever been identified.'

'And probably never will be.'

'How sad is that?'

'Is one Chrissie Streeter?'

5

Her senior Detective Sergeant Jacques 'Jake' Goodwin had obviously been at his work station a while when Inga Larsson arrived early the next day. In fact he looked as though he had been there a good while. Not all night as he didn't have the look about him.

Him of caustic humour, the one with defined ingrained principles about life and human behaviour, but no matter what, he was a first class copper. Unlikely to inspire the powers that be to want to promote him anytime soon, but he was an absolute rock she could always depend on.

Jake's sense of duty had been the lever to propel him into the police service. His companion in life had since an early age been his inbuilt moral compass. Black and white, good and bad and woe betide those who choose the latter.

He was fully aware how the police are seen by some sections of the community. Those who look at the rogue cops, those hit with disciplinary procedures after complaints from scurrilous Joe Public. Those only interested in nothing but rumours and lies of corruption on social media he made no attention to in his private life with Sally.

Jake Goodwin had always known he was different from his peers. He had been taught to read and could write his own name before he went to school by his French mother. He had been toilet trained which he knew was not always the norm nowadays. His mother had walked him to school that first day and from then on he walked or biked himself there and back. The bricks to build his early life experiences, cultivation and building of basic standards. All part of his in-built stubborn streak when dealing with today's wayward youth.

A combination of being born to parents from either side of the Channel would have more than likely been responsible for his standards and principles. He retained all the politeness of yesteryear and had been influenced by his time spent abroad. Jake was always been aware of how different the use of mobile phones is between the UK and other countries who lack the obsession. Another example of his uneasiness with today's society's behavior can be seen by him never having ever bought a to-go coffee. Purely because he had been taught never to eat or drink in the street. He was also influenced by Italian friends of his mother who would never grab a coffee to scoff as they walk, as this is simply not the way coffee connoisseurs behave. Jake is also aware how in most places in Italy such a service is simply not available. They simply do not serve their favourite drink in cardboard.

Not buying a coffee to-go of course was also a no no with Inga Larsson but for an entirely different reason. She could not stomach the tang of the plastic inner which affects the coffee taste..

Inga was not in any way surprised in how as soon as she had got her jacket off, sat down at her desk and logged onto the systems, checked the overnights and her messages Jake was at her door.

'Been having a think' he opened with.

'About how long it is since you got me an early start of day milky coffee?' He sighed and shook his head. 'I'll still be here when you get back.' She was always aware he would never leave the job at the door when he left for home as Raza Latif did. When he returned with two mugs she made a performance of looking all round hers. 'They sold out of biscuits?'

Goodwin patted his not over extended stomach. 'On a diet.'

'This official?' she asked and knew there were millions more in far greater need than him.

'Sally's idea, so how much more official do you want it?'

'I'll be watching you then, and if I spy any naughtiness I'll be having a word.'

'It's not a criminal offence having a Mars bar,' he said sitting down.

'I know but Sally's a nurse and one day she might just come in handy and I've no intention of getting in her bad books, those needles can hurt!'

'You women.'

'What was it you wanted to talk about?'

'Mindi Brookes.'

'Go on.'

'I've read all the reports, all the gory bits, ploughed through all the CSI stuff, and I know we've not got Jack Black's final analysis as yet but I reckon this Streeter wet the bed first, and...' he stopped when Inga grinned and began to nod.

'Snap!'

'You think so too?'

'Had it all sent home on the secure system, good bedtime reading which didn't amuse Adam I can tell you. Think you're right, but give me your version.' Inga sipped her milky coffee as Jake began.

'Let us assume the killer is this Christine Streeter female because at present we have nobody else. She turns up to see Brookes possibly pre-arranged with Kempshall going off to his rugby. During the chat when they made arrangements, this Mindi casually told her how Kempshall would be in London and she planned to call him at half time. When she phones him, this Streeter takes the opportunity to nip upstairs to the loo, except she does it in the bed and dries herself off on the duvet.'

'Carry on,' said a grimacing Inga when he stopped for a breath. 'Hadn't occurred to me she'd made the phone call as her opportunity, but it fits. Knows the coast is clear.'

'Probably be a case of come round Friday, Aaron'll be down in London, we can have a girl's night in.'

'Ned'll be at his rugby.'

'You're probably right. Assuming they know each other of course.'

'Could be a client, goes to her yoga classes.'

'You ever...?' was as far as she got before he shook his head and gave her a look. She really should have known better.

'She then goes into the loo and flushes so Mindi downstairs hears she's been to the toilet. When she comes down, if you remember the layout, Brookes'd have had her back to this Streeter.'

'Hang on. I've got an extra bit,' said an intrigued Inga. 'When she goes up to the loo she takes her bag,' put her head on one side. 'Ladies sometimes need to take their bag to the loo with them,' she received a knowing slow nod from Jake.

'Comes back downstairs,' he went on. 'Mindi has her back to her. Phone call finished and Streeter takes the knife from her bag, reaches over Mindi Brooke's right shoulder and plunges the knife into her chest, pulls it out and back in slicing her heart almost in two it says in the PM report, then out again and for good measure into her stomach.'

'Good man,' she smiled as she nodded. 'Be interesting to see what Jack Black comes up with.'

'All the blood is downstairs, there's none upstairs or in the kitchen area. Job done she probably wipes off excess blood on the cover over the dreadful sofa and walks out, all done and dusted.'

'Guess you've wrapped it up then,' said Inga before she took a bigger drink of her start of day caffeine. 'All we have to do now is find her and discover why.'

'You been thinking the same?'

'Pretty much,' she looked past Jake out into the incident room. 'One worry is a lack of fingerprints. I know we have the DNA, but if what we think really did happen she's been mighty careful.'

'But the fingerprints from way back, how good were they when they didn't have her alive or dead?'

'Always possible upstairs she pulled rubber gloves from her bag of tricks. Brookes'd never have seen her wearing them the way we see it panning out.'

'Just doesn't make sense to me,' Jake said slowly. 'Disappears knowing Brorowiak has been done for murder, stays hidden all this time which would have been far from easy, then just pops up and kills some totally innocent woman.'

'But is she innocent?' Inga queried.

'Why not?'

'Something to do with sport and leisure,' said Inga. 'Spent last evening going through the notes. Streeter worked for a small now defunct insurance company back then, sort of broker I suppose, but...' she waited a moment. 'Insurance?'

'Which is far removed from aerobics or whatever it is Brookes did.'

'Yoga Jake. There is a difference.'

It had been decided to bring the subject of Christine Streeter disappearance back into the public domain and the Lincoln County

Police's PR team had based the story they issued to the media on the fact they now had fresh evidence and were asking for the public to let them know of any sightings of the woman who would now be thirty-three years of age.

They made a great deal of the fact her poor parents Bill and Kathleen Streeter were still in a state of turmoil unaware whether their only daughter was alive or dead.

'According to him,' said Ruth. 'Their marriage has broken down as a direct result of their daughter's disappearance.'

'You'd think they'd need each other at such a time.'

'To be honest,' said a concerned Ruth. 'He is without doubt the strong one of the pair, and he was quite open about it all when I spoke with him. Says his wife resented the fact he could quite easily deal with it all to a certain extent, whereas she couldn't.'

'And she still can't?'

'Most certainly she can't. She is real hard work,' the new to the team DC told them all. 'I cannot imagine of course what she's gone through for all these years, but to be honest when I spoke with her it was as if it happened yesterday.'

'D'you say they're divorced?' Inga checked.

'Oh no,' said Ruth. 'Kathleen's very religious, or should I say has become even more so with all this business, and not divorced according to her husband Bill because she says her faith won't allow it. Think he's hopeful they might one day get back together, but after talking to her I don't see it.' Ruth hesitated to clear her throat. 'Don't take this as gospel, but I got the feeling he supports her financially, they just don't live together or associate socially anymore.'

'Has all this made her worse do you think?'

'When I spoke to Mrs Streeter,' said Ruth who always tends to have a serious look about her. 'It was as bad as it gets. The poor woman is going through the nightmare all over again now it's all been dragged back up. Absolutely wretched with grief for the second time and her husband said to me he thinks all this has hit her worse than all those years ago.'

'Years of being desperate for news must have built up inside her,' Inga offered.

'Every time the phone rings, every knock on the door.'

'And we still have no answers for her.' Ruth just lifted her hand and shook her head. 'How do you explain to somebody in the state she is in, yes we have her DNA, but no we're no further forward in finding her daughter?'

'Her life must have been on hold all this time.'

Ruth went on: 'Bill Streeter is tormented by the thought of Borowiak knowing what happened to her, and before long some do-gooders sat on a parole board will say enough is enough, he's been punished enough and he'll be let out on the say so of a bunch of soppy women.'

'You'd think people at her church would help,' Gillian suggested.

'Not if it's one of these happy-clappy places,' said Jake. 'Some of them are as close to being sects as you can get. They're all about using people, especially using the money you give them, but the moment you want help they'll not be seen for dust.'

'All smarmy walk-the-talk greasy bozos.'

'Got them in one,' said Jake to Raza Latif. 'All smarm and no charm in flared jeans.'

'This Bill Streeter, did he seem a decent sort of chap?' Kenny asked Ruth.

'Just one problem,' she answered. 'War games in a big way, but maybe just his way of dealing with it. Could be he gradually got more and more involved as a way to occupy his mind but all she's got are the lily livered at her church to remind her.'

'We came across war games once before,' said Jake Goodwin listening in.

'Just a lad doing it on line, this one is all about acting out great battles with tiny soldiers.' Jake sniggered and went to comment but Ruth had more to say. 'According to this Kathleen he and the group he belongs have spent the past four years re-creating all the major battles of the First World War. Actually plays them out a hundred years to the day they happened, all in absolute detail.'

'Be coming to an end next month I guess.'

'You haven't heard the best of it,' Ruth smiled. 'Told me in all seriousness he's heading up a sub-committee to plan for 2039 and the start of World War Two.' Nobody commented, they were so amazed except boss Larsson.

'Plan to do the same all over again, apparently,' Inga added stealing Ruth's thunder. 'Hundred years and go through it all. Dunkirk, D-day all the rest.'

'That'll not be for another twenty years!'

'I know,' Ruth smiled. 'Total obsession, he'll bore you to tears in five minutes flat. I know I've met him.'

'How old is he?' Gillian wanted to know.

'Mid-fifties must be,' Ruth said. 'Seems a decent bloke on the outside but it must be great fun to live with a complete dork like him. Not.'

'This a man thing?' Gillian asked amidst a chuckle.

'Complete idiot thing.'

'Selfish more like.'

'But if your daughter is still missing and possibly dead, his marriage has gone up the spout, what else has he got? Grand kids?'

'Just one thing,' said a reactionary Ruth. 'When I was talking to this Kathleen she did say something I thought was out of character and more than a little odd for her at the time. Said something like, d'you know if I had the guts I'd become a lesbian, but I suppose it would mean more of the fiddling about business,' she was struggling to continue without laughing. 'Not sure I want any more of all the mucky stuff.' It was no good, she just had to titter.

'What a strange thing to say,' said a serious Gillian.

'Seemed a somewhat rather peculiar thing to me from such a staid woman,' Ruth offered and kept her own thoughts to herself.

'Some people really are quite complex when it comes down to it.'

'Said she knew her Christine was never truly happy at school, almost as if it somehow didn't agree with her. Got the impression the way she spoke Christine's mind somehow rejected the institution. Told me had it been possible, they'd have schooled her at home.'

'She went to an all-girl school remember,' Inga reminded them. 'They're full of shortcomings of course, reason they're dying out. One reason is girls are put at a distinct disadvantage by not being able to communicate effectively with men.'

'With Borowiak?'

'Could well be,' Inga responded. 'Those sorts of places do tend to produce shrinking violets. Pleasant enough kind of young women but the sort who spend their lives being febrile, and I understand their lack of certain skills can result in bullying.'

'Don't have boys to rough them up. Knock them into shape.'

'Better not let the feminists' mafia hear you talking this way.'

On line versions of local media and radio carried the story to varying degrees, each seemingly coming at it from a different angle.

One of the detectives borrowed from PCT (Priority Crime Team) working for Jake Goodwin had come up with interesting information on Kempshall. He had not been to Harlequins Rugby Club before, so why that night? He had always gone to matches closer to home, even though his ex-school chum played for Quins. He was right in what he had said about going to watch Owen Edwards play two or three times a year, but not as far south as The Stoop. He'd even been up as far as Newcastle, and booked seats at Northampton and Leicester to watch matches which made more sense.

'Any mileage do we think in asking Kempshall why that day of all days he gets as far away from Lincoln as is possible?'

'I need to find a link between him and Streeter,' said Jake. 'His alibi is being miles away and on CCTV.'

'We have him at the Services getting on for two hours before he arrived back here,' Inga reminded. 'If we assume he never went to the rugby at all, we're talking an hour and a half from here to Peterborough assuming he went straight down and then another couple back including the stop. Can't have killed her as she didn't leave work until getting on for six and she was still alive then.' Inga thought to herself for a moment. 'Not a priority, but at some point would be interesting to find out why. If he didn't go to London, what was he doing? Visiting somebody else, up to no good?'

'Cultivating an alibi?' was Gillian.

Inga casually propped up against a desk shrugged. 'Add it to the list for the team but as an added extra.'

'Get an ANPR check done of him heading for Twickenham but much closer to the ground if at all possible. Cover all eventualities.'

'From what her girlfriends tell us remember,' said Michelle Cooper. 'Mindi was trying to get him to make things a bit more permanent. Looking to buy somewhere together rather than waste money on rent.'

'But if he'd got a floosie hidden away somewhere. What my mother used to call, or rather probably still does call loose women.' Jake Goodwin turned to the boss. 'Disreputable woman, free and easy, but not necessarily free,' he explained to the boss. 'Be a wanter,' he added. 'Another phrase from my mother's knee, want this, want that.'

'Still playing the field you think?' Gillian checked with the boss.

'Just a feeling I gathered talking to him on the night,' Inga responded. 'Serious lack of emotion and reaction, more concerned about Harlequins having won and not being able to get in the house than worrying about Mindi.'

'Something he didn't want us to find?'

'Got him for speeding twice in the past three years, nothing else,' said Jake. 'Admitted to me he smokes a bit of weed sometimes but said she didn't, in fact admitted Mindi got quite angry when he did.'

'We talking motive? Don't bring your stuff in here - you think?'

'Closest we've got so far, a pucker motive really is unclear.'

'Is whoever did this known to Kempshall? And he made absolutely sure he was well out of the way? Streeter did it for him or maybe he used a surrogate killer?'

'Who would have done this for him, apart from this Streeter woman?' Inga asked them all. 'Is whoever did this local, is he or she still in our midst? Is this person just going about their life as normal today?' She looked towards chunky Sandy MacLachlan. 'Anything from those we spoke to before?' was replied by just the shake of his head initially.

'Ones I've caught up with so far, have a job to remember what they told us back then, let alone having any new ideas.'

'No big payments from his account,' Jake advised. 'If you're thinking he paid somebody.'

'Would you do it for your mate? Go and kill his woman while he's out of the way?'

'If you're desperate for a few bob maybe. Bad debt, drugs problem.'

'You've got to be bloody desperate.'

'Millions are. Millions of folk are in debt remember.'

'Only because they want everything now.' Inevitably was a Jake Goodwin remark. 'When they've spent too much on a honking big tele. Don't get me started on all the down the drain cash spent on take-aways, rent and the bookies. Ridiculous amounts some of them spend, you know. Bet on anything some of 'em.'

'And wet the bed?'

'According to the eTeam there's a lot of talk on Twitter, but no names as far as they can see, just folk asking who and like us, asking why.'

Jake Goodwin admitted he had learned things about rugby clubs and the location of their grounds he had until then been totally unaware of. He'd known of clubs such as Wasps and London Irish but until this investigation had no idea where they were actually based.

Ruth Buchan and her team were all convinced to disappear to the degree in which this woman had, she would need a serious plan of action, considerable help and more importantly money. This was never something you can do on a whim, especially when within a matter of hours the whole nation knows about your disappearance.

'Creating a new identity is not really too difficult,' Ruth offered. 'The empty or non-existent property is a good start. Think we've come across people doing it before. Nicking stuff from letterboxes because the postman's too lazy. Emptying mailboxes in high rise. Take a gas bill, driving licence, anything in a give-away buff envelope. Even a tax return or tax coding notification can be gold dust as it'll have a National Insurance number on it.'

'Register of deaths is next I bet,' MacLachlan piped up. 'Find the name of a dead kid to match it. Too young to have a passport or driving licence and you're away.'

'ID cards would have sorted all this,' said an exasperated Jake and they all knew how right she was. 'And the damn terrorists.'

'Without them you can be who you like, when you like.'

'Except,' said Inga. 'The person we're talking about went missing before there was talk of ID cards.' She frowned. 'I think I'm right in saying.' Jake and Sandy nodded to each other.

'Doing all this wouldn't cost her a fortune,' Ruth offered. 'Just a lot of shoe leather be all.'

'Where did she live initially? What did she do for money? Especially as her bank account had not been touched from then onwards, except those direct debits to pay her household bills her solicitor eventually put a stop to. Her credit and debit cards had not been used. She even had Tesco Club Card points she's never claimed.'

'More and more questions than answers,' said dour Ruth.

'This is the bit I hate,' said a determined Inga. 'All these questions about Mindi and no answers. I know its early days but there's no indication as to why she was stabbed, and as we know the post mortem had it down as multiple stab wounds, but she had no defensive wounds to either hands.'

'As we thought,' said Jake. 'Came up from behind, big arc over her right shoulder, down and in.' He looked at the DI. 'Blade sharp side up, too.'

'So the poor lass didn't put up a fight.'

'Couldn't, more like,' Inga jumped in. 'First blow could well'ave pinned her to the crap sofa. All over before she knew what was going on is my guess.' She looked at Jake. 'Got a big knife in her chest before she could react, and by then it's too late.' Her DS nodded his agreement.

'Pathologist tends to agree with us.' Jake Goodwin looked across at Ruth. 'Streeter,' was all he needed to say.

'Can I just say,' Inga interrupted before Ruth could speak. 'This Mindi with all due respect and without being rude is one of life's nobodies. From what we can gather so far she's not known to us, apart from a couple of parking tickets and speeding four years ago but she was doing under fifty in a built up area. Apart from that most probably one of the decent folk who live by the rules, played life as it should be.' Inga nodded to DC Buchan.

'We're of the opinion,' said Ruth. 'If she is not dead, and the new DNA tends to confirm it. This Streeter must have created a whole new identity which makes all our jobs quite a bit harder. If she was escaping debts and to deal with those sort of issues she staged her own death so to speak, then it has illegal consequences, not least what all this has meant to Tomasz Borowiak.'

'Except,' said Lizzie. 'As far as we can make out she had no debts as such.'

'And,' said Gillian quickly. 'It appears she and Borowiak had separate money, no joint accounts according to the file from back then.' Slim tall woman despite two pregnancies, pretty with a gathering of freckles.

'Eleven year old new identity, not be something she's just trying out now. It'll be ingrained in her habits with the people she associates with. By now surely she'll actually be this new person.'

'If she had reasons to escape from Borowiak,' said Lizzie the HOLMES inputter. 'There are legal ways to change your identity. As far as we can see she did nothing, just took it upon herself to become somebody else.'

Inga was aware how Lizzie Webb herself had contemplated such a move at one time when she finally walked out on the brute who had left her with both physical and mental scars.

'She was surely not doing a vanishing act for no reason,' Inga surmised. 'Except spite maybe. Has Tomasz Borowiak been the problem all along? He didn't kill her or so it appears if this DNA is correct, but was he the reason why? Rather than go down the legal route to change who she was she chose another. Difficult they say to run away from someone and all the time keep looking over your shoulder, but if you pull a stunt so the police arrest whoever it is you're scared of, you stand a much better chance.'

'They do say ma'am. Keep your friends close but your enemies even closer, so you know what they're doing. You have to remember they know you, know your likes and dislikes and your habits and you know what they say. Habits die hard.'

'She knew exactly where Borowiak was and what he was doing. He was in nick.'

'Hardest thing to change,' said Lizzie. 'Your habits, all the things which clearly say who you are.'

'From what we can make out, one piece of sound advice is to abandon your car,' said Ruth. 'Leave the DVLA documents in the glove box, leave the door unlocked, even a window open and park it in an undesirable location for a thief to happen upon and then just chuck the key away.'

Inga was pleased Ruth was really taking an interest in these aspects of the case. Just wished one or two others she'd been stuck with in the early days of this case would buck their ideas up.

'Car's not been seen since, nor have the documents. Her driving documents, MOT, driving licence and insurance certificate, where are they?'

'Back then they put flags on everything,' Gillian advised. 'Her credit card, cheques, phone, passport even her National Insurance Number. Nothing and her car tax and insurance have never been renewed.'

'But how could she afford to just dump her car?'

'Not worth a lot,' said big Sandy who had been earwigging. 'We're talking a Mk 2 Seat Ibiza, few years old back then.'

'Got to say,' said a well satisfied Detective Inspector. 'You've all certainly got a handle on this disappearing business.' She sniggered. 'Now you have to get a handle on who she is now.'

'And how she afforded it.'

'Sugar daddy?'

'Now we're talking a whole different ball game.'

6

Lizzie Webb had phoned Inga Larsson at home the previous evening and thanked the DI for not mentioning how she had at one time had seriously considered changing her identity to free herself of the monster in whose hands she had suffered untold torment.

Lizzie was able to confirm how the sheer magnitude and rigmarole of changing identity had in the end put her off. The moment she started to list all the changes she would have to make she had realized how onerous a task it would be for a lone woman.

'Every time I thought of something new which had to be done, it then produced even more problems to deal with. My biggest worry was would all these people keep it to themselves. Would any of them decide to write to me at the house where that evil sod was still living? Would some tosspot decide to phone me up on my old number? Nightmare, let me tell you.'

'First thing,' said Inga to open her afternoon briefing. 'We've had an outskirts enquiry team on house-to-house all around the uphill area. Anything come of it?' she aimed at DC Kenny Ford him of the bald head courtesy of a razor.

'No ma'am. Nothing to speak of. Got a couple still out there going back to the no shows. All the neighbourhood streets have been checked, but haven't come across anybody who saw or heard anything that evening.'

'Think wider,' she came back with. 'No cars, but what about a bike or a taxi?' Inga looked across at Jake Goodwin. 'We done them?' Jake nodded and smiled. 'Thank goodness,' she said with a breath. 'Carry on Kenny. As they say, think bike.'

'Up there walking's the best bet,' MacLachlan suggested. 'Be out of sight in no time.'

'Time gentlemen for you to shine,' Inga announced after a glance at her notes. 'What have you come up with about both Borowiak and our rugby fan Aaron Kempshall?'

Sandy MacLachlan along with Sam Howard and Kenny Ford borrowed from PHU glanced at each other before Sam spoke.

'Thomasz Borowiak according to the file says he was night fishing by the side of the lake in Hartsholme Park. Claimed he left their house around ten-thirty and biked across there from Swanpool. Claims he was there until around five fifteen, packed up and rode to their flat which he found empty but in a bit of a mess...'

MacLachlan butted in. 'Seen the photos of Brooke's place. All as if there had been a struggle, with chairs knocked over, a cushion on the floor and a general untidyness. Nothing at all in the place Borowiak and Streeter shared. True they were taken some time after she must have walked out when missing person became murder.' He answered the question before Inga managed to ask it. 'He could well have tidied up of course.'

'And what if it has been staged?' Inga offered. 'Or haven't you been listening? Streeter we assume comes down the stairs with Brookes sat on the sofa with her back to her, attacks her from behind. There's no fight, no defence wounds. Remember. All done and dusted Streeter or whoever just upturns a couple of badly painted chairs, throws an appalling cushion on the floor,' she sighed. 'Been me I'd have thrown them out the window!'

'CSI photos are available if we want,' Kenny Ford offered. 'But they're particularly pertinent to the bedroom where there's nothing obvious until you pull back the duvet.'

'Good news for Borowiak,' said Sam used to acquisitive crime in PHU, day to day nonsense such as shoplifting and burglary. 'Chap in the next street just setting off for work in his car saw Borowiak on his bike come out of Almond Avenue and into Westwood where he lived. All exactly at the time Borowiak says he got back.' He smiled. 'Bad news for Borowiak, his downstairs neighbours were away for a few days so could not confirm any sightings of anybody else, or heard any noise when Borowiak says he was fishing or when he got home.'

'And the prosecution concluded what?' Inga asked although she knew full well what the files said.

'Borowiak did go off fishing, but he came back at some point in the night, killed Streeter, took her body and hid it somewhere only he knows. Or,' and he hesitated. 'He took her somewhere then killed her and buried her and went back to his fishing.'

'What about the suggestion he dug her grave in advance?' Inga threw into the ring.

'Defence,' Kenny Ford popped in. 'Claimed the prosecution couldn't prove any of it as they had no witnesses and no evidence, and said the neighbours on one side because they were in Whitby for the week were in effect defence witnesses because they could not confirm Borowiak had been back to the house to do the deed half way through the night. The same had gone for the Matthews on the other side who'd had friends round for the evening and claimed to have heard nothing. And the only other witness had seen him at exactly the time he said he was in the area and nobody else then or earlier. We're talking half five in the morning. Not a lot of folk about.'

'Two lots of DNA dominated the scene as you would imagine and one lot of blood which happened to be hers got him put away.'

'Phone call to 999 was just around twenty minutes after Borowiak said he got home and this guy in the next street says he saw him ride by.'

'Was Borowiak seen at the place where he was fishing?' Inga checked.

'Not actually there, but people did come forward and a private eye they used found witnesses who said they'd seen a guy on a bike with a load of clobber the previous evening.'

'If Borowiak never did go back to kill Streeter, then he had absolutely no way of proving a negative,' said the DI as she mused.

'Blood on his jacket he claimed was him just brushing against some of the blood in his panic.'

'Wet blood?' she queried.

'No just tiny bits caught up in the fibres.'

'Neighbours from downstairs may not have been there at the time but they were character references,' Ford could not depress a snicker. 'Said Streeter and Borowiak were always rowing, had to tell them to keep the noise down more than once. At it like cat and dog apparently.'

'Bet it was brought up in court!'

'According to press reports after he was sent down, he was asked in court about it. Borowiak just shrugged apparently and treated it as if it's just what couples do. Really didn't see it as an issue at all. In fact he lost his cool at one point in the witness box and turned on the prosecution counsel and asked how often he and his wife have rows.'

'Can I just add an observation,' Jake Goodwin asked. 'The defence it seems were unable to provide anybody who would claim to have called on Streeter after he left. No callers, nobody phoned, she made no calls and nobody communicated with her in any way.'

'We know her phone was last used over two hours before Borowiak left,' Inga reminded him.

'Instead of no contact by anybody failing to help him I think it is quite the opposite.' Jake could see the boss frowning. 'To my mind this all confirms this was a planned escape by her. Not only did she become invisible from the moment Borowiak set off to go fishing, in effect it confirms she became invisible to the outside world at least an hour or more before he even left, maybe longer.'

'The phone by the way just like her, has never been traced.'

'Nowadays she could have bought a new SIM from Poundland for next to nothing tossed the old one away and she's up and running.'

'But could you do such a thing back then?' saw Inga scribble a quick note.

'When Borowiak left she swapped phones or as Kenny suggests changed the SIM and somewhere down the line dumped it. Finger-tip searches, door-to-door carried out at the time and checking drains and all the rest produced nothing.'

'Which is worse, needle in a haystack or SIM in a sewer?'

Inga looked at the four men all sat together. 'Let me get this straight. Am I right in thinking...?'

'Borowiak is innocent ok?' the three thought amusing but the reason for their humour passed her by.

'Not wishing to be the party pooper,' said a smiling Inga. 'But can I just add a word?' She hesitated. 'Blood, her blood.'

'Won't wash,' said a confident Jake immediately. 'When I go for my annual diabetes review they take a blood sample, in fact they take two test tubes of blood. It's not rocket science, and given a bit of practice I reckon I could do it. Then if I'm Streeter when Borowiak has gone off fishing I just get the test tubes full I took out of my arm yesterday or the day before and spray it about. Just enough to interest CSI.'

'And where pray did you get such an idea Jake?' Inga smirked.

'Some American television crime series, couple of years ago.'

'And a partner who happens to be a nurse,' she popped in with a smirk. 'I bet.'

'Here's a thought,' said Howard. 'One woman leaves blood for CSI to find and another leaves DNA for them.'

'As if they both knew the system.'

'The blood back then gave us a DNA profile assumed to be hers and the urine now gives us a repeat.'

'Here's a thought ma'am,' said Sam Howard. 'How do we know the original DNA actually belonged to Streeter?'

'Her DNA was one of two major profiles all over the flat, hers and Borowiak.'

Inga had always been intrigued by what Jake called 'the come-overs'. Those like Sam Howard and the rest drafted in by Darke as required for major incidents such as this one.

They were always better behaved to the extent they were at times almost too good to be true. There was always a lack of banter from them. No pictures of their kids to adorn their workstations, no Minions stuck atop their monitors. Just homed into their task, with furrowed brows through concentrated effort. This was a real opportunity to impress, to shine in amongst a successful team all part of career projection for the ambitious keener ones.

Her team were well aware how the Swede would accept no truck from any of them, but her regulars were never going for the goody toe-shoes role in vogue for a day or two, a week or if things were really bad, a fortnight or more.

One downside for Inga always was the 'the come-overs' who never had a box of Jelly Babies, packet of Maltesers or tube of Smarties open at their station ripe for nicking one or two when they weren't looking.

Inga Larsson had become utterly frustrated by this time and hard pressed resources wasted on the no-hopers looking for their few minutes of fame. All the look-at-me reprobates who had responded to the media stories about Christine Streeter. Some skanks were so stupid they'd not bothered to check the facts before they emailed in claims to have seen her, met her or knew where she was. Many were still at junior school when the events took place, yet they spoke as if they knew her well and had done so for donkey's years. Truth was of course it was their parents who were the more likely to have had some contact and who just might with any luck recognize her now.

Three or four they had checked out but although the people had made contact with good intentions they were all crossed off the list of hopefuls very quickly. Except for one.

A man in his forties had walked into Worksop police station in Nottinghamshire claiming to have seen her at East Midlands airport. They swiftly got in touch with Inga and she made arrangements to phone him and record the conversation.

'This is the Steven Lawlor I told you about,' she told her gathered throng. 'From Carlton-in-Lindrick but used to live in Lincoln and worked in Newark at one time with Christine Streeter.' She started the tape. 'I'd already established all his details as had the lads over there.' She turned on the recording.

'My flight had been delayed and I was in the queue waiting to get rid of our suitcases, but they were being a bit slow checking passports and tickets like they do and that's when I was just looking all about bored to tears. I'm dying to get through so I could get a coffee and a bite to eat when I spotted someone, and thought I know you. Thought it was Christine Streeter in the distance.'

'You recognized her?' was Larsson's voice.

'Not necessarily the look, but the overall appearance if you know what I'm saying, sort of the gait of this person reminded me so much of Chrissie who I'd worked with of course. Looked older, but then she would be if it was her and her hair was dark.'

'She had the same look you remembered?'

'No not really. But remember this came right out of the blue. Be 2012 and we're on my way to Costa Brava flying to Girona and there was no reason why Chrissie should be on my mind. For a second or two it was somebody I thought I recognized, then in the time it took for my brain to work out who it was she was gone.'

'And you thought, it can't be her, she's dead.'

'Well sort of, s'pose I must have done.'

'*And you've not seen her before then or since,*' the Detective Inspector asked this Lawlor.

'*No not at all. Did look about after we got through security even had a look around on the plane when I went to the toilet, and at Baggage Claim I did make a point of looking at people just in case.*'

'*This was in Departures? Who were you with?*' Inga asked him.

'*My wife and my daughter.*'

'*Would they recognize her?*'

'*No.*'

'*So even if they had seen her it wouldn't have registered?*'

'*No not at all.*'

'*Did you mention it to them?*'

'*Might have. Might have said think I've just spotted someone I know.*'

'*But she was dead,*' she reminded him. '*Did you not think I've just seen a dead person...?*'

'*She wasn't was she? That's what all the fuss was about, that foreign bloke got put away without them ever finding a body. Based on circumstantial evidence seemed to me.*'

'*Circumstantial was it Mr Lawlor, things such as her blood?*'

'*You know what I mean. Had she been dead I might have said it was a bit spooky I'd just seen someone who looked like a woman who'd died. Without me being aware she might have turned up, how was I to know?*'

'*I think Mr Lawlor you'd have read about it had it been the case.*'

'*I don't follow the news, haven't bought a paper in donkey's years all opinionated nonsense, just boring politics got nowt to do with me lass.*'

'*Thank you Mr Lawlor.*'

'*They say everybody's got a double somewhere.*'

Inga turned off the recording. 'Drifted away to nothing from there.'

'Why when all the news stories said phone Lincoln County Police, did he go into Worksop?' Inga's perceptive colleague offered up cautiously. Nobody had an answer to.

'Good question Jake,' Inga paused thinking about his question she'd not asked. 'Asked him if he knew Kempshall and he said not. I went on to ask him if he still knew of any other people who would have worked with her. Just in case they'd seen her maybe. He says he'll have a look on his Facebook page see who might help us.'

'I know it's only been a few days,' said slender Gillian Brown-Reid. 'But since we started all this business with this woman, I've realised how away from work and home I've not seen or spoken to anybody from work I know in the street, in shops. Not something I've thought about before. Like people are invisible.'

Jake knew Gillian had come out with that line before. 'Anybody suggests Streeter's the Invisible Woman I'm outta here,' Jake joked.

'Might as well be!'

'Back to where we were,' said Inga. 'As you know we heard via his so called friends on social media this Lawlor had messaged people about a woman who he thought might be able to help.' She hesitated. 'But then he discovered she had died suddenly a few months or more back. Had her drink spiked this person Lawlor spoke to reckons, but she doesn't really know only what she heard.'

'Social media,' Jake sighed and looked skywards. 'Got a lot to answer for.'

'Dead woman,' Inga continued. 'Was at school with Streeter apparently, but not in the same year or anything and they seem to recall her saying she saw something about her on social media a while back.'

'We do seem to have moved away from our Mindi Brookes whose murder we would have been pinning on somebody by now if it were not for our Chrissie Streeter popping up out of nowhere,' were astute Inga Larsson's thoughts said out loud.

DC Julie Rhoades for the most part working alongside Jake, thought that had been aimed at her. 'This Mindi Brookes I'm afraid is very much a blank canvas. What we have come up with are about two dozen friends, except they're not friends really. They're more like clients or customers and because she works as a self-employed instructor she's not an employee as such. Just went to places, did her class and was off. Nobody went overboard and said she was the greatest thing since sliced bread, but then they probably don't know her that well. None of them appear to be bosom buddies, no inseparable friend but on that subject the feeling seems to be how our Aaron Kempshall had tended to move her away from any close friends to some extent since she got shacked up with him, or rather since he got shacked up with her.'

'Social media,' said Gillian to give auburn Julie Rhoades a break. 'She has sixty four friends on Facebook and even that's not very exciting because the number includes her two sisters, her mother, most of those we spoke to at her work and a few people who look like aunts or people her mother knows.'

'And no Chrissie Streeter listed I suppose?'

'Can I just say,' said Julie. 'We have one sliver of doubt regarding this Mindi. One of the women we spoke to said she understood Mindi had left a previous employer under a cloud, and it was then she went freelance.'

'Interesting. We heard about it from anybody else?' was received with shrugs, shaking heads and a lone 'Nope.'

'Looks like it could be worth a look.' Inga looked at this Julie. 'Can you take a closer look at what it might be all about? Be nice to find a chink in her armour.'

'You suppose right,' said Julie. 'About Christine not being amongst Mindi Brookes' Facebook friends. Not only that, we have asked every person we spoke to in person and on the phone, and nobody had ever heard of Christine Streeter in conjunction with Mindi Brookes. Yes the majority have heard of her recently because she's been in the media these past few days and be the sort of thing people remember if you remind them about Borowiak and no body and all the rest of it.' She hesitated to grimace. 'Linked to Brookes? No chance it seems to me.'

'In which case,' said Inga firmly. 'What is she doing there? How did her DNA get in the bed she had wet we think, on purpose?' she blew out a breath, and looked at Ruth. 'This is one of our Monday morning scenarios,' she said to make the chestnut haired DC giggle slightly and then realized she needed to explain. 'Some time ago Nicky Scoley and I were chatting over coffee at the end of a case and got round to thinking what people face when they go into work on a Monday morning compared to us having to look at a badly mutilated body in a field somewhere. As we do.'

'People who are chocolate tasters,' said Gillian. 'Or those made up to the eyeballs who stink to high heaven in big stores just inside the door trying to sell you exorbitantly priced perfume.'

'You get the idea,' Inga said. 'Footballers who face the horrors of kicking a ball about and doing spitting practice,' she offered and headed for her office.

Jake Goodwin was right behind her. 'Guvnor,' he said to get his boss to turn round before she reached her desk. 'Is it me or is there something going on?'

'How d'you mean?' she swatted back.

'I thought the Darke boss had taken on this Critical Incident Manager role with this case, but I don't seem to have seen him at any briefings, and…' he grimaced. 'I'd have thought with a case as high profile as this our Lord Stevens would have been crawling all over it too.'

Inga smiled. It always amused her the way even Jake phrased mention of Craig Darke at times as the Darke boss which Nicky Scoley has first come up with. 'Detective Super Darke is being briefed by me each morning and each afternoon, and I'm nearly drowning in his emails. As for Stevens, think the way technology is moving he's got his work cut out dealing with his own cases particularly those going to the CAT eTeam. Budget restraints means he can't take on staff, so they're a bit overworked I understand.' She chuckled. 'I can imagine he's not best pleased with all this going on down here, but you know what he's like, door will suddenly fly open and in he'll come.'

'All flashy tie and gawdy socks!'

7

'Let me hypothesize' Inga suggested at Thursday morning briefing. 'Our mystery woman kills Mindi for some reason we have yet to establish, having relieved herself in the bed.' She looked all around at the faces. 'Here's a good question. Who else has stayed over in their house, do people do such a thing on a regular basis? How often do people stay over at your house? Is this somebody playing games by saying, here I am this is me but you can't catch me? And why can't we catch her?' She left hanging, then answered her own question. 'Because she's...dead.'

'We saying Christine Streeter?'

'You got a better idea?' was sharp. 'You got anybody else's DNA in the house except Brookes and Kempshall? If you have then share it. Yes, bits and bobs like you'd find in any house, but only three serious captures. Fingerprints for two of them and DNA for all three.'

'And how do they know each other?'

'Leisure is a link. Brookes as we know did yoga, pilates and all the rest of it, plus she brought in a few extra pounds dog walking. Christine Streeter worked for an insurance agent now defunct, and was a swimming teacher in her spare time. They're not far apart surely. Go to any leisure centre you'll find both. I know Streeter basically worked for a small insurance company but she did have this swimming teaching sideline.' She smiled. 'Bit tenuous I agree but it is a link. Not exactly chalk and cheese.'

'And your pathway from here, bearing that in mind?' was Lizzie with her HOLMES hat on.

'If it is what a dead Christine Streeter did then it really is so surreal and difficult to take on board. Why come back now, why kill this Mindi and more than anything having achieved all she has why then leave evidence?' Inga shook her head. 'Makes no sense.' She sighed her frustration. 'Why not just make good her escape? We're only looking for her because she pointed us in her direction.'

'Christine Streeter is alive and has been all along,' Lizzie threw at her.

Inga just scanned the room. 'For God's sake don't tell the media or this place'll go daft.'

'If it really is the case somebody needs to free Borowiak from prison,' said Jake Goodwin. 'Red faces or what?' he smirked.

'This has to be the ultimate clean skins scenario,' said statuesque Inga. 'She's been so low key as to be invisible for years, for all intents and purposes appears to those who have been in touch with her to be normal every day citizen. In truth for more than a decade she's been invisible.'

'If you were her with a fairly unusual name like hers, surely first thing you do is change it. To something simple.'

'Such as?' made Jake grin.

'Next step?'

'Kempshall,' just one word emphasized how wound up Inga was. 'Interview Kempshall and put all this to him. Does he know Christine Streeter by sheer chance, did Mindi know her? Does he know somebody who looks like her but goes by another name? Did Mindi know her back in 2006, had she come across her recently? Does Kempshall know if people have stayed over before? Did she talk about people she no longer mixed with before he came along?'

'Could be she didn't actually stay over.'

'Appreciate that,' Inga acknowledged.

'I know people who've never had anyone to stay, who have actually never had anybody round even for a chat and a cuppa even, except close relatives.'

'Know an odd couple who only meet friends in cafes, never at home.'

'Wonder what people like them have to hide?'

'Does Kempshall know how often she washed the sheets? Does he know of any reason why somebody would behave in such a way?' Just as three were about to comment, Inga went on. 'Have you ever done something like that, stayed over in somebody's house and wet the bed?'

'No, to the last question,' said a smiling Brown-Reid with her stark pageboy hair as others chuckled.

'And I plan to get answers,' the DI shot at her. 'Starting later today when I interview Kempshall, in his own backyard.'

Blonde stunningly attractive Swedish Detective Inspector Inga Larsson had made a real effort as she did from time to time before interviewing men. Put them off their guard, give their brain something else to prioritize over, and while all that is going on creep in under the radar.

Wednesday had ended wet, but the new morning while not sunny and bright was at least dry, if overcast at times.

Aaron 'Ned' Kempshall was at work and Inga had phoned him to arrange to meet. Just enough warning to make him worry, but not enough to give him time to conjure up a sob story. His employer, a niche market provider of top of the range bathrooms and wet rooms for whom Kempshall was a surveyor come salesman was understanding under the circumstances and provided a small office for their use.

Sat either side of a desk, Inga started off by talking about bathrooms and his role in an attempt to put him at ease. She and Adam knew their bathroom was in need of a make-over but by the look of the displays out in the showroom the offerings were in a different league financially. Why people get all fussed about roll topped baths stuck in the middle of the room and Jack and Jill sinks she had never fathomed.

'Can we start with your life with Mindi,' said Inga. 'How long had you been living together?'

'Eight months or thereabouts.'

'And how long had you known her before then?'

'Couple, maybe.'

'You'd met all her friends I take it?'

Kempshall grimaced. 'Those she saw most of I s'pose, lot she worked with I'd not met.'

'Any reason?'

'Didn't mix socially.'

'What do you mean?'

'Any she saw away from work was always all girls together sort of thing. All the aerobics clan.' He smiled. 'You know what it's like. Be all the social media bags, shoes and baby nonsense.' Inga knew she was fortunate to have friends with more about them than that, but it certainly told her a great deal about Mindi Brookes. Part of the clone brigade as one of her friends called them, be all bothered about what her peers might think or say if she dared to be herself, be an individual.

'And you'd never met them.'

'No.' He pulled in a breath. 'Wasn't like she had a nine to five job in an office with workmates and all that business.'

'What about those who visited the house?'

Kempshall puffed out a little breath to hint at his annoyance and boredom. 'Same thing really, all girls together. Be all thin aerobics women is my guess, I bet.' He grinned. 'Used to make meself scarce before I became the subject of their derision.'

'How about people who stayed over?'

'Bloomin' heck,' he sniggered. 'Erm, maybe one or two possibly, not sure who now.'

'One called Christine was there do you think?'

'No idea,' he offered with a shake of his head. 'Not heard o'one.'

'Called Chrissie maybe?' he just shrugged away.

They had managed to track down a few friends of Mindi's and through them had discovered this Aaron lived his life almost entirely at weekends, which her friends claimed was her big gripe.

To her both Saturday and Sunday were lazy carefree days after the rigours of teaching her classes. According to these friends, she hardly ever took dogs for a walk over the two days, usually because the owners had more time to do it themselves. Lying in bed, in fact as often as not breakfast in bed, even if she did have to get up, cook it and take it back with her, was her idea of heaven.

Not Aaron apparently. It was as if he was transformed by hyperactivity the moment the calendar said Saturday. He'd be up and out early for a run often at the crack of dawn. Not just a scamper round the corner, this guy would do five or six miles often considerably more, and he'd have the rest of his weekend all mapped out as if he dare not miss a minute of it, would never stop for a coffee and a chat as Mindi did regularly. He was all go.

'Let's change the subject,' said Inga as she checked her notes on her tablet. She'd had her fill of his best 10K time and talk about stride patterns and fartleks. 'Do you have any idea how often Mindi would change the sheets on the spare bed?'

Aaron Kempshall just looked at her with his eyes partially screwed up. 'What?' was breathy. 'I've no idea,' he managed but was controlled by confusion. 'I don't understand.'

'Just bear with me,' she asked. 'After somebody stayed would you think?'

'S'pose so,' confirmed his lack of domesticity.

'Let's go back to these close friends shall we?' Inga suggested. 'Any fights, any falling out?' she had noticed a puff of a breath again before he spoke.

'Be usual girly stuff I s'pose.'

'You like your women to behave in such a manner do you?'

'How d'you mean?'

'Women who are into make-up and cocktails holding big bags cackhanded,' Inga sniggered.

'S'what they do,' he emphasized.

'So it is what you like then is it?'

'Dunno.'

'These all yoga enthusiasts or aerobic teachers?'

'Don't ask me,' he sniggered. ''Putting your right foot behind your left ear's not my idea of fun.'

'Unusual positions eh?' Inga teased and chortled.

'Sorry?' he grimaced.

'You and Mindi.' When it hadn't dawned on him the DI just let it go, but noticed there was no hint of blush to give the game away. 'Any of your friends ever stay over?' she posed to change subject.

'No.'

She knew Aaron Kempshall had a BSc yet could only find a job measuring people's bathrooms and flogging them copper baths, bidets they'd never use, high powered showers and all the must have paraphernalia some folk are into to impress friends. Was he deliberately acting confused or was there a hidden meaning?

'Have you ever met anybody from her past? People she used to work with, old friends maybe?'

'Be only in passing I s'pose. Bump into women in the street, she'd exchange a few words, say she used to work with them.' He shrugged.

'Nobody you'd regard as a good friend?'

'No, not really.' He really had no interest in Mindi's friends and to an extent Inga felt he didn't really know her.

'How many people would you think were in your close social circle?'

Inga waited for a reply. 'Not really sure there was one. Be her friends and my pals most of the time.'

'Tell me about going to the rugby?' had an effect on his face. 'Why Twickenham, why then?' she hurried in hoping the briefing on rugby clubs given to her by the lads would hold her in good stead.

'Northampton's nearer.'

'His club s'pose.'

'Where did you go after you left Peterborough Services?' She threw in.

'Sorry?' was him playing for time to think.

'We know you never went to Harlequins. We have ANPR records of you at Peterborough Services heading south and then later after the match heading north.' His eyes said he was crestfallen. 'Did you really not think we'd check? We know you bought a ticket off their website,' but it was never used because you never got as far as The Stoop,' she checked on her tablet.

Timing at such a critical moment was crass. There was a quick tap on the door and a female popped her head round. 'Tea, coffee?' she asked. 'Water?'

Inga wanted a coffee, providing it was decent, but when Kempshall said no thanks, she felt she had to follow suit, thanked the woman and they were back to the subject in hand.

'Gonna come out I s'pose,' was only mumbled. Images and thoughts rampaged through Inga's mind. If he now confessed to driving back to Lincoln to kill Mindi how on earth did Christine Streeter come into it all? Was she with him? A staggering thought from somewhere to swamp her brain to hinder concentration.

'Bin seeing someone.' Inga held her breath and waited ready to tap what he said onto her tablet. 'Met her at the Interior Design

Exhibition at the NEC in Birmingham.' He shrugged and then looked down at the grey desk.

'So, why did you say you'd been to Twickenham? Why did you sit in the police car telling me this half-baked story about rugby you normally probably reserved for Mindi? We told you the bad news, the situation with Mindi before we even got round to asking you where you'd been. Why keep it a secret?'

'Dunno.'

That was where the grey jacket and shirt came in. He'd worn those to visit some woman.

'You do this do you? See other women? Have you done this before which Mindi didn't know about?' There was a shrug again to confirm he had as far as Inga was concerned. 'How many times have you been unfaithful?'

He smirked. 'Unfaithful?'

'Yes.'

'You seem to be forgetting something. We weren't married or anything old school.'

'You don't have to have walked down the aisle to be unfaithful.'

'Do in my world.'

'Not a very nice world seems to me,' she said as she tapped her tablet. 'I need full details. Name, address, phone number, where she works, star sign, what size knickers, next of kin, you name it I want it.' She hesitated a second. 'Now!' The change in Inga's tone had an effect on him. 'And while you're at it, I'll have the full details of anybody else you've been seeing on the sly since you've been with Mandi Brookes.' Inga ginned at him. 'Your Quins sweatshirt gave you away, did you realize?' she told him. 'Done to fool Mindi was it? You all decked out for the rugby, then a quick switch on the way to meet some tart in your best clobber.' He looked astonished at what she was telling him. 'Let's start with her details.'

The fact he'd lied to her, then led them a merry dance for no reason was so annoying to her. All the time, money and precious resources spent checking him out, tracking him on ANPR and for why?

'And if I don't?' surly Kempshall asked.

'Then you'll be arrested, it's as simple as,' she said so casually as if it was an everyday event. 'And when we're done here we'll have our techy guys walking around inside your laptop and going through your service provider's list of all your calls for three months just to make sure.'

'What for? Is seeing someone suddenly illegal then? This another diktat from the bloody EU we need Brexit to get shot of?'

'Perverting the course of justice for starters, or with a suspicious death it could amount to a whole host of charges.' She had her tablet ready, finger poised. 'Full name...?'

Inga Larsson had got what she called another 'live' one from the eTeam techy-geeks upstairs when she got back, grabbing that missing coffee en route.

A Jessica Tindall in Retford had known somebody very well who at one time used to talk about the life this Christine Streeter led with Thomasz Borowiak. Unfortunately they would be unable to talk to the woman first hand as she had died a little more than a year ago.

A fact to make Inga want to carry out the interview herself. Two women somehow connected to Streeter who had died in recent times. Mindi Brookes and now this Amelia Evans.

Delegation she knew was the right and proper thing to do, and if the team was to develop as a whole she knew she had more and more to rely on them to carry out her wishes.

Decided to keep girls together for now and gave Gillian Brown-Reid and auburn Julie Rhoades the job of interviewing the woman, with curiosity ringing in their ears from their boss about the dead woman. 'Two dead women is two too many as far as I can see,' she told the pair more than once.

'Don't forget the one who had her drink spiked,' Jake added.

Gillian was not in the best of moods. With this murder suddenly appearing to change all her plans she was still annoyed at having to give tickets she and David had to see the Lady Antebellum tour in Birmingham on Monday to her sister. Not to mention the £120 she'd lost.

How would that have gone down? *"Thanks boss for allowing me to work with MIT, but I need to nip off early on Monday. Got tickets for this country band I must see."*

Now with a forecast of unusually sunny weather for the coming weekend, she knew work would curtail any chance of enjoying time with her children. David'll not be happy dealing with the kids again, but she was ambitious to progress, and so be it.

Grey brick two bedroomed semi-detached on a modern pleasant estate was the destination for the two detectives. One of those places where they've dug up the lawn and put gravel and paving slabs down in its place to make room for ropey old cars, which is bad news if it floods.

'When it were all in the papers she used to go on about it all the time, like.' Jessica Tindall laughed. 'She was not surprised at all with him being one of those control freaks and that.'

'When the case first came to light back in 2006 was she interviewed by police then do you know?' chestnut haired Gillian enquired.

'Think she were, but I'm not absolutely sure. They seemed only interested in things like the last time she'd seen her and Amelia said they was interested in busybody neighbours watching all the comings and goings and that.'

'How did this Amelia know Christine Streeter?'

'Worked together at one time and used to bump into one another now and again.'

'Be close enough to know about Borowiak you say.'

'You hear about them don't you? These control freaks and that.'

Julkie like most of us has met the self-opinionated about everything and anything, who quite often try to dictate the type of person the subject of their torment should be and who they can mix with.

'So basically your friend's friend Christine Streeter had to do what she was told?'

'Amelia told me more than once how Chrisie said she felt like a prisoner in her own mind as if somebody else was doing all the thinking for her.'

'They were really close then?'

'Not very close really, I don't reckon.'

'Did she tell the police all this before?' Julie with just a smidgen of make-up to cover freckles, but clean clear bright eyes, needed to know

'Like I said they was only interested so Amelia was saying, in the last time she'd seen her. Been a couple of weeks earlier think she said at one time. Think they coppers made up their mind he'd done it like.' She grinned. 'He had no excuse did he when it all came out? Got no alibi I seem to remember when I read it all in the Sunday papers.'

'The way he treated her. How did it all manifest itself?' Julie queried. 'Or would this just be what Christine Streeter had told her?'

'Hated surprises so she said, had to just make casual suggestions, not invite people over for example until he thought it was his idea.' She blew out a breath. 'What a way to live eh?' Julie didn't need telling. 'Think she once said Borowiak must have lived with unreasonable parents and guessed it had rubbed off.'

'Your friend Amelia,' said the DC. 'What can you tell us about her?'

'Lovely woman, real salt of the earth to be honest. Amelia Evans. Really sad, but seems such a lot of it about these days.' Gillian was about to ask the supplementary when this Jessica went on. 'Bowel cancer done for her in the end. Be getting on for two year must be now, think it had spread as well in the end I heard, as it seems to and that.'

'Did your Amelia ever meet Borowiak do you know?'

'Difficult to tell really. This were all a bit back now duck.'

'Story was of course he'd gone off fishing.'

'He'd expect things at home to be just so when he came home and wobetide her if they were no. Be about what it seemed like to us at the time'

'No doubt she'd feel she had to please him all the time. In their relationship there would be only one opinion and no prizes for guessing it'd be his.'

'I don't suppose you'd have any idea where Christine Streeter might have gone if in fact Borowiak didn't kill her?'

Jessica blew out a breath. 'Such as where?' she smirked.

'Just one aspect we're looking into.'

'Why?' she shot back. 'Somebody saying she's not dead are they?' She sniggered to herself as if the whole idea was absurd. 'Think it's what he said if my memory serves me right, claimed he'd not seen hide nor hair o' her that night. Jury didn't fall for it all and no mistake,' she chortled and her body wobbled with it. 'Not sure they always get these things right, but they did to my mind as far as Streeter was concerned, poor lass.' She looked at Julie. 'Hope you're not siding with him like how you lot seem to do these days.'

'There's still no body, no proof,' said Rhoades.

'Where would you suggest she is then if Borowiak did in fact kill her?'

'How should I know? Could be anywhere.'

'Can't be too far if you think about it,' said Julie. 'We know when she left work, we know what time Borowiak was spotted heading for the lake and we know what time he arrived home.'

'And the prosecution case,' Gillian added. 'Suggested he stopped fishing, rode back home although there were no sightings, killed Christine Streeter dumped her body some place and then went back fishing.'

'And how much open space is there in the county I ask you? Turfed her in a drain some place I s'pect or dug a hole in the woods beforehand, found a place where folk never go. Plenty o'places round 'ere like that me duck.'

Her comment remained with slim Gillian. It had been something the boss had casually mentioned at one point, how it was always possible Streeter's grave may well have been one Borowiak dug sometime earlier.

8

DC Ruth Buchan felt somehow she had been handed the short straw. Was this deliberate by the boss or just a coincidence? Perhaps this was the boss testing her, putting her in her place, reminding her of her worth.

Inga Larsson was aware how Ruth always had this need to prove herself. Set her a task and she was key-tapping almost before the request had landed. Being multi-skilled she'd retain a conversational presence, type yet at the same time slip a Malteser into her mouth.

She'd been packed off to talk to the thoroughly distressed Christine Streeter' parents and now was back on the road down to Grantham to talk to Mindi Brookes' mother and father. The family members she guessed who would be suffering the most tremendous emotional pain.

Ruth had spent some time serving as Family Liaison Officer and had undergone all the training necessary to deal with parents overcome with the trauma of bad news foisted upon them at a moment's notice. She'd heard how Larsson had admitted to somebody how she did not have the temperament and patience to deal with such matters, but not hers to wonder why. If her career was to progress she knew full well she would have to take on board whatever was thrown at her.

Did it say something about her she wondered? Having been chosen ahead of Julie another fully fledged specialist in all aspects of bereavement and what about that Gillian foisted on them, she was always dead keen.

And DS Jake Goodwin? What was wrong with him doing this interview, after all he was supposed to be overseeing everything for the boss?

Ruth knew he was good at delving into bottomless pits searching for information on this, that and the other through his laptop or the in house systems to move cases on. She guessed him trundling down the A1 a bit to deal with the tearful and distressed was not his forte either.

Blue sky at times on the way down was a bit of a bonus. There appeared to be nothing untoward as she approached the house, but the doorbell push ignited a pretty little tune she was sure after a while would get on your nerves. Correction. After the third time you'd want to chuck it in the bin.

Hard going from the moment this bald bearded bloke opened the door to this detached property on a busy road. Ruth had always wondered why people would do such a thing.

Buy a house on what is quite obviously a busy road with traffic day and night then spend their lives moaning and complaining they can't reverse out of their drive?

Ruth did wonder what it was had attracted the Brookes couple to ignore the serious access issues, which had forced her to park round the corner in a quiet cul-de-sac.

'What now?' she was asked as soon as she had introduced herself. Wasn't the fact beards had become the in vogue nonsense the very reason why sensible people did not grow one? And to make matters worse this goon had shaved his head to tell the world he couldn't for the life of him make his mind up or as is often the case his wife made all such decisions for him, not something he'd ever admit to.

'We are following up a number of leads with regard to your daughter Mr Brookes, and we would very much like to discuss with you any disputes she may have had with anybody, about her employment history and relationships with friends.'

An abrupt 'What makes you think we'd know all that?' sounded less than grateful for all their efforts.

Ruth Buchan with her delightful plaited up chestnut hair gritted her teeth. 'Because you're her parents.'

'What's this all about?' a woman's voice asked then she pushed Brookes to one side.

'Police bothering us again, dear,' he sighed.

'Don't just stand there pet, come on in,' was not an instruction she could easily ignore and Ruth stepped across the threshold squeezed between Brookes and the wall and followed this tubby woman in slippers as she led the way along the hall and turned right into a really decent lounge. 'What'll it be?' she was asked as the woman motioned for her to sit down.

'We're trying to ascertain...'

'Tea, coffee or cold?' was blunt.

'Tea, please,' said Ruth who knew from experience it might be weak and willing but people tend not to make too much of a pigs ear of a cup of tea as they quite often do with cheap-jack coffee off the warehouse floor and cream.

Ruth in her navy blue suit was left alone and she could just about hear whispered mumblings coming from the kitchen, which then stopped shortly before the pair arrived back.

'Mrs Brookes,' said Ruth once the cup and saucer had been placed on a glass topped low coffee table in front of her. Somebody had certainly got a good eye for design and colour. Although the room was not to her taste at all, she could see where they were coming from.

'Libby please,' she was instructed.

'Libby,' she opened with this time. 'We need to ascertain if your Mindi had any bad relationships, in her personal life or at work at all.'

'What good will it do?' her husband asked. Ruth noticed he'd got a can of lager in his fat hand and his lower jaw wiggled about after he spoke almost as if he was trying to adjust his dentures.

'It might point us in the right direction.'

'To finding this Streeter woman?' was assertive, except he mispronounced her name. *'Stratter'* was a peculiar rendition. 'Seems what all papers are full of, sod our daughter, let's get all puffed up about her.'

'We don't know at this stage whether this matter has anything to do with Christine Streeter or not. We need a motive and is basically what I'm trying to establish.'

'Not that I know of pet,' Libby Brookes replied.

Background notes supplied to Ruth on her iPad said how Richard Brookes owned a security company which had turned out to be nothing more elaborate than a three man business fitting burglar alarms and then serviced them which is where they make their money. A money for old rope sort of set-up.

'So what is happening with this Streeter?' he persisted and mispronounced. Strange thing to do when every television and radio report she had heard made a point of correct pronunciation after all it wasn't very difficult. Maybe he only read the scurrilous media rags. Millions mispronounce names such as Adidas and Nike so it was no real surprise.

'We have a team looking into every aspect right now,' was not entirely true. 'But even if they are able to resolve such issues we need to establish particularly for the CPS what had been going on.'

The mother frowned. 'True what they say is it? They found this DNA business they talk about. In the house must have been, was it?'

'They certainly did.' There was no point in fudging the issue, it was what social media were obsessed with.

'Why do you think something had been going on, as you put it?' Libby Brookes slid in.

'There are some crazy people about,' said Ruth while Brookes supped from his can. 'But not many enter somebody's home intent on doing what happened to Mindi, There has to be a reason. Could be anything. Someone she upset even something like road rage which is a real problem these days. People she had issues with at work maybe, somebody she fell out with on social media,' Ruth knew was unlikely with the little she appeared to be involved according to the eTeam.

'I hope you're not suggesting our daughter'd be one of these...well, you know, these dreadful people what allus cause internet trouble nowadays.'

'Trolls you mean?' Ruth hoped she'd guessed right, lifted the cup in readiness to give the tea a try.

'Think they're called, something like it.'

'Unlikely, but some people do take umbrage very easily on social media, get upset about the slightest thing, read stuff out of context, get half a story.'

'Get up backside first,' he chuntered. 'Too much o'this political correct nonsense seems to me.' Brookes is one of those jowly men who need a diet to start from the top of their head, shaved and bearded or not.

Ruth sipped and was pleased it was fairly strong as she took on board the remark her own granny had used. 'Too often people start a message halfway through the story which can cause all sorts of problems. Not sure at all why they do it.'

'D'you use those things pet?' Libby asked.

'Not extensively but can prove useful in cases like this at times. For work quite a bit, but not personally. Got fed up with so much of it to be honest.'

'Always makes me laugh all this social media twaddle,' Brookes suddenly piped up. 'Would have us all believe their lives are full to overflowing these bits of girls. Truth is it's full of little more than meaningless drivel, which means they have empty lives. Quite funny really when you think about it. Deluded to my mind.' He sniggered. 'And you think our Mindi was up to some'at?'

'Not up to something Mr Brookes, just may have fallen out with somebody like people do from time to time, got in with the wrong crowd or even knew of people who were up to no good, not that she was involved herself.' She sipped a bit more. 'Trouble with social media is you don't really know who you're dealing with most of the time. Not at all the same as meeting people face to face.'

'I was going to say.' There it was again jiggling about with his mouth.

'What about work?' Ruth asked when he never did say.

He raised an eyebrow. 'I shouldn't imagine so.'

'I don't know Rich,' said Libby and he made a face. 'She did have a really bad time back at the Spa place if you remember.'

'We're not bringing all that up again, surely. It was ages ago.'

'Where was this?' Ruth enquired as she realized there was an issue between the pair.

'What was it called now?' said Richard Brookes who seconds earlier had been against it being brought up.

'Phase Mindi went through I'm afraid,' said Libby softly as if she was ashamed.

'All youngsters go through it to some extent they tell me.'

'Not like she did!'

'Enough now,' made Richard look daggers at his wife. 'Our daughter didn't actually go off the rails so to speak, just her hormones doing their worst if we're honest. Just walked out on her decent job and got one working on a caravan site out at the coast for a summer.'

'Two.'

'All right, two.'

'What was the problem, do you know?' Ruth asked, then drank more of the tea.

Brookes cleared his throat. 'She was a Duty Manager,' he nodded his bald head slightly and gave the impression he was proud of the fact.

'Senior Duty Manager.' The antagonism continued.

'This was at a caravan site?'

'No,' said Brookes with a snigger as if she was stupid. 'What was it called now?'

'Northwater Manor Spa Hotel,' Ruth was sure some of her chums had been there on a day ticket at one time or was it her sister who had been with girls from work?

'Had trouble with a member of staff, but as usual the powers that be wouldn't back her. Typical bad management practices, too much of this university business not enough person to person one-to-one skills seems to me. Not backing your staff, see it time and again these days.'

Ruth was tempted to ask if it applied to his staff of two.

'In the end poor Mindi had to resign on a matter of principle. Always the same, seems to me,' said her mother soberly.

'Must have been the stress of it all,' said Brookes. 'When she went off the rails a bit,' he added.

'Richard,' said Libby and motioned with her head.

He just ignored her. 'To be fair she did manage to turn her life around after a while, got back into the swing of things. Think whoever it was Mindi caught was on the fiddle, place didn't want the police involved, worried sick about the bad press and all this PR nonsense they go on about.'

'Nothing else for it in the end, had to resign.'

'Got to say,' Brookes leant forward. 'Big believer in standing up for your principles me.'

'When was this?' Ruth dared.

'Five or six years ago.'

'Any names?'

'Now you're asking,' said Richard. Then just head back and he gulped down his lager in one go.

'This Northwater Manor, is this the one down south of Stamford?' Ruth asked having waited for him to finish. She had noticed during his drinking this Libby had rolled her eyes instead of making known her feelings verbally.

'Dear me no.' Ruth waited for more from Brookes and for him to stop licking his lips. 'Up in Yorkshire some place.'

'You're right,' said Ruth when it came to her. 'One I was thinking of is called Southwater Manor.'

'All part of a group, miss,' he advised.

'This is a long shot but do you recall Mindi mentioning anybody called Christine recently, who might have been this Streeter?'

'Bit old fashioned if you ask me,' said Libby Brookes. 'Be the kinda thing what them frim foak go in fer. Bit like Doreen and Glenda, not exactly all the rage with such an old fashioned name.' This from a woman who'd called her daughter Mindi, left Ruth wanting to say something but knew she daren't.

'I'll take that as a no then.' She wasn't a baby called Ada, Florrie or Maud, this Christine would now be into her thirties.

During their conversation Ruth had gradually gained the distinct impression this Libby would be very much concerned with what her friends and neighbours thought. Be the kind who'd have coughed up a few bob for a hot tub to impress friends and the nosey folk next door. Sort of thing she could really see no sense in as she knew enthusiasm lasts around six months, but one would fit nicely in the impression stakes with a gym membership which she knew has an even shorter shelf life.

'After the caravan park, what then?' Ruth had to delve.

'Went self-employed with her yoga business. All the rage they tell me, don't see the sense in it myself.'

Richard Brookes offered very little more and simply left it to his wife to attempt to give Ruth what she could remember about the Spa place neither of them had ever been to. They both advised how they were unaware of any dispute at her previous place of work where she had been for over five years working for an offshoot of Anglia Water. When Ruth eventually left with only the bit about the spa to go on this Richard Brookes was still quite obviously not a happy bunny.

Ruth Benson was indeed relieved to have got it all over and done with and to have come away relatively unscathed. She had been warned by the boss of the one question likely to be thrown at her as was frequently the case. .

When would the body be released? What's going on? What are you doing to her? Why d'you need to keep it?

Nothing was mentioned, and although she had been prepared, it was still a relief Richard Brookes had not made an issue about it as she had expected.

The body she was well aware is primary evidence, and remains under the care and control of the coroner normally until such time as the accused has been identified and charged. Then and only then can it be released, and that is particularly relevant when talk of cremation has entered the arena.

It was never a worrying aspect but the can of lager had gained her attention because beside his chair was what she surmised was an empty can. Did this guy have a drink problem? Mindi'd not taken after him as far as she was aware as the tox screen had said no alcohol in her blood.

Inga was cheered a little with the information about a dispute at the spa place.

'Anything out of the ordinary with them do we think?' She asked Ruth.

'He's not happy, thinks we should all be out combing the streets for Streeter and neither of them gave any indication they are at all upset they will soon be burying their only daughter. I trod very carefully knowing what a minefield it can be and expected a few tears, but nothing. Could have been talking about a woman down the road.'

'You saying they couldn't give a fig about their daughter?' Jake Goodwin checked.

'About the size of it.'

'Usually a given,' said Inga. 'When can we have the funeral? What's the delay? Poor parents need closure. All those and a lot more are thrown at us at every opportunity.'

'Except for these two.'

'Seems to me we're chasing moonbeams,' said a very serious Jake. 'What worries me is they are the very same moonbeams this force was hunting for years ago. Are we being arrogant I wonder thinking we can do better this time around? We're not talking about a cold case from the dark ages here, we're talking 2006, in our fairly recent past.'

'Not too out of the norm really. Mindi Brookes catches somebody on the fiddle but the boss won't back her up, gets in a bit of a strop and walks out. How many times do such things happen in the workplace? Hardly earth shattering news.'

'Then you say Brookes went off to a caravan site?' Ruth nodded. 'Doing what?'

Ruth knew she'd not actually asked the Brookes the question. 'Don't think they actually know, think they disapproved. He in particular was a bit snooty about her working somewhere he probably considers beneath them. And at the same time finished off a can of lager while I was there.'

'Sort who turn up their nose at shopping at Aldi or look down at folk going to car boot sales.'

'About the size of it.'

'Be alright in the summer I should imagine.'

'A can of Heineken?'

'No,' Inga sniggered. 'Caravan site.'

Inga Larsson had considered victim association first because it is an established fact most murders are committed by people well known to the victim. In this case all they had was the DNA of a dead woman. Said to be dead, but not proven and as far as they could gather may not be known to the victim.

No forensics for her live-in lover boy, her parents, aunts or uncles, the next door neighbours, a work colleague, jealous jilted ex-boyfriend. Just had to be a one off, this was a murdered woman.

Larsson was well aware she could link scene assessment to the victim and to the perpetrator. She had timelines for Brookes and one for Kempshall now they had dealt with his lies, but no timeline for Streeter. Dead people in the most part tend not to have them.

Once she'd finished checking the overtime returns, Inga knew would not please Darke, it took her a minute or two to bring her team to order to put suggestions of what he could do and thoughts of discrimination to one side and concentrate on the matter in hand.

'Before I bring you all up to date with Kempshall, tell me how we're getting on with a disappearing act?' was aimed at Gillian Brown-Reid and Rhoades.

'Seems to me, disappearing people has become an epidemic,' said Gillian. 'Jessica Tindall who Julie and I spoke to out at Retford talked about this woman she knew who is inconveniently now dead.'

'I understand this sort of thing is not as uncommon as we would imagine.'

'Certainly not' Gillian responded. 'I've come across another one just a couple of months after Streeter,' she sniggered at the look on Inga's face. 'Don't worry, no connection.'

'I was going to say!' the Inspector reacted. 'Another woman murdered but no body?' she checked.

'Lihau Cao was Chinese and met her rich husband in London,' slim Gillian read from her monitor. 'She was last seen alive in October 2006 and her husband was eventually charged with murder six years later. In December 2013 he was sentenced to life with a minimum of twenty two. Just like Borowiak he's still inside, as far as I know.'

'Again no body?'

'No body, as yet,' Gillian confirmed. 'One good line was the trial judge saying "When there is no body, the bereaved will suffer agonies of false hope," which is exactly what Streeter's mother Kathleen is still suffering even now.'

'Anymore?'

'Did ours just decide to re-boot her life some other place than Lincoln?'

'When I started looking into this I never imagined there'd be so many done for murder without a body. There's loads to be honest, 'specially in America of course. One was only in 2012 and in that case her husband is now doing seventeen years for it. Found a Canadian woman and another from up in Elgin and as I say, plenty in America.'

'And in all these cases, nobody knows for sure if they really are dead, or just did a runner to get away from some skurk of a husband?'

'Like people still missing from the twin towers.'

'About the size of it boss.'

Gillian, pleased to be in the limelight nodded at Julie the dark redhead. 'On the subject of disappearing, one suggestion I've read about is,' she said. 'You book a flight to somewhere where you have no intention of going to and tell nobody of your plans.'

'Reason?' a frowning Inga posed.

'To confuse everybody in particular the authorities, such as us.'

'Be even more pertinent now. We get told the one we're looking for was booked on a flight to Mexico ten years ago, our enquiries would go off at a different tangent altogether.'

'And if they didn't check it out ten years ago?'

'Then we're scuppered.'

'Next,' said Inga, but Brown-Reid hadn't finished.

'You have to plan for every eventuality is the advice,' said the stark haired brunette. ''But will never...erm manifest itself,' she boggled over the word. 'In anything we're looking at now all these years later. Just imagine trying to think of everything likely to happen in your life and being prepared for it. Be an absolute nightmare.'

'You need to create a back story of your life,' said Ruth. 'Create a false family you have left behind. Take my case for instance, if it was me I'd need to create a sister just like I have.'

'Why have the same, surely you'd change your family?'

'Not so,' Ruth responded. 'Just suppose I added a brother to my story for my new life. It'd be so easy to forget in the early days and casually refer only to my sister, when all your new friends have been told you have a brother as well. Change the names of course, but make it easy on yourself without giving the game away. Create schools you have attended and this back story is the basis of everything your new life is built upon.' Ruth smiled. 'I'm telling you it must be an absolute bloody nightmare. Sort of thing spooks and the undercover people have to do I bet.'

'Then you need places you have worked, but they mustn't be local because you need to tell your story to everybody you meet in your new world.'

'Think I'm getting the message,' said Inga who when she caught Lizzie Webb's eye she read the *"Told you it was a bloody nightmare"* message. 'You're doing well, keep it up. I've had a breakthrough too with Kempshall,' she said not wishing to be outdone by the women in her team. 'Problem number one is he told a pack of lies about going to Harlequins as we already knew, but if he told lies without reason what about the rest? ANPR caught him out with the rugby, but CCTV stops him killing Mindi. But is he telling the truth about our Christine and was visiting this Erika Parker woman down in Kettering doing nothing more than providing him with an alibi? Was she being used by him?' the DI grinned. 'Tell you what I think is amusing. He's flogging these bathrooms, all roll top whirlpool baths and all the up-to-the-minute silliness, yet the one in the place he shared with Mindi tells me exactly why nobody he knows ever stayed over.'

'Bit cobblers shoes is it?' Inga ignored.

'Grow tates in it?' at least made her smile.

'Admitted seeing this woman on the sly and his whole attitude was, so what? As if it was inconsequential. Cheating on his woman and he thinks it's no big deal.'

'Got two more likely hits on the reaction to the media story we've dragged from the pile of nonsense,' said Sandy McLachlan. 'One is another positive sighting a few years after she skedaddled, and a woman who was at school with Streeter.'

'Could do with a sighting for last week.' Inga Larsson quipped then hesitated. 'Do we really need to spend our time being told what she was like at school? We know all there is to know about her, this shy weak woman the file tells us.'

'Woman we spoke to reckoned Borowiak was a bit of a control freak.'

'May be so, but as it now appears he quite possibly didn't kill her, what use is it to us?'

'What's happening about the whole Borowiak business, ma'am?'

Inga pointed to the ceiling. 'Pen pushers, CPS, Appeal Court and goodness knows who will be dealing with it, but I doubt very much whether anything will be done seriously until we find Streeter alive and kicking. All pure speculation so far, and most of it by the media.'

'Nobody has mentioned this Chrissy being harmed they know about,' said Sandy. 'But it could have been mental torture.'

'The smell of fear to the control freak they say is like a rich perfume.'

'Basking in the pleasure of not destroying her physically, but doing it psychologically, could be a turn on.'

'He knows where the body is,' Inga suggested. 'And all this is quite possibly part of the pleasure right now he enjoys alone in his cell.'

Had to be done, another stone Inga knew she daren't leave unturned. Raza could be a tad too abrupt in interviews, but if she sent him he was reliable and he'd cross every t.

Inga welcomed all the enthusiasm but at the same time was well aware how tedious and monotonous the work could become. Taking statements from a whole range of bozos, crunching data, going down blind alleys, checking names and addresses, collating intelligence. She knew more than likely they'd reach a point where enthusiasm would wane and it could quickly all become a dull routine chore. Then she knew it would be down to her to lead them eventually to the promised land.

'This woman who knew her from school,' she mused. 'This from the eTeam?' she asked MacLachlan who nodded. 'Where is she?'

'Sheffield.'

'Might be worth a punt,' she shrugged. 'What else we got?' she said carefully as she looked to her left. 'Give it a whirl please Raza. Stop you twiddling your thumbs. You got much on?'

'I can let him go,' said Jake before Raza could think up a daft excuse.

'Take Sam with you, go up and see Stevens' eTeam geeks and get everything you can from their snooping and arrange to call on her.'

'You want us to do it by phone?' Latif hoped.

'No I don't,' Inga insisted. 'We're struggling as it is with the waste of spacers calling in. Need every snippet we can get and you never know she just might come up with more names. First one we've got from the original case, could very well just come up with something she didn't think of before. Do we know how many callers they've traced?' Inga asked nobody in particular.

'All the world's weirdoes as usual,' said MacLachlan. 'All looking for their fifteen minutes of fame. Sometimes wonder how many crimes some of these neds have admitted to.'

'Thirty eight,' said a smiling Jake. 'Only two or three they took any further, as Sandy said the rest were the usual gubbins. Talk is they're trying to track down one woman whose not answering her phone.'

'Dropped it down the toilet, I bet.'

'Could do with a break through.' Inga looked over at Julie and Gillian. 'Any chance you can come up with one?' she sniggered. 'How about this control freak business, what's it all about?'

Gillian let Julie Rhoades lead on this one almost as if she was reading the boss's mind. She did well, after a nervous start freckled DC Rhoades went through almost everything they'd been told from memory and from her notes.

'Somewhere we must have a heading for reasons why. Reasons why this Streeter did a bunk, and we can put control freak at number one.' As she was talking Sam Howard closest to any of the white boards added *Reasons Why She Left* in blue under Streeter information in a space left. 'If its right like any of us, she'd be fed up to the back teeth with all such nonsense from Borowiak. Would be interesting to know how the prison authorities see him. Plenty of wierdos inside I know but is he one they have down as a control freak which of course as we know are in effect also controlling themselves, so it could be the prison officers may have an opinion on Borowiak's attitude.'

'If he really didn't kill her my guess is he'll be kinda angry by now.'

'I'd be a darn sight more than angry!'

9

Less than ten minutes after DI Inga had sat herself down at her desk, logged in and started reading the serials the computerized system listing each and every crime committed overnight DS Jake Goodwin walked into her office with a mug in each hand.

She'd briefed Darke on her way in when they'd bumped into each other in the car park. In his usual style he slid another option for her to consider into her mind, as if it wasn't bunged up enough with unanswered questions.

'Bodies,' he'd said as they strolled in. 'Are usually as you know, kept in the morgue until they have been identified, even if we know the cause of death by circumstance or through the PM procedures and toxicology. What you need to consider is how from time to time cadavers are not identified and remain in the freezer. Have you considered this might have happened to this Streeter woman? Is she in fact bed-blocking in a morgue, lying some place just waiting for some kind soul to recognize her and claim her?' He grinned as they parted. 'I'll leave it with you.'

'I'm liking it,' Inga said to Jake as she peered up. 'This could become a habit,' she tittered as he placed a mug of her milky morning coffee on her desk, and sat himself down after closing the door.

Another late evening of nothing but Wedding plans at home with Adam had left her exhausted. Phone calls to her mother Christal back in Stockholm and she couldn't imagine how much they were all costing her.

Inga had not been at all surprised when Adam took a keener than normal interest in this latest case from the moment the discovery became lauded on Twitter, his clients had been more than a little curious about.

Unlike her parents still married, living together back home in Sweden, still so in love as they had always appeared to her, Adam had not been anywhere so lucky.

His parents had separated when he was young and in the intervening years after the acrimonious divorce his father with whom he had very limited contact played an increasingly insignificant role in his life.

Somehow his mother had kept in touch with two or three friends in order to keep abreast if news on Reginald Kingsley's life. When two of her ex-neighbours moved away and the key witness then passed away her link with her past life ran out of steam.

What Adam had known for more than fifteen years was how his father had moved away, married again and the coupling had produced a daughter.

With no link to his former life remaining any attempt by the physiotherapist to trace his father and sister had produced nothing of any significance.

Adam Kingsley had no real interest in Christine Streeter he was simply because of his own situation keen on the processes the police use to trace missing people.

Very much against the rules Inga had surreptitiously entered both Reginald and Mavis Kingsley into PNC which had drawn a blank.

With no family to speak of Inga could understand Adam's frustration and his keen interest in how they were searching for Streeter a dead woman when he couldn't find a live one or assumed they both were.

'Two words,' Jake said with the hint of a smile. 'Witness Protection.'

'Sorry?' she grimaced, mug in hand.

'What if Christine Streeter is on the Witness Protection Scheme?'

It took Inga a moment or two for her brain to process what he had said and for her to come up with a response. 'And what is she supposed to have done, or supposed to have witnessed?'

'Haven't got that far yet,' he smirked. 'Remember, people see things they then can't un-see. They hear things by sheer chance, not their fault any of it, just lady luck or ill luck in many cases affects innocent bystanders.'

'Where on earth did this come from?' she asked and he looked somewhat sheepish. 'Go on.'

'Well,' he hesitated and looked a trifle sheepish. 'Sally got a box set of *Shetland* for her birthday, and one we watched last night was about witness protection., just got me to thinking about why Streeter has never been traced.'

Inga sipped her milky coffee. 'If you're right, then Borowiak must have been up to something very serious indeed you think? You don't get witness protection because you've seen somebody shop lifting.'

'Here's one for you,' said a grinning Jake. 'Borowiak's not inside.'

'What?' was inside a breath.

'Be all part of the subterfuge. Yes, they went through the process but he's been paid off and released donkey's years ago. Now making sand castles on a beach in Rio.'

'And the high profile court case?'

'All part of the process, building up the cover, telling whoever's after her, how she's dead.'

'But surely they would keep all this business under wraps, but in this case the media have been crawling all over it for all this time a bit like Lord Lucan and now they're back onto it.'

'But,' tall dark Jake said seriously. 'This is not just her trying to stay hidden, the Protected Persons Service will be looking after her. They would have done their level best to make her new life as close to her old one as possible.'

'Reason why she'd have no trouble getting a passport and all the rest of it.'

'Why she easily could be abroad.'

'Sunning herself somewhere and laughing her socks off.' Inga took a tiny sip. 'She could be with him. Could be sunning herself...' she stopped when Jake nodded.

'Except, if it's true how did her DNA get uphill?'

'Over on holiday?' was a guess.

Inga sipped her coffee and looked seriously at her senior Sergeant over the rim of her mug. Was this the right moment to talk about Darke's frozen cadaver idea in mortuaries nationwide, which was nowhere near as bizarre as Streeter getting a tan with Borowiak some place? 'Must say I'm not convinced about witness protection, but having said that it can't be ignored.'

'Want me to have a look see what high profile cases were going on at the time she might have been a witness to?'

'You get on with your search and I'll have a word with the boss,' said the DI realizing she'd need to find some other willing servant for the cadaver theory.

'She'd have been relocated by the National Crime Agency depending on the level of threat, and from what I've read this morning Streeter would have had a say on where she went to.'

'Thing which worries me, is what part did Borowiak play in all this?'

'Nothing,' said Goodwin with mug in hand. 'He was paid handsomely to be the wally who took the wrap. Plasterer without two ha'appenies to rub together got himself a few grand. Maybe a witness protection for him too. What's the betting he's not in Wandsworth or Ford but as you say he's also sunning himself some place running a beach-side bar?'

'You sure you've not been watching *Spooks*?' she chided.

'But they could be involved. She could have been a witness to anything by chance. Murder by a top politician, goings on by the Royal Family or in this day and age something to do with terrorism.'

'But this was eleven years ago,' Inga reminded him.

'After 9/11.'

'You're right,' she said and downed more of her lovely warm drink. 'Leave it with me.'

Detective Superintendent Craig Darke had taken some persuading but in the end he agreed to offer time for Jake Goodwin to put his case about witness protection.

It was Darke who had suggested they bring in the one person in their midst with more experience in such matter, the dapper DCI Luke Stevens much to Inga's chagrin. Dressed in a navy blue Paul Smith with the silk tie as ever in a hue of the correct candour.

'I'll be perfectly honest with you,' said Darke for openers. 'I'm not at all convinced, but even so this case is a burden on our operational capability and most importantly our budgets. We could very well be spending our hard earned resources on a wild goose chase. We scour the country and the NCA are doing their level best to keep her hidden.'

'And laughing their socks off,' said Stevens. 'Knowing them.'

'Purely on the basis of budgetary restraints I think we should at least consider this.'

'Have to say, sir,' said Stevens. 'This does sound a bit far-fetched, but the moment you start to think in such a manner is when the world of spooks and terrorism comes into play. They could well be up to goodness knows what and in the present climate anything is possible.'

'But surely somebody would have warned us off,' said Darke. 'If that were the case.'

'Isn't ...' Jake tried.

'Exactly the opposite,' Stevens rode roughshod over him. 'It only emphasizes the story the PPS have created about her.'

'Only they know she is now Freda Jones married with three scratty kids living in Pont-Rhyd-y-groes,' said Darke, then realized he had to explain with a smile. 'Had a holiday cottage there once.'

'Her being so high profile does concern me somewhat,' Inga offered.

'Think it's always a case of thinking out of the box,' Luke Stevens told her. She'd not had sight of his socks yet, but Inga knew they'd certainly be very colourful whatever the pattern, the four colour zig-zag tie was certainly new to her. At least he was never awash with cologne. 'Rather than spend all their time keeping her name out of the media, in this case they made her high profile, to do the exact opposite.'

'Never been any suggestion she was involved in anything or witness to whatever it was.'

'Been proved right,' said the DS.

'In effect they concentrate everybody's minds on the fact this woman was a victim and Borowiak is paying the price.'

'Allegedly,' said Stevens and blonde Inga sensed he was enjoying being brought into offer his opinion. 'I became more involved in this sort of thing in the Met of course.' Now he was bragging.

'We put out feelers then do we think?' was Darke.

'I'll do it, sir.' Stevens popped in quickly. 'Few folk still owe me favours,' was typical Stevens and Inga caught a look from Jake. He glanced at his watch and got to his feet. 'Be all for now?' the DCI checked and once Darke had nodded the smoothie was gone.

Inga had become increasingly aware how PR had gradually gained the upper hand in policework. Senior officers were forever desperate for the public to be kept informed about what they were doing. At times she felt it was not at all easy when there were issues for operational reasons they should not divulge for any old Joe Soap to scan on his phone.

She was well aware how the top brass didn't actually mean it, but at times it felt as if they would authorise her to just slap the cuffs on any passing waste of space so the public relations team could put out good news to keep the moaning minnies at bay.

Wetting a bed would she knew have had some of the tabloids drooling and going into overdrive over what they could make of it, and screw up Operation Lancaster at the same time.

10

The semi-detached red brick house in Daffodil Road in Sheffield was on one of the hills which dominate the city. Part of what had been known locally as the Flowers Estate at one time, the property had the look of original post-war council houses having been refurbished over the years. Be the sort of place way back with an outside lavvy.

Dark, swarthy and slim DS Raza Latif who always looks as though he needs a shave let slim mother of two DC Gillian knock on the door.

The woman who answered was wearing an old fashioned wrap around pinafore of the sort likely to have been popular when the house was built. Apologized for her get-up by explaining how she was busy baking. This was even though she knew when they were calling and they were just about on time.

Rather than invite the two officers into her front room to offer them tea in dainty cups as often happens, they were instead ushered into her scullery to stand and watch her as she continued to make pastry at a formica topped flour infested green wooden table.

Although to the two officers it was irrelevant to the reason for them being there, it was almost as if she thought she had to give them her life history. Married with a boy and a girl but now on her second husband and from what they could gather he was the reason for their moving to Sheffield to be close to his job, which she never went into in any detail about. Her accent was not from somewhere around Yorkshire and just like Raza her speech tended to be abrupt in manner. Friendly enough but brash.

She then went on about her daughter's autism and how she needed to attend a special school as if it was all important to their enquiries. Raza did wonder if she had mistaken them for social services, by the way she appeared to be justifying her life situation.

Took quite a while and a degree more of this idle chatter before they could then move Angela Gray off the death of Mindi Brookes and what she had read in the media and heard on the radio and onto Christine Streeter, the reason for their visit but even then it was hard going.

'We understand you went to school with Christine Streeter,' Raza Latif tried when she took a breath.

'Like I said when I phoned. Never seemed the sort to me.' The pair waited for more.

'What about after you left school?' Raza was forced to ask.

'Not really.'

'How do you think you can help?' Brown-Reid tried. 'Is there anything you can remember from back then which may be relevant and assist our enquiries now?'

'Just knew her. Didn't seem the sort. Really didn't.'

'In what way?' Latif asked.

'Long time ago now,' she told him. 'I was born in eighty-six, year the *Sun* said Freddie Starr had eaten a hamster,' was to Howard a most peculiar thing to say. 'Went to Forest Girls School was when I first came across her.'

'And this is where?' came right out of the training manual. Ask a question you know the answer to as if you don't.

'Lincoln, well not actually in the city of course, but close by.' This women was determined to continue with her baking despite their presence. 'You from Lincoln?' she asked peering up from her endeavours.

Raza's annoyance was quite evident as this Gray and Gillian started chatting about where she and David lived, about this woman's sister just outside the city and then involved him in idle chatter about schools.

'Were you close?' he tried to break the deviation.

'No. Not close, didn't live anywhere near me, just in my class for a lot of things.' She stopped rolling, spun the pastry round and started again.

'What d'you remember about her?'

'Well,' said this Angela slowly as she worked away with her wooden rolling pin, as if she was about to release a long tirade of information. 'To be honest only stood out because she was so weak and woolly, little Miss Muffet we used to call her. All prim and proper.' She stopped rolling and looked up. 'Quite ironic really when you think about it,' left Howard wondering if he should ask why. 'How years later,' she then went on. 'She got mixed up with the foreign bloke they locked up, he must have been the spider who sat down beside her,' she thought was funny.

'Anything else?' was Latif's curt way to show he was not amused.

'Saw Chrissie's mum and dad at school things, didn't know 'em of course.' Angela Gray stopped what she was doing, stood up straight and folded her arms. 'Good chance she was bullied of course. Don't know for sure, but be the sort. The weakling, the one who won't fight back, too scared to tell teacher, pick on the weakest of the litter. Sort these days who'll give teacher a Christmas present like they do.' She lifted her head enough to peer at Latif. 'Your kids. Boys, girls?'

'Two. Got two daughters.'

'There's bullying in most schools don't you think?

'Never affected mine,' Latif retorted.

'That you know of,' she sniggered annoyingly. 'What they called yours?'

'Dania and Tiana.'

'Nothing silly like Mindi then,' she thought was amusing.

'You know she was bullied for certain? You saw it?'

'No. Not for certain, but just saying she was a likely candidate. Bullies have always got some reason to pick on people, easy targets are the fat ones these days, but they've certainly got plenty of choice,' she sniggered. 'Ginger knobs, fatties, posh ones too mind,' and she was back to her pastry. 'Ones with flash phones and not enough likes get a bad time these days I reckon, what say you?' was ignored.

'So, the main thing you remember for certain is she was quiet.'

Most kitchens Raza had been in were either white, cream, grey or teak; this one was certainly different and old fashioned. Had to be the first green kitchen he'd ever seen, bit tired looking and in need of refurbishment.

'Think soppy is a much better word. A bit dozy and languid, just right for someone like him I bet. She'd be the meat in his sandwich, though there wasn't much meat on her to be honest. Well, not then there wasn't.'

'Someone like who?' Gillian slipped in, as she maneuvered the pastry onto the top of the pie.

'That Boro...Borove...whatever his name is.'

'Borowiak.'

'He's the one.'

'In what way?' Gillian asked.

'Did you know him too?' Latif queried.

'No, not him,' she said with a shake of her head. 'Just what I've read over the years. My guess is she was probably under the thumb I should imagine.' Angela Gray began to clear away her utensils, and then turned to the sink behind her to run hot water.

'Why would you think that?' slim Gillian wanted to know.

'Her being the lily livered little thing and him being one o' these foreigners. Plus stuff I've read.'

'He's not actually foreign.'

She smiled at Raza. 'You know what I mean. These foreign types then, not the same are they, not same as us and no mistake? Not a reet Yorkshire lad were he?' Howard caught a look from Latif. 'Different values, too stuck in the past those places abroad are aren't they. Very much all behind the times. Work the fields with oxen and all that business I hear tell just the sort of nonsense we're paying for through the EU.'

'What do you think happened to her?' swarthy Raza Latif asked instead of reacting.

'Dead,' she said sharply as she lifted utensils into her green washing-up bowl and added a quick squeeze of own label washing-up liquid. 'Has to be. Dumped somewhere in the middle of nowhere I should imagine, but she'll turn up one day when she's least expected I bet.' For some reason she glanced out of the window. 'Bury her up on the moors be worse than a needle in a haystack. Be a helluva job to take on, where d'you start?'

'We have reason to believe she might well still be alive.'

'What?' she shot back and turned away from the sink grimacing as she did so. 'How come?'

'Only a theory at the moment, but something we're looking into.'

'You think?' she looked at Latif. 'You think she's been hiding away all this time? Somebody's got her maybe, what you're thinking? Read about them don't you, people being held captive, used as slaves. Even in this day and age eh?' She shook her head. 'Guess it'd be those greasy foreigners too I bet, usually is. Just imagine, dear oh dear. Must be awful.'

'Not only foreigners.'

'Read somewhere in a couple of magazines how some of these poor women get involved in sexual exploitation and domestic servitude. Is it right when they get stuck as slaves in some o' these big houses they have to provide sex as well?'

'Anything's possible,' said Raza Latif. 'In such an environment I should imagine,' he added in need of a change of subject. 'And we obviously have an open mind at this stage.'

'Poor woman. Not the sort I'd have ever been pals with you understand, but you don't wish it on your worst enemy. Be better than dead though. Anyway, how's all this fit in with this Mindi woman I've been reading?'

'Just a snippet of information came to light around the same time. Like us being here today, we get calls all the time in situations like this, particularly with unexplained deaths, people pop out of the woodwork with all sorts of theories and ideas.'

'You don't think…no.'

'What were you going to say?' Gillian queried.

'Just thinking out loud. The name Mindi. Guess it came from Mork and Mindy, what d'you think?'

'No idea.'

'Got to be a real thankless task at times,' she said as she took a towel and began to dry her hands. 'Anything else I can help you with?' she checked. 'Not the sporty type, remember. One of those you get who are too girly to get a sweat on.'

'She didn't play any sport then?'

'She could swim, but then we all could pretty much with a big pool at the school of course. Be a given. Something I believe in to be honest, with us all living on an island, so it should be mandatory on the curriculum like Maths and English.' She spread her hands wide, one still clutching the towel. 'How many kids drown every year, far too many if you ask me?'

Raza Latif produced a card from his top pocket. 'If you think of anything else, please let us know. All helps build a picture.'

'Just have to hope,' she said as she read the card. 'In the end you don't find she'd been imprisoned somewhere. How awful would it be?'

'Certainly.'

'All seen stuff on TV haven't we? Just finish up with a pile of bones, be awful being on your own in a tomb, dying slowly day by day. Just imagine it eh? Take months I bet.'

'Thank you Mrs Gray,' said Gillian Brown-Reid as they both turned to the open door which would lead them back to the wallpapered hall.

'Tell you who you could try,' said Gray to stop them. 'Lottie Elliott.' Both detectives looked at her waiting for more as the name had caused a spike in Gillian's interest. 'Last heard of her somewhere near Lincoln she was at school at the same time she'd know of Christine, sure she'd remember probably more than me, think they were quite pally for a while.'

'Any idea where?' the DC asked.

'Lincoln way somewhere, and her old man was a carpet salesman if I remember rightly, well back then he was. Think if my memory serves me right he stood for the council at one time. Don't think he got in but may have done later of course.'

'Thanks for that,' said Gillian as Raza made notes. 'Don't suppose you'd have a number for her by any chance?' he hoped. Angela Gray just pouted and pulled a face and shook her head.

'And before you ask I've no idea if she's on social media,' she grinned. 'Just not my scene at all or d'you think I look fifteen?' Howard went to respond to her grin. 'All soppy photos of toddlers seems to me and what should you never put on the web?' she raised her eyebrows in anticipation. 'Photos of your kids' she sighed obviously to make her point and shook her head.

'See ourselves out,' and they just walked down the hall out of the front door with Gillian closing it behind them and up the short path to Raza's car.

'Could have asked what made her call us,' Gillian suggested in the car.

'She knew Streeter.'

'So what? She knew her at school, since then nothing. What use is all that? Not like she saw her last week in the queue at Aldi's. Wonder what made her call in?'

'I'd had enough, it was all going nowhere except we've got another contact. Especially when you went off piste with all that personal stuff.'

'What I've been taught. Not always a case of asking closed questions. Let them talk, you sometimes pick up snippets, learn something basic questions will never give you.'

'Whatever,' was surly Raza. 'Kitchen could do with an update.'

'Latest thing so I'm told'

'What is?'

'Making it look tired and unloved. All the fashion.'

'It's certainly that all right,' Raza scoffed and had to remember what she had said. That'd stop Ghada wanting to spend a fortune on one of the new all singing all dancing bespoke things she'd got her eye on.

'Why is that name ringing a bell?'

'Dunno. Heard it somewhere before, and recently too.'

'Better be a darn sight better or Inga'll not be best pleased.'

'Bet it was her fifteen minutes of fame, now on Facebook telling all her girly mates I bet. Thought she was bloody ignorant to be honest carrying on making that pie thing with us there.'

'Talking of Facebook, why she want us to keep off? What it seemed like to me.'

'Give it a check when we get back.'

'Bit odd must confess.' Gillian giggled to herself. 'Born the same year as Freddie Starr ate his hamster. What was that all about?'

'Talking of something to eat, we stopping?'

'Services down at Blyth be our best bet, want me to turn off?'

DS Raza Latif left it to Gillian Brown-Reid to report back to boss Larsson about the woman in Sheffield. All about her not stopping making a pie during their chat but more importantly how she considered Chrissie Streeter may well have been bullied at school. He had decided that on the basis of providing co-opted Sam with an opportunity to impress the boss.

'What's she like this Angela Gray?'

'Dark haired, pleasant enough about Ruth's height I would guess. Very much a mummy figure there busy making a pie.'

'At least she can cook and tea won't be straight from a packet in the freezer. Nice place was it?'

'About average for around there; nothing special really. Former council house semi I should imagine, be where steel workers used to live, up on one of the hills.'

'We learnt anything do we think?'

'Only this bit about bullying. Her description of Streeter fits what we already have. Sort of mealy mouthed little thing wouldn't say boo to a goose we've read in the case notes. She was a bit nasty about Borowiak being foreign or at least she thought he was. Saw him as a bully which maybe fits with the control freak info.'

'Racist issues?'

'Not really, just an attitude.'

'Did you ask her if she can remember who did the bullying?'

'Not sure she did, more along the lines of bullying goes on and she was ripe for it, being the way she was made her a target.'

'Way she was?'

'Drippy.'

'These days of course it'd all be done on social media,' Inga reminded him.

'Even if she does know who was responsible, if it happened at all of course, we'd have hell on now trying to find whoever it was.'

'And she reckons Streeter could swim,' said Sam from his notes. 'Well, she said they all could. Even if there was no need to explain she reminded us there was a pool at the school.'

'Ruth,' said Inga to catch her attention. 'Mrs Streeter. Any thoughts from her about Chrissie being bullied?'

'Never mentioned it.'

'Make a note somewhere on her file please. If we have reason to talk to her again we could do with mentioning it.' Inga turned back to Gillian. 'Anything else of interest?'

'Married, two children everything appears pretty average, sister lives off Newark Road somewhere, just wanted to add her four pennuth.'

'What's her husband do, d'we know?'

'Didn't ask.'

'Anything else?'

'Yes,' he grinned. 'She wore rubber gloves to make pastry. My mum always says you need warm hands to make pastry. You don't see a baker kneeding the dough in Marigolds.' He laughed. 'Apart from giving us the name of someone else who says might know about Streeter, but no contact number.'

'Except,' said Raza quickly to join in. 'Got the feeling she tried to put us off going on social media to look her up. Might be nothing in it of course, but you never know.'

'Lottie Elliott,' said Gillian. 'Said her old man was or still is a carpet salesman and once stood for the council.'

'Lottie?' she queried to all and sundry.

'Charlotte,' said Julie Rhoades. 'What Lottie's short for.'

'Thanks Gill.' For somebody used to dealing with shoplifters and burglars down in PHU she was doing just fine.

'Hang on boss,' said Jake Goodwin concentrating on his PC, but she took no notice other than to glance round still reflecting on a peculiar observation a man had noticed about a woman making pastry, then shrugged her shoulders very slightly. 'Got it!' said Jake loudly and clapped. 'Good news and its Friday 13th!' he shouted. 'Charlotte Elliott is the name of the woman who died after going to a wine bar in Peterborough a few months back, remember? Claims at the time were made about her drink having been spiked by some low life but the toxicology suggested the chances are she'd taken something.' He grinned at the boss. 'Knew the name rang a bell.'

'What's the situation now?' Inga wanted to know.

'Still under investigation.'

'Where is she from?'

'Scampton.'

'RAF?'

'Village.'

'But is it the same one?'

11

The Home Office system of information technology administrative support, HOLMES for short, had on this occasion been brought in purely due to the sudden appearance of Christine Streeter's DNA.

Normally reserved for serial killings or a multi-million pound complicated fraud case for which it was originally designed, this discovery had moved its application to the forefront of their procedures.

Civilian Lizzie would at times of least data streams simply input idle information just as she herself says *'to see what pops up'* and in fact Inga at acute times like this would frequently ask for a 'pop up' from her.

'Have you considered separating the issues?' Lizzie asked after Inga to make her stop and look back. 'Think the waters are being muddied by this DNA. Not my place I know, but from where I sit, punching in all this data we do seem to have moved away from who killed Mindi Brookes.'

Inga made no comment, turned back and bent down slightly to talk to her very able lieutenant Jake Goodwin.

'Stevens' eTeam have two more for us to check out.'

'All we've got, just two?'

'No,' he assured her. 'The less likely are being dealt with by PHU to free us up to trace those with more of a marker.'

'Let's hope they're better than the last one.' She chuckled to herself. 'Did you know she was born in the year when Freddie Starr eat his hamster?'

He just grinned as he shook his head. 'What can you say?'

She nodded and grinned at his reaction. 'Been thinking we go back to Lawlor who says he saw her at the airport. He'd made contact with somebody on social media who had something to say about a woman who might know but is dead.' He looked at his boss.

'Charlotte Elliott surely is the one he talked about on social media, and that's the name of the woman down in Peterborough. Not just a sad case of her inconveniently dying this could well be murder, or so they reckon down there.'

'We can't talk to her though, unless you've got an Ouija board.'

'No. But we can get everything from the lads down there. See what they've got.'

'Is it me or is this all a series of blind alleys? None of these people lead us anywhere and now we find some of them are already dead. CSI Leicester are dragging their feet with the urine.' She saw Jake's grimace. 'Asking them how old it is. This fresh or this old pee from somewhere?'

'Can they do that easy?'

'Easy for them I bet, I'd not want to be doing it.' She hesitated to blow out a breath. 'PHU are tackling the guy from East Midlands.'

'Steven Lawlor.'

'Don't hold out much hope with Lawlor. Surely we all see people we think we recognize, but then realize we're mistaken when we get a proper view. My guess is he just saw her walking away in a crowded airport, could've been anybody.'

'Case of waiting on one of ASBO's minions if he ever clambers out of the dark net.' Inga Larsson sat back hand behind her head. 'Week tonight since the phone call about Brookes.'

'Look on the bright side,' Jake suggested stood in her doorway with his jacket on. 'Waiting for the geeks gives us a decent chance over the weekend to do more checking and double checking.'

While her team would spend the weekend going through the list of actions Inga had dealt them, she was already aware she'd be busy waiting.

Waiting on the age of urine, waiting on Forensics reports she'd asked for and the second wave of door-to-door statements. Knew she'd need to catch up on other ongoing cases all at various stages dragging their way up the judicial ladder rung by rung.

'Just our luck going to be a really nice weekend.'

'Indian summer they say.'

'What chance we got of enjoying it?'

DI Inga Larsson had been pulled into having her daily early morning chat with Detective Super Craig Darke to update him on the situation with the Mindi Brookes case and equally importantly the possible sudden appearance of one Christine Streeter.

She knew Darke would have had the Chief Constable on his back and he'd not be the only one. All those with fingers in the historic city pie would be expecting a quick resolution to the Mindi Brookes murder as if it were childs' play this homicide business.

They'd be worried about the effect such events had on the stain on the city's character and importantly of course on their wallets.

'Here's what we're doing,' Inga just loved it when he said "we" about something he'd not go within a mile of. 'This Streeter business will be high profile whether we like it or not. The scandalous media have of course all but forgotten Mindi Brookes poor soul and are hell bent on finding this Streeter woman. How long before one of the red tops claim to have spotted her sunning herself in Spain?' Inga was given no chance to answer. 'I've instructed DCI Stevens to put Adrian Orford personally at your disposal. I know he normally can be found living in cyberspace and the dark net and all that business, but some of this is likely to be beyond your team. Use him, even for the basic checks if you wish. He thinks differently from you and I.'

Inga knew this was all about PR. Adrian, better known throughout the force as ASBO was Luke Stevens' top puppy dog techy-wizz and he'd be none too happy with him being given specific duties away from his CAT team role. Craig Darke had spoken, so be it, which she knew in itself would annoy Stevens.

By the time Inga had wandered back along to the MIT incident room she discovered Raza Latif had been called away with an important issue concerning his daughter at school. To make matters worse Gillian had phoned in about her car being vandalized overnight.

Inga was forced under the circumstances into a quick reshuffle. Planning to send Ruth Buchan along with Julie Rhoades to a hotel south of Nottingham for an appointment with a Susan Sewell, and Raza and Gillian back to Sheffield she had to change tack.

Rather than sending another pairing for the Sheffield trip to see Angela Gray again, being two down Inga gave both jobs to the girls. Across to Sheffield then M1 down to Nottingham.

Another box ticked, after Darke boringly yet again had mentioned budgets earlier. A life of continuous tedium it seemed to her. Budgets from Darke endlessly and Brexit on the radio, on TV news and headlines in any paper she spotted and now two short.

'We're a couple short this morning,' Inga informed the remainder of the gathered throng who were already aware Raza was missing. 'Ruth and Julie have gone to talk to this Sewell woman who claims she went out with Borowiak before Chrissie Streeter did, after they've double checked a few things with that Gray woman in Sheffield we saw on Friday.'

'Be my turn for a trip out when Hurricane Ophelia arrives.'

Inga just ignored the quip, but knew the forecast was for unusually warm sunshine for the girls. 'Our friends up in Stevens' world have come up with a bit of a coincidence I was worried might be heading our way,' she sniggered, tablet in hand. 'And you know what I'm going to say. Like Father Christmas and fairies at the bottom of the garden, I don't believe in them. In the context of a murder enquiry I'm sorry but there's no place for coincidences.' She hesitated to just peer down at her pad. 'Charlotte Elliott is dead. Just had confirmation from the crew upstairs how she is the same person as the one who popped her clogs in Peterborough,' she said very plainly. 'It happens of course, but remember that Amelia Evans is also dead.' Sandy went to respond but a hand stopped him. 'Evans died from bowel cancer couple of years back. She was the one the woman in Retford said had known Streeter when she was with Borowiak. Now we have this Angela Gray putting us onto a woman who is also dead. Both in their thirties, so we're not talking old age here.'

'Can't we ignore Amelia Evans?' Jake suggested. 'After all dying of cancer is a good enough reason to me. Scratch her name out and we just have the one the Gray woman put us onto. Sorry guv, but whatever way you look at her, this is never a coincidence.'

'And if Gray's not been in touch with this Charlotte recently and she lives in Sheffield, chances are she's not heard what happened down in Peterborough.'

'So you're all ganging up on me,' a spirited Inga shot at them all.

'Not at all, ma'am,' said Jake earnestly. 'I'm sure we feel the same as you do about being buffeted from pillar to post, but you know from experience the tide will turn. Right now we're ploughing our way through the bad news we always get with the territory.'

'And to stop you becoming morbid, how about you look into Charlotte or Lottie Elliott for us? Easy enough start just steal whatever Cambridgeshire have come up with. Talk to DI Ralph Higgins tell him I sent you,' her look told Jake she was enjoying the banter. 'See what more bad news you can bring to the table.'

Inga had wondered about making use of a better link. Nicky Scoley late of her parish who was now working for Cambridgeshire, but then she remembered she was actually based in the city itself not out at Peterborough.

'More bad news,' said Michelle Cooper with a wry smile towards her boss. Tidied bobbed brown hair and to a degree an anonymous attractive scrubbed face. 'Every system we can think of checked, all social media and only seventeen people with the name Christine Streeter. Nobody even comes close to fitting the bill, and just to give you some idea. There's a seventy-three year old suffering from an inability to care for herself so she's been shoved in a care home by her kids. There's a teenager with the regulation attention span of a gnome and a vicar attending some wives club at the church hall.'

'A vicar called Christine?'

'What world are you living in?'

'To my mind,' said Inga. 'If it were not for her past history and parents still alive it would be very easy to see her as a cleverly constructed false identity.'

Inga was not at all sure whether the news from on high was good or bad.

According to Detective Super Craig Darke the whole conundrum regarding witness protection had been checked out by DCI Luke Stevens and he had confirmed to the boss how his National Crime Agency contacts had assured him categorically how they had never had any involvement whatsoever in the disappearance of Christine Streeter.

Stevens had also discovered she was not the subject of an official anonymity order to keep her hidden. Those orders they all knew were for nationally known killers like Jon Venables and Mary Bell, not for somebody who might have seen or heard something. It was good of him to double check, thought Inga.

What Darke had added, she had not repeated to Jake Goodwin was how they regarded the Borowiak/Streeter case as so unimportant in the big scheme of things and more suited to folk out in the sticks as not to be anything they would ever dirty their hands with.

What did surprise both Inga and Jake was how dapper Stevens had not made an appearance to be plauded for his efforts or to poke his nose further into their case.

12

Raza Latif's report on his visit with Brown-Reid to Sheffield had even given a good description of the house in Daffodil Road even down to the fact the front door had been painted royal blue.

Odd thing about Latif. In a person to person situation he always tended towards being abrupt and gave people short shrift, but set against such negatives were his reports. So often his observation skills were second to none and in his reports he included the finest detail, particularly about people.

This case was no different. He described her as a pleasant fairly attractive woman with good deep brown hair and what he described as refined make-up. Which for a bloke like him probably meant she hadn't put her slap on with the garden trowel. He put her down as a typical stay at home mumsy. Fairly unusual in this day and age, but he was pleased she was baking for her family and not planning to just rip open another packet to shove in the microwave.

Julie Rhoades knocked on the door and it was opened fairly quickly by a black woman whose big brown eyes darted from Julie across to Ruth and back again.

'Yes,' she said and sighed with a degree of annoyance.

'Angela Gray?' Rhoades asked and presented her warrant card.

'No,' the woman said and shook her head.

'I'm Detective Constable Julie Rhoades and this is Detective Constable Ruth Buchan from Lincoln County Police. Is she in?'

'Is who in?'

'Angela Gray.'

'Never heard of an Angela Gray. You sure you've got the right house?'

Rhoades just glanced at Ruth Buchan stood beside her. 'Our colleagues were here on Friday and spoke to Angela Gray, and we're here to ask a few follow-up questions.'

'Not here they didn't.'

'Can I ask?' said Ruth who was going to whatever she replied. 'How long have you lived here?'

The woman grimaced. 'Four years and a bit. What's that got to do with anything?'

'And you are who?'

'Hope Parkes,' she said as two distinct words with an emphasis on the 'p' in each case.'

'And you say you don't know an Angela Gray.'

'Not sure I know anybody called Angela.'

'What about Angela Wilcox?'

This Hope shook her head.

'What school did you go to?' was their next question.

'What?' the woman gasped and screwed her face up.

'School?'

'Senior School?' she asked to which Ruth responded with a nod. 'I went to King Edward VII as it happens, Kind Ted's and I'm an Old Edwardian. Why?'

'Live here alone do you?'

'Why d'you need to know that? What's this all about?'

'We're carrying out major enquiries into a very serious case,' said Julie Rhoades. 'Angela Gray who lives at this address has already provided useful information.'

'What are you talking about?' was louder. 'Not her, she's not.'

'I'll ask again,' said Ruth with a much firmer tone. 'Do you live alone?'

'As it happens, no.'

'And?'

The woman shook her head and sighed noisily. 'I've already told you, I've never heard of an Angela Gray I have no idea what you're talking about. Might I suggest you go back to square one and next time get your facts right.' She glanced left and right down the road. 'Or find the right address maybe.'

'First,' said Ruth. 'We need to eliminate you from our enquiries. Do you not think it might be a good idea to invite us in? Always possible you are completely innocent but the neighbours just might make more of the situation as people often tend to do'

'Innocent? What situation?'

'Us standing on your doorstep. And we really do need to establish you are who you say you are.'

'I need to check your ID,' she suggested to Ruth, who produced her warrant card again and this Hope Parkes woman made a big issue of checking it.

'Come in,' she said reluctantly and stood aside to allow the DCs to walk into her hall. 'Turn right,' she suggested and they walked into a small front room furnished with a mix of new and old. New and pre-owned by many before. 'Now what?' she threw at Julie when they were all three stood there in the middle of the carpeted room.

'Do you have any form of ID?' Ruth asked and Hope Parkes spun round.

'Don't see why I should, thought this was a free country,' and left the room. Both women looked at each other, unwilling to speak in fear of being overheard by the woman or anybody else in the property but showed by their expressions their frustration at their situation.

'Driving Licence and my Hospital pass,' she said when she returned and handed both to Julie.

'Hospital?' Ruth tossed at her.

'I'm an Operating Department Practitioner.'

'And what does the work involve?'

'I work mainly during anaesthetics but also in surgical and the recovery phases.'

'Like a sort of nurse, do you mean?'

'My husband is a staff nurse,' she answered. 'I'm a degree educated professional, as it happens.'

'Children?' Julie asked as she handed the IDs back.

'A son.'

'Just out of interest,' said Ruth very softly. 'Do you know anybody around here who has a daughter who is autistic?'

'Not round here, not in this street I don't think.' She hesitated. 'Well, not I've heard of anyway.'

Ruth caught the look on Julie's face. 'And today you're off?'

'Worked all weekend, took today off. Why?'

'What were you doing last Friday?' Ruth asked. 'Friday 13th.'

A moment's thought. 'At work, all day from early on.'

Ruth glanced all around the room. 'You buying this?'
'What's it to you if I am?' was sharp.
'Think you need to calm down. We're just asking.'
'Not yet.'
'What do you mean?'
'We rent it at the moment,' she sighed obviously. 'But there may be an opportunity to buy the place, we're weighing up the pros and cons of whether to buy somewhere we know or go the whole hog and look for somewhere new.'
'Seems to be about it then,' said Ruth. 'We're sorry to have troubled you. Please accept our apologies for the intrusion and we'll need to get back now.'
'To sort out your cock-up.'
'Something's obviously awry.'
'Awry?' she chuckled. 'It's a darn sight worse than that!'
'We may turn out we have to call on you again.'
'Whatever,' she said languidly as the pair shuffled out of the room, Julie opened the front door and they stepped out.
'Thank you for your time,' Julie called back.
'Explain that to me,' said Ruth when they were in the car. 'What a bloody cock-up!'
'Raza was specific, and it's the only blue door I can see.'

He was in a hurry, just as the situation required but he was far from the realms of panic. Years of training had taught Raza Latif that much.

Having parked up at the far end of the school car park designated for staff only, he'd hurried across to follow signs to the entrance. Raza pulled one of the pair of double doors and pushed past the inevitable schoolkids dragging themselves towards him, strode on to the signed Reception area and a woman stood with elbows on the counter gazing at nothing very much.
'My daughter has an issue, I'm her father,' he told the woman.
'And you are, sir?'
'Raza Latif,' was abrasive.
'And what exactly appears to be the issue?'

'I understand there's a problem, can you point me in the right direction?'

'To where, sir?'

'To where my daughter is,' he insisted.

'And who might she be.'

'Tiana Latif.'

The unconcerned woman lifted a file from the counter just below and began to flick through two or three pages.

'Don't think so, sir.'

'Excuse me,' he said curtly. 'I got a call to say Tiana had a problem and could I come down here as soon as I could.'

'Who was it from, sir?'

'From here. From the school.' His annoyance was by then very clear.

'Yes, but from who specifically?'

'Her teacher I presume,' was sharp.

'Form teacher would it be?'

'I don't know,' he responded to this annoyingly casual manner he faced. 'Whoever it was, phoned the station and the message was passed to me by control.' The woman frowned. 'I'm Detective Sergeant Raza Latif.'

'So you didn't actually speak to anybody?'

'No not personally.'

'Do you have any form of identification, sir?'

Raza Latif pulled out his warrant card and opened it for the woman to read. She read and shook her head at the same time and then sucked in a breath of caution.

'Not got anything down here,' she said and then picked up a phone, tapped three numbers. 'Muriel, got a...Detective Sergeant Raza Latif,' she said slowly, 'in Reception. Been told there's an...issue with his daughter,' she put the phone to her chest. 'Her name was again, sir?' she asked Latif.

'Tiana.'

'Tiana Latif,' she said into the phone whilst looking at Raza who nodded. 'Thanks,' she added, then spoke to him. 'Just checking. Be honest nothing's come to me this morning. We get all sorts of course,' she smirked. 'Doctor's appointments always make me chuckle. As if I ask you. Wish I could get one so quick, what say you? Throwing a sickie often as not, dentist all sorts, even family bereavements a time or two.' This woman then leant into him. 'Some I'm sure have had more teeth out than they've got. Even had one had to go to the vet with a stupid hamster week or two back.' She was then back to the phone. 'In class you say...yes...yes...no problem.' She put the phone back on the rack. 'Your daughter's in class, doesn't seem there's a problem, but somebody's off to just check.'

'Can you point me in the right direction?'

'Sorry, sir. They'll not be long.'

'The way to the classroom, if you please.'

'Can't allow that, sorry.' She pursed her lips. 'Too many issues I'm afraid,' she said and sucked in noisily in real jobsworth fashion. 'Child protection, health and safety, you know what it's like these days.'

She came very close to getting both barrels but for once DS Latif put his daughter first, when he really wanted to throw his weight about and give this tawdry woman some of the Latif way she'd not have liked one little bit. He stood there arms folded, back against the Reception counter for a good ten minutes, before this tubby woman in sandals with bare feet and varicose veins appeared through swing doors to his right, strode up to the desk and spoke with the woman.

'She's in class, don't know what all the fuss is about, to be honest.'

'Are you saying Tiana Latif is safely in class?' Raza threw at her.

'And you are?'

'Detective Sergeant Raza Latif, I'm part of the county's Major Incident Team. Now what's going on?'

'As I just said,' she threw at him. 'I've just taken the trouble to go to her class and she is there. And your issue is?'

'My control received a call earlier to say my daughter had an issue here at school, and could I attend as soon as possible.' He put his head on one side. 'Here I am. Next question?'

'Seems a lot of fuss about nothing, as if we haven't got enough to do.'

'Somebody from here made the call,' he insisted.

'So you say.' She said. 'That it Amanda?' she asked the woman behind the counter.

'Thank you Deidre.' And this chunky going on plump woman just plodded away.

Raza handed this Erica a card. 'If there are any more issues, please call me directly.'

'Shouldn't image there will be,' she said, just slid the card to one side and was back to leafing through a magazine.

13

The two policewomen were shown to a small conference room just off the hotel foyer close to the M42 south of Nottingham. Within a couple of minutes the door opened and in walked what could only be described as an off-the-peg businesswoman. She had the 'look', the very dark brown coiffured hair which will never move, immaculate but heavy make-up with plucked angry eyebrows, the crisp pale blue blouse, fine worsted suit and black very high heels and regulation nobbly calves to go with them. Unusually she wore black rimmed designer glasses, which surprised Ruth who would have expected her vanity would have insisted upon contact lenses.

As soon as she closed the door behind her a thin hand was stretched forward to shake hands first with Ruth. 'Good morning, I'm Susan Sewell,' she said, before she had managed to get fully to her feet and then Julie. 'Pleased to meet you.'

Sewell sat down, laid her smart phone very carefully on the table in front of her, crossed her legs and just tugged at her skirt with her fingertips to place it in perfect position.

'Good journey?' she asked Ruth.

'Fine, thank you. Bit of a hold up on the motorway but apart from that.'

'You want to know about dear Tomasz then,' she said as her fingers interlinked around her knee. 'Good job we can't see into the future,' she said and smiled. 'Goodness me no,' she chuckled to herself. 'Tomasz Borowiak hmm. Well let me see. We were together towards the end of my time as a holiday rep. In fact it was how we met out in Tenerife to be honest, so as you can imagine it was never a full on living together happy couple sort of relationship, and to be honest I think he was seeing others on the side, so to speak.'

'Did he always do that?' Julie Rhoades piped up, as Ruth looked at the woman closely. She had no eyebrows, they'd been shaved off and were drawn in very heavily and starkly. Be a fad no doubt she thought sat there looking at her, trying to be snazzy or some other daft reason for it.

'To be honest I don't know. I'm in Tenerife remember and he's over here. Then I was offered a job by one of the hotel groups and of course it meant I was over in the sun virtually permanently rather than primarily the summer months and although we never discussed it, it was what drove us apart and provided the opportunity for young Miss Streeter to slip herself under the duvet, so to speak.'

'Were you ever interviewed by police at the time of her disappearance?'

'No,' was firm. 'But to be honest I'd wrapped myself up in my new role as I began to climb the ladder and it was around the time I had started with the hotel group I'm with now,' she looked all around the room as if there was a need to establish her position. 'Of course it meant a great deal of travelling and as a result I tended to lose track of family and friends and to be honest it's only in the past six months or so I've begun to interact with old friends again. When you're in Istanbul one week, then New York and Qatar keeping up with the old school pals and girls back home is never a priority,' appeared to amuse her slightly. 'They were on silly school-run business no doubt and I'm in conference.' She grinned. 'Different worlds as you can imagine.' She leant forward. 'There is always a degree of homesickness no matter what some people will have you believe. All to do with a need to be comfortable in certain surroundings rather like the womb.' Ruth went to speak but she was having none of it. 'Yes I know in this day and age technology can work wonders what with Skype and all the rest of it, but it's never quite the same. This is particularly true as people you know get older.'

A tap on the door, and it opened inwards to reveal a young Asian looking waitress complete with a tray, jugs of coffee and milk, sugar cubes, three cups and saucers. She was followed by a nervous young man with a fine selection of unusual biscuits and the requisite number of white plates. His behavior was almost as if he had suddenly been thrust into the presence of royalty for the first time.

'Thank you, dear,' Sewell said to the girl as the trays were placed on the low table.

'Thank you Miss Sewell,' said the waitress and they were gone, with the door being closed slowly almost silently. A curtsey would not have been out of place.

Ruth was well aware they'd be what companies euphemistically call 'colleagues' but in truth they are nothing of the sort and are probably on zero hours contracts, minimum wage, foreign and in the main treated like nothing more than the hoi polloi.

'Please help yourselves. I ordered coffee but if you wish to be terribly English and would prefer tea just say, it's really no bother at all.' She poured a minor amount of milk into her black coffee and sat back. 'In the early days I did miss my good old cup of tea, but over time I learnt to live in a world of coffee rather than stomach what some places offer as tea but is nothing of the sort.'

'Coffee's just fine,' said Ruth for the pair of them. It certainly smelt good enough.

'Where was I? Oh yes. I find it better if I keep contact with my home life quite separate and for the most of the time treat it almost as if it no longer exists. Otherwise you feel, or at least I do, feel as if you are somehow missing out on everything which is going on back here. Truth is of course nothing special is going on.'

'Thomasz Borowiak,' said Ruth as a reminder.

'To be honest I can't remember where I was when somebody told me Tomasz was in trouble, and then it was months later of course I heard the case had come to court and then I got it all but in dribs and drabs which is pretty much always the case. Just makes no sense, sorry but what I have read about the case was most certainly not the Tomasz I knew.' She sucked in a breath, allowed her head to shake before it was released. 'Never could get my head round them finding him guilty of murder without a body. Most peculiar I have to say. Sort of way one expects some regimes deal with the proletariat.'

'Fishing?' Ruth queried. 'It was his alibi,' she said as if it made up for there being no body.

'Yes, he went fishing certainly but not something he did morning noon and night by a long chalk. His way of relaxing now and again to be honest, more than anything else.'

'Can we ask you about a suggestion somebody has made?' Ruth queried. 'We've been told by someone who knew Christine Streeter around the time how Thomasz Borowiak was very much a control freak.'

'What?' Sewell chortled. 'Utter nonsense, dear. Who spun you such a yarn?'

'I'm sorry,' said Ruth. 'Unfortunately we're not at liberty to say at this stage.' She added milk to her black coffee.

'Well, I can certainly assure you the Thomasz I knew if anything was too laid back, if there was any sorting out to do as there usually is with men, all he needed was a good kick up the backside, to get on and sort his life out. All his potential just going to waste.' She smiled as if an image of him had just appeared in focus in her brain. 'Good looking guy mind,' she shrugged. A fact Ruth was aware of from photos at the time. Mug shots maybe, but he was still a piece of goods despite his obvious forlorn look. 'But you can't build a strong relationship on looks alone. Otherwise all these celebs wouldn't be chopping and changing like they inevitably do, for that very reason.'

'How well did you know Christine Streeter?'

'Can I just say before we move on,' said Sewell. 'On the subject of Thomasz and how he was, looking back now I cannot imagine our relationship would ever have worked long term due to his languid ways. Really nice guy, don't get me wrong but he just lacked any sort of ambition, just happy with his life just bobbing along.'

'Christine Streeter,' Rhoades reminded her, cup in hand.

'I didn't, plain and simple. Never met the woman.'

'Not at all?'

'Tomasz and her were over here canoodling and I was making the most of the sunshine and more importantly the career opportunity.' Ruth just managed to catch Julie's eye as she peered over her cup as she drank. Her career had been thrown at them more than once. Control freak and this Sewell woman were most probably better acquainted.

'Are you still in touch with any of your old school pals?' Ruth asked. 'People who might have been around at the time perhaps.'

'Why this sudden interest in the woman, I thought she was supposed to be dead? Surely it's why poor Thomasz has been locked up all this time.' She looked at Ruth. 'Are you saying...?'

'We're not saying, save to say our enquiries have led us to believe Christine Streeter may well still be alive.'

'She been seen about or something? I don't understand,' she posed with a frown.

'Information has come to hand recently.' Ruth drank some of her coffee.

'You really are a strange bunch,' said Susan Sewell with a self-satisfied look on her face. 'You're almost a stereotype of police on television rather than the other way round. All this need to know business I find so very amusing. If you are serious about gaining knowledge from people like me who might have vital information, you'd be better off coming clean. Always been my policy to lead with the truth, good or bad at every opportunity. Be up front with people, position them on your side. If you were to tell me how you've reached your conclusion it might help my thought process.'

Ruth shrugged. 'Sorry,' she said as this Sewell lifted her cup to drink. 'Old School friends,' she said to remind her and change subjects. 'You were about to tell us.'

She knew what they say of course about high achieving women feeling the need to do twice as well as men for them to be thought half as good. Was that what all the get-up was about, for her and others like her? If Sewell had been a man would he have been decked out in anything much more than his normal suit, collar and tie, although these days even such items are no longer a must. Ruth wondered why this woman was all dressed up to the nines and how long it might take her to get ready of a morning, with the pristine hair and make-up?

As Ruth sat there looking at immaculate Sewell she did wonder what remarks there would be across the incident room if she ever turned up for work in such a state?

Susan Sewell sat there, white cup held in both hands almost as if she had a need to warm her manicured fingers made so obvious by the black nail varnish, as she pondered. 'Be a case of those I can remember if I'm honest.' They waited as the thought process continued. 'There'd be Angela Wilcox and Paula Turner,' she sucked in her breath. 'And....erm,' she looked at Ruth. 'These are the names I knew them by of course back then. What you have to remember is I was not in the same year as Streeter, I'd have been two years behind.' Her wistful expression suggested more. 'Trying to remember why I recall those two. Maybe good at netball.'

'Would your Angela Wilcox be Angela Gray now by any chance?'

Sewell shrugged and grimaced at auburn Julie Rhoades. 'No idea, could be of course.' A moment or two of contemplation. 'Rebecca Odling, any use to you?'

'Might be,' Ruth replied as Rhoades made notes. 'Put them through the system when we get back and see what pops up.'

'All technology based now of course, you'll have it all at the tap of a key no doubt.'

'What is it you actually do?' Ruth asked using the boss's tip of changing subject without warning normally used by her for scrotes in an interview room.

'Futures Senior Executive,' she said.

Ruth was forced to ask the obvious. 'Which means what exactly?'

'When one of our hotels has been refurbished I'm responsible if you like for bringing the final version to market. A brand based role also linked with customer care and our launch services teams.'

Ruth just looked around. 'And here?'

'Oh dear me no,' Sewell said firmly. 'I'm actually heading for Birmingham and our new Spiceal Grand close to the Bull Ring and New Street Station,' she said. 'New concept entirely and certainly a big project and an even bigger launch.'

'Exciting I bet,' Rhoades suggested.

Then 'Unusual name,' Ruth offered.

'Comes from one of the street names at the turn of the century and our concept team like the link to special, for it most certainly will be.' Ruth wished she's never mentioned it as she knew she was about to get the whole hog of nauseating nonsense you inevitably always get from people like her. 'To be honest after launch we will change Birmingham forever from a good city to a great one. The Spiceal Grand will be iconic, the sort of place where people have no need to pray for their dreams to come true for we will guarantee them. Something we take for granted with it simply being built into our DNA.'

'Seems very special,' from Rhoades annoyed her colleague..

'Gracious service for a city deserving of the very best only we can deliver.' She was going through the whole spiel now. 'We waited until this time in order for us to be able to be the fairy atop the tree so to speak. Exactly what England's second city has been crying out for. Spiceal will most certainly be…special.'

'Commonwealth Games heading there too they tell me.'

'Exactly.'

'You'll be busy,' oh how Ruth wanted to tell Julie to stop as this woman wagged a thin finger at her.

'But every launch also has too much champers and too many wild mushroom and parmesan vol-au-vents,' she chuckled at. 'I say that, but if the parmesan is actually produced in Reggio Emilia, they really are to die for of course, as I'm sure you'll agree.'

Ruth refused to get involved with any comment, even though 'pretentious prat' was running amok in her brain. She really couldn't be doing with all the sort of showing off nonsense, and she downed the remainder of her coffee. Nothing really special about it, but to be fair the biscuits were above average. Not good enough to make your dreams come true but a very fair choice.

'Anybody else you've thought of from your schooldays?'

'Really can't think,' Sewell responded. 'May I ask, what will happen about poor Thomasz if she is found?'

'Not up to us of course, but that's not to say how as a force we won't have an input even if it is only at Home Office level.'

'But it could mean he has been in prison for no reason. I'm sorry but I daren't think what he's gone through. After you called I Googled him and from what I can gather he has pleaded his innocence all along and still does as far as I could make out.'

'So we believe.'

'Why now?' she asked. 'Why on earth didn't this all come out ten years ago.'

'Sorry,' was Ruth with a smile.

'You know something, I take it.'

'I'm afraid it's all for others, at this stage we just get to interview people,' Julie Rhoades looked down at her notebook. 'Probably some of the names you've given us will be our next few calls.'

'Some'll have got married of course,' Sewell smiled at what she was about to say. 'And divorced no doubt, so names may not be exactly as I knew them.'

'We have teams of little nerds who just love any sort of unpicking task set before them.' Julie saw Ruth's tiny nod. 'Time for us to get back to them and see what they can come up with.'

'Give my regards to any you manage to find.'

'We certainly will,' said Ruth as she got to her feet, and held her hand out down to Susan Sewell. 'Thank you for your assistance,' she told her as they shook. 'And good luck with the launch in Birmingham.'

'Thank you,' said DC Rhoades and she too shook hands with the woman. 'And many thanks for the coffee.'

'My pleasure,' said Sewell. 'Actually the hotel's pleasure,' she said and smiled.

'Why do people like her get right up my nose?' Ruth asked as Julie pulled away from their car parking space down the side of the hotel. 'She's a high-ender if ever I saw one.'

'Doing all right for herself by the looks of it.'

'Might be nice thing to do to start with, but is going to Paris one day then Toronto then Melbourne and some place in Mombasa such a thrill when you've done it all hundreds of times? Think of the packing and unpacking, another airport, aircraft food, hotel room looking just like the last one. I'm not too sure it's all it's cracked up to be.'

'I don't know but I'd like to give it a try, especially the sun bit!'

'But nowhere is home.'

'S'pose you're right.'

'I bet some of those she was at school with looked down their noses at her getting a job as a holiday rep at the time, when they were swanning off to uni no doubt. Bet they're not so cocky now.'

'Probably why they're no longer in touch with her.'

They drove on in silence for a few minutes as Julie found her way off the motorway and heading for Lincoln whilst Ruth phoned back to Inga Larsson at Lincoln Central to report their findings.

'Expected better coffee,' Ruth suddenly admitted.

'Really?'

'Fancy dan like her with a pot of coffee, least I'd have expected from her was some cranky artisan coffee they serve on a piece of wood with holes in it.'

'Do what? You serious?'

'Here's a tip, don't waste your money.'

'What's with the wood?'

'You tell me,' Ruth sneered. 'Just all chic silliness and the coffee's not up to much. Typical to my mind of those who give women a bad name,' said Ruth. 'But at least it wasn't a no show like Sheffield. Think the boss is putting the eTeam lads onto it so we might know more when we get back.'

'But the neighbours said Hope Parkes is who lives there. They know her, their kids play with her lad.' She threw out a sigh. 'You don't suppose…'

'Raza and Gilly got the wrong address?'

'But they went there surely, they said they spoke to the woman.'

'And we know we got it right.'

'Do we?'

14

It was very obvious DI Inga Larsson had been waiting on their return.

'My office if you please,' she said and as Ruth and Julie walked past their boss and stepped into her office as DS Latif and Gillian joined them. Four detectives were stood waiting for their boss to walk in, close the door, go to her chair and sit down. By then all four were looking more than a trifle concerned. She pointed at Raza Latif.

'Let's start with you,' she said firmly with more than a hint of anger. 'Are you absolutely sure you went to the correct house in Sheffield?' Brown-Reid went to speak and then thought better of it. 'I take it you did go there, this is not some scam you're on which has backfired on you? If it is, now's the time to come clean. Come on, out with it.'

'If we went to the wrong house then Angela Gray was in the wrong house. We didn't ask for ID she was expecting us, she answered the door, apologized because she was cooking and we spoke to her in her kitchen. She never said, sorry you're talking to the wrong person.' He allowed his head to wobble from side to side. 'If I'm honest I thought,' he looked at Gillian. 'We thought after it was a bit odd she was doing the cooking when she knew we were coming.'

'Ma'am,' Gillian dared without being invited. 'She knew all about Streeter, in the way you would if you'd been to school with her or knew her well. Even gave us names of other girls who were there at the same time.'

'She mentioned phoning in about Streeter.'

Inga Larsson sat back. 'Then explain to me how this morning there's this Hope Parkes in the house. Has never heard of Angela Wilcox as she was then or Gray now?'

'And went to school in Sheffield miles away from the one Streeter went to,' from Julie Rhoades was not best received by the look on Inga's face.

'What did you make of the green kitchen?' Raza asked in an attempt to catch them out.

'Didn't see the kitchen,' Ruth admitted. 'We were shown into the front room.'

'Needed a serious makeover.'

'No it doesn't,' Gillian snapped back. 'It's what interior designers call distressed. It's made to look that way deliberately, like it's all 1950s.' Raza was far from convinced, to his mind it all just needed freshening up but he'd not say. His wife Ghada would tell anybody who cared to listen how the natural look of creams and whites are in with all the colour depicted through utensils and accoutrements.

Inga turned her attention to Julie. 'And you two are as convinced about Hope Parkes as these two are about Angela Gray?'

'One thing's for certain,' she said. 'They're not the same person for sure.' She looked sideways at Ruth. 'Your Angela Gray was brunette, so was Hope but there's only one problem. Hope has black skin, what about this Angela of yours?'

'You're joking!' Raza gasped. 'Black?'

'Yes. Very. Black hair naturally, big brown eyes and a bit on the chunky side. Not fat mind you, just chunky and certainly intelligent.'

'What did you say she does?' Inga asked for the others to hear and Ruth checked her notes.

'Operating Department Practitioner, I think is what she said.'

'Like a nurse?'

'But not actually a nurse apparently.'

'And married to a staff nurse she said,' Julie added. 'With a son, and the neighbours confirmed they'd been there a few years and their kids play with the son.'

'Gray?' Inga asked Raza and Gillian 'What about her?'

'Two kids,' Sam shot back. 'And one has autism she made a point in telling us.'

'Did you check with the neighbours?'

'No reason to.'

'Ma'am,' said Raza. 'This makes no sense at all. When we went to see her I phoned to explain the situation and checked when she'd be in, then when you said we needed to go back and ask more questions I phoned her to make the arrangements. As it happens in the end I had to go off to the school on that cock and bull story about Tiana so Ruth and Julie went instead. Yes, I'll be here she said. But make it before two thirty.'

'Clearly she wasn't was she?' Inga shot back. 'Use whatever means are available. Go back to the eTeam and see what they came up with in the first place. If you have to, get in touch with her and arrange to meet up again, but this time make it somewhere neutral. One way or another we need to get to the bottom of all this,' said the Detective Inspector thrusting a finger towards the more senior Raza Latif in particular.

'But ma'am,' said beleaguered Raza. 'I wasn' there today?'

'But does she know?' Inga threw at him. 'Tell her you kept the appointment, where was she? Let's see what she says.' She turned to the other three. 'Find out everything there is to know about Angela Gray nee Wilcox. Name, rank and number, check her on PNC. I know kids are not involved but do a DBS check if she works at a hospital she'll be cleared. I want schools, jobs I want the complete works, what she has for breakfast even her shoe size and where does she buy her knickers!' She looked at the two women. 'Hope Parkes and her husband must work for the NHS I'm guessing in Sheffield, get onto the Trusts up there and get me everything there is to know about them. Failing that get onto the private sector and the agencies who rip off the NHS.' She hesitated a moment. 'And, to cover all bases let's check immigration, always a chance people like her could be an illegal. Has been known. Phone,' she said when they thought the demands were all over. 'Ask the eTeam to have as look at Gray's phone, who owns it and where.' She just waved her hand at Raza and Gillian. 'Get on, get on with it.' She looked at Ruth and Julie. 'Tell me about Susan Sewell.'

'You'd have loved her,' Ruth started as the two disgruntled men trooped from the office. 'The complete works, starched hair, too much make up, suit obviously cost an arm and a leg, high heels and self-praise with everything she said.'

'But knew about our man?'

'Thomasz Borowitz. Most certainly, oh and her phone was one of those ones to probably wakes you in the morning with a freshly brewed cuppa and an egg sandwich!'

'Get eTeam to check hers out anyway if they haven't already. What about Streeter?'

'Claims she never met the woman, Streeter was Borowitz' piece on the side if you like.'

'He was seeing this Sewell and Streeter and never the twain shall meet.'

'So it seems,' said Julie. 'But although they went to the same school Sewell was a couple of years younger.'

'Why didn't it last? What did Sewell reckon was wrong with Borowitz? Any chance he threatened her?'

'No chance I wouldn't think, not the slightest suggestion anyway. Too laid back, did go fishing but not over much according to her, not the self-starter she was after, said he lacked the get up and go she demanded. Looks like she left him behind rather than dumped him. Sounds as though he was up to naughties on the side out of sight, out of mind.'

'And this was where?' Inga asked as she shuffled through papers on her desk.

'Assume he was back here in Lincoln, but she was abroad being a holiday rep bearing in mind how they met, then she got a job with a hotel group and was off climbing the ladder to the top and he was just being a bloke.'

'Why she never met Streeter,' Julie explained even if there was no need to do so.

'He did what for a living?' Inga asked. 'Got it somewhere.'

'Plasterer.'

'That's right.'

'Not exactly high flying is it?'

'What about this Angela Gray, any chance your Susan Sewell knew Gray?'

'Yes. Said she knew her from school but had no idea where she might be now. In fact she knew her as Angela Wilcox which she would of course.'

'But they've not kept in touch?'

'Knew of her at school ma'am, not knew her.'

'With her swanning off all over the place she admitted family and friends have had to take a back seat over the years, can't imagine keeping up with a few old school friends would be a priority for someone like her.'

'To be honest,' said Ruth. 'When she was just a holiday rep I might have kept in touch see if I could get a cheap holiday, but not now. She really thinks she's the bee's knees. Staff at the hotel were almost bowing to her.'

'So at least this one was pucker.' Inga smiled at last as she sat back in her black chair for the first time. 'Back to it. Get what you can on this Parkes woman please, include what you can about the house. Is it rented, housing association maybe or are they buying? I want the last ounce of info on her to set against this Angela Gray woman.' Julie and Ruth turned and took the two paces to the door. 'I suppose you've heard about Raza's wasted trip to the school.'

'No. What happened there?'

'Kids messing about seems to me. My guess is his girl upset some kid at the school and thought he'd get his own back. I say he, but it could well have been some nasty little madam.'

'False alarm?'

Inga nodded. 'Be some kid practicing to be a troll, probably what he's told the careers teacher he wants to be when he grows up. What on earth do they get out of behaving in such a manner?'

'Probably the son of a local dumbass thinks buggering the police about is a good laugh. Hiding behind the bike sheds having a good giggle when poor old Raza turned up.'

A fitting moment to end the discussion. 'Thank you ladies.'

Searches by Ruth Buchan and Julie Rhoades with more than a little help from the nerdy eTeam had produced results they were more than pleased with.

Hope Parkes it turned out was a UK Passport holder born and brought up in Yorkshire employed as an Operating Department Practitioner at the Royal Hallamshire. Her husband Richard worked for the Rotherham NHS Foundation Trust as a Staff Nurse. They were renting the semi-detached house Ruth and Julie had visited and had done so for four years from a property company through a local estate agent. Further enquiries along those lines had provided even more information to confirm Hope Parkes was indeed telling the truth. The estate agent confirmed how negotiations for Hope and Richard Parkes to purchase the semi from the present owner were in the early stages.

On the other hand Raza Latif and Gillian Brown-Reid had no such luck. They went back to the original information the eTeam had gathered from all those who had phoned in claiming to have information from which they had chosen Angela Gray along with others.

They had a transcript of the phone conversation in which she said she'd been at school with Streeter and knew another women from the same era. When the pair listened to the play-back they confirmed the voice was that of the woman they had spoken to in the green kitchen in Daffodil Road.

'And?' was all Inga said as Raza walked into her office.

'Nothing,' he admitted. 'Dead. According to the geeks she could have pulled out the SIM and swapped it for one she got from Poundstretcher.'

'And it tells us what exactly?'

'We've been conned?' was more a question than confident statement, but she spoilt it with a gentle chuckle.

'Exactly, and now we have no idea where she is or quite frankly who she is.' Inga closed her eyes and was biting back a sigh. 'Great!' she uttered as he re-opened her door he'd only pushed to.

Raza just turned round and ambled away to leave Inga sitting there pondering. Did it make Hope more of a suspect or less?

'Change of emphasis boss,' said Jake Goodwin. 'Your DI pal Ralph Higgins has been back to me from Peterborough. He's not exactly dealing with the Charlotte Elliott case, but he has spoken to those who are, and he'll get them to fire over a resume of the case when they've got a spare few minutes. Apparently, there are two people a man and a woman captured on CCTV they have yet to trace. Post mortem and toxicology are leaning towards her having her drink spiked. Apparently around then a hen party had invaded the wine bar and it was squeeze time. Anybody could have popped something in her drink.'

'Thanks Jake, good work. Ruth!' she called out as Jake left to go back to his station. 'Here's what we do,' she told the chestnut haired young woman as she entered. 'I want you to go back up to Sheffield unannounced, I want you to take Gillian with you this time and I have a few questions you can ask that Hope Parkes.'

'She works shifts I guess.'

'Sorry, but go there and wait for her to come home if she's not there when you first arrive. I want Gillian to confirm it was the house she and Raza went to, and I want him to confirm this Hope is not the Angela Gray they interviewed.' She put her hands up. 'I know, I know one's black and one's white and they should be able to tell the difference, but I also want you to ask this Hope woman what she knows about this Lottie Elliott and the other one that Sewell woman gave you.' A finger came up to stop Ruth. 'When you ask about Elliott, play it cagey because I want to know if she knows if the woman is dead.'

'I thought the eTeam were delving into Paula Turner, Rebecca Odling and some Green woman they've now got?'

'Yes they are, and so is Lizzie because now Stevens tells me they're suddenly too busy, but put those names to this Hope. The eTeam no matter how clever they think they are with their Browser Cache, Sandbox and Cookies and all their nonsense, they'll never be able to come up with her natural reaction. Let's just see how happy this Hope is when she comes face to face with those names.'

'Julie?'

'Plenty back here for her and Raza to do don't you worry about that.' She smiled. 'He's off back down to his daughter's school in the morning to see the head teacher. Wants to know quite rightly if there have been any other incidents. Wants to know why the head allows phones into school at all and does he by chance have his suspicions about who might have been responsible.'

Ruth was pleased to have been given precedence over Julie and p[aired with Gillian it was this new pairing off up to Sheffield, to Daffodil Road on one of the hills overlooking the steel city.

'The blue door?' Ruth asked when they parked a little along the road and Gillian nodded. 'Now you are sure?'

'Why? Isn't it where you went?' she queried.

'It's exactly where we went. Took a bit of effort to get inside but it certainly is the house.'

Gillian Brown-Reid warrant card in hand, knocked on the blue door but nobody answered, and if she were the particularly suspicious type she'd have thought the whole road was ominously quiet.

The pair of them moved the car further away from the house, but close enough so they could see if anybody approached the front door. They were neither of the mind how perhaps one of them should linger about suspiciously out in the cold just in case she arrived home via the back door.

Back at Lincoln Central Inga Larsson had reports back from the nerdiest geek himself when for once in his life ASBO (Adrian Simon Bruce Orford) left the confines of his cloistered open-plan office and the array of monitors and gadgetry they all sat before to venture down to the MIT offices.

First time Inga could recall such a thing happening. Was this a reaction to Stevens suddenly suggesting his gang of geeks was too busy and ASBO had slipped out unnoticed?

'This Susan Sewell's phone tells me she's in Birmingham, in the city centre to be precise as it happens, do you need it any closer?'

'No Adrian that'll be just fine, and ticks a box for us. One down many more to go no doubt.'

'Other one belongs to somebody who is either a very private person or they don't wish to be traced. Of course you can do it fairly easily with Android as you know.' Inga had no idea as it happens, a phone was just a phone to her. 'All we get is whoever owns it is telling us number withheld so the chances are it's not a cheap-jack clockwork one off the market, it'll be an all singing all-dancing top of the range quite likely.'

For just a millisecond Inga wanted to ask if it would be the sort to make a cuppa and iron her blouse, but thought better of it. All just go over his head no doubt. Not strong on jokes his sort and Adrian in particular especially concerning his beloved technology.

'Thanks for that.'

'But,' annoyingly ASBO carried on. 'Another alternative is what you probably know as a burner phone.'

'Explain.' Inga had heard the phrase.

'What TV people call them I'm told. Burner phones. Always pre-paid and used specifically for one purpose usually unlawful of course. Job done they're then dumped when considered burned or too risky to use, too hot.'

'You think in this case?'

'Not necessarily, just saying. After all, people use burner phones for dating.'

'What do you mean?'

'If you're organizing a first date say and not sure how it will go it saves you having to block unwanted calls after.'

'Very nice.'

'There's an app of course.'

'Of course,' was her sarcasm. Perhaps Adrian visiting was not such a good idea after all.

'The app allows you to create multiple numbers on the phone you keep for these dubious activities. Through that you can easy delete a number any time you like and it also allows you to create as many numbers as you want.'

'Interesting,' she observed. Pleased it was his job to work his way through that sort of minefield. 'What about the others we're looking for? Anything on any of them?' she looked down at notes on her pad. 'Turner, Odling and is it Green?'

'Working on them. More's the pity you've not come up with another Streeter, names like those are ten a penny, takes a bit of time to go through them all, but we're getting there.'

'Thank you for taking the time to pop down.'

'Boss in one of his funny moods,' he grinned and grimaced. 'Easier face to face than email,' was a surprising thing for someone like him to admit to.

Inga knew there were many women who'd give anything for a figure like Adrian, but maybe not to the extent of having what looked very much like a concave chest. Did he know how visually he had very little going for him as he was painfully thin, pasty faced and had little or no dress sense. Was this the reason he had become so totally engrossed in his dark world both at work and at home. Somewhere out there would be a lonely geeky spotty female who would welcome him with open arms. Problem was getting him out into the world to be noticed in the first place and stopping his mother from cutting his hair with her kitchen scissors and ironing a crease in his jeans.

'Something I'd like to put to you,' he grimaced as if what he was about to say was seriously bad news. 'We have to consider illegal immigration.'

The DI waited for him to continue and when he didn't she was left with no alternative. 'Go on then.'

What this strange guy had to say next had Inga bring him up short, as she waved Jake Goodwin into her office to have a listen. 'Can we start again?' she insisted.

'Illegal immigrants,' Adrian said and she saw Jake frown as he took a pew. 'Ask yourself this. How do they survive over here, bearing in mind before this Brexit business started they were just flooding in? One way of course is living hand to mouth, four to a grotty room or in some cases half a dozen in a shed for exorbitant rent and the rest.'

Inga had always sensed how away from the tiny world in which he excelled he always appeared apprehensive, nervous and most unsure of himself. Here almost as if she had put him up on a pedestal he was an altogether different character.

'There is an alternative,' he said with the hint of a smile. 'Live hand to mouth for long enough to get a few pennies together. One aim in mind, to gather enough to buy yourself a false passport.'

'Hang on,' said Jake. 'Are you just suggesting Streeter got herself a false passport in order to go abroad?'

'No,' was most indignant. 'Just hear me out,' he said quite forcibly. 'Just let me explain what goes on and it could be something to consider in Streeter's scenario, explains why we can't find her, why she's vanished off the face of the earth.'

'Sorry Adrian,' said Inga on behalf of her Detective Sergeant. 'Carry on,' she urged.

'You buy yourself a false passport,' Adrian said directly to Jake. 'Not one you want to get you through airport security or customs and all that business, but one to provide you with an identity. Hasn't got workable holograms and the other nonsense. But,' he emphasized. 'Has the name you want to be known by and has your photo. With that you can apply for a Provisional Driving Licence,' he lifted a hand to stop Jake interrupting. 'Then take your test and suddenly you're up and running with a full UK Driving Licence, a real pucker official document with your photo on it.'

'Which a lot of people will accept as ID,' said Inga.

'Because the brain dead turned down ID cards.'

'Exactly,' Adrian responded to Jake's remark and now he was seriously on his soapbox. 'Such an incredibly stupid decision played right into the hands of all the world's crooks and anybody wanting to damage and exploit this nation of ours, like illegals. Chances are people who were against ID cards were pro-Brexit which is a serious case of make your mind up time.'

'All the namby-pamby human rights, freedom of the individual, politically correct nonsense and all that old baloney,' said Jake. 'No wonder we're in such a mess and because we have no real form of identity we've made it dead easy for them to merge into the black market.'

Adrian was back to it. 'With this real pucker Driving Licence in your pocket you can open a bank account, get a credit card, rent property and get a decent job. One minute you're a down and out called Petru Vasile looking over your shoulder living hand to mouth living in somebody's garage and in no time you're a fully-fledged upright Marius Albescu we'll call him, a seemingly UK citizen with a vote.'

'You suggesting this is what our Streeter did?'

'Or a Romanian Vasile,' he just rode roughshod over Jake's remark. 'Changes his name to a Polish Dariusz something or other Kowski.' Inga had to wonder what sort of brain produced all these random names.

'Is that risky?' she had to ask.

'If you said you were from Denmark,' said Adrian. 'Why would I think any different?'

'So we're buggered if she's done that.'

'I'm only suggesting its one road she could have gone down. Christine Streeter has become Alice Wonderland or anybody she likes from anywhere.'

Inga could sense there was more. 'Go on, what else?'

'Could have changed sex.'

'What?!'

'For the driving lessons and photo for the licence. Easy for a woman to look like a young man. In fact there's been a few cases where they choose a name which could be either meaning they only need to be dressed like a bloke for officialdom.'

'Just gets worse.'

'Especially as we don't know if she did or not.'

'Or if she is dead or alive.'

15

After two hours, DCs Ruth and Gillian had reported back to Inga Larsson how there was nobody at home and no sign of anybody. It was wishful thinking by the pair if they thought the boss would relieve them of their duties and give Ruth time just to pop into Meadowhall.

It was gone four-thirty when eventually a small cream Peugeot pulled up and out stepped the woman Ruth knew to be Hope Parkes accompanied by a young lad of about nine or ten who she took to be her son. The pair watched and waited, gave them time to get indoors before they walked slowly from their car along Daffodil Road and Ruth knocked once again on the blue door.

It was opened in a flurry, as if the occupant was annoyed by someone disturbing her within moments of arriving home.

'Yes?' she threw at them, recognized Ruth and she could see the woman's whole persona sink. 'What now?'

'May we come in?'

'Do you really have to? I've just got home, my lad needs a bite to eat...' what else she wanted to say just drifted away on the breeze as she stepped aside to allow two detectives to enter her home yet again.

'Sorry to disturb you but we just need to go over a few important issues,' said Ruth in the kitchen once Parkes had coaxed her son Samuel upstairs to keep him out of the way. 'Can you tell us what you were doing on Friday 13th?'

Parkes frowned and looked at Ruth for a moment or two before she pushed past the pair, closed the door and ran her finger up a calendar hanging on the back.

'Surgical Theatre 4, means I'd have been in around 7.30.'

'Be there all day?' Ruth checked.

'Most certainly, probably later than today. We got on well with the list this morning, so I'm home a bit early, picked George up and here we are. I can get you a list of the procedures we had on that day if you insist and the names of the surgeons and an anaesthetist or two plus....'

'Won't be necessary,' said Ruth to stop her, smiled at the woman who was not. 'Thank you.'

'Angela Gray,' Gillian said and Parkes just looked at her. 'Friend of yours perhaps?'

'No,' she appeared to reply honestly.

'A good cook?' Ruth popped in and Hope looked bewildered.

'Do you know of her?'

'No,' she replied shaking her head to emphasize.

'What about Charlotte Elliott, Paula Turner and Rebecca Odling?' she read quickly from her tablet.

'Should I?'

'You tell us.'

'What's it in connection with?' Parkes wanted to know.

'Serious crime,' Ruth advised.

'And you think I'm involved? With these people?' she said loudly and chuckled. 'How dare you?' Hope blew out a breath of frustration. 'I was done for speeding about three years ago, Sammy was ill, and I was late for work if you must know. That's it,' she raised and lowered her shoulders. 'No shoplifting, no drunken brawls, no weed, no smacking coppers in the mouth, nothing. So you're quite safe with me.'

'Good to hear it,' said Ruth just as Parkes went to speak but the detective beat her to it. 'Thank you Hope for your co-operation, you have been most helpful. We'll be on our way, and I doubt whether it'll be necessary to disturb you again.' Ruth turned. 'We'll see ourselves out.'

'Thank you,' said Gillian to a bemused and confused woman.

With renewed energy Hope asked 'Who are these people?'

'Just people we need to trace, if you suddenly realize you know any of them, please get in touch,' Ruth urged and handed her a card.

'No bloody way!' said Gillian confidently once they were in the car with the doors closed. 'There is no way she was here before. It's the same house, the same damn green kitchen,' she said as Ruth pulled away. 'It was bloody spooky too. Why did she show us into the kitchen just like that Angela Gray did? What's wrong with the front room an easy chair and a cup of tea? Eh? Tell me that.'

Ruth sniggered. 'Someone's done a great job with that kitchen. It is old but they've made it look all distressed like on these programmes, paint it then rub it down or something. Not sure about green though.'

'It was green when Raza and I were here before.'

'She's the woman Julie and I interviewed before and for your information there's not a dead body in the front room which is where Julie and I talked to her. To the very same woman, the nurse.'

'This is like one of those magic shows, where it's not at all what you think it is, you think it's one thing and it turns out to be another. She's not really black she's white with dark hair and cooks all the way through the interview all covered in flour. She knows people who went to school with Streeter.' She stopped his rant. 'I could do with a coffee.'

'But did you see Angela Gray's two children? Were there any photos of her family?'

'There weren't any photos of that woman's kid either.'

'You got family photos in your kitchen?' Ruth asked.

'No.'

'But you saw George, you saw them arrive home and remember she had no idea we were coming. You saw him being sent upstairs, he was in school uniform and she called him Georgie. What d'you know about Gray except what she told you? What are her kids called, can you remember?'

'Don't think she said.'

'Once again it's only what she told you.'

'You think the Parkes woman is all above board?'

'Why not?'

'In that case what was another woman doing making a pie in her kitchen when the one we've just spoken to says she was at work? Saw her with my own eyes remember and I have a Detective Sergeant to back me up.' Gillian was relishing the moment.

'If this is some set up, if this Parkes woman is involved, then why did Angela Gray need to make a pie? Why didn't she just show us into the front room and answer our questions?'

'If this is some big con, then my next question is why?' Gillian glanced at Ruth weaving through the traffic. 'And the chances it'll be exactly what the boss will be asking.'

'Better have your answers ready then.'

The remainder of the journey back down the A1 and then A57 across to Lincoln was a very quiet affair and it gave Gillian time to think.

Truth is of course Gillian had no answers. She'd initially witnessed a white rabbit popping out of a hat, but next time she saw the same blue door trick it was a black rabbit but she had absolutely no idea how the trick was done, if that was what it was.

'Are we of like mind?' Inga Larsson asked her whole crew. 'Can we cross a few names off the list? How about we start with Aaron Kempshall?' she asked Jake Goodwin and his men. Inga was in effect telling her team what was going to happen like it or not in the form of questions.

'A bit of a philanderer,' said Sam Howard.

'Can I just say,' Ruth interrupted. 'He sounds very much like the Borowiak Susan Sewell described to us. A plasterer who is quite happy plastering your kitchen but Sewell probably wanted him to bid for plastering Buckingham Palace. Kempshall sells bathrooms to people who need an avocado bathroom in their semi, but he doesn't try to sell enough to win the contract to fit out all the bathrooms in one of Sewell's hotels.'

'Geeks upstairs have trolled through Kempshall's laptop and found nothing much, his phone had calls to and from this Erica Parker he went south to see on the rugby pretext and one other,' she checked her note. 'A Georgie North they've checked. No Streeter,' said Inga. 'Absolutely no Streeter.'

'Don't throw the cat amongst the pigeons!'

'Just saying that's all,' chirped in a disgruntled Ruth. 'They're strangely like two peas in a pod, Borowiak and Kempshall.'

'Except one's behind bars,' Jake reminded.

'Kempshall goes then?' Inga asked and received nodded replies. 'While she's been mentioned, what about Susan Sewell?'

'I've still got to phone her,' Julie reminded the boss. 'To see if she can point us in the direction of any of these other women she mentioned.'

'Fair enough,' Inga responded reluctantly. 'Give her half a tick. Hope Parkes?' she said. 'Think we have a dissenting voice.'

'It's just I've been in the green kitchen twice,' said slim Gillian leaning forward in her chair, arms on her thighs. 'Why should I believe one rather than the other?'

'Because Parkes says she doesn't know any of the names we put to her,' said adamant Ruth forcefully. 'Because she was working in an operating theatre at the Royal Hallamshire Hospital at the time, all of which we have checked out. She went to the King Ted School, she is married, she has a son we've met and more than anything else she doesn't have a clue what we're talking about.'

'What if Angela Gray asked her if she could borrow her kitchen for an hour?'

'What?' Jake asked nobody in particular as if he'd suddenly woken up.

'Gilly,' Ruth responded. 'As you said yourself, why not do the interview in the front room if this was some gag, why go to all the trouble to cook a bloody pie?'

'Why?' Inga asked Gillian and looked at Raza as well. 'Why go to all the trouble to ask a stranger if you can use her kitchen? Why not do the interview with you and Raza on a park bench, in a coffee house or down their local nick? What does Parkes expect to gain by pulling such a stroke if that's what it was?'

'She really was there you know,' said Raza to the doubters. 'This is not a figment of our imagination. Brunette *white* woman cooking a pie.'

'It's a helluva scam if that's what it was,' Jake suggested.

'But what the hell for?' Inga responded quickly.

'Can't see what she'd gain, in fact if this is some gag it's backfired because we're talking about her making this pie, when a casual chat in the front room would have left no impression and we'd be crossing her off the list.'

'If we put Parkes to one side for now as a maybe, where do we go with her?' Inga queried. 'The eTeam have already looked at her meagre social media interaction and nowhere can they find an

Angela Gray, nor do any of the photos look like the description for Angela Gray and surprise surprise many of the people she's in touch with are coloured.' The Detective Inspector took a breath. 'Answers on a postcard please and while you're pondering it all, if we leave her on the list where do we go with her?' She nodded at Jake while she took a sip of her cool coffee.

'Looks as though we can cross all the men off the list. Borowiak and Kempshall appear to be the same sort of people but one's inside and the other we know couldn't have killed Mindi.'

'Mindi,' said Gillian. 'You name it we've been there and so have the geeks upstairs. Checked her bank and credit cards, nothing untoward. Not on any databases we can find which might suggest she was involved in anything. Dabbles a bit on Instagram and she made her last call to Kempshall at 8.36. We assume he told her to so it would coincide with half time or thereabouts,' she hesitated to smirk. 'Except of course he wasn't at the rugby as we now know. There are only two things. One is the scenes of crime evidence and what we understand the Streeter woman left.'

'Any evidence she might have known anybody else?' Inga asked, although she knew the answer.

'Just the business her mother told me about,' said Ruth. 'Had a set to with somebody at that spa place, then worked at a caravan park her father obviously thought was beneath them.'

'No connection after she left school with Charlotte Elliott, with anybody called Angela Gray or Hope Parkes or any of the other names we've been given.' Gillian glanced at Julie. 'I don't send Christmas cards to any of the people I went to school with, they're not my friends.' Julie nodded her auburn head to say she agreed.

'I know two I went to school with,' said Ruth. 'But really only through the fact they live near my mum, apart from them...' she shrugged.

'Guess where it leaves us?' said Inga stood there white cup in hand. 'Christine Streeter who wets the bed who nobody has seen for years and the law assumes is dead. An Angela Gray who claimed to the two who say they spoke to her she went to school with Streeter, knew this Elliott woman who it turns out has died suspiciously, has a phone which also has mysteriously and conveniently died, who we seem unable to connect to anybody or anything and half a tick for

Hope Parkes. To be honest I'm only keeping her on the list because we think she has a link to Gray who is the big mystery, but I think even that's clutching at straws.' She dragged in a tired breath and let is drift out. 'Brilliant!'

'You still want us to speak to Susan Sawyer?' Ruth asked. 'Phoned her earlier but she said she was tied up and will call me back.'

'Not for her, but she looks like our only hope in tracking these other women who were at the school. 'Anything she can give us will be a bonus, where they live, what they do, may even get a link if she knows what universities they went to if any, plus married names would be useful.'

Inga held Raza back when the rest left to go back to their work stations.

'I asked PCT to go through the old witness statements from 2006. Go and chat to them, see if they've come up with anybody who might be able to give us an insight into how it was back then. Have people had second thoughts in the intervening years about Streeter? Did they follow the party line last time because it all seemed to be the thing to do?' Raza motioned to speak. 'I know it's not going to be easy, people have moved house, changed jobs, got married, got divorced even changed sex some of them.' She pointed at him. 'Just give this a good craic.'

Always the same in the incident room in the early stages of a major incident with all these odd bods helping out. Already as Inga looked out of her office there were the dropping shoulders and the black bins already full to overflowing with all sorts. From sweet wrappers and plastic bags to half eaten sandwiches wives had got up early to create and seemingly an endless amount of binned paper, screwed up or torn up.

'Here's what we've got from the Cambridgeshire lads,' said Jake Goodwin as Inga sat down beside him and crossed her legs at his PC. 'This is the CCTV from the wine bar that night the analysts down there have pinged up. Used to be a pub called the Bull and Dolphin.' He pointed at the screen as he set the footage running. 'There's our Charlotte Elliott they all call Lottie. She's part of a group of women who Peterborough describe in their briefing notes. One witness said it was the end of a shitty week and some of them wouldn't have gone but it was somebody's leaving do. Another, not part of the group though, thought it was a hen party.'

'Doesn't look like much of one to me,' Inga scoffed, knowing they'd have to drag her screaming to such a tawdry event.

'Think they're just using the phrase because as you can see there's no dressing up, no rabbit ears, no symbolism, in fact it all looks pretty tame to me, although of course I've never been to one.'

'I have,' she admitted. 'Never again.' Inga heard a stifled snicker somebody could not depress and looked to spot the offender. The return looks abounded with pure innocence.

'I can imagine.'

'I doubt very much if you can, believe you me!'

'Watch.'

Inga studied the group intently around the bar and counted seven women, who appeared to all be looking further along the bar at somebody or something. As she watched two men sidled up behind them with their backs to camera, then they were joined by a woman. Average height and build with what looked like blonde or white hair on the black and white, but all they got was a back view.

'She grey haired?'

'Apparently not,' said Jake. 'Witnesses who noticed her seem to think it was white but she's not old.'

'Not albino surely.'

'Dyed they reckon.' Inga just shook her head in dismay.

Ten seconds later the woman had by then pushed herself sideways between one of the men and two or three women. It stayed with her and then as quickly as she had arrived she and one of the men just moved back and walked off down the bar. No faces to be seen, no body language clue to either of them acknowledged the other and certainly no sense of them talking.

'According to the lads down there, witnesses who had even seen the footage couldn't remember the woman. She and the two blokes she appeared with are the ones they're still trying to identify.'

'What are they all looking at, what's taking their attention?' Inga wanted to know, as Jake played the sequence again.

'By the way, I know with these sort of things you always get hangers on, but this is early on in the night and they reckon nobody of her description was invited. People Peterborough have spoken to suggested she was probably just a punter in the wine bar.'

'Staff?'

'Nobody recognized her.'

'And why were they all looking that way, conveniently? Could it have been a set-up, like pickpockets operate, one takes your attention while the other does the nicking? You don't think they've set something up further down the bar so nobody watches those two?'

'No such luck. Some bit of a kid off one of these reality shows was there. Nothing to do with the hen party, just happened to be in the bar, and they were all gawping. As people like their sort do.'

'Not only do tatty programmes like those ruin my Saturday nights in, now they've even messed up a major enquiry.'

'Not good is it?' Jake suggested. 'And no it wasn't a hen party as such, turns out it was somebody leaving work, getting a bigger better job somewhere.'

'Just so called hens on a night out.'

'And not all rat arsed and vomiting either.'

'Not yet they're not. Sadly I've been to one or two hen nights and to be honest there are so many really good much better ideas on the market these days.'

'So why does the average wassock just want to dress up daft and get hammered?'

'Because they know no better, it's their idea of a good time. I went on one where it was all about tasting unusual cocktails, but properly done not just sloshing it down your throat. To be honest it was really quite good. You can go parachuting, bungee jumping and in all sorts of places, here and abroad.'

'Only ones Sally's been invited to seem to be big on pink, big on pina colada and big on puke.'

'We have hen parties back home of course,' Inga advised. 'But I have to admit the one's I've heard about do tend to be much more civilized, all based on giving the bride a good time not turning her into an alcoholic overnight.'

All about enjoying the experience of something like scuba diving, but to be honest I don't see why you can't do it all when you're married.'

'I'd have thought there were more opportunities not less,' Jake suggested. 'Certainly have been for Sally and me. Anyway, where were we?' he sighed. 'Oh yes. Next morning this Charlotte's mate was due to go jogging with her and they had a routine where they text each other first thing just to check all's well. Except it wasn't.'

'I've heard.'

'This pal of hers instead of heading off to where they run from, drives round to her flat rather than wait in the park for nothing. Front door key's taped under the window sill, goes in and there's this Lottie on the floor in her main room, dead.'

'With her body sliced about.'

'Somebody played noughts and crosses on her stomach with a knife, well scalpel the pathologist reckoned. Deep crosses and like a deep twist of the knife for a nought.'

'And now?' Inga grimaced as she asked.

'Nothing. No clue, no DNA. Felt ill at the pub, went home, sick as a pig on the floor. Hemlock it turned out to be.'

'Been slipped in her glass they think?'

'So they reckon. Timing seems about right.'

'By a woman and some guy at the pub you saying?'

Jake nodded. 'But that's not all. This was sadistic. Lots of games had been played with the crosses winning every time.'

'And that's a clue we think?' Jake could only just shrug his reply.

'Two games down each thigh, one across each breast and inside her arms.' He smiled weakly.

'Very nice of whoever,' said Inga as she shook her head at the thought of what horrors had gone on possibly when she was still alive.

'In the wine bar is the Peterborough theory.' Jake raised his hands. 'Their only theory to be honest, but what else is there?'

Inga sighed. 'Keep pinning our hopes on these things. Got people dying around us like this Elliott which is just a bit disconcerting don't you think? More than just a case of dying, with games of noughts and crosses.' She hesitated. 'Was she?'

'Dead you mean?'

'Yes.'

'No, at least not when the cutting started, but she'd be in a hell of a state, vomiting, paralysed so she'd be in no state to fight back according to the pathologist down there.' He put his head on one side. 'The extras on her arms and legs, were done so the report says post mortem.'

What a pity it had not been local with Dr Bonagh O'Connell overseeing the post mortem. She was always so focused and methodical yet at the same time very human and at less intense moments chatty.

'That another clue, the noughts and crosses?'

'Like crosses winning? Could mean anything, and she's not here to tell us.'

'Did she?' Jake frowned. 'Play noughts and crosses.'

'Not said if they know.'

'Sick, whatever it's about.' Inga thought to herself for a moment. 'Plus we have one who died from cancer. Wonder how many of my old school friends are dead? In this case, one died, one had her drink spiked. This the normal ratio you think?'

'You've forgotten one. Christine Streeter, because officially she's dead too.'

'Three then. Dead percentage is getting bigger.' Inga continued to peer at the screen of a still of the woman. 'But we're not talking three out of the whole school, we're talking out of the group who knew Streeter really well.'

'And we know Borowiak can't be responsible for more than just Streeter.'

'Any more we've not heard about you think?'

'Might be worth seeing if there are any figures on the matter. Perhaps get Lizzie to jump start her machine and see what it throws up.'

Inga spotted Sandy MacLachlan and gestured him to join them. 'You look like you've spent a wet weekend in Skegness,' she told him. 'You got anything yet on people who were interviewed back when Streeter went walkabouts?'

'Those I've managed to trace are about as much good as nothing at all.'

'Trouble is these days people move about so much.'

'And I'm sure most of those I've tracked down were just looking for a few minutes of fame. Didn't know much back then and even less now.'

'Keep at it,' she told him. 'Only need one good one to pop up.' As Sandy turned she smirked. 'And cheer up.' He just shrugged. 'I had the Darke boss at morning briefing suggesting it was time Streeter fell foul of something. Told me about some scroat who'd been missing for simply ages. Said he finally got nabbed when he tried to get a ride on a tram without a ticket.' The look Sandy gave her needed an explanation. 'Mobile fingerprint scanner.'

'Unlucky!'

'We could do with a bit of that sort of luck here.'

Inga kept reminding herself how statistically she is often reminded, murder in the UK is still quite rare. She was also well advised of something much rarer, but not the sort of thing the average man in the street comes across, or reads about with any regularity.

People being held against their will, captive to a degree, usually in a country they do not know and a language they do not understand and as a result live in an environment where recognizable speech is never heard.

With no passport or papers, running away to freedom would not be an option as it more than likely would be utter madness to even try.

Was it what had happened to Streeter? Was she right now being held against her will as a slave say within deepest Peru? Hidden away in some remote village off the Inca trail maybe? Or was the truth much closer to home with her being holed up in the basement of some dank dingy flea-ridden nasty run down crumbling property in leafy Surrey. Held against her will by goodness knows who.

Why not? After all none of the things normally associated with missing persons applied to Streeter. Breakdown in family relationships was always top of the pops, particularly with regard to surly teenagers storming out in a fit of pique. Talking of pops, the step-father always gets a bad press, but neither of these applied in her case.

DC Gillian Brown-Reid was back working in the incident room after all that business in Sheffield, looking into Mindi Brookes for Jake.

She'd been introduced to Adrian ASBO when she was in need of shady searches, and was hopeful of a move to MIT one day soon, if and when a vacancy arose. Like many of her colleagues down in PHU and PCT she was fed up with dealing with a constant stream of low life involved in growing cannabis, mouth smacking because of booze and shoplifting to fund an inevitable habit.

'Five years ago she left the firm she was working for under a bit of a cloud,' Gillian briefed Jake Goodwin. 'Guy who runs the show now says it was treated as a clash of personalities, but understandably didn't really want to talk about it over the phone.'

'What did she do exactly?'

'She was a Duty Manager at this Spa place up in Yorkshire which Ruth told us about from what Brookes parents told her. But what I was going to say was, when I mentioned this is part of a murder enquiry he changed his tune this regional manager chap. Says he's willing to help if he can if we care to visit.'

'Nice little trip for the boss and Ruth or somebody I would imagine.'

Not how it worked out. Not how it worked out at all.

16

In very much the same way we all would, Ruth Buchan imagined Susan Sawyer at the other end of the telephone when she called back as promised. Not a hair out of place, make-up perfect and the finest of clothes. Every inch a businesswoman but very much stereotypical. Something inside would not allow her to be individualistic, stick out from the crowd, whereas the really successful quite often are.

'We appreciate you gave us a number of names when we spoke, but to be honest we could do with a bit of a prompt, need to put flesh on the bones.'

'Before we get onto them, there's one I've remembered. Judy Green.' Ruth kept her counsel. 'One for the boys, skirts far too short, bit of a tease if the truth be known but I doubt if it's at all what you're after. She was good at languages I've remembered. One of these people where it all comes naturally. Me? I travel the world and all I use is a sort of pigeon Chinese,' was chuckled.

'University you think?'

'Oh most certainly I would imagine, probably took a degree in Serbo Croat or something similar and combined it with isiZulu probably. Could quite easily be a translator now I should think.'

'Relationships, family?'

'To be honest she was one of those I didn't know too well at school because they were older, just remember her because she'd swear in every language you could think of. Bit of a party piece I remember, to get her noticed by the boys.' Ruth was about to speak when this Susan continued. 'Family,' she said as if she was thinking. 'Not sure I knew them even then.'

'How about we try Lottie Elliott?' and for a moment Ruth held her breath.

'I feel awful,' was the response. 'It's as if I should know all this, but I think my problem is I spent all that time two or three years after leaving school living and working abroad and lost contact. Lottie was a tall gangly sort of girl, really nice though, very kind, do anything for anybody.' She chortled. 'Joke was she didn't live up to her name. Lottie by name but not by nature sort of thing. Not a lottie of her they used to say, with her being tall and thin. Best I can do is her dad worked for one of the big carpet stores. Think he was a salesman, sort of person who can work out how many square metres you need and what's the best underlay. Think Lottie's gawkiness came from her mother, she was all sort of wiry and had this fly-away hair.' Ruth waited for a second or two. 'Not being much help am I?'

'Every little helps, as they say.' The noughts and crosses were not for the public domain.

'Rebecca Odling,' said Susan without being prompted. 'Good dancer if I remember, but Ballroom stuff like they do on that *Strictly*. Feeling somewhere in the back of my mind says I was told at one point she married her partner. Just give me a moment,' she said and Ruth waited patiently. 'Think he was at City School, think we put him down as gay, but I can't swear by it. Maybe what I was told had got lost in translation and in the end he was gay and they were just dancing partners and not life partners. Could be it was the word partners used in completely the wrong context as it so often is today.'

'Only a couple more,' said Ruth.

'Mother was Welsh,' was suddenly there. 'Where did that come from?' Susan tittered as she questioned herself. 'Remember now, always said see after everything. I'll be going now see and I'm holding her bag see,' used to make us laugh. Bit to go on there, lived somewhere off Hykeham Road.'

'Paula Turner.'

'This one I know about or rather my mother remembered when I asked her. Paula is a make-up artist, done very well for herself by all accounts. My mother's quite sure her parents still live off Skellingthorpe Road. Last I heard she was in London or thereabouts working in television and films apparently. No idea about a husband and kids and all that though '

'Can't be many called Paula Turner doing such a specialist job at that level, surely'

'Probably find her name on the credits for EastEnders. And now we come down to Angela Wilcox.'

'Seem to be getting better as I go along,' she commented and Ruth imagined a smile at the other end. 'Angela would probably by now be a leader of men so to speak. I mean she could easily be a trade union official, think her parents were very left wing, and she'd probably have quite a few kids whether she could afford them or not which is the way of the world for some.'

'Was she in charge at school do you remember?'

'Always at the forefront shall we say, and if she's not running something then I reckon thinking about it she could be a chef. She'd make things like battenburg which always looked like it was shop bought and ours would be just a complete mess.'

'Could be a chef running a restaurant.'

'Could very well be. But unless she's changed never be a money making entrepreneur, very much in it for the good of the community.' There was just a hint of a giggle. 'People like her always make me chuckle. All very much for the working man yet they had quite a decent house with a mortgage no doubt. Make your mind up time with so many of these people, don't you think?'

'Any personal details come to mind?'

'Dark and sultry, too much make-up when I saw her out and about in the couple of years I went through quite a few jobs before I jumped ship so to speak. Her mother fancied herself as well, used to go clubbing which must have been a real embarrassment to Angela. Sort of thing most people grow out of when they leave their teens, but not this one. Not Monique.' Ruth noted down. 'Something in the back of my mind says there were children mentioned somehow. Something different. Only guessing here but she could have had twins or maybe triplets or one was disabled. Just something is ringing a bell somewhere.'

'You've done very well.'

'Lot of this of course is stuff my mother used to say when I came home or would scribble down in a letter to bring me up to date, most of which went in one ear and out the other. You know the sort of thing, guess who I saw last week, you'll never guess who's had twins.' She hesitated. 'Think that's about your lot.'

'Might I thank you for your help? Much appreciated and I'm sure we'll be able to make something of all this.'

'Been my pleasure.'

'How was the launch of the hotel?'

'Magnificent even if I say it myself,' brought wild mushroom and parmesan vol-au-vents to mind.

'Exhausting I bet.'

'But worth it in the end.'

'No doubt. Thank you Susan.'

'Can I just ask,' was cautious. 'Do you really think Chrissie Streeter is still alive?'

'Just one theory we're working on.'

'Really? Bit like one of those cold cases you see on television. How exciting, makes my life seem a bit humdrum.'

'Not as exciting as launching a new hotel.' Ruth heard Susan Sawyer laugh. 'Goodbye.'

'Was Angela Gray heavily made up when Raza and Gillian talked to her? Who will know the names of make-up artists in film and television? Have we come across an interpreter anywhere? Was this Lottie Elliott woman all gawky?' Ruth glanced down at her notes. 'Paula Turner's parents could still be living on Skellingthorpe Road.'

'And this Susan?' Inga asked. 'How was she?'

'Being as helpful as she could be, knew bits and pieces, sort of things her mother used to tell her to bring her up to date with people she once knew. Forgot to ask her where she's off to next.' Ruth looked up at her boss and smiled a knowing smile. 'Reckons Angela Gray could well be a chef by now.'

'Which means she'll be good at making meat pies.'

'Exactly.'

'So she is real.'

'Seems like it.'

'Just have to get Parkes out of the back of my mind,' the Detective Inspector grimaced. 'Feed it all into the team, anything we get stuck on have a word with our friend ASBO upstairs.'

It had been another evening for Inga to be dominated by one subject. Her wedding to Adam in Stockholm getting closer and closer.

The previous evening it had been all about wedding favours. Not a tradition at all in Sweden and never as over-the-top as in America. In the end after discussions with her mother Christal she and Adam decided they would give presents to the bridesmaid and to the best man. Rather than just some glitzy silly 'favour' more of a useful worthwhile present. Another wedding box ticked.

Inga had created a tick box system on one of the white boards in the MIT incident room. The names of, as it turned out, the nine or so women they had been investigating in one form or another.

She was just stood there in a quiet moment looking at what was developing and becoming increasingly maudlin, a reaction very much unlike the Swede. She absolutely hated coincidences, but this was what she faced.

The state of mind had not been helped by Det Supt Craig Darke at their morning briefing when he had suggested the possibility of there being a serial killer on the loose.

Three had a blacked out square against their name: Mindi Brookes of course, Charlotte Elliott and the Amelia Evans they'd been told about by that Tindall woman from Retford. All dead, two suspicious deaths and one cancer.

Then there were green ticks to bring some comfort against a number. Paula Turner was indeed a make-up artiste working ironically on a new TV adaptation of a series of science fiction detective stories.

Rebecca Odling was another they could discount. From what they could gather she had indeed been an amateur dancer of some repute but when her partner on the dancefloor but not in life was jailed for fraud she had found it impossible to discover the same degree of success with others. Now married to a guy working in IT with two left feet, as Rebecca Liddle she lives quite happily on the outskirts of Norwich.

None of them when interviewed had been able to offer any further information, particularly on Christine Streeter as generally their schooldays were far behind them, literally in another time and most cases in another world.

Susan Sawyer was a green tick they knew all about and on the list next was Hope Parkes with a red question mark against her name.

Left them with Angela Gray nee Wilcox and Christine Streeter as the two live ones people were working on, except Streeter had both a black square and a red question mark. The really bad disconcerting news was about Judy Green, the one Susan Sawyer suggested had been good at languages at school.

The black box against her name was the very reason Darke had suggested there might be a real problem. Inga was loathe to admit he could very well be right.

It was not Serbo Croat and isiZulu she had studied, but with considerable forethought had plumped for Arabic which in recent times had kept her gainfully employed as a translator and as a Professor of Languages she was also fluent in all the usual array such as German, French and Spanish.

Enquiries into her death had revealed she was teaching herself Hindustani in her spare time. Beats playing Zygolex.

Killed in a hit and run in her home village of Radley near Abingdon in Berkshire. The old Ford Mondeo when found abandoned and burnt out two days later in Newbury turned out to have been owned previously by a very dubious motor trader who had sold it well over the odds to a woman he admitted he had never met before, for cash with no questions asked.

Just walking down the road with her Schnauzer this Judy Green had been hit from behind and killed instantly when the Mondeo mounted the pavement. Just seemingly mown down in cold blood, by some boy racer scrote, not insured no doubt, with no licence, no tax and probably not hurt and frankly not really bothered.

And then there were three and a half: Mindi Brookes stabbed to death in her own home, Charlotte 'Lottie' Elliott had her drink spiked in a wine bar, Judy Green mown down in cold blood and Christine Streeter, dead for ages and now apparently risen once more.

Amongst the ideas buzzing around Inga's brain was one to search out ten people who she had been to school with, to see where they are now. Was four out of nine a good percentage she wondered? How many of her old school friends had died or been killed in the ensuing years? Or was this collection of bodies just too much of a coincidence, especially when one had been considered by all and sundry to be dead for over a decade?

'Penny for them,' asked Ruth as she sidled up to her boss.

'I don't think you'd want the complete mess my mind is in at the moment.'

Some parts of Ireland had suffered badly from Hurricane Ophelia on Monday, but now it had all moved north and away and driving in that morning had been windy but not been full of the hazards envisaged at one time.

This was a good job, because the bad news for Detective Sergeant Jacques 'Jake' Goodwin was it was to be him travelling north to investigate the reason why the murdered Mindi Brookes had left her role at the Northwater Manor Spa Hotel.

The good news was his boss, Detective Inspector Inga Larsson was up for the ride. Across to the A1 and up before turning off near Northallerton and they then wound their way with their sat nav assistant shouting instructions to this rather imposing hotel complex. Had no doubt been a grand family home in its heyday in acres and acres of land.

They were shown into a very comfortable yet not sumptuous room and served both coffee and tea in white pots, from which they both chose the coffee option they had to pour for themselves.

'It's the smell I'm not happy with,' said Jake. 'Like walking into a big department store and when you come out your clothes smell like a Turkish whore's armpit. Or walking past one of those soap shops that stink to high heaven.'

'You're not into volcanic stone massage or chakras and centres of energy.'

'I am most certainly not.'

'You never thought of treating Sally to a weekend away at a place like this?'

'All floatation chambers and mud wraps. No thank you.' He wasn't at all au fait with what went on, but had just scanned a leaflet on the low table in front of him.

'I've only been twice,' said Inga. 'Not here of course, but had a hot massage with fabulous oils.'

'And any men you meet are likely as not called Julian or Vivian.'

'Once a woodentop hey Jake, always a woodentop.'

'I don't go in for all the grooming nonsense either. Can't imagine what my old dad would say if I turn up to his place for Sunday lunch smelling like a...'

Inga was leafing through a brochure. 'Says here they have people to read your aura.'

'Read your what?'

'Here's one might suit me,' she said. 'Learn to swim in five days.' She blew out a breath. 'I'd want to swim in the Olympics for that sort of money,' was her final say before the door opened and a well suited and booted tall man entered and made straight for the pair of them.

'Laurence Haffenden' he said and shook hands before Inga could get to her feet. She immediately recognized his need to be in control and became wary. 'Pleased to meet you,' he said and Jake was on his feet. 'Stay where you are, please. Enjoy your coffee,' he said and sat down followed by the detective 'Any reason we can't talk in here?'

'None at all,' said Inga and delved into her bag for her iPad, as Goodwin produced a note book.

'Tell me. How may I help you?'

'Laurence may I call you that?' she asked to annoy him and he nodded. 'In a couple of words, Mindi Brookes.'

'Yes of course, bad business,' he said and crossed his legs. 'Mindi was a duty officer here at one time. Good at her job mind, but not exceptional so I'm told, but left with a bit of a stain on her character I'm afraid. Not one we'd look to move up the ladder in a hurry. If I'm perfectly honest with you, there were issues with another member of staff to be honest.' He stopped grimaced and let his breath drift out. 'Actually she was a sub-contractor if you like. We call them business friends, but sub-contractor is more along the lines of what you're used to no doubt.'

'This what the Duty Manager was?'

'No the other person. The one Ms Brookes was in conflict with happened to be a business friend.'

'What exactly would a Duty Manager be responsible for?' Jake asked.

'The whole spa complex, mate. Always a hotel manager on duty of course, but all the day to day matters concerning the spa are dealt with by the Duty Manager. Dealing with customer queries, ensuring all the staff are in place, properly attired and a hundred and one other things. Everyday bits and pieces.'

'And the staff member...' Inga stopped. 'Sorry, this Business Friend, did what exactly?'

'Quite a few things I'm led to believe as she more than likely had a wide range of skills. We use top of the tree masseurs, podiatrists, manicurists you know the sort of thing.'

'Sorry to change the subject Laurence,' Inga said. 'Just out of interest. What can you tell me about this learn to swim in five days you advertise? You swim all day, is that it?'

'Not exactly. It is intensive, but a skilled teacher can run two courses at the same time, side by side.'

'Hard work for an instructor.'

'Helpers in the water. But like all our Business Friends we'd make sure those working with our clients have terrific people skills. Makes all the difference.'

I bet thought Inga, and reminded herself of the ridiculous price. 'I see,' she said. 'How many on a course, out of interest?'

'Fifteen.'

'And the dispute?' she switched back as she did the mental multiplication quickly. Something she had long considered doing, but not at a ridiculous price.

'Personality clash is my guess,' and this Laurence had his elbows on his knees and hands steepled. 'Can I just add at this juncture I wasn't actually here at the time, and I've had to ask about for any information I am able to provide.'

'Appreciate it,' said Inga.

'To be honest, it was suggested this Mindi Brookes was forging our clients' credit cards and using that information to make purchases for herself on line.'

'How would anybody here know what was happening?' was Jake Goodwin on full alert. 'We're talking organized gangs here surely. Is this what you're saying? It's not something one of your women could set up I shouldn't imagine.'

'As I say,' Haffenden hesitated and looked at Jake. 'You see, I wasn't with the company at the time, but that does seem to be the essence of what was happening.'

'What actually happened then?' Inga urged, knowing Jake Goodwin would not be so calm.

'To be honest so I understand it was felt best for all concerned if we asked her to leave. You see, it was Miss Brookes apparently who suggested it was this other woman who was on the make, had been found out by her and had tried to accuse Brookes. Miss Brookes retaliated by threatening to call the police.' He sat back in his chair and folded his arms. 'Got very messy for a day or two so I'm told.' He sighed. 'I'm sorry, but times were not good in all honesty, and it was felt it would be best to let them both go. Cause least harm to our image. In fact the Business Friend involved left almost immediately, but Mindi Brookes threated to take the company to an industrial tribunal for unfair dismissal and a whole host of other things.'

'You paid her off is what you're saying? Paid her to keep her mouth shut?'

At this, Laurence Haffenden looked forlorn, and just sat head down, nodding.

'The reason why we are here Laurence,' said Inga.

'Surely you must understand guys,' he almost pleaded. 'Please understand that was the reason why the company dare not let this become official, not let it out into the public domain. The bad publicity could have killed us, well this hotel at the very least. Just a hint of a scandal in a place like this and we're dead in the water.'

'This business friend. What was her role?'

'Sorry, but it could have been a whole number of things, Front of House, Beauty Therapist or even a Hair Stylist.'

'Where is she now do we know?' Jake enquired.

'I don't know. Time ago now, long gone, just packed her bags and went. Assume we paid her up for what we owed her.' Haffenden then poured coffee into the spare cup from the jug and then added just a spot of milk. 'Never actually discovered how it was being done, but I understand we did have clients complaining their cards had been cloned here.'

'And you just dealt with it all in house?' Jake checked.

'Apparently so.'

'Would you have any further information on file at all?' the DS requested.

'It could be our head office does of course. I assume they must keep HR records for some time, maybe in our archives or on a database somewhere.'

Inga guessed he was not going to offer. 'Would it be too much trouble to ask you to look into it for us? Get what information you can. All a matter of ticking boxes with an investigation such as this, as I'm sure you will appreciate.'

'Sure thing, guys,' he said without any enthusiasm and then sat forward to pick up his cup and drink. 'As I say, I wasn't with the company at the time but when it was all in the papers about a former employee being murdered it was all people wanted to talk about around here.'

'I can imagine.'

'You seem fairly busy today, at least the car park is quite full.'

'Yes, the good times may not be back to where they once were, but we're certainly on the up.'

'What people are looking for,' Inga suggested. 'A spot of luxury now and again, to take us away from the humdrum of emails and the dreaded phone.'

'Certainly.' Haffenden downed the remainder of his coffee in a few gulps. 'Would you like a tour?'

'That would be very nice,' she said and received a look from her colleague as she got to her feet.

In the car on their way back down south Jake was fingering through a brochure Laurence had given him.

'You were wrong,' Inga told Jake. 'He wasn't called Vivian.'

'Maybe not, but he was damn rude!' she knew was coming. 'Mate!?' He almost screamed. 'Since when have you been a guy I want to know? At least we didn't hit rock bottom with yawright mate garbage.' Jake was seething.

'Did call me a guy though, but at least he didn't try for a hug.'

'And he'd not bothered to have a shave. Whatever happened to customer care for god's sake? Mate? What's that all about? How rude.' Inga drove on in silence, knowing there might be more to come and understandably so. 'Have you read some of this?' Jake asked as he tapped the brochure on his knees.

'Only glanced at it really,' Inga commented.

'Our sumptuous iconic treatment day provides you our esteemed client with a body experience to delight your senses and ensure you live in harmony with your individual well- being.'

'Just the thing I'd have thought for Sally for her birthday. Better than the usual top from Next.'

'Probably cheaper,' he quipped. 'This Iconic Spa Day is only £210.00'

'Very reasonable.' They both laughed as Jake tossed the brochure over his shoulder and onto the back seat.

'But you get called mate for free.'

17

Inga Larsson still had the previous evening's late TV news on her mind on Wednesday morning. Stories concerning how Britain had been battered and bruised by the tropical hurricane followed by the continuing saga about the lack of progress with Brexit had been pushed aside in her mind, and had still been with her over breakfast.

Thoughts of how many millions had been wasted investigating two super-dense stars colliding only 130 million light years from earth, had enraged her.

Such pointless mind-numbing nonsense had always annoyed her. To be told these so-called neutron stars had burnt out stars so dense a teaspoon of them on Earth would weigh a billion tons was to her mind just utterly fanciful bilge fit only for *QI*.

Why she was still asking herself when she pulled up at Lincoln Central, do governments spend vast fortunes on measuring vibration in space when millions of people the world over die annually through a lack of something as simple as clean drinking water?

As Inga walked into the incident room she was immediately brought down to earth with a nod of DS Goodwin's head and his eyes steering her towards her office. It was a wary Inga who pushed the door fully open and walked in to find Adrian Orford the eTeam chief geek and their tame navigator of the dark web waiting for her.

General chit-chat that morning was about Lincoln City winning away at Swindon the previous evening, but never likely to be a subject for her techy visitor.

'Found you a live one,' he said before Inga could acknowledge his presence, get round her desk or check the overnights. 'Only conceptual and probably there's a degree of abstraction.' He looked at the grin on Inga's face she was never going to explain.

'Good morning Adrian,' she said to slow down the tirade of information he was more than likely to spew in her direction.

'Had a call checked out and it permutates. Been through the invert systems, even had a bit of a flirt with ambivalent military sites.' He said and put his index finger to his lips. 'But to be fair she looks a good 'un.'

What was it with people like Adrian and these star gazing geeks on the news getting all excited about gobbledegook?

'Who does?' Inga enquired now seated and firing up her PC. How complex she had wondered more than once were this guy's thought processes. One minute he's pontificating about invert systems and ambivalent military sites whatever they are, then in a flash he's back to phrases such as "she looks a good 'un".

'Angela Wilcox,' he said as if it was obvious. Inga stopped tapping keys instantly and left her login half completed just hanging there and peered at him.

'Be serious. Where did you find her?'

'Not her,' he said hinting at a smile. 'This one's a military doctor,' he said in the languid almost dreary tone of his. 'Lieutenant Angela Chloe Wilcox actually, been with the British Army Training Support Unit, just back from her tour of duty. Her mother told her about Christine Streeter being in the news and as a result she phoned in. She's genuine despite what you might think. You have my word.'

Inga was tempted to ask why he had popped down to see her again despite Stevens saying how busy his geeks were. Twice in a few days was more than he had probably visited in his lifetime.

'Say that again,' was her in need of confirmation.

'Angela Chloe Wilcox. To give her full title, Lieutenant Angela Chloe Wilcox BSc, MD.' Inga just sat there looking at him. His hair looked as though it had not seen a comb since his mother did it before he left for school.

'Another one?' she said and waved Jake Goodwin in from the incident room. She was pretty sure it was the first time Adrian Orford had ever smirked in her presence.

'Thought you'd like that.'

'Why, how...explain,' she said as Jake walked in and she pointed to the one spare chair in the office which he took temporary residence in.

'Phone call from this Lieutenant Wilcox...'

'Angela Wilcox,' said Inga to bring her DS up to speed.

'Another one or what?'

'She's a doctor in the British Army,' was ASBO with an answer of sorts. 'Been in Belize. Posted back I assume, but in her phone call she said when she got home her mother had told her about Christine Streeter being in the news and we were asking for the public to phone in, so now she has.'

'And you've checked her?'

'Every inch. Absolutely pucker, only thing I've not been able to establish is a photo for security reasons obviously. Same age as Streeter, born and brought up in Lincoln went to Forest Girls School. Studied medicine at university then joined the army. Think she may have been army sponsored. Been back just over a week.'

Inga looked at a puzzled Jake sat there. 'Make sense of it if you can.'

He screwed his eyes shut. He knew of the demotic urban comprehensive back then. 'If my memory serves me right the only people who have mentioned Angela Gray nee Wilcox or Angela Wilcox have been the woman in Sheffield who then turned black and appears to have done a runner, and Susan Sawyer.'

'When we checked her phone it was unobtainable.'

'It can't have been this Angela Wilcox.'

'And how many girls called Angela Wilcox were at the school at the same time?'

'I've emailed you everything we found,' said Adrian as he pushed himself to his feet.

'We're having a coffee,' said Inga with a knowing hinted look towards Jake. 'D'you want one?'

'Only drink hot water,' he said and her eyes switched back to Jake to receive a quizzical look in return. 'I'll be off, need any more you know where I am.'

'Thanks Adrian,' said DI Larsson and sat back in her chair.

'Coffee it is then?' said a grinning colleague. 'Unless…' the look he got was still with him as he walked off.

'Couple of weeks ago,' said Inga as Jake plonked a white mug of coffee on her desk with the liquid inside doing a very good colour match impression. 'I was in the canteen and your friend Adrian was talking to someone about bitcoins. Going on about them as if this cryptocurrency I think he called it, could easily run alongside sterling or euros.'

'I can just imagine popping into my local Spar shop and saying I want to pay for my milk through something which only inhabits cyberspace.'

'Nearly as crazy as this business,' she said motioning towards her monitor. She took her first sip. 'Thanks.'

'Why d'we have to have all the nonsense from these nerds? Other day when I popped up to see him he went on about onion browsers, like it's something everybody talks about to their missus over tea.'

'It's only a phrase they use for a technique to communicate anonymously.'

'I know now because I took the trouble to look it up.'

'Just layers of encryption like the layers of an onion, that's where it comes from'

'But I don't talk to him in some sort of secret language.' Jake sighed and sniggered. 'Where we going with this then?'

'Going to interview,' Inga pointed at him and then at her own chest. 'Has to be us.'

'Where is Belize exactly?'

'Just googled it. Between Guatemala and Mexico in the Caribbean Sea.'

'One thing boss, the day can only get better.'

'Really?' The pair of them sat there in silence with Jake sipping his strong coffee and Inga just holding her mug in her hands on her desk.

'The team looking for Streeter all that time ago, did they come up against all this sort of nonsense?'

'This somebody taking us off the scent, deliberately? Playing games for some reason?'

'Perverting the course of justice is what this is. Not to mention wasting police time.'

Inga sipped her drink. 'It can only be Streeter who wants to keep us at arms' length. Who else doesn't want her found do you think? Even Borowiak has no reason to keep her hidden, she's his get out of jail card.'

'Who would gain having her on everybody's mispers list?'

'Or on the dead as a dodo list.' He drank more as his boss tapped keys and scrolled down on her monitor. 'Potterhanworth, is where we're off to.'

'We?'

'No cock-ups this time, no pulling the wool over our eyes. Angela Wilcox you've got a few questions to answer,' she said and took a decent drink of her milky coffee. 'Finish this first, give her a call, set the tasks for the day and you're driving.'

'One question before we start,' said a grinning Jake. 'Would she have gone to Forest Girls if she lived in Potterhanworth? Wouldn't it be Branston Community College or whatever it's called these days?'

'Just the level of thinking we'll need with this.' She downed a tad more of her coffee, put down her mug, glanced at her watch then picked up her desk phone.

Jake got to his feet. 'I'll do a spot of research, can you ping ASBOs report across to me?'

Inga laid the receiver down, went back to her PC and having done as requested picked up the phone, punched in the numbers ASBO had come up with and waited.

'Angela Wilcox?' she asked when her call was answered.

Before they left Inga had issued Operation Lancaster tasks for the day or at least for the bulk of the time she expected her and Jake Goodwin to be away.

Actions she had set were all based around new lines of investigation. Some of the material they were after had been archived and it had been a case of calling the records office and waiting for them to retrieve the files, hopefully later that morning.

DS Scott Doyle and DC Kenny Ford she had paired together for once despite the fact they so often were inclined to rub each other up the wrong way. Inga had decided after a recent episode the only way to deal with it was to put them together not keep them apart.

Scott's Yorkshire bragging annoyed the whole team at times but Kenny in particular for some reason. Referring to Scott as 'Me duck' out of his hearing was something Inga had needed to have words about.

A spell with PHU due to sickness had given the team some relief from his bluster and constantly singing his county's praises. Now Doyle was back after working lately with a small team of local idiots passing off over-the-counter pills as Class A drugs. Now of course as is his way he was a world authority in all things skanking.

The pair had been tasked by the DI with going out to Forest Girls School to ask them to search through their archives to establish just how many Angela Wilcox's had been at the school when Christine Streeter was there. If they were not able to come up with the answers there and then she had instructed them to make arrangements to revisit as soon as possible, or to even offer to do the search themselves.

First thing to strike Inga was how amenable this Angela Wilcox woman appeared to be and yet at the same time how disciplined. Has to be combination of medical and military training. Not sure she'd want her as a pal, be too formal she guessed and not one she'd fancy letting her hair down and having a good laugh with.

Up front it was the discipline which got in the way as she tended to be very formal, but then once her mother had produced a pot of tea and chocolate biscuits she became less detached. This woman had wanted to know Inga's nationality, almost as if it was a laid down military must ask. Inga explained her Swedish birth, followed by UK education and university.

When Wilcox explained what she was doing at home the ice seemed to be broken.

'Could only happen to me,' she said sat there in a navy blue Army track suit and Adidas trainers. No earrings, no jewellery, not even a ring. 'Medical officer and what happens? I'm the one who gets a snake bite,' was not at all what either of them were expecting. 'Fortunately we weren't too deep in the jungle and I had immediate attention of course but the powers that be in their infinite wisdom felt it best if I came home. My tour was due to end in a couple of weeks, so it's not a big issue.'

'You all right now?' Inga asked.

'Yeah fine. No lasting damage.'

'Poisonous I take it?' Jake enquired.

'Rattlesnake,' staggered them both. Be something for Jake to report to Sally.

'You're joking!' he gasped. And this Angela just grinned.

'First things first,' said Inga. 'How do you think you can help?'

'Basically because I was at school with Christine, we were very good friends during our last couple of years at Forest.'

'Can I ask why you went to Forest Girls and not to Branston?' Jake slid in.

'It was closer and...sorry...' she smiled. 'We lived in Lincoln back then. Parents have been out here about six or seven years, once Peter and I had flown the nest.'

'Peter?'

'My elder brother.'

'What do you know about the Christine Streeter story?' Inga enquired before she tried the tea. At least it was tolerable and this Angela had described Jake's as NATO Standard to her mother. Jake knew many nations in NATO don't drink tea, so what was such ingrained silliness all about?

'I knew she had been murdered of course and her body has never been found and to be honest as awful as it was I thought that was that. Then when I got home the other day my mother told me it had been on the news talk of her possibly not being dead.'

When she paused for a breath the Detective Inspector took advantage. 'So you phoned us?' She nodded her reply. 'How do you think you can help?'

Inga didn't know for certain but some of the furniture looked to her as if it had come from IKEA or other similar stores,

'Mother said you were asking people to contact you. Not sure I can be of any great use having been out of the area for such a long time, but I knew her, we were very close. At school anyway. Least I can do.'

'Did you know Tomasz Borowiak?'

'No. Be when I was in Medical School. We'd sort of lost touch by then.'

'What information can you give, do you know the names of people who were about at the time for instance?'

'Before you answer,' was Jake. 'Were there any other girls also called Angela Wilcox at the school around the same time?'

This Angela frowned. 'Not any I know of, not in my year I know, but not sure about lower down.'

'Others girls you can remember?' Inga reminded.

'Been thinking about that,' she mused. 'Rachel Somers, Becky Odling, Carly Hills.'

'Charlotte Elliott by any chance?' Inga asked but Jake's mind was searching for any memory sighting of the other three.

'Yes, but not a friend as such, in fact Christine and Rachel were the ones I was closest to. Knew Becky and Carly but again not as close friends because they were in my set for some subjects. Something about Carly but I can't for the life of me remember what it was.' She sighed. 'Can't be important.' Jake was so infuriated by her and decided to bide his time.

'This Charlotte Elliott what can you tell us about her?'

Angela pouted as she thought then sucked in her breath. 'Just not my cup of tea if I'm honest.' Inga guessed she was being very cagey.

'Tell us about Christine,' said Jake.

'Probably shouldn't say this but her parents were the trouble, or at least her mother was. Too molly coddling, treated her like she was still in a romper suit, wouldn't let her grow up.' Angela sucked in a breath noisily. 'Under the thumb is a nice way of putting it, wanted her daughter in a pretty party frock when we were all in jeans and sweats.'

'Anything else?'

'To be honest yes.' They then had to wait and both detectives took the opportunity to sup their tea. 'First got to know her when I found her crying one day,' everything she said was back to being deliberate and disciplined. 'Never actually admitted it but I'm pretty sure she was being bullied. What they do isn't it, pick on the runt of the litter so to speak?'

'Do you remember Judy Green by any chance?' Inga asked from her notes

'Only by reputation.'

'Good, bad?'

'Bad most certainly.'

'Which manifested itself how?'

'Two fold really, always showing off with being able to speak fluent French and she was a nasty piece of work. Her and Lottie, made a right pair.'

'In what way?'

'Only what I heard of course, never tried it with me. Bullying, picking on the weakest or people with an issue.'

'Such as?'

'Weak ones, younger ones or like Amy Devonshire who had a cleft lip.' She shook her head slightly. 'Get my hands on them now they'd know about it.'

'Guess so,' smiled blonde Inga. 'Anybody else?'

'There's always the girl who died of course,' said as if they knew who she was talking about and her look of enthusiasm had departed. 'So awfully sad.' Inga glanced at her colleague who grimaced slightly out of sight.

'Tell me about her.'

'Killed one half term, well the last February half term if my memory serves me right. What a stupid man he was,' the detectives were finding it difficult to fathom as Angela shook her head. 'All this outward bound is all good stuff, but don't just go off piste as it were.'

'Skiing?' Jake checked.

'No, no, sorry just a turn of phrase. Idiot macho father took her water boarding in February in seas you'd not go near even if you were Horatio Nelson. What a stupid stupid man.'

'Think you mean body boarding. Water boarding is torture.'

'Whoops! But it's what this was. Bloody child abuse if you ask me.'

'What happened?' Inga posed to her.

'She drowned. He did his best to save her, or so he said and somebody had to jump in to save him in the end. What a waste. What an absolute idiot.'

'But she was okay when she was at school with you?'

'Not a close friend and certainly not one of the Troika.'

'The what?'

'What some of the girls called them,' she smiled broadly. 'Silly really, there were the three of them. Lottie, Judy and Helen. Things you do eh? Somebody called them Troika because it was Russian and had something to do with three horses I think and it was supposed to be to do with Judy saying how she could learn any language you care to name in no time.' Angela dipped a chocolate biscuit into her tea signifying to Inga she had relaxed more.

'Anything else about them?'

They had to wait a moment for her to finish her biscuit. No beautifully crafted nails and most certainly no varnish.

Inga was fully aware of the increasing attention being paid to the matter of transgender, about people living in the wrong body type.

Was this Angela Wilcox such a person in how she had no more of a female figure than any young man, had hair shaved very short, and no suggestion of make-up or a skirt. Did she really want to be one of the lads?

Inga knew enough about it to know gender identity is one's feeling of being male, female, both or a mixture which individuals express through such matters as their clothing, hairstyle and behaviour.

In front of her was a woman who dressed like any man, particularly in fatigues she guessed, had her hair shorter than many men and was an Army person through and through. Looking at her in an armchair legs apart, she could easy be a bloke.

Was it why wanting to enter the medical profession, she had also plumped for the Army. Would she find life easier, closer to what she wanted to be rather than becoming just another 'Lady Doctor' on the wards with the NHS?

'Thought they were the be all and end all, those three. Come across people like that in the Army, but we soon knock it out of them don't you worry.'

'Did Christine get on with them?'

'Certainly not.' She leant forward as if she was going to speak in confidence. 'Christine always kept everything deep inside,' she laid a hand flat on her meagre chest. 'Truth is she was probably being bullied and it could be her palling up with me meant she was tormented a lot less.'

'Bullying?'

'Probably what the Troika were all about. Like you sometimes get in boys schools where the players in the Rugby 1st XV on Quarter

Backs in America treated like gods, it was the same with these three. Except they gained control by being nasty, not because they were hot shots at hockey or anything like that.'

'Any chance you know what happened to the three of them?' Jake queried.

'Judy's probably a Russian tourist guide,' Angela chuckled and then shrugged. 'Other two, no idea to be honest. I'm sorry.'

'And you think this Troika bullied Christine Streeter.'

'Got no proof, just what has come to mind over time. Nobody'd tried anything with me, but when I came across it once at Medical School and then later in the Army once or twice it just got me to thinking how maybe it had been Christine's problem.' She blew out a breath. 'Then of course we have that Borowiak comes on the scene later,' she looked earnestly at Inga. 'Certainly gets you thinking.'

'Not sure it helps us find her.'

'I'm not saying she could well have brought it on herself, but her upbringing couldn't have helped, could it? If I'm being honest and not wishing to be unkind she was best described as being mealy mouthed.' She sighed. 'Guess I felt sorry for her and as it happened she was a lot better at a couple of subjects I struggled a bit with.'

'Anything else you can think of?'

'Was one thing I've remembered,' she said. 'My mother told me there was a woman at the door year or so ago asking after me. Said she was in the area just called on the off chance. Mother explained I was in the Army, says she thinks it quite caught her by surprise.' Angela took a big drink of her tea to empty the cup. Inga could just imagine her downing a big mug of hot char in the NAAFI being one of the boys. 'Said she'd known me at school, then mentioned some sort of get-together but never left any information. Don't even know if it ever took place. Just thought it a bit odd at the time when she told me as I've never lived here, and wondered how she knew where my parents live.'

'And she was who?'

The answer was in the form of a shaking head. 'Didn't give a name and my mother only realized she should have asked her after she'd gone.'

'Do you know anything more about this Helen?' Jake took from the list he was compiling.

'Nevins. Helen Nevins.'

Suddenly, there was the name accredited to the phone from where the incident was called in. 'Where, what, how?' he hurried.

'To be perfectly frank I've no idea.'

'If you were in our shoes, knowing all these girls, well women now, which avenue would you go down to find her if she is still alive?'

Rather than answer, she had a question of her own. 'Can I just ask, why did you want to know if there was anybody else at Forest called Angela Wilcox?'

'The name has cropped up.'

'As being at the school?'

'No, but it was always a possibility and we didn't want to be chasing the wrong one.'

'We're talking about what? Fifteen, sixteen year old girls in when? 1999?'

'I left in 2001,' which Jake made a quick note of. 'And what was it, five years later when Christine disappeared?' He reckoned it would make Streeter 22 at the time.

'Yes.'

Angela Wilcox had her arms folded and just sat there looking down at the deep blue carpet which provided Inga with an opportunity to wink at her sergeant.

'Lottie Elliott,' said Inga gently aware all these names was becoming confusing. Angela peered up. 'Did you know she had died?'

'No.'

'Unexplained apparently, down in Peterborough. They think her drink was spiked.'

'My God!'

'Still looking for a couple of people who are possibly involved.'

'Usually used to put women at a disadvantage. Any idea what it was?' was the doctor in her and a look of disbelief across her face.

Jake shook his head. 'Read the main toxicology points from Cambridgeshire Police, sorry I can't remember what it was now.'

'You think it was deliberate?' she frowned.

'We have no idea at this stage. Still an ongoing case.' Having a game sliced on her stomach was certainly deliberate.

'This recent?' Angela asked Inga who nodded. 'Don't look at me,' Angela grinned. 'I was in Belize.'

'Just out of interest,' said Inga. 'Does noughts and crosses mean anything from your time at school?'

Wilcox pouted and shook her head. 'Not my scene at all I'm afraid.' She looked towards the door. 'What old folk do eh?'

'Can we just go back to this Helen Nevins?' was Jake. 'Any clues to whereabouts perhaps?'

'Sorry,' she shook her head slightly. 'Like the rest, sorry no idea. Haven't a clue.'

Time to thank the Army woman for all her help and hospitality and head back to Lincoln.

'Wonder why people do that? Want to be a doctor but add Army to the baggage as well. Wonder if it's double the stress in their world.'

'Sally has enough problems as a staff nurse, let alone being a soldier as well. In this day and age with the state of the NHS she has a whole assortment of stressful scenarios on a daily basis. The tardy staff no longer anything like dedicated as they once were. Demands of uncouth patients, arrogant consultants stood alongside her head of nursing and hard pressed admin with little or no medical experience. Not to mention paying over the odds for agency nurses.'

'Can't image how bad it must be these days. A&E has to be a complete nightmare.'

'Sally's constantly frustrated by government cutbacks, ridiculous staff shortages, pointless targets to give Whitehall mandarins a job and ludicrous snap inspections.'

'This little lot'll keep my friend ASBO busy,' said Inga as she read Jake's notes as he drove them swiftly back to Lincoln Central on a calm day after the storm.

'At least we now know Helen Nevins is real.'

'Shame we can't say the same about her address.'

'I don't care what anybody says, our mystery Angela Gray nee Wilcox from Sheffield is not the Angela Wilcox we've just met.'

'Little job for Adrian, he can find us the marriage of Angela Wilcox to somebody called Gray.' Inga knew Adrian would check each one thoroughly even down to their bra sizes but doubted whether he might be at all interested in such macho facts.

'Not at all sure Stevens will be happy with us giving his lad all these run-of-the-mill tasks. Surely any of ours could cope easy.'

'Think there's something going on between Darke and Stevens and this is the boss using his authority to bring he of the gawdy socks down a peg or two.'

'Do we know what?'

'Not yet. But all the time he's giving us ASBO to piss off Stevens I'll take advantage,' she sniggered. 'Don't you worry I've got some for the team to chase up,' Inga looked down to check the names Jake had scribbled down. 'Rachel Somers, Becky assume Rebecca Odling and Carly Hills.' She glanced at Jake. 'Charlotte Elliott, Judy Green and this Nevins woman in this Troika thing. How interesting is that and how stupid she must think it all sounds all these years later.

'Oh to see ourselves as we were back in school.'

'You're not the only one. Two of them are dead we know of, and it's not natural causes or anything else we can tick a box for. Next on the list for Adrian has to be this Helen Nevins.' Inga was pensive for a moment. 'Except he's been there before with the phone.' She smirked. 'Must remember to tell Nicky about this one today when I see her next.'

'What?'

'We had this thing about what people face when they go to work in the morning, how life must be grim for some and an absolute breeze for others. Got a new one for her. Met a woman this morning who'd been bitten by a rattlesnake at work,' Inga chuckled. 'Beat anything Adam's dealt with today I bet.'

'Have you spoken to Nicky at all?' Jake queried.

'Not for a while.'

'When I spoke to her about what was going on in Peterborough said she's up this way from time to time seeing her parents and her brothers.'

'You got her number?'

18

The techy-geek Adrian Orford heading up the eTeam never gave the impression of doing anything in haste. This time might very well have been the exception in having arranged for one of the two people he had found off Inga's list, to be interviewed on Skype.

Ask no questions and you get no lies was Inga's policy with Adrian. They had all their systems from a simple PNC checks and a link through to DVLA but she was sure the eTeam must be able to access Census records not normally available to the public for a hundred years. She was sure the geeks would delve into National Insurance, Births, Marriages and Deaths and of course the HMRC databases, not to mention GCHQ, the Home Office and naturally these days their Immigration websites, and they were only the ones she could surmise about. What of the so-called dark net he was quite possibly more than very familiar with?

Inga could never fathom why people keep spouting about CCTV cameras peering into their movements and their liberty when everyone with half a brain knows the authorities keep track of people anyway, and to her, so they should. It is after all for their own good.

Only the guilty need to hide.

Inga had to go up to sit beside the eTeam guru for this Skype interview. According to Adrian he claimed to have located a Helen Macritchie nee Hardaker nee Nevins now living in the Highlands of Scotland, most certainly a heck of a long way from Forest Girls School in downtown Lincoln.

She had been one of those who had contacted the police, in her case Police Scotland, when she heard they needed to speak to anyone with information on Christine Streeter. Helen Nevins as she was back at the school despite the fact her name was linked to the original phone call, had been dropped down the pecking order once they realized she lived so far away and her current knowledge would be less likely than others.

Inga speculated in her mind quite often how old school coppers would deal with major investigations these days. All these apps, downloads and digital footprints. DNA lists, content warrants, cyberspace, the Scene Evaluation Branch, data sifting and not forgetting the dark web.

She also frequently sat in her office watching out into the incident room wondering how they would have coped. The sound of mobiles playing good, bad and awful ringtones, whiring printers, the chatter and laughter which never seemed to stop. What about the food? Crisps, Monster Munch and Mars just seemed to be chomped endlessly around the room. Jelly babies, bottles of water, crème eggs and those dreadful cardboard coffee cups filling the bins in double quick time.

Back then she guessed they'd have coped with black heavy telephones she'd only seen in films, thick white cups of tea with saucers, regular pints at night at the close of play in the pub on the corner. Plenty of fags of course and a bag of chips on the way home.

The moment Adrian had popped in the names Inga had given him from her chat with Angela, there was a link.

Once the introductions were over, the DI decided rather than go starkly into the Christine Streeter questioning she'd discover how come the former Helen Nevins was now in the far reaches of Scotland.

'Can we please go back to 2006? Were you ever interviewed about Christine Streeter disappearance back then?'

'No,' she said quite bluntly.

'You seem very sure.'

'I should be,' she retorted strongly. 'I've never been interviewed by the police about anybody. I didn't know this Borowiak and had nothing to do with her once we left school.'

'In order for me to be able to get my bearings,' said Inga gently. 'Could you possibly give me a précis of your route from Lincoln to the Highlands?'

'Is it really necessary?' Inga saw her sag with a deep breath. 'Thought you wanted to know about my relationship with Christine Streeter for some reason.'

'Please humour me,' she said. 'We are dealing with an unexplained death here in Lincoln and at the same time looking into the possibility Christine Streeter might be alive.'

'How come?'

'You knew she was missing then?'

'No. Just heard she was dead. But that was ages ago.'

'So can we please just fill in the intervening years as far as you are concerned? We've already spoken to a lot of your former school friends in order to build a picture. Could do with your input.'

'I really thought I'd escaped. You know,' she shrugged. 'Thrown myself into a new world far away from all the nonsense going on and now up you pop out of the blue.'

'But you contacted Police Scotland.'

'I know.'

'If we weren't looking for Christine and hadn't been given your name by Angela Wilcox you'd still be incognito if that's what you're after.'

'Am I in any trouble?'

'I shouldn't imagine so. Why, do you think you might be?'

'Just wondered as its Christine and what happened to her.'

'Think if you were in trouble you'd find me stood on your doorstep not chatting on Skype.' Determined Inga waited and watched.

Deep breath and off she went. 'Did the usual. Left school, went to uni, got my degree for all the good it's been. Got a boring job, met somebody I stupidly fell for because he was charming and good looking when I shoulda known better, went through a nightmare few years, got the hell out of it, met another guy by sheer chance and here I am.'

Adrian Orford had established this Helen Nevins that was, had been employed as a Business Coach, the sort of role which always worried Inga. Why could people not do real proper jobs, something to help the world go round, contribute to society?

'Any chance you can put a bit of meat on the bone?'

'Which bit? If you want the whole gruesome story we'll be here all day.'

'Let's go from any contact you've had with former class mates and then run me briefly through your relationships and then bring me up to date with your situation as is.'

'Think it'd be halfway through uni when I lost contact with the last of those I knew at Forest. To be fair I broke off contact if I'm honest. Not proud of some of the stuff what went on, things we got up to, but my excuse is I was immature. Thought I was the bees-knees but as we all know I was just a silly schoolgirl. At least that's what I tell myself.' Inga looked at the screen as this redhead looked left and right almost as if she was seeking guidance from somebody off screen.

'What can you tell me about Troika?'

Helen Macritchie looked shocked at the question. 'How utterly stupid it all sounds now. Almost as bad as admitting we bought Beyoncé records.'

'And?'

'Don't realize at the time how what you're doing has serious consequences, but when it happens to you if you like, it all came home to roost.'

'In what way?' Inga was struggling to understand but was wary of butting in too much.

'When you're the one being used, bullied in my case is not too strong a word, but then when your life's a nightmare it comes home to you. Sometimes I just wished to God I could go back and put everything right.' This Helen Nevins that was, looked as though she might burst into tears so Inga let it be. 'Then I went through the nightmare with the shit I married, took an aunt's advice to get away to re-think my life.' She went from looking sad and upset to the hint of a smile as she looked straight ahead.

'Where were you living by this time?'

'Grimsby's near enough.'

'And it turned out to be the right decision? To get away from him.' Inga realized how the Troika business had been skipped over very quickly and scribbled a quick reminder.

'I should say so.'

'Am I right in thinking you were in a violent relationship?' she guessed.

'To be honest no. Avid football supporter, football on TV day and night, expensive season ticket, travelling to matches here and abroad what with Champions League and all. Air fares and hotels cost a pretty packet. We could afford a new home and away shirt for him but no new clothes for our daughter except a stupid replica shirt of course. Then there were the moods when they lost and in the end he actually became violent when they lost in some semi-final thing.' A concerned Inga watched her clear her throat. 'Sorry, about as much as I could take.'

'Tell me about life now,' she didn't really need to know but felt it just might help to relax her and keep her on line.

'Logan runs a small niche biscuit company which is expanding thanks to the internet. I have my daughter with me plus we have one of our own and life is good.' She looked down and then back up again. 'Until you came into my life.'

'It's not you we're investigating,' Inga assured her gently. 'But tell me about the bad times at school, please.'

She had to wait.

'Don't know how it started, just sort of drifted into it somehow, four of us initially if my mind serves me right but finished up with three.' She shrugged visibly. 'Got too damn big for our boots to be honest. Picked on new kids, then the weak.' Helen cleared her throat. 'Sorry, bitch of the week doesn't come close,' she said and just sat there with her head down. When her auburn head came up there were tears in her eyes, a glistening of her cheeks. 'Not proud of it, we were bullies. No other words for it, and I'm ashamed, been ashamed for donkey's years, just have to hope it didn't do any lasting damage because I now know what such nasty can do to you.'

'You say there were three of you.'

'Yep.'

'Any chance you can recall the names?'

'Lottie Elliott and Judy Green.'

'And you?'

'I'm sorry to say.'

'As you can imagine with Christine Streeter having been missing for a long time now I am particularly interested in how people manage to achieve that status and why. You appear to have been successful in dropping out of society. Would you be willing to tell me your story?'

Inga watched her on the screen pick up a pen and just tap the top on the surface in front of her while she gave the question some thought. 'Marriage from hell to be honest,' she started. 'Just wall to wall Liverpool bloody football if I'm honest. Nightmare, absolute nightmare, there really was nothing else in his life or ours to be honest. He'd been a supporter when I met him of course but it just seemed to take over his life; just got worse and worse. Plucked up the courage from somewhere, just grabbed my daughter and got out. Should have done it years before if I'm honest and when I eventually plucked up the courage ran to my aunt up in Wakefield with bloody Roger threatening all sorts. Then a few months later my aunt Marjorie was heading to Scotland to visit an old friend of her husband, my uncle who'd died.' She puffed out a breath. 'Asked me to go with her. Went to this very Scottish evening with bagpipes and neeps and tatties and Scottish dancing and all the usual touristy business,' her look had improved as she spoke. 'Then this big guy just came over to me and suggested we were somehow the odd couple, being the only ones under about sixty, took me into the bar for a drink.'

Then a man's heavily bearded face appeared by the side of Helen and he just said 'Hello, I'm Logan.'

'And that as they say, was it?'

'Kinda,' Helen responded as Logan disappeared.

'And now you're married with a child of your own?'

'Not married. Felt Roger was getting too close and making more threats in his bid to get his hands on Lisa, so I just changed my name to Mcritchie and joined him here. Never looked back.'

'And you've not had any more trouble from this Roger?'

'Still probably trying to trace me.' She looked to her right. 'Be honest I haven't married so there is no record of Helen Hardaker getting married, just changed my name and for business purposes I use my second Christian name. Too easy to track people these days I guess what with the internet and all the other business.'

'Has he been stalking you?'

'Possible I s'pose,' she shrugged.

'But you don't know for sure.'

'Dunno.'

'Have you by any chance got a pay as you go mobile?'

'No,' was all Inga thought she was getting. 'Did once upon a time years ago.'

'What happened to it?'

'Goodness knows.'

'Have you ever lived in Leeds?'

'No,' she sniggered as if it was an outrageous suggestion.

'Whilst we're on the subject of names and places, can I throw a few at you? Just say what springs to mind.'

'One I've just remembered,' she stopped and Inga watched her bite her bottom lip. 'Poor Susan,' she mumbled then looked up and blinked as if she had shaken herself out of her memories. 'Drowned on holiday out doing something utterly ridiculous with her father in the sea in winter. Be that water boarding is it they call it, could've been surfing. Whatever.'

'Susan you say?'

'Yes, Susan Sawyer,' opened a stream in Inga's brain. 'Men eh?'

'I realize this might seem a stupid question,' said a shaken Inga Larsson. 'But were there two girls called Susan Sawyer at the school at that time?'

'Not that I know of.'

'Where does she fit into everything?'

'In our class, in my set for some subjects, not a particularly close friend or anything along those lines.' She stopped to take in a breath. 'Went to her funeral, well a lot of us did of course.'

Inga just wanted to scream at the complexities of this case, but had to make sure she gave nothing away and decided it might be best for all concerned to change subjects.

'What about Christine Streeter, the reason for us contacting you? What do you remember about her?'

'Nice girl, but a bit timid, just ripe for it if you're a bully I'm ashamed to say. We used to steal her pocket money and her sweets, I remember forcing her to buy Snickers for me more than once.' She closed her eyes. 'Having said that you'd not wish what happened to her on your own worst enemy. Not actually an enemy, more a victim, sadly.'

'More than once it appears.'

'Now I wouldn't give you tuppence for a Snickers.' Her head was just shaking slightly from side to side. 'Could have been me of course when I think about it. Vicious relationship only hers went too far I guess. Often think how lucky I've been in truth.'

'Tell me,' Inga dared. 'How would you go about it? Getting her to buy you Snickers?'

'Fags as well I've just remembered,' was no answer. 'Threatened her with all sorts.' she watched as Helen shook her head.

'Violence?'

Helen shrugged. 'Yes I'm sorry to say.'

'What else?'

'Stole her little bra once in the changing rooms, had to spend the rest of the day without it.' Inga watched the screen as she closed her eyes, bit her bottom lip and smiled to herself. 'Bit ridiculous now thinking about it. Some of the girl'd be in real trouble going about without one, but not her, got nothing much to put in it to be honest.'

'Anything else?'

'If she didn't do as she was told we'd do things like pushing her in the showers fully clothed, that sort of thing.' She looked up. 'I know, I know, I feel so ashamed, I really do.' She let out a long sigh. 'This is worse than being in the confessional,' she said. 'Not that I ever have.' She then went on. 'Think to be honest she probably had to steal money to keep us at bay, probably robbed her mum's purse and all sorts of things. Once in science we held her hand in flames so she got badly burnt. Thinking about it now, just awful isn't it?'

'What did the teacher say?' Inga just spotted this Helen look off camera and mouth 'Sorry' she assumed to Logan.

'Nothing. Stupid girl'd not say what happened, said it was an accident, her fault.'

'Now you'd do it all on social media,' Inga suggested.

'With death threats no doubt or force her to pose naked on her phone for all the lads.'

'Or the whole internet.'

'Could have been worse is one way of looking at it, I s'pose. Never ever be something I'll ever be proud of though. Psycho-babble merchants'd put it down to youth and hormones and any number of excuses, but the truth is there is no excuse for such behavior.' She bit her bottom lip. 'Paid the price I suppose with all the horrors I had to suffer later.' The DI watched her sigh and glance to her side, to Logan again she guessed. 'Saying I've picked up up here, is God doesn't pay his dues in money,' was linked to her head just shaking slowly from side to side. 'We may have been young but you have to remember like all women at the time we were influenced by the Bridget Jones culture. Being laddish meant everything. Was everything.'

Inga jumped in to move her on before she uttered more tripe. 'Angela Wilcox, what can you remember about her?' was next in line from her notebook. Be easier to assimilate as she'd met her.

'Bit of a swot, but good at netball.' She smirked. 'Be no good trying to bully her, she'd certainly give as good as she got!' She laughed. 'Would she!'

'Charlotte Elliott, Lottie?'

'Bit gawky,' Helen said and hesitated. 'With a big pony tail. Looking back think she made up for being shall we say, less attractive by being downright nasty. Certainly not liked by any of her peers. Taller than everybody which gave her an advantage. Had two brothers as I recall who were always up to no good, and they lived on what would then have been called a council estate. Think her old man wasn't as good as he should have been, did a bit of trading in scrap and all sorts of shifty goings on I seem to remember.'

'Now you're a million miles from it all.'

'Yes,' she responded. 'Business is doing well, the internet of course has been an absolute boon with people surfing the web. We're pretty much self-sufficient, live in a delightful community and life's good.'

'Last but not least, what can you remember about the Judy Green you mentioned?'

'Are we being recorded?' she asked but didn't wait for a reply. 'Hope you'll excuse the phrase but Judy was so good at languages she could say things like,' she took a breath. 'Do you fancy a shag, to all the boys in about nine different languages?' She looked embarrassed. 'Sorry.'

'That's quite all right,' Inga smirked and looked down at her notes with the name Susan Sawyer still running amok in her mind.

'S'pose now you'll tell the authorities where I am and I'll soon have Roger beating a path to my door.'

'Sorry. None of my business, I've got too much on worrying about dead and missing women, to be spending time on old domestic issues.'

'Do you really think Christine Streeter is still alive after all this time?'

'There are issues which lead us to believe she very well may be.' Inga glanced down at her notebook one more time. 'Troika?'

Macritchie looked aghast. 'Oh God.'

'You were part of it I take it?' The answer was mumbled. 'Think that's about it for now.'

'For now?'

'We don't know how this will all pan out. There are no plans to contact you again but if something vital crops up and we need answers I'd hope we could call on you.'

'Please don't pass my details onto anybody.'

'Certainly not,' Inga assured her. 'Thank you for your assistance, and good luck with the business. Always love a good biscuit,' made Helen smile.

'Excuse me,' stopped Inga from asking ASBO to close down the circuit, and there facing her was this heavily bearded fella she now knew to be Logan Macritchie. 'Helen's been having trouble with her IT, think somebody's infiltrated it, if she's perfectly honest Helen thinks it might be that Roger and...'

'Sorry,' said Inga to stop him. 'We're the police, you need to get onto your internet service provider. Have you got anywhere up there can fix whatever the problem is?'

'You don't seem to understand,' he insisted. 'Helen's been getting emails, nasty emails from someone.' *Don't we all,'* thought the DI. 'She knows as well as I do who it might be. And gets weird messages on her Facebook page.'

'Do you know who from?'

'No, but we can guess.'

'What proof do you have?'

'We don't but we don't need many guesses. Only one person's got it in for her. Done my best, and got a pal who knows about these things reckons we've been hijacked.' Inga saw ASBO beside her grimace and then visually suggest it could be real.

'Are you saying you think, and Helen thinks she's been receiving emails and Facebook messages from Roger Hardaker, is that what you're saying?'

'Who else? And they're threatening too.'

'What proof do you have they are from him?' The response was just a shrug. 'If it happens again come back to us...' ASBO nudged her and began to scribble a quick note. First time she'd ever seen him actually write anything down. 'Hold on,' she said and read what ASBO had written. 'If you get any more such messages don't delete them, leave them on your system and I'll see if one of our techy team can look into it, but please remember we're not here to save you a trip to PC World.'

'Susan bloody Sawyer, what in god's name is going on there?' Inga quipped to Jake and Adrian ASBO the moment the line was cut. 'I've a good mind to get Raza to work out how many coincidences we've had with this bag of worms.'

Raza she knew was never good with original thinking but he was reliable and a constant in her team compared with the come-overs dragged in when the balloon went up, and good with sulky dregs in interview.

'She the big cheese with the hotel group?' Adrian asked.

'Yes, and interviewed by two of my team,' she shot back. 'Looks like I might have been a bit hard on Raza and Gilly over being conned by the Angela Gray woman in Sheffield.'

'Who turned out to be Angela Wilcox we interviewed yesterday in Potterhanworth who was in faraway Belize at the time of the murder.' Jake shook his head as he blew out a tired breath. 'You couldn't make it up! A bit ago, the boss gave one of these unexplaineds to...' he looked all around the room at the geeks all beavering away. 'Luke Stevens. Wish to God he'd given him this one. And I'd had the forethought to book leave.'

'You and me both,' Inga plopped in. 'Now it's looking very much as if Ruth and Julie were taken for a ride too.' She sighed and sagged. 'According to them apparently she even wore a badge with her name and the hotel group logo and everything on it. It's not real.'

She'd read somewhere recently how in Germany geeks are known as gecks when they talk about the unfashionable amongst us and the socially awkward.

'What on earth has this all got to do with Christine Streeter?' Jake Goodwin questioned.

'And why are we spending all our time worrying about her and not who killed Mindi Brookes?'

'Because they could be one and the same remember.'

'Oh I remember don't you worry.'

'This Troika had three members and two it seems are dead.'

'And the third one is virtually in hiding.'

'Suggests she's in hiding from her ex-husband, but is that all? Been told so many lies I'm beginning to doubt everything anybody tells us.'

'Can we do a complete check on Helen Nevins,' she looked down at her tablet computer. 'Hardaker and now Mcritchie. Can we look at Roger Hardaker and find out what he's doing now and where he is.' The next question was to herself as much as Jake and Adrian. 'Do I need to have a word with Police Scotland? Not talking about protective custody or a safe house, just a word of warning.'

'If she hadn't phoned in and been on the list,' said Adrian. 'We'd have had a heck of a job finding her.' He looked at the DI. 'Changing her name without it being on official records is a smart move.' He looked down at his tablet. 'Susan Sawyer?' Adrian asked.

'I think you've got enough on, give her to my girls and Lizzie can get HOLMES fired up.'

The Home Office Large or Major Enquiry System had proved vital in the past and with Lizzie Webb in-putting it was a serious 'must have' for almost every murder.

'I'll find spare screen time for one,' he spun his head to look to his left at an IT wiz just staring into space. 'Investigate Nevins more to make absolutely sure and another one to track down Mcritchie, just need to give this Logan of hers the once over.'

'Hardaker?' said Jake, but his boss was beaten to the punch by the normally languid ASBO.

'Leave it with me,' he offered to surprise them both. 'I'll find somebody to delve into Liverpool's Season Ticket database.'

If nothing else this odd bod was always very thorough. Inga just couldn't imagine what either Logan Mcritchie or Hardaker had to with all this business, but it was worth a check. At least it would keep a nerd off the streets.

'We've only got her word for her story.' Inga scrunched up her eyes. 'Beginning not to trust anybody the way it's going.'

'Interesting it was Logan who mentioned computer issues and not her.'

'I'll delve into Susan Sawyer and her hotel,' Adrian continued.

'Spiceal Grand in Birmingham,' Inga quickly brought up on her screen, then stood up. 'Now I've got to explain this to the team. Probably no connection but we do have issues on another case up towards Grimsby. Do we have his address?' she asked them both.

'I'll email that, even if we finish up doing nothing he'll think we are.'

Inga was well aware she'd have to explain a series of cock-ups to Detective Super Craig Darke, the one being hammered relentlessly by the Chief Constable all concerned with public image.

The events of 2006 had returned to haunt the powers that be in the city. To now have the name Streeter return to expose it once again to the horrors of being splashed across the modern media would be as much as some of the self-obsessed could take.

The police chief would be apoplectic once he heard what she had to admit, and knew his suffering would more than likely bounce all the way down onto Craig Darke's desk.

She doubted whether Darke would ever have the guts to admit it to the Chief but the odds on finding Streeter second time around were not good. Not good at all.

19

As was very often the case, a verbal briefing to Craig Darke finished up with Larsson heading off at a tangent. He wanted more information on what Adrian Orford hoped to gain by looking into Macritchie and Hardaker. She guessed it was all to do with budgets and had his reasons for suddenly wanting ASBO to be back working solely on eTeam cases. That and moans from Stevens.

She wanted to make as much use of the IT guru as possible, especially as he appeared to be in a really good mood which was not always the case, yet at the same time Inga had no desire to upset Darke or give Stevens dressed like an investment banker an opportunity to poke his nose in.

The DI was aware how this Adrian could so easily interrogate people's laptops without their knowledge. Scan emails and texts at will. She had to assume the program he used Darke had told her about, was of the sort used to keep an eye on terrorists. According to the boss, those being investigated would never be aware their system had been turned on and off and compromised. Completely oblivious to the geek watching and listening into their private world. She was of course intrigued to know how the geek had got his hands on such a thing, but knew the answer would be simple. Don't ask.

'Correct me if I'm wrong, but are you suggesting that with wi-fi you can just log onto anybody's system if you've got the right piece of kit?'

'Password,' was all he said as if it was a guessing game.

'You need a password?' Inga asked the geek in all innocence.

'No,' he said and sighed with frustration. 'You can log on as long as it's not password protected obviously.'

'Obviously,' she shot back. 'And?' Why was it often like this with techy ASBO, you had to keep pressing. Interested in a subject for its own sake.

'You get a wireless router which is a bit of hardware which'll cost you a hundred and it puts out a signal. Then anyone with one of those within range can log onto the internet through it.' He raised a finger. 'As long as it's not password protected.' Hardware Inga has always understood and it made sense, but wondered why software was called that when you have no idea if it is. What exactly did they mean by soft? Do they mean soft and weedy or soft in the way marshmallow is?

'Like when I first go in? First thing I have to do is enter my password?' she was just checking.

'Yes,' said ASBO in a conciliatory manner as if she was a real computer refusenik.

'Let's get this straight,' she said slowly. 'If I've got one of these...'

'Wireless router.'

'Wireless router,' she repeated and wondered how big they'd be. 'If I were to walk down the road where I live I could just log onto anybody's system and onto the internet?' She hoped it was small enough to carry about or he was about to make her feel stupid, again.

'As I said.' His look brought her up short. 'Password, remember.'

'Which means it's free,' and the moment she'd said it she realized was a stupid thing to say. ASBO didn't react but his look said it all. 'Why would the average man in the street want to do that?' she asked. 'Hump one of these things about.'

'If you're out somewhere and decide you want to pick up your emails. You can just do it.'

'You are sure about this? Are you saying it could be this Hardaker goes all the way up there, sits outside their house and picks up what's going on?'

'Done it myself,' for a moment the DI wondered if it was strictly legal, bit like cannabis farms short circuiting the electricity supply, does the same apply to the net she wondered? 'Had my laptop open,' he said casually as if it was something everybody did. 'Suddenly I realized I'm on line. My system picked up a signal, meant I could download whatever it was I was after.' He said as if it were just an everyday event.

'And you'd be doing it to save money?' got her a nod, but then supernerd ASBO sucked in hard and noisily. 'Go on,' she encouraged.

'If you're lowlife and you want to make any message you send as difficult as hell to trace, you could do it that way.'

'Just how difficult would they be to track down?'

'You'd need to be a bit of a geek for sure. Ginky on overload more like.' Inga found it hard not to chuckle to herself having considered it a somewhat truly remarkable statement from someone like him.

'You really done that hidden messages bit?' She had to wait for a delayed reaction. 'Might I ask why?' she queried after the slight nod.

'See if it works,' he grinned.

'So you know for certain it's not an urban myth, not some on line rag and bone story.'

'Oh it works alright. And if you're up to no good,' he just grimaced. There was no need for anything further.

'Let's think about this,' she said. 'Hardaker has an issue about his daughter and not having access because she lives hundreds of miles away. What is to be gained by going all the way there just to poke his nose into their emails? It won't get him access next time school holidays come round. In fact she suspects it's him, so it'd make her even more determined she should ensure he doesn't see her.'

'Of course it could be somebody like Hardaker has hijacked her IP address,' would need an explanation for Inga. 'Of course autonomous systems often ISPs will usually use designated IP prefixes to...'

'Enough now.' ASBO almost looked hurt that she should stop him before he'd got going on this new tack.

'If somebody took control of your IP address,' he stopped and looked at her.

'So far, so good.'

'If they've done that your IP address can then be used for nice things such as spamming and stopping you working on your system as normal.'

'But it's only her laptop, her email address apparently. Not the biscuit business system where someone could do real damage. Stupid question,' she popped in before he went off again. She knew almost anything she asked King Geek here would be considered stupid. 'How IT literate do you need to be for all this business?'

'Google anything you want and if you know a computer mechanical student or some geezer working in IT, be easy.'

'You don't need to drive the way up north for this option?' ASBO shook his head. 'So it is possible he's just making her life difficult, putting the frighteners on her, but is never actually turn up there or do anything physically damaging.' ASBO just sat there looking at her, almost as if what she was saying was of absolutely no interest to him.

'Could be fraud,' he said suddenly, as if he had a need to get back on subject. 'Has somebody infiltrated their business maybe.'

'He said it was her personal laptop one she uses for emails and Facebook.

'Still,' he leant his head to one side. 'Maybe they don't know somebody is poking their nose into their business and into their accounts. Any chance of blackmail? Remember internet routing nodes have no conscience, they're not like people, they wouldn't know fraud from a jelly baby.'

Rumour had it this ASBO had developed two mobile apps to earn him more than a few pennies on top of his salary.

Inga was well aware this strange guy spent his entire life trawling, worming and crawling through people's lives. People who had absolutely no idea he was ever there. Yet as far as she had been able to gather he had no proper life of his own. Not even a gaming freak as he'd told her more than once he hates them, everything they stand for and what they get involved in with a vengeance. Stevens had told her one day when she'd queried his stance, how it was all to do with war. ASBO is an out and out pacifist and wants nothing to do with boring war games, battles to the death or fighting stupid childish monsters.

According to the lads in CSI he regularly breaks his way through folk's carefully constructed impenetrable firewalls to poke his nose into their world. Probably because he appeared to have no life of his own.

According to Jake Goodwin he'd been reliably informed how people had seen ASBO operating in front of people's eyes just like a techy version of the invisible man. He'd told her a tale about Orford over coffee one day.

'D'you know what his most sophisticated system of comms involves?'

'No. Tell me.' Inga knew anything was possibly the answer.

'Says it's the perfect way,' Jake had said. 'He uses...phone boxes,' and Inga scrunched up her face in sheer disbelief. 'Calls from say an old red phone box out in one of the villages because they can't be scanned. GCHQ have no idea what you're doing, who you're calling.'

'You serious?' but knew Jake was, he was hardly ever anything but.

'Call lasting thirty seconds might as well have never happened.'

'All this,' she'd had to stop to giggle. 'Ultra wizzo technology from the next century and just like vinyl the old systems still prove to be the best.'

Inga knew there was to her mind always an issue allowing this Orford to go off on a tangent of his own volition, especially as he was on Stevens' team. If through his mysterious hacking techniques he emerged from his little cyber jungle with information of a seriously dubious and sensitive nature she knew she'd have to find a way to explain. How they'd come up with data said to be beyond everybody's reach in court when asked by a clever-dick barrister was never just a case of asking the fountain of e-knowledge to explain how he'd got his mits on it.

Lie is what she'd have to do. Lie convincingly.

It was a while before Inga had given her answer to the question Jake Goodwin had posed on their way down to MIT. "How do you plan to explain this?"

She spent the intervening period holed up in her office with just her PC for company before she emerged to make her announcement.

Inga Larsson clapped her hands. 'Team briefing in five,' provided the occupants of the incident room with the opportunity to end phone calls, log out, reach a convenient point on their enquiries to pay attention, to slip their cheese sarnie into a drawer and swallow the last lump of Twix

'Remember when we first started out investigating the murder of Mindi Brookes and CSI discovered fresh DNA for a woman who had been dead about eleven years?' she asked and paused. 'Remember some of you interviewed Susan Sawyer some sort of Futures Executive for a major hotel chain?' She looked at Julie and Ruth in particular. Julie nodded but Ruth looked more sceptical.

'Go on,' she just had to utter.

'Susan Sawyer who went to Forest Girls School back sixteen or more years ago...' Inga smiled and hesitated to create an effect. 'Drowned in 2000.'

'Bollocks!' said Ruth before she covered half her face with her hand and peered at the boss with one eye. Julie bless her soul just sat there with her mouth open.

'But she's a big cheese and she's...'

'Launching a new hotel?' a smiling Inga jumped in shaking her head. 'Is she buggery? She died on 26th February 2000 whilst on Half Term holiday with her parents in the Isle of Wight. I have here a print out of the death certificate and if you so wish I can no doubt get you all the details of the cremation including the hymns, and I have even spoken to one woman who was there. At the cremation, who informs me many of the girls from the school also attended the funeral.'

'I don't understand,' said Ruth, looking about for help in her confusion and anguish.

'You're not the only one,' the DI responded.

'Why would you phone up and say you have information on this Christine Streeter, go to all the trouble of organizing a meeting with us in her hotel and...' she stopped when Inga's head began to shake.

'Guess what?' Jake jumped in. 'She doesn't work for the hotel or the hotel group. They have never heard of a Susan Sawyer and apart from the fact the owners of the hotel you went to know nothing of anyone by her name, they do not have a Futures Executive. In fact they asked me what the title meant. Plus I'm sorry to say they have no plans to open a hotel in Birmingham and there is no Spiceal Grand in the city nor is one planned.'

'But the staff,' said Ruth and looked at Julie. 'Were all cow towing to her, like she was God.'

'Quite a performance then,' said Inga still with more than a hint of a grin. 'I've spoken to the hotel and they tell me the room and coffee and biscuits for three were reserved by...a Susan Sawyer.'

'So,' said Jake slowly. 'If we'd checked up, they would have confirmed a Susan Sawyer did indeed have a booking with them.'

'Exactly.'

'Why be so elaborate?' dour Sam Howard from the back asked. 'Again.'

'Think someone asked at the time why didn't the Angela Gray you met organize the meet somewhere like Starbucks or wherever, why go to all the trouble to make a pie, same with this woman. Why be so painstaking?'

'Angela Wilcox,' said Jake Goodwin as a reminder.

'As most of you already know, Jake and I met a woman called Angela Wilcox, which was Angela Gray's name before she married. The name she had when she was a pupil at the Forest school. Had her checked out,' she said stood there with her arms folded. 'She most certainly is in the Army, she has just served a tour of duty in Belize and she is a Lieutenant medic. She's real, she all adds up according to none other than the MOD.'

'She told us about a group calling themselves Tri...sorry got in a muddle. I nearly said triage,' Jake smirked.

'You're spending too much time with a nurse!'

'Troika, I meant to say. Who bullied girls at the school,' he went on. 'And a woman in the north of Scotland has confirmed to us she was one of the three bullies, along with...'

'Two more dead people,' Inga could not resist.

'Lottie Elliott and Jane Green.'

'The woman in the hit and run?' Raza just checked.

'What in god's name is going on?'

'She had the works,' said an obviously annoyed and obviously conned Ruth Buchan. 'She really did look the part, a real off the top shelf executive. The hair, the designer glasses, the heavy make-up, the suit and shoes. The shiny all-singing-all-dancing phone with the Man in the Moon on speed dial if you want, I bet.'

'Perhaps it's what she is,' boss Inga suggested. 'Not in the hotel business, but something else.'

'So why not be herself?' Julie asked. 'If you're a senior sales executive for a chemical company or a media executive for Sky why pretend you're in the hotel business?' She blew out a breath of frustration. 'Had me fooled and no mistake.'

'So our tame geeks can't track her down,' Inga replied and pointed to the ceiling. 'We've spoken to the real life Angela Wilcox remember.'

Inga strolled into her office and laid out neatly across her desk side by side were printouts she guessed were from Adrian who must have called in whilst she was in the loo.

'Boss,' said Raza Latif at her door. 'You did mean what I think you mean?' he asked as she looked up. 'Do you really want to know who Liverpool were playing the day Streeter disappeared?' she nodded. 'It was a Friday, so you want the Saturday fixture?' Inga nodded again and added a smile.

'Helen Nevins husband's a Liverpool fanatic and she now thinks he may well be checking up on her.'

'Checking up now,' he said. 'Then it becomes stalking, then he puts saucy photos of her on the net and...'

'You get the picture,' his boss chortled. 'Long shot I know but this is all such a mess we need to check every little snippet. Could he have been involved? Tell you what, check who they were playing on the date the one had her drink spiked in the pub too.' She turned her attention back to Adrian's gift on her desk.

'How...?' Raza dared.

'I don't know how he might be involved,' she replied strongly. 'But if he's not I just need to cross him off the damn list,' Raza must have accepted and trudged off. Be the sort Inga guessed the media would describe as a *lovable rogue* when in truth he'd be a complete dickhead as they usually were.

Back to the gift. There was a birth certificate for a Helen Eve Nevins, a marriage certificate to Roger Hardaker, birth certificate for each of her daughters. Lisa Gerrard with Hardaker named as the father in 2009 and Catriona Helen with Logan Macritchie as daddy just a little under four years ago. When she lifted a couple of sheets to read she discovered more information hidden underneath. A birth certificate for Logan Angus Macritchie told her he was forty one.

She then discovered an email from one of Adrian's minions telling her all about the Macritchie artisan biscuit business, about the shortbread with a difference and oatcakes he produced along with Bannocks and Black Buns. She was pleased he'd taken the trouble to explain. For someone brought up on Brunscrackers and the team's favourite cake she made for them occasionally Princesstårta. These were certainly new to her. According to this self-confessed nerd a Black Bun is a "type of fruit cake topped and tailed in pastry", and a Bannock is flat quick bread. What he emphasized was how all products even down to the very basics of his biscuit range were all true to original recipes some dating back centuries he had discovered from somewhere.

It was a relief to put two more people to the back of her mind along with the Army's Angela Wilcox.

Next up was her pal Lizzie the HOLMES wiz walking into her office and sitting herself down without so much as a by your leave thrusting a self-satisfied grin in her direction.

'Go on,' she sighed. 'Out with it.'

'Heard all about this Susan Sawyer business and got to wondering why somebody is posing as her. See it dozens of times in movies where the baddy takes the identity of as dead person. Susan Sawyer drowned, so I wondered if she'd been used.'

'And,' said Inga expecting and prepared for more bad news.

'I traced her details back from the police reports on the drowning. There has never been a passport issued to Susan Sawyer, no National Insurance Number issued, nothing with HMRC and all I've managed to find is her National Health Service Number which has not been used since her death.'

'Just using the name then?'

'Seems like it.'

Inga managed to catch Ruth's eye out in the room, and she walked in. 'You've got more identity info have you?'

'Just historic really. There's the harrowing story I've come across about over forty babies who once had their identities stolen by the Met.' Her boss released a breath noisily at the mention of the name.

'Was it where they scoured cemeteries all over the place for details of children who'd died and would be about the same age as the undercover cops who needed a new ID?'

'The very one,' Ruth responded. 'Apparently parents are still seeking answers.'

'They've got no chance,' was Lizzie. 'Not with the Met.'

'If they could manage to do it to forty or more kids it must be possible for someone like Streeter to do it with one poor mite. Go to the local paper archives on line, see what little girl died around when she was born.'

'I know we need to use false identities,' said Inga languorously, 'but doing it wholesale and still keeping quiet all this time later is more than gruesome.'

'What is known as the Jackal Run.'

'Sad thing is, some of these poor people may never know if their babies' identities have been stolen,' Ruth advised. She had not of course been involved, but her time with Family Liaison told her how those parents would suffer.

'Thanks,' Inga sighed.

20

Years of dedicated work with the HOLMES system which ironically had been set up for major fraud cases because of their complexity and the hunting of serial killers, and Lizzie Webb had come up with a few more answers. She was however first to admit how she regarded it as a team effort, a feminine team effort she emphasized to boss woman Inga as there had been considerable input from Julie, Gillian and Ruth.

'Before I get onto my reason for this, can I just say all the way through this process, the basic scenario has been devoid of any serious hits to take us forward.'

Inga guessed it was the 'no body' when they scanned over databases which brought up next to nothing. Her job, his job, descriptions, him out fishing all produced hits but the moment the lack of cadaver was added they all just slid away.

'Other elements when added instead such as betrayal, revenge, reprisal and grudge-bearing were providers of previous cases until the no corpse was plopped in to sink the bounty.'

'All the time we include no body it's as if HOLMES is telling us something.'

Rachel Somers was first up when Lizzie got on to her reason for being there. Rachel Amanda Somers to give her full title, had been Rachel Gillespie for five years but had now reverted back to her single status as her Bobby had done a runner with a slapper from work.

'This one is a blank,' said Lizzie.

'Does nobody stay married these days?'

News on the radio on her way in told Inga how divorce rates had soared, which had then been dispelled when the reporter explained how these days same-sex unions are included to skew-whiff the figures and make it another non-story.

Lizzie smiled and carried on. 'Got a new kid by her new bloke and she's the sort you can see filling up coffee shops most of the morning with their pushchairs and hogging tables piled high with feeding bottles and nappies desperate to me a yummy mummy. She's well into all this having missed out first time around as apparently this Robert Gillespie announced just after they wed how he didn't want kids at any price. Now she's making a meal of being mumsy. As they do.'

'Mornings are the worst,' said Julie when Inga wished she'd kept quiet.

Inga was constantly worried how as a result of a truly horrific and brutal relationship in her past, Lizzie Webb now had a downer on some young mums. The DI would be first to agree how at times it can feel as if they want to take over the world and consider nobody but themselves. Other selfish mums and the wee things they drag out in all weathers to completely the wrong environments appear to assume they have right of passage.

Inga doubted very much whether her badly damaged pal Lizzie would allow a man into her life ever again, such was the horrors she had suffered and the miscarriages she had endured as a result. This meant she would most likely remain childless, a sad sector of the community these giggly mummy types seem cruelly quite unwilling to recognize quite often. As far as they are concerned having babies is just a given.

Inga was also aware how she might just be unkindly comparing some young dregs she sees about with young mothers from her homeland, where there is an entirely different attitude and mix of sexes. A way of life many young couples possibly hanker after, but she is aware how only a real insight into a different mindset and ingrained attitudes will enable change to take place.

In Stockholm it is unlikely the new young mums would corral together in the way she and Lizzie are used to seeing. She cannot recall having ever seen two dads out together in the UK feeding their babies and chatting over Americanos.

She was used to a greater gender mix rather than the "them and us" feelings these young women engender as if the male of the species is a necessary evil they are forced to endure

As it turned out this Rachel Somers when interviewed could hardly remember the names of anybody she went to school with save for one or two, and when prompted really had no idea what had happened to them.

The names of those she did have an inkling about were never on the case radar and she had very quickly been disregarded.

'And her story is,' Inga prompted.

'The berk she married was an habitual adulterer,' happily married Gillian Brown-Reid advised. 'But that wasn't the worst of it. Unbenown to this Rachel one of his loves, although there probably wasn't anything approaching actual love, had got pregnant. When it became plainly obvious and she was told who people thought the father might be, she finally kicked him out.' Slender brunette Gillian put a hand up to stop any interruptions. 'Now the useless sod who wanted nothing to do with babies has a son he'll be playing football with before you can turn round.'

'Really get my goat some of these,' said Lizzie. 'Did your mother spend half her life supping some ridiculous coffee with cream and chocolate sprinkles? Saw half a dozen of them last week,' said Lizzie. 'Really put me off my latte. Sat there covered in sick taking selfies of this little kid with a stupid big pink bow in her hair. God I really felt for the kid lumbered with a useless mother like her!'

'Rebecca Melanie Odling,' said Inga to move angry Lizzie on from the subject of her envy before she started going off on one about young mums and forward facing baby slings she knew actually frighten the children in them. Alas Lizzie having a rant was never going to stop these peer pressure controlled young mothers.

'Why do people have such complicated lives?' Lizzie asked nobody in particular. 'This is another one. Rebecca Odling. Got some of the chit-chat from PC Barry Dendy's wife.' She looked up from her tablet. 'They live in the same road,' she said to explain. 'Rebecca Odling so the story goes works shifts in a care home, was married but it went toes up when she got pregnant by her boyfriend, who then cleared off.'

'What has it got to do with the case?' Inga asked firmly as officers grimaced at one another.

'Nothing,' said Lizzie. 'Lived out at Eagle when she was married, now shacked up with some new much younger lover boy off Monks Road still works at a care home.'

'Cross her off the list,' Inga dismissed.

'Reason this little list has taken a while is the last one,' said Ruth. 'Even then we had to seek the help of the upstairs geeks.'

'Carly Kirsten Hills,' said Lizzie Webb. 'Which she still is,' she said as she flicked down on her tablet. 'Here goes,' she said when she found what she was looking for. 'Left school at the same time as all the rest including our Christine Streeter, but within months she had left these shores for Canada. Her father was a high flying senior accountant for a major player in the car hire business worldwide. In the last two or three years of her time at Forest School he had commuted down to London on a weekly basis to their UK office. Then he was head-hunted by their head office in Toronto.' Lizzie lifted her head. 'Gillian, you've got the next bit.'

'Carly Hills went first to catering college and then took a degree in hospitality in Canada. Now we have tracked her down to her role as Manager of a catering francise in a huge baseball stadium complex. Dealing apparently with everything from popcorn to hoagies.'

'What's a hoagie?' DI Inga had to ask.

''Submarine sandwich,' said Gillian. 'With meat or cheese or whatever takes your fancy.'

'Someone once told me,' Julie added. 'A real hoagie should be made with Italian ham and salami.'

'Think this Carly has her hands full with that lot.'

'Deals in everything from nachos to candy, burgers, hot dogs and ice cream not to mention all the beers.'

'Never likely to have popped over here messing about and having anything to do with Christine Streeter.'

'When we caught up with her the other day she said she could just about remember Christine at school, but had no idea she had been missing all this time. Said for a year or two she'd kept up a sort of pen pal relationship with a couple of old school chums but like they do it soon drifted away to nothing.' Ruth sniggered. 'Then she said she'd suddenly remembered how some called her Princess because she was so precious.'

'Not heard that before.'

'So it was all a waste of time,' Julie sighed.

'Not exactly,' said Inga. 'Those three names we've had mentioned none of whom it would appear had any involvement years later in what happened to Streeter. Might be only three but its cutting down the field.'

Inga's last message for Julie and Ruth when they set off from MIT to interview a woman about Mindi Brookes was plain and simple.

'If her hair won't move even if you kicked it, if she has too much slap, scary eyebrows, black nails and heels she'll regret one day. No arguments bang the cuffs on her.' She sniggered. 'If she offers to bake you a pie you do the same!'

It had been a real team effort and certainly a case of out of acorns with them finally coming across a woman who claimed to have information about Mindi Brookes sudden exit from a job. With Inga's words ringing in their ears and stark memories of their meeting with Angela Gray nee Wilcox and Susan Sawyer they were determined not to get hoodwinked again.

They were both aware this interview could so easily be carried out by telephone, but at the same time they didn't need Inga to remind them of exactly why this had to be person to person.

This woman who had worked for some time at the Northwater Manor Spa Hotel complex at the same time as Mindi Brookes was somebody Laurence Haffenden, who'd annoyed Jake, had discovered for them.

It was back up the A1 in dull and dank weather for the pair to meet this Beth Casey now running a hairdressing salon on the outskirts of Harrogate.

Altogether too much, too rabbit-in-the-headlights alarm on her face when they were introduced which immediately had Ruth asking why. Threading, trimming and Hena tinting were all listed in the quiet corner of the salon away from the hair stylists.

Beth Casey's hair was pale brown going on blonde and could have been very attractive for someone in her mid-forties if it were not for the hideous stark black eyebrow creating the inevitable angry look.

Looking at her Ruth felt safe in the knowledge they were dealing with exactly who she said she was and who Haffenden had said she was.

They quickly got down to the pre-amble about why they were there and had to put up with how she had moved from the service she provided at Northwater to now running her own salon although she did no actual hairdressing.

'Mindi Brookes,' said Ruth eventually.

'Oh her,' she scoffed.

'What can you tell us?'

'Up to all sorts that one.'

'What exactly? Any chance you can be more specific?'

'Guess it'd be the credit card scam business what finally got her the poke lass, and not before time either.'

'Why do you say that?'

'Queries with petty cash, stock being nicked, stuff disappearing. Real bad lot and no mistake.'

'Tell me about the credit card business.'

'Like a lamb to the slaughter couldn't have happened to a nastier person, denied it of course then tried to blame the swimming teacher woman who was about around that time. Picked on the wrong one there.'

'The swimming teacher?'

'No,' she laughed. 'The secret shopper.'

'Secret shopper? You saying she…'

'Scammed his card or whatever it is they do,' she chuckled again. 'How stupid was she? Ridiculous. We all knew what he was, stood out a bloody mile like, except that silly bitch. Real good laugh gotta say.'

'Hang on,' said Ruth to stop her. 'Think you need to start again. We've had swimming teacher and secret shopper. Are you saying this was how she was discovered through a secret shopper?'

'Yeh, and tried to blame the teacher.' She stopped as if that was all.

'Are you saying Mindi Brookes was fiddling the credit cards and was caught out by a secret shopper?'

'Yeh. Can't for the life of me remember who she was?' Beth shrugged. 'Not important anyway it was Brookes what got kicked out in the end and not before time let me tell you.'

'Can I just ask,' was Julie. 'It's some time since you were at Northwater, so how were they able to get in touch with you?'

'Me niece works there. They was asking about like and she mentioned it to me. I remember all that business,' she said as if she wore those events as a badge of pride. 'Well, you would, wouldn't you?'

'Guess so.'

'As well as the credit card business, you say she was stealing as well,' was Ruth's next question.

'Had no proof, but soon as they showed her the door all that sorta thing stopped. We'd had our suspicions coz of what she was like. Worse thing you can do steal off your workmates I reckon.'

'You didn't get on?' Julie tried.

'Certainly not. Too highfalutin for my liking.'

Exactly what the boss was after. Confirmation of the late Mindi Brookes working at Northwater and had left under a cloud. Ruth could not recall anybody else suggesting this Mindi Brookes was trying to be something she was surely not. Different people, differing views and opinions.

DS Jake Goodwin had been waiting in drizzly rain sat in his car right outside the home of Roger Hardaker when he arrived home from work at a small engineering firm in Grimsby.

The house where he lived in Waltham south of the town was ex-local government property someone had bought off the council some time back and had no doubt made a good wack when they sold it to Hardaker.

First thing Jake noticed was no obvious reference to Liverpool or even to football. He was not one of those who live in their replica shirt, had not given the house a name like Anfield or had stickers and scarves adoring the rear of his Micra.

Mariesha Kurzawska his partner wore the trousers in their household of that Jake was absolutely certain from the moment he was invited in. Roger might well have left the Detective Sergeant stood on the doorstep but Mariesha was the one to invite him in, make him feel at home. She was an absolute delight, offered him a choice of tea or coffee and a plate of digestive biscuits she placed on the table as he was talking to Roger Hardaker.

It was obvious to Jake Goodwin how this guy wasn't the one who had taken control of Helen Macritchie's IP address. Unless they were both acting well enough for a BAFTA they only had rudimentary knowledge of IT between them. She used Facebook to keep in touch with her pals through a tablet, when she brought up her page at his request for Jake to see. He mentally made a note of just 34 friends, and Roger claimed he didn't bother with social media. For the first time football was then mentioned when Roger admitted in the main he used the internet to keep an eye on football matters, scores and the like.

The moment he began to delve into that aspect of the man's life it was obvious this Roger was still a Liverpool supporter, but he was living a new life amongst different people and even admitted being a complete prick earlier in his life. Yes he would very much like to see his daughter living in Scotland, but these days with a young son and Mariesha pregnant again he was quite willing to wait until Lisa became old enough to make her own decisions about him.

'What made you stop heading for Anfield every fortnight?'

'Stupid money,' surprised the copper as he expected to be asked how he knew.

'To get in?'

'Nah just all of it, mate.'

'How do you mean all of it?'

'Football's not what it was,' Hardaker said. 'Even call it stupid footie these days, whas that all about? All to do with money from damn foreigners who own the clubs to the multi-millionaire players with daft haircuts. And don't get me started on bloody agents what 'ave ruined the game.' Just happened to be very similar to what Jake thought of football these days. 'You gotta team?'

'Fraid not,' Jake admitted. 'Well, Lincoln I suppose.'

He knew there was no connection with Liverpool playing when Mindi Brookes was murdered as it was when internationals were being played. Nor was there any connection with the death down in Peterborough as that had been out of season.

'Better off without if you ask me. Just not fit enough seems to me. I could easy to go to a game only to find some of the poor darlings are too tired from a mid-week Champions League game they can't possibly play on Saturday.' This Roger sighed with frustration and shook his head. 'I could be paying a small fortune to watch half a dozen reserves coz the fancy dan foreigners are not fit.' Jake went to add a word about wishing he only worked ninety minutes a week but was beaten to it. 'Take those Brownlie lads in the Olympics, bet they swim, run and bike every day. Not jog around a field once a week. But then I bet they don't roll out o'nightclubs in the early hours,' he sneered.

'Think you're probably right.'

'Bill Shankley'd turn in his grave if he knew what was going on,' at least there he was quite likely spot on.

This was to all extent and purposes a changed man from the one Helen Mcritchie spoke about. He had grown up and matured. Lived for his partner, his son and their soon to be bigger family. This Roger held down a decent job as far as Jake could gather and offered the name of his boss if he needed to check him out. Admitted he'd been to see Liverpool play just twice the previous season and smiled when conceding he'd actually attended double the number of Grimsby games.

'You know your daughter's in Scotland then?'

'Yeh.'

'You ever been up there?' Jake posed.

'No chance.'

'Why did you say that?'

'Can't stand 'em.'

'Can't stand who?'

'Scots, 'specially that fish woman whatever her name is.'

'Sturgeon? Nicola Sturgeon you mean?'

'Yeh she's the one. No tuition fees, prescription charges, get loadsa things we don't get down here and it's our money. Whas that all about?'

'So you've not ventured over the border?'

'No bloody chance. Steer well clear of blokes in skirts let me tell you,' Hardaker released a snicker. 'Can't understand a bloody word they say, and their football's crap too.'

Jake thought of asking his opinion of the Welsh and Irish but decided he'd more than likely have a biased view of them.

He sensed how this Roger Hardaker could easily lose his rag over next to nothing as his ex-wife had suggested when Liverpool results went against him. Yet on the other hand on his way back Jake did wonder if Helen for some reason had made more of their marriage difficulties than was entirely honest. Was a bad marriage the reason why Roger had become intolerant and difficult to live with? Always possible he decided Helen was the bad apple in some form rather than Liverpool Football Club?

21

Ruth Buchan had arranged to interview Hope Parkes at work on the basis it would be difficult for her to deceive both her and Julie Rhoades again.

Typical UK weather. Lovely unusually warm weekend when she was working, then the wind from some hurricane, back to calm and now pouring in less than a week.

Sitting there in her green scrubs and a red and white bandana, arms resting on the table and hands clenched together, Hope Parkes was not at all happy. Her greeting had been curt.

It was a small office, obviously used for meetings of some sort and consisted of just two tables with metal legs and a dozen chairs stacked in one corner. They'd had to pull a chair off the pile each before they could sit down. No tea or coffee, not even a jug of water. Could have been anywhere but the smell was a giveaway, it smelt like a hospital, the unique smell all their own.

'My husband says,' she began. 'I shouldn't be meeting you on my own, says this is starting to amount to police harassment.'

'What gives you that idea?' Ruth asked gently.

'You turn up at home asking for somebody I've never heard of, then you came back I assume because what I told you wasn't good enough.' She sighed and pointed a finger at Ruth. 'I told you the truth, it's who I am. My mum told me time and again when I was young. Life might be hard at times pet, but if you always tell the truth nobody can accuse you of anything, like they'll try to do.'

'Would you like a union rep with you?' Julie asked.

'You're joking. Don't want everybody knowing my business.'

'But if you feel you'd be better if someone was...'

'Just get on with it,' she snapped.

'Fair enough,' Ruth sighed and shrugged.

'If you didn't lend your house to Angela Wilcox, who did you lend it to?'

'Is it against the law?'

'No, but I still require you to answer the question.' Ruth had seen Hope as a particularly strong woman, but all of a sudden she had gone and so had her stance and all replaced by tears. They both waited.

'Didn't work did it?' she sniveled. 'I told the truth I answered your questions truthfully. Been better off if I'd lied I reckon, eh?'

'You tell us.'

Hope sniffed. 'Never get the house now will we? Oh dear,' she sighed and the two detectives realized she was struggling with how to react, what to say as she looked all about as if searching for salvation.

'Why is that?'

'Can't raise the deposit,' she said sounding more composed. 'Every day which passes the price of houses goes up and it's like chasing the cat's tail all the time, we never quite manage it. We raise an extra hundred, price goes up hundred and twenty. Raise interest rates next I bet, then we've got no chance.'

'What has all this got to do with somebody using your house?'

'That was the deal,' Parkes said as if it was obvious and with heavy breaths her head hung and she let it swing from side to side.

'What deal?'

'Borrow the house for an afternoon in exchange for the deposit.' Ruth could have done with an instant replay as she wondered if she'd heard right.

'You were offered the deposit for a house in exchange for allowing Angela Wilcox to use your house for an hour or two?'

Julie checked what sounded as incredulous. 'Is that really what you're saying?'

Hope Parkes just sat there with her head just wobbling from side to side. 'How many more times?' she gasped and with her head now raised she looked at Ruth with a look of anger. 'I don't know any Angela Wilcox,' was louder. 'I asked my husband and he doesn't know anybody by that name. Worked with an Angela once yonks ago, he says. Like I said, I told you the truth before and it doesn't matter how many times you ask me, how you ask me, however you twist it to suit, I do not know Angela Wilcox. Why won't you believe me?'

'We're only...'

'Hang on,' Hope interrupted loudly and sat back in her chair and folded her arms. 'Would you be happier if I told you a bunch of lies? Is that what you want, this how it works? Be what you're used to criminals doing eh?' She blew out a big breath of utter frustration. 'Not like this on the tele.'

'Please,' said Ruth softly. 'We are only interested in the truth.'

'And it's what I've been telling you for crissakes!' was shouted. 'Just fuckin' listen will you?'

'Please Hope,' was gentle when Ruth wanted to be the opposite. 'You say you lent your house to somebody but if it wasn't Angela Wilcox. Then who was it?'

'It was,' Hope hesitated and looked at the officer. 'Carly Hills,' she said softly and reluctantly.

Two minds were like helter skelters spinning round and round searching for the name, as they glanced at each other.

'In exchange for what?' said Ruth trying hard not to show how the name had landed. 'This Carly Hills was doing what for you?'

'Paying our deposit.' She tutted and sighed. 'Not as straight forward as that. She owns the house, one of those lucky sods who can buy up houses people like us have to rent. We rent it off her and doing this told us we won't have to save any more for the deposit, she's knocking it off the price.' She shook her head. 'Was.'

'Why d'you say that?'

'Not likely to now is she,' Hope said without a glimmer of enthusiasm. 'This'll probably get us kicked out.' Hope Parkes closed her eyes and tears rolled down her cheeks. 'What a bloody mess!'

'This Carly Hills,' Julie chipped in. 'What does she look like?'

'Part from the hair, she's very normal really. Got those jeans with rips in the knees seems all the fashion with some. Just ordinary really.'

'You say apart from the hair.'

'Sort of pale blue, like kingfisher blue and black.'

'Tall, short, fat, thin would you say?'

'Slim, bit shorter than me.'

'Did she say why she wanted to use the house?'

'No, just asked if I'd do her a favour, said she had to meet someone on neutral ground.'

'How often do you meet...Carly Hills?' Ruth enquired.

'Only time, well twice. Once when she popped in to make the arrangements and once when she called to pick up a spare key.'

'And you'd not seen her before?'

'No.'

'Has your husband met her?'

'Richard? No.' Hope looked at each detective in turn quickly. 'She in trouble?'

'Be up to our boss,' Ruth advised. 'Does this Carly Hills deal with your property personally or is it through an agent?'

'Agent. First time I've ever met her, didn't know it was a woman owned it.'

'Can I ask,' was Julie who was going to anyway. 'Did she threaten you, did she say if you tell the police you won't get the house?'

'What? Blackmail you mean?' Julie nodded slightly. 'No, never said anything, certainly never mentioned police or anybody. Just thought we were doing her a bit of a favour for some reason.'

'Do you have the name of the agent who deals with your house?'

'Got their card in my wallet, but,' she patted the sides of her legs. 'Wallet and everything is in my locker I'm afraid.'

'Can you remember the name?'

'Yeh, no probs.' Ruth slid her notebook across the small table and with a pen Julie provided, Hope Parkes wrote down the name and address. 'Not absolutely sure about the email though.'

'That's fine,' said Ruth as she took the pad and pen back.

The two women detectives made a half-hearted apology for having needed to speak to her again, made no assurances about the requirement to talk to her again and headed from the complex round into the car park.

'The boss will go ape shit! Carly Hills!' Ruth shouted. 'If I'm not much mistaken, she's the one in Canada. What in God's name is going on?'

'Carly Hills property owner, buy to let, we have the agents address. Beggars belief this.'

'Next stop. Need the sat nav for this.'

'Smell of hospitals really gets to me. Almost as if it's done on purpose so you know for sure where you are. Sort of a danger aroma, this is where they cut you open, here's where people die.'
'Lodoform.'
'What?'
'Think it's a form of anaesthetic, they sometimes use as a disinfectant. Lodoform I think the smell is.'

'Please miss can I dip out next time?' Ruth said to her boss Inga stood in front of her desk. 'Every time I come back I feel like a naughty schoolgirl stood in here facing the head.'
'I'm starting to get fed up with this too.'
'According to Hope Parkes this one's got pale blue and black hair.'
'Be easy to spot then.'
'But no,' said Ruth leaning forward slightly. 'One of the things I've learnt about taking on a new identity with the amount I've read, there are those who say keep as dull and normal as possible just do your best to become part of the crowd. Then there's another theory about how things like hair and clothes take people's attention away. If this Carly Hills walked down the road, all people would remember is the hair. They'd never go home and say they saw a woman in town with a pert little nose or a nice pair of lips. I'd be, saw this odd ball woman with blue hair.'
'And not have a clue what she looked like.'
'What they reckon anyway.'
Inga looked down at the papers on her desk. 'Hope Parkes specifically said Carly Hills had borrowed her house for an hour or two, but when you went to speak to the agent he said he didn't know a Carly Hills, never dealt with a Carly Hills. The house in Daffodil Road is owned by a buy to rent property company registered abroad and according to our friend ASBO the IPC address of the website and email is registered to an address in Leeds.'
'Which is where we've been after seeing Parkes.'
'And number 147 doesn't exist,' said Inga looking down at the sheet in front of her. 'For a second bloody time!' She screwed her

eyes tight shut, then lifted her head. 'Same bloody address we had for the phone in the name of Helen Nevins!'

Ruth was seriously struggling to get her head round all this. 'The agent Parkes put us onto says they do everything on line with these people, and asking about seems all this buying and selling property is done on line these days. Nobody writes letters back and forth, so the address not existing is no problem to them. They don't need one and never use it.'

'There's a scam I think we came up against one time, where they know the postman drops letters for say a missing 147 through the door for 145 rather than take them back. What's the betting this Carly Hills is paying the person at 145 to collect mail for her?' Inga chuckled at the look, on Ruth's face as she allowed herself to slump down in her chair.

'Do I have a choice?' Ruth asked quietly. 'Wait for the postman to turn up?'

'I don't think so. If she does the majority of her business by email which seems quite likely these days, how often will there be letters? You could be sat outside forever and a day and I'll have the boss rattling my cage about wasting the budget again.'

'Bit like a merry go round,' said Julie. 'Every time it spins round somebody else jumps on.'

Inga waved to Detective Sergeant Jacques 'Jake' Goodwin out in the incident room and they all waited for him to join them. 'You heard about this?' Inga asked him and he nodded with a huge grin. 'It's not funny,' she smirked.

'No ma'am.'

'Where we going from here?'

Ruth Buchan had put her boss Inga onto a website about how people disappear or rather the process they go through to make finding them almost impossible for the layman and in many cases the authorities.

She and Adam were at their dining table, glasses of red to hand reading about people all over the world wanting to evaporate, to forget their past, the good as well as the bad and head for what a great deal of people would regard as a meaningless future.

One person's guide the pair of them had read included the suggestion of wearing ill-fitting shoes to make your gait different. Losing weight was another idea but often easier said than done.

Some people she realized have good reason to seek pastures new. To free themselves from a criminal record which of course can permanently hold them back in life or a seriously bad credit rating. Run away from a violent father, husband or partner or just to lose all the emotional baggage and detritus we all gather over the years and carry around with us.

How good would it be to wake up one day to discover all the emotional silliness, the grudges, the enemies, sexual abuse or people you simply cannot abide have all gone in a puff of smoke.

Problem is waking up on the streets or some dive somewhere would be good news mixed with bad and in many cases frighteningly bad.

Get away with it and you can design a new you, in fact create for yourself what businesses pay a fortune for, become a new brand. Inga knew every month many people decide for reasons best known to themselves to simply vanish.

Inga had read about a number of very strange events Adam found particularly intriguing.

A man in Colorado disappeared at half time during a Broncos American Football match in Denver.

Of course Inga was well aware people understandably do a runner if they know they are likely to be sent to prison, particularly those without a criminal record.

There are some who actually go in for pseudocide, to fake one's death to make people believe you have committed suicide. Difficult to achieve Inga imagined without a body. Others do go to the trouble of faking their own abduction.

One such guy was reported missing after going swimming and had never returned to shore to the people he was with. A body was never washed up and his friends and family assumed he had been abducted. His attempt at deception didn't last too long as weeks later he was stopped for speeding.

Debt is one heck of a very good reason to do a runner and of course so is life insurance if you are in cahoots with someone who will benefit.

Naturally the military have people who can no longer face the rigours of seemingly pointless conflicts or the constant unnecessary discipline but are of course in this day and age still called deserters for some reason.

Julie Rhoades had reminded Inga there are folk all over the country with a missing loved one who they keep their bedroom like a shrine for. Completely untouched waiting for their return, no matter how long that might take. Ruth had wondered if Kathleen Streeter had done so even though her daughter had already left home when she went missing. They'd never thought of checking when they had the ideal opportunity early on and wondered if back in 2006 anyone had done a check of Catherine's bedroom.

Many people live under a cloud for years when the police, friends and even family are suspicious when their husband or wife goes missing. Inga knew in such cases the police often have a difficult decision to make. Has this person gone missing in suspicious circumstances or do they simply not wish to be found? Are they in truth just fed up to the back teeth with life as they know it and indeed no crime has been committed?

'If it wasn't for the blood and his lack of alibis, the Christine Streeter case would never have come to court.'

'Could be,' said Adam, glass in hand. 'Like these we've been reading about, she just cleared off.'

'Got pissed off with life with Borowiak for some reason. Decided enough was enough and she was off.'

'Except for the blood.'

'Except for the blood.' She sucked in a breath, then took a sip of her Rioja Reserva. 'Think it was Jake who suggested she could have done it herself.' Adam turned his head to look at Inga. 'How difficult is it to fill a needle with your own blood, then splash it all about?'

'Now you come to mention it,' he mused. 'Why would you do that if you've got blood like hers?'

'What d'you mean, blood like hers?'

'On some social media thingy today apparently talking about her having a rare blood group.'

'Who told you?' Inga shot at him as she moved her head away to look at her man.

'Thought you'd know. Lydia was saying today.'

'I wonder where this stupidity comes from half the time,' she said as Adam pressed keys on his phone. She sat there sipping her wine as he asked this Lydia one of his receptionists where she had seen the item about the Streeter blood group.

From phone to iPad and Adam was hunting without a confirmed website to aim for, as it appears this Lydia had come across it by chance.

'You're half right,' he said after he'd read a few lines. 'Doesn't seem stupid, but you do have to ask where does some of this stuff come from. Who would know?'

'Hematologists.'

'This says they knew back in 2006 she had a rare blood group.'

'How rare?' Inga asked, but annoyingly the reply was a question.

'You sure you don't know?'

'We've not been looking at the case, you any idea how thick the case notes were? We've concentrated on her disappearance, and a lot of that's been on how anyone can just vanish.' She closed her eyes as Adam went back to scouring for more information. 'D'you know, looks as though we've spent too much time chasing moonbeams on the dark net and got all too involved with the geeks. Should have remained with the basics like blood, fingerprints and DNA.'

'You had all three.'

'I know that.' The look Adam received was a frequent visitor, and his slight nod was all the encouragement she needed.

'I reckon she didn't know she had a rare blood group,' said Adam as Inga picked up her phone.

'Jake?' Inga asked even though she had chosen his name on her phone and knew it was him answering. 'Apologise to Sally, but just a quick one. Did we know Streeter had a rare blood group?'

'No. Since when?'

'Since always.'

'You saying we've known all these years?' Jake asked.

'Looks like it,' said Inga. 'Only going by what we've found on some scurrilous social media site, between talk of fund raising for transgender dogs and stupid women sharing photos of their little kids to keep paedos happy.'

'About par for the course,' he commented. 'And nobody put out an all-points bulletin to every hospital, lab or blood testing centre.'

'Or did they?'
'And nobody has come forward in...eleven years?'
'Little job for the morning.'
'Thanks.'
'No problem, see you tomorrow.'
'Patient confidentiality,' said Adam the moment the phone left Inga's ear. 'Could be a serious issue.'
'But if we'd put out a plea for information,' Adam was shaking his head. 'She was missing presumed dead for god's sake!'
'I know, but it's still not acceptable. That's why it's there, patient confidentiality is paramount. If somebody had leaked the information to the police she could have sued them from here to kingdom come.'
'But we were on her side.'
'Makes no odds.' Adam downed the last of the wine in his glass.
'More?' he asked as he waved his glass in front of her.
'Not now. No.'

'Detective Inspector. Are you seriously telling me nothing has come of the fact this missing woman has a very rare blood group, that nobody checked this out with any of the medical authorities, with the National Blood Bank or the medical profession?' Inga went to attempt to answer, but Darke had not finished. 'No doubt the medics did what they regularly do and closed ranks, just in case this dead woman might sue them? That what you're saying?'
'Seems that way,' she admitted. 'Remember they had nothing to compare it with.' Darke's bark was always worse than his bite but his mood this time was up a notch or two, but not aimed at her. She knew despite not being involved at all back in 2006 she'd just have to stand there and take it. 'But staff who knew would most likely keep their mouths shut. Is it worth losing your job over?'
'Probably right,' he said. 'But you really do have to wonder how some of these coppers ever solved crimes, how they ever had anything like decent clear up rates when this sort of thing was going on.'
'Adam suggests it's all to do with patient confidentiality.'
'Poppycock!' he shouted. 'That's just hiding behind utter codswallop!' The Detective Superintendent pointed at her. 'Did

nobody think to suggest to them this was a murder enquiry, and what about the Borowiak chappie languishing in jail? Did nobody give him a moment's thought?' Inga was fighting to get a word in edgeways. 'They'll come out with some clap-trap about human rights no doubt and being politically correct. Well, what about his human rights? People like them never seem interested in the victim.' He just sat there looking all around his office, his mood so evident for all to see, but she was the only person present. 'Sometimes I do wonder if it's all worth it, you know. We work our butts off and all the while there's these half-baked so-and-so's doing their level best to make sure justice is *not* served.'

'Almost as rare as you can get apparently,' Inga advised and wondered how much he had suffered in the hands of the Chief Constable and one or two others higher up the food chain.

'Don't even know what my blood group is. Told what it is once upon a time, but...' he just shrugged.

'Her parents never knew,' she told him. 'We've checked with them. News to them as it was to us. So my guess is it never became general knowledge and as a child she never had her bloods taken, so nobody knew.'

'Should have been her big mistake,' he said and he sank back into his big black chair. 'They all make an error somewhere down the line as we know, and that should have been hers. Think you're right, she spread the blood back then, we should have picked up on it.' The DI was pleased he was calming down.

'Trouble of course this time, we've had no blood so it never became an issue.'

'D'we know where all this came from?'

'Adrian Orford is onto it. Somebody on social media asked why we hadn't picked up on her having a really rare blood group.'

'How rare are we talking?' a much calmer Darke queried.

Inga looked at notes she'd brought with her Jake had come up with. 'Apparently your blood group is decided by the genes each of us inherits from our parents.' Darke motioned for Inga to sit down, so she took him up on his offer. 'Your group will be either RhD positive or RhD negative, which means you are one of eight types.'

'You're confusing me already,' he tittered.

She read on. 'These eight types are identified by antigens and antibodies. The four groups are...'

'Wow, wow hang on. You said eight, now it's four.'

'Eight types,' said Inga with a wry smile. 'It'll make sense in a second or two. 'The groups are A, B, O and AB and each one of those four can be positive or negative making the eight.'

'That's better.'

'AB negative is found in only one percent of the population of the UK.'

'And Streeter?' Darke asked.

'Not so fast,' she cheekily told him. 'She only has to lack a single antigen and her blood becomes very rare indeed.'

'We're that close,' he said. 'Now we have to break down barriers to get at her no doubt.'

'Advantage of course from her point of view is, being seriously rare your blood is hardly ever needed.' She folded her notes. 'If we're right in what we say she smeered her own blood, she probably had no idea how rare her blood group was.'

'Possible she still doesn't know.'

'Has to be somebody in the lab from back in 2006, or somebody with an axe to grind in haemotology.'

'Looking for their fifteen minutes of fame, like every silly bugger these days.'

'More like five minutes. Everything you watch is done in flashing images.' Inga got to her feet.

'Keep me posted please.'

'If she's not had her blood tested of course we'll be no further forward.'

'Don't say that,' Darke said almost sadly and she guessed what he would face from those above him were it to be the case.

'We now just have to hope she's needed a blood test somewhere down the line. If not,' she shrugged. 'We're still screwed.'

'My guess is at the time they put out an all-points bulletin to the medical profession to look out for her rare blood. Over time it'll have just gone off the radar.'

22

North Yorkshire Police had reconnoitred the cottage for Inga the previous day, with a local patrol just casually calling at the property to ask if the woman they spoke to had by chance seen a stray horse they were searching for.

Now it was time for the DI to pay the occupant a visit, to come face to face hopefully with the woman with very rare blood. She had persuaded the local bobbies to hold back, take a break and park up their patrol car half a mile or so from their destination.

It would have been so easy to go rampaging into Dovetail Cottage. Scream to a halt in clouds of dust on the single track road, fling open the van doors for two dog handlers to scramble out in their Sunday best of black jackets and trousers and the ubiquitous matching baseball caps emblazoned with POLICE. Front runner with the red battering ram, followed by a further mob suited and booted in body armour and helmets with visors down.

There could have easily been a mob of them. Three cops round the back ready for a bust and more at the front of this picturesque building with the dog handlers struggling to calm their over eager German Shepherds.

None of that.

Inga Larsson and DS Jake Goodwin were in the lead unmarked car, escorted by the one with a three litre engine and covered in the garish decals housing two chunky uniformed cops.

They had no command to wait for, no screaming and shouting, no radios, no megaphones or tasers, no dogs looking for someone to bite and all that malarky.

Inga used the old wrought iron knocker to mark her arrival at the front door and just stood back waiting patiently.

There they were looking for all the world just like any man and woman in suits visiting for an appointment. In truth they were both just desperate to see who might well open the door.

Twice more the Swede made her presence felt by using the old heavy knocker. No reply. No sign of life.

This was not the bad and mean streets of south London or the chav and slut infested areas of Manchester you can still find sadly. It was unmistakably Fangdale Beck an absolutely delightful hamlet amongst quite outstanding countryside close to the River Seph in the North York Moors National Park were it not for the dank overcast going on wet weather.

Looked to Inga despite what Sandy would call dreich weather as they wandered around the side of the whitewashed former farmhouse, as being absolutely ideal as a holiday cottage. To one side as the pair discovered was an orchard with apple trees and they then came across a stone patio area to the rear. All very well maintained and when they peered into the lounge and kitchen they could see it had undergone considerable modernization at some point in recent years.

They stayed for half an hour just in case, then released all the bored coppers with them before reluctantly they themselves headed for the A1. Sat in Costa with a coffee and toasted sandwich each it was Inga's phone to bring her news.

The very person they were looking for according to DS Craig Darke on her phone had walked into the Lincoln County cop shop complete with two solicitors. Their trip to the North York Moors had been as it turned out a complete waste of time and resources.

Not Christine Streeter. The woman who had walked off the streets and was awaiting Inga's return claimed to be somebody calling herself Carly Hills.

All the way back to Lincoln when Jake Goodwin was not chuntering on about this, that and the other of little interest Inga's mind was back as ever into the planning of her wedding.

The church near to her parents' home just outside Stockholm had been chosen, and the timing by tradition in the afternoon had been set.

She'd had to explain to Adam how in Sweden the bride is not given away like some chattle by her father. She and Adam would enter the church together arm in arm.

'Please allow me to explain the situation to you,' said DI Inga Larsson in a very controlled manner. 'I happen to be the Senior Investigating Officer into the death of a young woman here in Lincoln. During my investigations your name has arisen with the discovery of your DNA at the site of the victim's body. Whilst looking into this matter my team have arrived at the conclusion that you were at school with two or three other people who have been the subject of unexplained deaths as part of Operation Lancaster.'

Yes the title did appear nonsensical, but she'd not chosen it, and the snigger across the table probably confirmed what she herself thought of these odd ball names the computer comes up with.

Inga knew from experience the more tedious she made the opening in such circumstances the more frustrated both the offender and her solicitor would become.

The booking-in procedure had as ever been lengthy and been followed of course by a disclosure session for the solicitor which always seemed to be a serious case of wasting Police time to satisfy do-gooders sat at home in their chunky knit cardigans and pink fluffy slippers.

More than once she'd been shouted at. "Get to the point!" and "Cut to the bloody chase!" she'd had thrown at her but not in such acceptable language, which made her even more determined to bore them into submission.

She knew it might very well be a slow process and the clock was ticking before she would be forced to charge her or release her, but so be it, if time were of the essence in the end she had a plan.

On this occasion Christine Streeter who had now been missing presumed dead for more than eleven years was sat across the dull grey Interview Room table from her but in a different guise.

First hurdle the Swede had to overcome was the stench of perfume and make-up. No doubt Jake beside her had some manly words on the subject of whores and brothels to describe the smell, but for Swede Inga it was just completely over the top and wholly unnecessary.

The woman sat opposite was claiming to be one Carly Hills, glowering at her but avoiding eye contact.

'For the purposes of this interview you will be regarded as and addressed as Christine Mary Streeter which is your given name according to your parents and recorded on your birth certificate.'

To the right of Streeter positioned to ensure she was in the least attractive position, was her solicitor who had been the one to deliver her. Not as is often the case one who has been almost dragged off the streets to deal with a case against somebody he had never met previously.

Inga knew he must know about Christine Streeter, her story having been all across the media now for some time, and there was no need to be too techy or au fait with social media, she was known to even those who still read the red tops, The Times or listen to Radio 4. Despite what he thought of his circumstance this might very well be something this badling Dugdale could boast about over a glass of Chablis with his pals.

Once she had filled enough time with legal nonsense and had hinted an untold gathering of information, Inga got down to naming names.

'Can you please confirm you are Christine Mary Streeter?'

'I see you're starting with the difficult ones!'

Inga ignored her remark and chuckle being unwilling to go down the silliness path immediately. 'Shall we start with Mindi Brookes? Tell me about her and your relationship?'

'Who on earth are you talking about?'

The heavy sculptured make-up was certainly well done, with well blushed high cheekbones, vivid puckered red lips and a little pointy nose. The big brown fedora hat and the nose could so easily have been borrowed from a witch and with Halloween so close seemed quite appropriate. The blonde tumbling locks down to her shoulders were quite obviously not real, not because the wig was not good, but because Inga had been told by both Ruth and Julie she was very much a brunette when they'd met her as Susan Sewell.

'She's a woman who unfortunately had you urinate in her bed, or on her bed and probably all over her bed and her best Dunelm duvet.'

The solicitor didn't look aghast as they often are when details are revealed, but just sat there po faced. Inga reckoned it was not at all what he was expecting and she imagined he was desperate to create this picture in his mind of what had gone on.

'Not exactly what you expect when you invite somebody round is it?' Jake Goodwin quietly slipped in then turned to boss Inga. 'Friend pops in for a coffee and a slice of cake and then wees in your bed. That ever happened to you?' he asked his boss.

'Not lately,' Inga responded.

Jake her stalwart supporter grimaced and shook his head. 'Different, I'll give you that,' he told the DI.

'Nice friends you've got obviously,' grinning Streeter thought was amusing.

'We've got a couple more friends, in fact three, we need to ask you questions about,' Inga went on. 'Charlotte Elliott, Judy Green and Helen Nevins. All of whom you went to school with coincidentally. We can forget Helen Nevins for now as she unfortunately for you is alive and well and living in…' There was silence for a moment, then Inga said, 'think we'll leave it there shall we?' she teased and smiled.

'Can we now talk about the guy you lived with, Thomacz Borowiak?' Jake asked as Inga tried to place the sickly sweet perfume. There was a touch of Botox too by the look of her.

'What kind of question's that?' Streeter sniggered and fidgeted, a sure sign of agitation and the signal Inga needed only once to start pushing her.

'One you haven't answered…yet. Who is currently languishing in jail having been sent there for murdering you,' he grinned to illustrate the absurdity of the situation.

'I think you'll find Detective Sergeant, if anything, it is actually manslaughter,' the solicitor piped up to prove he was still awake. 'He was, might I remind you found guilty by a jury in the Crown Court.'

'Murder, manslaughter does it really matter?' Jake shot back at him. 'After all, do you think Christine Streeter sat beside you,' he pointed at her with his pen. 'Looks as though she has been dead for more than eleven years? Looks a tad peeky maybe.' Dugdale made no response. 'After all, it is what murder and manslaughter are all about surely. There is a statutory requirement in law stating the victim actually has to be dead.'

'To be fair, she looks well on it don't you think?' Inga cheekily tossed at the poor man.

'In law they are actually quite different,' and the goon then went off on one about points of law and suggested to his client how all the time reference was made to murder she had no reason to respond. It all became very tedious with the lawyer quoting cases and then as if that was not bad enough in length quoted principles behind what had made the law he was quoting. When he began to pontificate and waffle about the merits of the law in question, Inga for one had switched off.

She took this tedious opportunity of him trying hard to score points to have a real good look at Christine Streeter aka Carly Hills.

'Let's get back to the girls from school,' said Jake when he got fed up with point scoring. 'Two of whom are dead, and to them we could also add a third if you like who is also no longer with us who you decided to impersonate, to take her identity. You used the name of a dead girl from school, her birth certificate and then everything else we need in life to help you hide your true identity for over a decade. Even down to sitting in a Police interview room.'

All Christine Streeter did was blow out a weary breath of frustration as her shoulders sagged as if highlighting the fight had gone out of her suddenly.

'Charlotte Elliott and Judy Green,' said Inga clearly and carefully for the tape. 'Tell me about them.'

Christine blew out a breath , as if the air she sucked in as a refill gave her a boost somehow. 'Girls I knew at school.'

'But not girls you have remained in contact with over the years.'

'No thank you.'

'And why is that?'

'It dawned on me how these women who'd made my life an absolute horror story were all going to carry on living a life. Just carry on for maybe another sixty years without a care in the world, with no thought whatsoever for those whose life they'd made a living hell at that blasted school. It was obvious this evil pair were planning to thoroughly enjoy not quite the sort of life I'd choose for myself, but a life all the same.' She shook her head and raised her voice. 'Not in my time they're not, there's no way they're getting off scot free and having the last laugh. Sorry ladies your times up, fun's over, it was my time to have a bit of fun. My time to be a bully, not denegrade some poor young wretch with a simpering dozy bitch of a mother, one with a last century home life with a so-called father playing with fucking toy soldiers! No way!' was almost shouted.

'Christine...' Inga tried as she digested what she had just been confessed.

'Me?' she yelled: 'What was going to happen to me? Always the bloody victim, the one they always took the piss out of. Never the netball captain, always the poor little bitch nobody wanted on their team, always the one with PE kit which was never quite right. I was always the one forced to wear trainers from the bloody Co-op round the corner. Never Nike, never going to be a hoity-toity prefect, and no chance I could swear in fifty bloody languages. Not me.'

'Can I just say...?'

'Number one had to be that Lottie bitch,' she sighed loudly, pushed out a breath and just ignored Inga trying to talk. So she just sat there studying the woman again. Acres of a free flowing sleeveless black chiffon dress over what could have been a grey t-shirt all hiding what Inga guessed as being a burgeoning figure. Black thick tights she'd seen earlier and black pumps. 'What sort of crap name is that I ask you? Sounds like somebody's dear old great grandma from the big house,' she thought was humorous with a glance to her left proving pointless. The solicitor just sat there without a flicker of reaction or emotion towards what she had said. 'See that bitch Lottie over there, there's a lottie of her!' she was the only one amused by her remarks.

'Did you know her family at all?'

'Name like that trying to be something they're not seemed to me.'

'Did you know them?' the blonde DI tried again.

'Didn't all make life easy for me I'll admit, but the Lottie cow'd got a real drink problem. She knew how to shovel down the red and no mistake, went down so fast it'd not touch the sides I bet.' She smiled at Inga. 'Her own downfall you could say. If she'd been a bit pretentious and one of those silly sods into all this smelling the roses round the door at the vineyard and taste of cow muck and tarmac off the road she'd have spotted some'at was up.'

23

'Can we please talk about Tomasz Borowiak still languishing in jail?' Inga asked and spied no reaction. 'Or maybe Mindi Brookes, who didn't go to Forest School. What was your gripe with her?'

'No bloody way!' Christine reacted firmly. 'You're not leaving those bastards out of this, I'll not have it, do you understand?' For the first time she pointed a thin finger at Inga. 'You want the full nine yards, you're gonna get it, but you get it my way, or no way.' She sat back and folded her arms. 'First come, first served.'

'Christine,' said the lawyer. 'I really think you...'

'Just button it, will you?' she scythed him down and his look of hopelessness was not lost on the Inga and Jake pairing sat side by side.

'Tell you what,' said Inga suddenly to surprise her colleague. 'We'll do it your way, you choose the running order.'

'Is it always skank tea round here?' Christine put to Inga. 'Or if I'm a good girl will I get a decent coffee and biccies?'

'We'll take a break shortly,' Inga advised acting the good cop. 'First we need more information from you, so shall we talk more about Lottie Elliott then?'

'Her name's Charlotte dear, her stupid mother used to say. What'd he do?' she threw out. 'Sold carpets, big deal how snobby posh is that? Not.'

'Did you know her brothers?'

'No,' was sharp. 'Horrible gawky kid, one of those who have trouble controlling their legs, like their brain's too far from their feet sort of thing.' Inga refrained from giving her the satisfaction of agreeing with her. 'Why pick on me, why not pick on my stupid mother? She's the one who always thought she knew better, not my bloody fault.' Christine stopped turned her head slightly to look at the blank wall as if she was picturing her situation back then. Clothes and shoes never quite right, hair lacking in style shorn short probably by her mother with the kitchen scissors.

'How did she pick on you? How did it manifest itself?'

'Hang on,' was not the answer Inga was expecting. 'One of the brothers, called him Nicholas. See, like I said another stupid swanky name. No Nick, oh no. Always had to be Nicholas, dear.' She laughed over much. 'Bet his other name was Peregrine!'

'Can we talk about her picking on you?'

'You ever been picked on?' Streeter shot back.

'No.'

'Wouldn't bloody dare,' Jake so wanted to add.

'To just say it was all the usual makes light of it, but it's never that, let me tell you. Reckon this bullying is more mental than anything else. Not necessarily the pain from a punch or a kick it's all the rest of it. Called me names, laughed about my clothes and stuff I never had what everybody else took as a given. Somebody once told me how the Lottie bitch had spat in my lunch more than once.' She gave a weak snort. 'What do you do then when you get your lunch next day? Do you decide it was a lie and eat it or decide it was most likely true and then what? Eat it and retch, go without and bloody starve?'

'Had she?' Jake had to ask.

Christine shrugged with her hands pushed down between her thighs. 'Next thing I started to self-harm,' she almost sniggered. 'Couldn't even do that properly', she smiled. 'Just made scratch marks I told my mum I'd got in PE.'

Inga knew she would have been within her rights to ask this Christine aka Carly to remove the big brown hat, but as she'd faced a whole raft of unwashed skurks over the years all with hoodies or baseball caps on back to front, what did it really matter?

They were usually worn by those with body odour issues, compared to this revolting sweet pong being ushered forth across the table.

'You say it was a lot to do with things you didn't have. Was it because your family was not well off?'

'We's all right, just my old lady had her own ideas, all old fashioned out of touch stuff and she allus knew better. That and praying to God.' She leant forward. 'Listen, every damn kid in the bloody school had a backpack, all the latest, best there were, and me? I had a stupid brown satchel the daft cow got from a jumble sale!'

'Did you tell the teachers what was happening?'

'And what good would that have done? Remember, I wasn't the teachers' pet.' She leant onto the grey table. 'Bit they don't tell you about, but switched on mothers soon hook up with. Be teacher's pet, give her an Easter Egg, a pressie and a bottle of wine at the end of term and any amount you can get away with at Christmas. Bain of my life having a mother who never had a clue about any of it. All passed her by this education politics I think they call it these days. Only bloody kid I should imagine who didn't get taken to school by car except the social housing lot who couldn't afford one. Wish someone would tell me what that's all about?'

'What do you mean exactly? Why didn't you tell a teacher?' Inga asked.

'I had to walk to school?' she chuckled. 'Hadn't got a back pack? What you on about? What do you take me for?'

'No,' said Jake. 'The bullying you say you suffered.'

Christine just ignored what he'd said. 'Some people can get away with anything, like the ones who buy teacher a present at end of term, ones who are friends with the girl's mothers.' She shook her head. 'Bet my stupid mother couldn't even tell you any of the teachers' names.'

'But surely if you'd spoken up, it's possible something would have been done,' suggested Inga.

'Yeh right,' she scoffed. 'What planet are you living on?' Christine threw at her. 'Cloud cuckoo land?'

'Unless...'

'Teacher teacher they've been picking on me, miss,' said Christine in a silly girly voice with her hand in the air. 'What's in it for me teacher asks with her hand out?' She shook her head as her hand came down. 'Yeah I should coco.'

'Unless you spoke up nothing would have ever be done. They're not psychic.'

'Yeah right,' she managed before she released a tired breath. 'None so blind as they who don't want to see.'

'This is the reason you murdered Charlotte Elliott is it?'

'Never said I murdered her.'

'You said she liked a drink which tells me you must have been studying her and guess what. She had her drink spiked, and we just happen to have you on CCTV in the bar at the time.'

'No,' she threw back. 'What you have at best is possibly a doctored film of somebody who looks like me. CCTV proves nothing and you know it. No fingerprints and no DNA you lot hold so much stock by these days. When you've got those you come back to me. Until then...' she sniggered. 'Go whistle.'

'You murdered Charlotte Elliott and it appears from what you say it was because she spat in your lasagne.'

'You've got a vivid imagination,' she chuntered. 'And you musta gone to a posh school if you had bloody lasagne. Crissakes what d'you get for starters? Stupid avacado?'

'Far from it. We're working from facts and from witness statements.' Did Inga right there and then spot just a hint of surprise in her eyes?

'Where you from anyway?' Christine Streeter asked.

'I was born in Sweden.'

'Our cops really in such a bad way we have to import foreign buggers now? Portuguese nurses, Poles and Lithuanian plumbers, what the hell's wrong with this damn country?' Streeter leant forward. 'Brexit's coming and you'll be on your bike lady.'

'Back to the subject,' Jake Goodwin urged. 'How about you do us all a favour and we tick a box for Charlotte Elliott. You confirm for us right here and now you were responsible for her death and we can move on.'

'You'll be lucky,' she scoffed.

'You need to think seriously about what lies ahead of you Christine. Life in a cell let me tell you can be far from comfortable.'

'Is that right?' Streeter sniggered her arrogance. 'While I'm thinking about what's clearly *not* going to happen you need to give a great deal of thought to the Human Rights lawyer I've engaged who'll ensure I don't ever see the inside of a cell, anywhere, any time.' The look she gave Inga deserved a smack in the mouth, nothing less. She'd picked on the wrong one there. Inga's father Stefan had sent her to unarmed combat lessons when she was young, a skill she had retained.

She glanced at the solicitor expecting him to be confused and bewildered by the woman.

'Let us move on then to Judy Green.'

'Quelle surprise!' was an attempt to be clever and ironic.

'Tell me about her.'

'Probably sitting in a booth at United Nations now translating codswallop from a bunch of foreign warmongers about all their airy fairy religious nonsense.'

'What did you do with the Peugeot you bought off a bloke in a pub for less than a grand or from an advert in the paper?'

'You serious? A Peugeot? What d'you take me for, a boy racer? Every time I see some driver acting bloody stupid odds are it's a Peugeot driver.' She folded her arms. 'What you think of me then is it?' She shook her head. 'Dear oh, dear.'

'You bought one, we know that.'

'Don't be ridiculous!' and with that Christine Streeter stood up. 'Toilet please.'

Inga knew her sort tend to try to mock others with what appear to be tailored clothing she no doubt considers to be a label of power and position.

The Swede knew otherwise from her stringent upbringing how such gauche creatures are in truth those regularly nominated for establishment revulsion.

DI Inga Larsson with her deep blonde hair up, wearing her favourite deep blue suit, bit off the end of her Bourbon biscuit and then drank from her mug of white coffee sat at her desk.

She'd just remembered she still had need to contact her uncle Nickolaj. In Sweden at the party after the formality of the wedding ceremony there are always many toasts. Her uncle would organize it all for her, decide in which order would be most appropriate.

'What's all this Human Rights lawyer business about then?'

'Search me,' Jake Goodwin responded as he dipped his second biscuit in his black coffee. 'They told me he's the one waiting for Darke when we walked in.' More biscuit. 'Just need to be careful that's all.'

'Never had human rights at a murder interview, what's she up to do you think?'

'Why hand yourself in with two members of the smarmy brigade?' Goodwin queried. 'What's that all about?'

'No idea, but what worried me is this could take forever and a day. We only had the 24 to start with, the way it's going we'll need a hundred hours to get to the bottom of this.'

'And that's just for starters.'

Inga sipped and savoured her coffee. 'What's with the stink?'

'Just checked with Ruth,' said Jake. 'And she reckons there was nothing too smelly when she met her at that hotel.'

'Like walking into one of those department stores and the awful pong hits you to make you gag.'

'Not politically correct but poofs parlour comes to mind,' added Jake and stifled a snort.

'D'you get the impression she doesn't want to talk about Borowiak?'

'Very much so.'

'Think what I'll do, unless you have a better idea,' Inga said. 'Is to get as much as we can about Charlotte Elliott, so if we struggle to meet deadlines we can at least charge her with one.'

'Plus what Peterborough have will build the case.'

'Exactly, then move onto the others once we have her safely behind bars.'

'Solid tactic.'

'CCTV backview stand up in court d'you think?' Inga asked her senior DS.

'Not looking the way she did today. Looks like that in court we'll all have a problem.'

'If *Daily Star* get a shot of her in the hat thing on her head the shops'll sell millions! Be fedora fever.'

'Why do folk do that?' he asked. 'I'd steer clear of stuff like that, but Joe Public has to buy any old tatt in the news, clothes the Royal kids are paid to wear and all sorts of nonsense. What's it all about?'

'Got to follow the herd for some reason when you and I make absolutely sure we steer clear.'

'They lack confidence,' he reacted. 'But this one spent all this time hiding, then out the blue hands herself in and turns up dressed like...' Jake just blew out a breath.

'We'll see how it goes, may decide to let her go then re-arrest her. Looks as though this is all about bullying at school, but if it is the case where does all this leave Borowiak he'll be chaffing at the bit to get out and what about Mindi Dodds, she never went to the blinking school at all?'

'Could be we finish up with just a plain and simple serial killer?'

'But why all the subterfuge? What about the business of baking a pie, using Hope Parkes, shafting Ruth and Julie with the story about working for a hotel group which doesn't exist and all the rest of it?'

Tap on the glass in her door and Julie half opened and poked her head in. 'Boss is in a conference apparently. Says he can't be disturbed under any circumstances.'

'Thanks,' said Inga. 'One minute he wants to be briefed every five minutes, now we get to the crunch he's off on one of his meetings,' she giggled. 'Then when I see him next he'll start on about merging crime scene management parameters, improving the effectiveness of major crime initial complex case response.' She just shook her blonde head.

'I've asked ASBO to check if the real Carly Hills ever had a National Insurance Number issued, bearing in mind before she started work she'd gone off with her family to Canada.'

'Ruth's just done it,' said Julie. 'She's just gone on the government website and applied for a National Insurance Number for Carly Hills. As easy as falling off a log she reckons, just filled it in, gave her old address, made up a date of birth.'

'She's actually applied?' Inga blurted anxiously.

'No,' said a smiling Julie. 'Just filled everything in, but stopped at actually pressing send. She could if you want her to.'

'I think we'd better not, but maybe I'll get ASBO to actually apply as her, or perhaps make up a person.'

'He could apply as Susan Sawyer, see what happens.'

'Good thinking.'

'Great thing about that is,' Jake said. 'You don't have to come face to face with some government official.'

'Makes life so easy.'

'Bloody clever I'll give her that,' said Jake. 'Lizzie was right, the obvious thing to do would have been to take Susan Sawyer's identity, the one who drowned.'

'Instead she just used the name as and when but plumped for Carly for the full make-over, the one hidden away selling burgers and fries for the baseball.'

Jake Goodwin drank down the remaining half of his coffee in one foul swoop. 'We've got our hands full to get through all this.'

'Reckon we won't get half of it until we get to court.' Inga joined her DS in downing the remainder of her coffee and stood up. 'You take it to start with this time, might put her off her stroke. See how she reacts to a man.'

'Expected it to be a lot harder, almost as if she suddenly caved in.'

'But not admitting anything, in effect she's putting up her defence. I was bullied she's claiming.'

'But we already know she was,' said Jake quickly. 'Well,' he said and just hesitated. 'Maybe not actual bullying, but threatened, which I suppose some would say is the same thing. And we know who by.'

'But she doesn't know we know.'

'Bit concerned at how confident she appears.'

'But we don't know what she's really feeling inside.'

'Not giving off a vibe of knowing the game's up.'

'Over confidence, probably the trait which has turned her into the killer we know she is. How often do we see the guilty in interview all full of bullshit, then suddenly it all comes home to roost and their world comes tumbling down.'

'Got a lot of bottle I'll give her that, the way she manipulated us and the audacious strokes she's pulled off.'

'Why now I keep asking myself,' said Inga stood there in her office arms folded watching her team still beavering away. 'Why did she wait all this time from running away from Borowiak to killing...'

'Allegedly.'

'Allegedly,' she acknowledged with a grin. 'Killing three women.'

'And if Helen whatsit hadn't by sheer chance run away up to Scotland and lived with a bloke she desperately wants to marry but daren't, it could easy be four.'

'Only one way to find out,' said Goodwin and held his boss's door open for her.

At the last second Inga remembered she had to ask Uncle Nickolaj, and quickly made a note on her pad before she left.

24

Comfort break over and in no time Goodwin and Larsson were back to continue where they had left off as they noisily dragged out their chairs opposite the pair and sat down in different positions in Interview Room 3 with the tape and video running. Back to the sickly sweet smell.

'Tell me about being bullied,' said Jake Goodwin for openers. He saw Christine Streeter's big eyes roll across to look at Inga then back to him showed the switch had put her off her guard.

'Kept telling me how my dad wasn't my dad and she knew who was.'

'Who did?'

'Hell Nevins I called her, well not to her face of course, just to myself mind,' she grinned. 'She was a nasty piece of work.'

'And you're an absolute charmer of course.'

'Proper name?' Jake remembered to check for the tape.

'Helen Nevins, or hell on earth.'

'What happened with her then?'

'Said my mum had always put it about. Told me I was fat which is ridiculous when I think about it now, but in such situations your mind's not your own.'

'Had she?'

'Had she what?'

'Had your mum put it about shall we say?'

'How dare you!' Streeter screamed.

'Excuse me,' said the silent Solicitor. 'That really is most uncalled for.'

'Not uncalled for,' sneered Christine. 'Ridiculous! If you knew my mother you'd know how bloody daft that is.'

'Just trying to establish the facts Mr Dugdale, after all this girl must have had a legitimate reason for saying something like that.'

'May well be so, but your attitude is quite unnecessary.'
Goodwin ignored Dugdale by not even bothering to look at him. 'That it?' he asked Streeter 'You call this bullying? Bit of tittle tattle seems to me, just how life is at school.'
Christine Streeter then once again criticized her mother, this time at length covering everything from making her wear her hair in plaits at Primary school, to banning make-up from the house.
'You lived with someone like her would you go home and tell a nasty bitch like her you'd been bullied?'
'She might have gone to the school about it,' quiet Inga offered.
'You really are the limit d'you know that?' she threw at the DI. 'You just don't have a clue. How d'you get through life being so naive is what I'd like to know? Being foreign won't help.'
'Because we don't make a fuss about unimportant things which just don't matter.'
'You been bullied?' she shot at Jake, her face full of anger.
'Do I look as though I've been bullied?' he retorted with a grin. 'Just playground silliness, all girly stuff, there's nothing in it.' He hesitated momentarily. 'Your mum's screwing the milkman,' he imitated a girl's squeaky voice. 'Hello fatty,' Jake shook his head and looked straight at Christine Streeter. 'Be serious, please. That sort of thing goes on day in day out in every playground the world over. If you were upset by such nonsense it's a wonder you turn on the news at night, or watch anything tougher than CBBC.'
'You've really got no idea what it's like, have you!' she shouted. 'Typical, absolutely bloody typical. Men huh.'
'Because I've got more about me, and I don't go round killing girls who call me a fat cow? It's all just silly school kid sticks and stones nonsense seems to me,' he grinned at her again to annoy. 'My ears were a bit sticky out when I was at school and some kids took the mickey. So what?' he shrugged.
Inga waited a few seconds, not long enough for Christine to recover from the tirade, but long enough for her to take in what was being suggested.
'Judy Green. Tell me about her, tell me about running her down in that car.' Inga sat there arms folded and waited.
'No idea what you're talking about,' said Christine still churning over what Jake had thrown at her.

'So the DNA we found in the car matches the DNA we found in Mindi Brooke's bed and matches the DNA we still have on file from when you did a runner from Thomasz Borowiak. Not yours then?'

She laughed quietly. 'Don't be stupid,' and waved her head about. 'You can't get DNA from a burnt out car, everybody knows that,' the moment she said it a realization crossed her face.

'You know the car was torched then?' Jake looked at Inga beside him.

'You'll not get DNA that's for sure.'

'Think you're a bit behind the times,' said Inga softly. 'Back in the old days I'll admit you couldn't get DNA from a burnt out car. Things, unfortunately for you, have moved on quite a bit in the world of forensic science.'

'Called DNA polymerases retrieval,' said Jake, and although she'd never heard of such a thing DI Larsson was impressed.

'So?'

'Your DNA in three places so far,' he said calmly. 'Want me to go on?' Christine just shrugged. 'As you know you kindly allowed us to take a sample of your DNA here today. Now being fast tracked through what we call CSI Leicester. Results in no time to add to the list. It's all stacking up against you.' He tapped his pen on the desk to annoy the boss. 'Want to tell us about your blood?' he asked. 'Thought not,' he added before she could consider a reply.

'Can we get back to Judy Green and why?' Inga got in before she could react but had to wait, and it was as if this Streeter was weighing up her options.

'Had this sort of boyfriend for a few weeks until that lot told him I'd been cheating on him which was really stupid as I was still a virgin and had not been out with anyone else. He then called me a slag to add to it.'

'That lot? Who are that lot?'

'Lottie, prudy Judy bitch and hell on earth. Called themselves by a stupid name, God knows what it was all about, just showing off's my guess.' She grinned. 'Troika, have you heard the like?'

Inga was surprised how every now and again she'd talk about the situation as it was, or how she was telling them it was back in Forest School.

Jake Goodwin sighed noisily. 'Please. We're not back to all the childish handbags at dawn bullying nonsense are we?'

'Just shut up!' Streeter shouted. 'You have no idea what it was like. At times it really was non-stop as they obviously got some sort of nasty evil pleasure out of it all.'

'So you decided after all this time to get your own back.'

'Not go on Facebook or Snapchat and tell the world what a bunch of evil young women they'd been to you,' said Jake. 'Do what everybody else does these days and expose them to the world. You decide to teach them a real lesson.'

'If you like.'

'Are you admitting you killed Judy Green?' Inga swooped allowing her voice to rise into a shout.

'No.'

'These girls who you say bullied you,' said the DS quickly. 'Did you never speak to any of them about it after you left school?'

'No.'

'Because I guess you realized how ridiculous you'd look. It was just childish silliness and really not worth making a fuss about. Talk about it over cappuccino and they'd all laugh their socks off.'

'Talking of coffee I'll have one now.' When they'd had the previous comfort break Streeter had turned down the offer of a drink and the dopey Solicitor had seen fit to join his client with a negative response.

'All in good time,' said Inga to rile her on purpose. She guessed the stupid woman had refused a drink earlier but now wished she hadn't. 'It would appear your poor mother couldn't afford the latest Nike trainers or ridiculously priced fancy designer backpack and other nonsense. Combined with a bit of girly pigtail pulling fun it seems made you disappear for years on end then kill three of them just for the fun of it.'

'Fun of it!' she screamed back. 'Where did you go on holiday when you were sixteen eh? Come on,' Christine urged. Inga momentarily considered explaining how at the time she was living in Nottingham and going on holiday back then would mean returning to Stockholm to stay with relatives.

'Abroad as it happens,' was the easy way out. 'Jönköping and Göteborg,' she then said in Swedish to annoy and confuse. 'Are two I remember in particular.'

'Bet wherever it was it wasn't a Christian holiday home dump in wet Wales! You want to try being bored senseless for a fortnight in your teens You want to give it a try sometime, book yourself into one of their horror holidays where you can enjoy the real pleasures of life with like-minded dopey kids. Try prayer study every evening with a cup of cocoa before lights out in a bloody dormitory with kids crying for their mummy, and walks in the countryside. Where you end up sitting there on a tuft of wet grass being told about the Sermon on the Mount in great detail or other really exciting and interesting things all your class mates back in school will be really envious of.'

'Time for coffee,' said Inga as she gathered her paperwork together and stood up. 'Biscuit?' she asked and received a genuine look of surprise in return. Anything to get her away from the stench.

Back in the safety of her office DI Inga Larsson had one question for her senior Detective Sergeant.

'Tell me. DNA polymerases retrieval, what's that all about?'

'Utter cack.'

'What?' the Swede threw back.

'No idea.'

'You've no idea?'

'Sounds good though, what d'ya reckon? Polymerases are enzymes which I understand create DNA molecules, I remembered from somewhere,' he sniggered.

'But we can't get DNA from a burnt out car?'

'Not that I know of.'

Inga was nodding. 'But of course she doesn't know it.'

'And nor does the dick with her.'

'This is all very peculiar the way she keeps denying, yet spent ages decrying her mother, and goes on about the bullying.'

'Almost as if she wants us to understand why she's behaved the way she has. Being bullied constantly must have got to her.'

'And what seems like a lousy home life.' Inga hesitated a moment. 'Almost as if she's creating her life story, building her defence in advance.'

'We know the bullying is true of course from what Helen Nivens admitted.'

'She's very much ashamed of now of course.'

'What I don't understand is why now? Why after all this time has she in effect come out of hiding and killed three women? Chances are if she'd not wet the bed we'd still be none the wiser. Can't still be the bullying surely, but as far as I can see it's all that appears to link two of them.'

'If it really affected her so much all those years ago, why didn't she do something about it back then?'

'We've hardly scratched the surface,' Jake admitted.

'That's what worries me.'

'Not got a good word to say for her mother,' said Jake. 'Wasn't it Ruth when she interviewed her, said she made one or two strange remarks?' Inga motioned through the window to Sandy to ask Ruth to join them.

'Streeter is saying a lot of this is her mother's fault,' she put to Ruth by the door. 'Tell us what you made of the woman,' Inga asked her.

'Quite sure she thinks the jury got it spot on. She truly believes Borowiak killed her Christine and dumped her body. No love lost between those two, Kathleen and Borowiak.'

'Does she have any idea what he might have done with the body do you think?' Ruth just shook her head.

'Very religious,' made Jake look at his boss. 'Bit of a control freak I should imagine around the house, what she says goes and I think the father's so laid back he let it all wash over him. Be the sort to light a candle on Christine's birthday, you know the sort of thing.'

'But not divorced, if I remember,' said Inga.

'But surely he's the turnip trying to re-create the whole of the Second World War in miniature.' Jake just sat there shaking his head at the thought of it.

'Her faith stops her agreeing to a divorce apparently,' Ruth went on. 'But I think he's still hopeful of them getting back together and my guess is he supports her financially although they live apart. He's in not much more than a rented scruffy one bedroomed flat and she's still in the house.'

'And he's into this war games business?'

'Think it could very well be a big bone of contention. Not at all sure her religion and his wars go together.'

'Christine's mentioned it a couple of times.'

'We've had her going on and on about her mother,' Jake advised. 'Always had to wear the wrong clothes, less hip shall we say, cheap jack trainers not Adidas all that sort of thing.' He hesitated. 'But most wars are based on religious infighting surely.'

'Old fashioned satchel not a backpack, was one thing she mentioned.'

'House was a bit old fashioned,' said Ruth. 'But not actually stuck in the seventies or something odd. Just a bit tired if I'm honest. I've seen a lot worse.' She looked at the two sat there. 'Did you have the best of everything when you were young?' They shook their heads. 'Thought not. So, what's so special about her?'

'Just her mother's way maybe, doesn't like change. Father being involved in all these old wars can't have kept them up to date I shouldn't imagine.'

'Didn't you say she said odd things at times?' the DI asked her detective.

'One I remember without looking at my notes was about thinking of being a lesbian, seemed the oddest thing out.'

She chuckled. 'Thanks Ruth.'

'Just seemed a strange combination really,' Ruth went on. 'Sometimes look at couples and wonder how on earth they ever got together. There's Kathleen Streeter all into her faith and married to a bloke who is into war games. She's all peace and love and forgiveness and he's planning the Battle of the Somme.'

'What you seem to be forgetting,' said a serious Inga. 'Is how the vast majority of wars come about because of religion, seems to me as an outsider they are bedfellows. Without all these conflicts what would they all do with their time?'

'How about doing good?' was offered with a wry smile.

'Don't be silly.' Inga stood up and stretched her arms high above her head. 'Time to get back, kind sir,' she said and the pair of them were soon back downstairs in the cramped room facing a refreshed Streeter.

'Tell me about Mindi Brookes,' said Inga to get them going once all the formal preliminaries were over.

'What's to tell? The bitch was on the fiddle, just blatantly stealing money from people. You hear about these gangs sticking cameras in cash points and recording your pin or looking over your shoulder and all that. One case I saw this bloke watched this old man key in his number while his mate snatched the bloody card. This bitch was doing it to people she knew. Doing it right there in front of them.' She blew out a breath in a short puff. 'Tried to blame me when she got found out, the cow. I'm not having…'

A sharp tap on the door, it opened and when Inga's head spun round there was Detective Superintendent Craig Darke as large as life.

'A word if you'd be so kind.' Had it been anybody else who had interrupted an important interview they would most certainly in no uncertain terms got their head in their hands to play with.

'Sorry?' was all she managed.

'My office if you will,' was stern. Then Darke looked at a bemused Jacques Goodwin. 'I'm sure our visitors would welcome a cup of tea. Thank you Detective Sergeant.'

Inga and Jake looked at each other fleetingly and both pushed their chairs back with their legs, and got to their feet. Inga grabbed all her paperwork and walked out of the interview room with Darke holding the door for her, leaving her senior DS to close the interview, explain as best he could into the microphone, turn off the machines and act as waiter.

'What's the problem, sir?' she asked looking back to him.

'All in good time,' was no answer. 'Nothing to worry about, but my office first.'

Inga decided there was no point in trying again. She knew his moods and this was one you didn't want to mess with and his assurance helped her relax a trifle.

25

Inga Larsson stepped smartly aside to allow the Detective Super to open his office door and then usher her in. Sat at the small cramped conference table in the corner were two people she knew by sight. One considerably more than the other. Biggest shock to the system was the pair of them being there after closing time on a Friday evening

'Take a seat, please,' he said to Larsson as Darke dropped into his big black chair. 'Harriett I'm sure you know of course,' Inga nodded at the woman she knew by reputation but had never actually been introduced to before. Harriett Delaney happened to be the Chief Crown Prosecutor which meant they were rolling out the big guns for some reason. 'And Marcus I do believe you know.' Yes she knew Marcus Spence, the sort of solicitor who looks as though he has just stepped off a legal TV series. He has the cut of his clothes and the look they'd go for which is so far removed from real life in the Magistrates Court. Dark, manly and certainly what some would call a dish with a mop of black hair straight from public school. Larsson sat down beside him on the only empty chair. 'Marcus, if you'd be so kind.'

'Thank you Craig,' this Marcus said and then turned to look at Larsson. 'Inga. I do believe you've been interviewing a Carly Hills.'

'If it's what she's calling herself this week,' was a sardonic remark to gain her a look from Darke. She guessed this Spence could very well be the Human Rights lawyer Streeter had been talking about.

'Can we please put all your interview room nonsense to one side, please?' said Harriett Delaney from the Crown Prosecution Service. It was a question but Inga knew from experience it was never likely to be a matter open for discussion.

'Carly Hills,' said Marcus Spence again very calmly. 'We have asked, due to her circumstance, that she be granted police bail which I'm pleased to say Harriett here has agreed to.'

'Hang on, hang on,' said Inga with her eyes closed. 'We're talking about somebody who has been missing for eleven years pretending to the world she is dead, who's former partner has spent all this time languishing in jail and...'

'I think you'll find,' said Harriett interrupting Inga who opened her eyes fully as she turned her head to look at the woman. 'Thomasz Borowiak will be released in due course.'

'In due course?' she shot back too loudly.

'Yes dear,' a phrase Inga hated. 'There are procedures we need to adhere to and he will be set free all in good time.'

'Let's not forget the procedures,' Inga muttered. 'But what about Mindi Brookes?' she threw at this Delaney woman all made up to the nines. 'You know as well as I do,' she said and somehow stopped herself from poking a finger in her direction. 'She killed the poor woman and our evidence points to her killing two more, and far as we can make out Carly Hills, Christine Streeter, Susan Sewell and goodness knows who else she's been masquerading as, is as guilty as hell.' She sighed her frustration. 'We're talking about a serial offender here, not some bit of a druggie off a sink estate.'

'Inga please,' said Darke to calm her. 'Your concern is fully justified, but please allow Marcus to explain.' Inga came very close indeed to swearing in Swedish and including one universal four letter word they would have all have recognised. 'In return he is willing to divulge all the information he has on the whole case.' Inga spotted this Harriett woman nodding out of the corner of her eye.

Why Inga wondered, do people like this Marcus Spence have to make a statement just with what they wear. She'd not ever seen the like of that mushy-pea coloured suit. Was this him desperately trying to dress casual? He was usually awash with pin stripes and a teenie weening knot in his silk tie.

'We can give you the whole nine yards, I have information from Christine Streeter which will I am sure answer all your questions, and in fact if you still have unanswered ones I'm sure we can do our very best to assist you. I will be first to acknowledge how this has been a very complex issue covering many years, and I can assure you my understanding is such that Thomasz Borowiak will be well compensated for,' he hesitated. 'His inconvenience, shall we call it.'

The voice inside was screaming at Inga to give him a mouth full, to scream the office down. Inconvenience? The poor bastard had been locked in a cell probably twenty three hours a day for getting on for eleven years. Her crazy brain told her amounted to over four thousand days and nights he may well have cried himself to sleep over something he knew he had not done. Eleven birthdays and eleven Christmases. Eleven years he would never get back, ever.

'That's it is it?' she threw at this Marcus. 'We just forget it all, pretend it didn't happen? This being pushed under the carpet I suppose?' Inga spotted Darke shaking his head before she looked at Harriett Delaney. 'You telling Mindi Brookes parents?' She sighed deeply and shook her head. 'No I guess not, be our job no doubt.'

'Inga,' was Darke and motioned towards smooth Marcus.

Inga had spotted three cups and saucers the moment she walked in, and when she sat down a plate of biscuits the like of which she'd never seen Darke offer to anybody before. In fact she was used to him nicking spare biscuits from her team given half a chance.

'Christine Streeter I'm sorry to say has terminal cancer,' shook Inga rigid and as it sunk in Craig Darke slid a letter in her direction. 'Truth of the matter is, and as I say we'll go into the detail of this shortly, I'm afraid it would appear this is behind what has been going on recently.' Her eyes quickly scanned the letter confirming what the smooth git sat beside her had said.

'Why didn't somebody say?' she asked loudly. Was it what all the make-up and pong had been about, had the cancer done its worst and this was her giving herself a boost?

'The unfortunate death of Mindi Brookes, of Charlotte Elliott and Jane Green are all linked to two things,' Spence went on. 'Bullying and cancer. I believe she cannot face the prospect once again, as has always been the case throughout her life it would appear. She is once again playing the role of the victim.' He hesitated a moment, as if he found the whole business upsetting. 'She said to me in a number of the private conversations we have had. I've only ever been the sacrificial lamb, the muggins,' and he shook his head in a sad motion. 'The perpetrators as far as she was concerned would be getting off scott free once again. Those at school, the man she lived with and a guilty woman at work all of whom wanted to turn Christine from a completely innocent bystander who knew right from wrong at an early age into a victim once more.'

'I do have to say,' said Harriett. 'Her upbringing from what we've heard from Marcus here couldn't have done anything but harm. Some people really shouldn't be allowed to have children. From what information I have been able to gather her mother in particular virtually set her up to be bullied.'

'As some do of course,' said Marcus Spence and looked surprisingly solemn.

'Surprise really,' said Craig Darke. 'She didn't have her mother on the list.' He nodded his head as Harriett went to speak. 'Yes I know, which would have led us straight to her of course or at least told us she was still alive probably.'

'And she's clever enough to realize it.'

'Are you saying Streeter held onto all this bullying business all this time,' Inga queried. 'Had done nothing about it then or since and waited until somebody told her she'd got cancer and decided she'd not suffer on her own anymore?'

'About the size of it,' said Darke.

'Terminal,' said Marcus. 'Let that not be forgotten.'

'The trigger you could say,' said the CPS woman.

'Borowiak has served including time on remand getting on now for eleven years,' said Marcus. 'He's the one who bullied her, beat her black and blue who she didn't kill, but she certainly made him suffer.'

Inga pointed to her right. 'I've got a team along there who've been battling with this for ages, their brains have been turned inside out by it all. Meeting people who were not who they thought they were. None of which made sense.' she told Marcus in particular. 'All the acres of stuff I've read about taking on a new identity says chose a new you and stick with it. Not her, not Streeter. My team were told by more than one person about this timid weak thing at school, since when they have met a woman supposed to be at home cooking a meat pie, two more met an astute brunette businesswoman. Are you telling me those two and the one downstairs right now in full make-up with curly blonde hair...' She stopped when Marcus started to chuckle.

'Sorry,' the grinning man held up both hands. 'But she's been playing games with you.' He bit his bottom lip. 'Her last big fling you could say.'

'Going out with all flags flying,' was unnecessary from a grinning Harriett Delaney

As far as a furious Inga was concerned, they were taking client confidentiality too far. How long she wondered had he been party to all she was getting up to? She glanced across at Craig Darke and his sombre face clearly had a message. Was Spence in talks with her before she killed Mindi Brookes she wondered? And the CPS, how long had they been in cahoots with all this? How legal was all this she wondered. For a fleeting moment her brain told her the media would pay an absolute fortune to be a fly on the wall.

'What happens now? Think as we speak my DS is making her another cup of tea,' even Inga had to chortle at when she imagined Jake still wading through the guff of the sickly pong. 'With a biscuit,' she added as a hint Darke didn't pick up on.

'We need to run through the statutory procedures,' Harriett Delaney advised firmly. 'You will need to formally charge her, she will then be bailed into the custody of Marcus here and in the morning she will appear before the Magistrates who will have been briefed and they will remand her.'

'Tomorrow?' Inga asked. 'Saturday morning?' she reminded them all.

'Special session before the scurrilous media get wind of it,' astounded Inga.

How much had that all cost, how long had these bastards been organizing it all, Inga wanted to know? Her team had been driving themselves insane and all the time they knew, they bloody well knew!

'Think what we have to bear in mind,' said Craig. 'Is the amount of media attention all this will create. High profile cases such as this always cause the Home Office and beyond that the government, great concern. We need to be seen to carry out our procedures as we would for any similar case, but we have to consider a vast proportion of the public will inevitably see her as a victim.'

'We realize,' Marcus took over. 'How a considerable number of column inches will be written after her demise, and it will of course all come out about her family, how she was bullied at school, then by Borowiak and finally at work.'

'Not to mention cancer to add to the mix.'

'Always a very emotive subject.'

'And after she's been in front of the magistrates?' Inga really wanted to know as she tried to get her head round all this she really had no wish to be party to. Opening the court on a Saturday in the High Street, getting staff in, organizing security and a co-operative magistrate, all that and the prison van when all she got were constant reminders about her budget. A budget she had been wasting carrying on with all this nonsense!

'The government has what amounts to a hospice for such cases,' Harriett said.

On behalf of joe public Inga wanted to protest about so much. Prisoners were normally sent to prison and if there were health issues they'd be dealt with on the hospital wing. Taken to the local hospital, often in handcuffs for specialist treatment. What was so special about bloody Streeter?

'She'll be driven away in a security van of course,' Darke took up the story. 'Before they get a chance to get photos of her through the windows for some reason I've never managed to figure. Then we have arranged for her to be transferred out of sight to a car and driven to her remote destination.'

Inga sat there was astounded by the fact she and her weary team had been chasing this woman all this time. Until a matter of minutes ago she and Jake both starving hungry had been sat in the soulless interview room battling for a confession and all the time the powers that be had irons in the fire sorting out what was going to happen to her. She so wanted to ask this Marcus how long he had been her client, how long had he been in talks with Streeter while her team were scratching their heads to bring the whole matter to a conclusion?

Next time Darke dared to mention budgets she'd remind him of this very expensive debacle.

She was worldly wise enough to know if she did ask she'd not get a straight or honest answer from any of them.

'In case you are wondering why she is being dealt this way,' said Craig surprisingly. 'From our point of view, it really is all to do with the force's image I'm sorry to say. There is little to be gained by us slapping her in irons, dragging a dying woman through the courts and throwing her into a prison cell when she has less than three months to live, at the outside.'

'Can I just say,' said Marcus Spence. 'By doing things this way there are people who will most certainly benefit. I have been given the sole rights to her story. Since the day she was diagnosed, Christine has been writing her story right back to her bad times at school. Which is now in my possession and I will in due course be selling it to the highest bidders obviously for book rights. Plus I should imagine TV and film rights no doubt.' He sucked in a breath in a most unbecoming manner. 'All proceeds, and I would expect them to be considerable, she has asked be given to an anti-bullying charity of her choice.'

Inga was sat there still struggling to take this all in, and she wondered how long Craig Darke had also been party to all this.

'You'd better start thinking what actress you'd like to play you in the movie,' was Harriett being frivolous, but it was certainly an intriguing thought.

'I'll order more coffee, if it will suit everybody,' said Darke. 'Then perhaps we can give Inga here a run through of the elements she has missed out on in her enquiries.'

26

First thing Inga Larsson noticed was a distinct lack of those dark chocolate chip biscuits from the previous day when she entered Craig Darke's office early doors the next morning with Jake in tow. In fact, there was not even a smell of coffee.

'Good morning,' said Darke sat there at his desk, as the pair took their seats. 'Have you seen the papers?'

'No,' was all Inga managed before he went on.

'How in God's name did they get wind of all this?' he said as he picked up a copy of the *Daily Mail* and waved it about. 'Serious questions being asked on the one hand and yards of sympathy on the other as you can imagine.'

'And we'll have weeks of it. Be worse than Brexit.'

'Not sure anything could be that bad,' he offered. 'I've sent you the first part of the report from Marcus Spence,' said Darke. 'Certainly thrown up a major surprise.' He smiled and nodded his head just slightly. 'I can see now why there was so much confusion, wonder she didn't tie herself in knots, let alone us.'

'Assume nothing has changed overnight,' Inga said.

'No. Everything as is,' he looked at his watch for no reason. 'Due in court around eleven and I'll poke my nose in just to make sure.'

'D'you not trust them, sir?' Jake asked.

'Not a matter of trust Jake, but to a degree this is unprecedented. At least in my experience.' Craig Darke gave a hint of a shrug. 'This is just a PR exercise to be honest.' The newspaper got another wave. 'Can you imagine what social media's like this morning?'

'Trolls'll must think it's Christmas!'

'What this is all about,' and he stabbed the paper with his forefinger. 'No idea how far up the ladder this has all gone but I can guess.'

'Not unprecedented surely,' Inga suggested. 'Prisoners have gone into hospices before and wasn't a Great Train Robber in a normal NHS place or somewhere for ages?'

'But in those cases they'd at least served a term in prison. Remember the nearest she'll come to a cell will be in the hour or so journey in the security van later this morning. I'm sure they're only doing it for the press.' He put a hand up. 'I know, I know,' he said.

'Don't look at me,' said Inga. 'I probably agree with you. We should have got to her sooner, got her a spell on remand at least, then go to a hospice or whatever it is.'

'Wishful thinking,' said a smiling Darke. 'Back to it,' he said reading from his monitor. 'When she left Borowiak she changed her identity to Susan Sawyer, because the poor kid had drowned. It's the old ploy we've seen a hundred times, take up the identity of a dead person, and in Sawyer's case of course she was young enough not to have a passport, no National Insurance Number, no driving licence. She was perfect.'

'What I'm saying is, how long has Marcus Spence been part of all this? How much of a head start could we have had if he'd spilled the beans?'

'He's a lawyer,' Jake scoffed.

'Yeah right.'

'Think there'll be plenty screaming on social media for an enquiry into CPS's involvement.'

'I think you're right Jake, but I do think both Marcus and Harriett Delaney have come into this late, since the death of Brookes at least.'

'That what they claim?'

'No, just my feeling.'

'Somebody will find out I'm sure,' said Inga pointing at the newspaper on Darke's desk.

'Be the Sundays.'

'You can run but you can't hide from social media nowadays.'

'Anyway,' said Darke wanting to move on. 'She set her life up as Susan Sawyer, she's a real person with a real identity. Bank account, National Insurance Number, property owner, phone in her new name and all the rest of the things we have in life.'

'The one my team met twice.'

'But,' said Jake. 'Different people. Remember two of the lads met her as Gray in Sheffield were not the same as Julie and Ruth the two who met Susan Sawyer.'

'And that didn't happen by chance.'

'All will become clear,' said Darke. 'For some reason she decided to take on another persona.' He raised his left hand in a gesture to stop further interruption. 'Don't ask me why,' he pointed to his screen. 'Not explained why in here, except it says she became somebody else.'

'Yet.'

'Be in the film no doubt,' Inga sighed. 'Something happened I bet and it occurred to her how having a second identity would be useful.'

'She became Carly Hills,' he said calmly. 'She used the name and the blonde get-up and everything you saw yesterday to play the part. But, only when there was no officialdom involved. For anything to do with banking, legal stuff, paying tax, buying and selling the properties she was still Susan Sawyer, but to the local people she was Carly Hills.'

'What we have to remember is, people were looking for her. Could be she had an inkling somebody was getting close.'

'She was Carly Hills to that Hope Parkes,' Inga popped in. 'And, she worked for the spa as one of their business friends – have you heard the like - as a Carly Hills.'

'Clever,' said Jake. 'No National Insurance needed, no pre-employment checks, she was in effect a casual subbie.' He turned to Inga. 'Sub-contractor.'

'To the Parkes woman she was Carly Hills from the property company she was running, but companies house have Susan Sawyer down as the owner.' He smirked. 'Looks to me as though to all official purposes Susan Sawyer was employing Carly Hills. It was Carly Hills who dealt with the estate agents, and as you say with the Hope Parkes woman.'

'Why do that?' Jake Goodwin asked. 'That would drive you insane?'

'Wouldn't mind going back up to the cottage of hers and asking about. I bet the locals think she was Carly Hills who rented the place off Susan Sawyer.' Inga blew out a breath. 'It's mind boggling.' She sat there thinking as Darke peered at his monitor again. 'Worked though didn't it,' said Inga.

'Only by sheer chance we ever heard of a Carly Hills,' Jake suggested. 'Who was it mentioned her in the first place?' he asked his DI.

'Must have been Angela Wilcox,' she replied slowly after a slight pause and looked at her boss. 'The Army woman.'

Jake chortled. 'That's ridiculous!' he said. 'If she hadn't been bitten by a rattlesnake we'd never have found out she even existed.' He just shook his head.

'She's only back home now because she was bitten by the snake,' Inga told Darke. 'They decided in case there were complications to be careful and sent her home.' She could see what was going through his mind.

'Do you ever stop to think how amazingly complicated life is?' Darke asked. 'If it were not for a rattlesnake over in...'

'Belize.'

'Belize,' he repeated. 'Biting an army officer, we'd not have known about a Carly Hills and...' he just allowed to drift away.

'Turn right at the next road junction leads you into a different life to the one you encounter if you turn left. Decide to become a paramedic rather than a policeman, choose not to go drinking with your pals where you would have met a handsome young man.'

'That's life.'

'Just a small example of how complicated life is,' said Darke.

'And why with the help of Chrissie Streeter, Susan Sawyer and Carly Hills and....'

'D'you know, I'd almost forgotten about Christine Streeter.'

'And isn't it exactly what the world did and Susan Sawyer was able to take over?'

'Is it any wonder we had our work cut out?'

How is Streeter feeling right now? Inga wondered sat in her office with the door closed wondering how she should deal with it all? This is one guilty woman who won't have to suffer the indignity of a prison cell and all the loathsome goings on you find in any prison. She also won't have to face the judge with his black cap and some vicar insisting he calls on her no matter what her religious feelings to pray with her the night before. Last Rites would be a better bet. Christine Streeter will never have to suffer as the politically correct hangwoman stands there and slowly slips the black hood over her head. By then your minute is down to a few seconds before the big drop. She'll not have to suffer the racing beating heart, the inability to think straight, the last breath, the ...

Amongst the Major Incident Team there will be those she is aware of who will be sorry this Chrissie doesn't face the death penalty like those shouting the odds on social media.

Inga had just not bothered to bring up Twitter or any of the other sites she scarcely bothered with, but she could imagine how *#Chrissie Streeter* was trending right now worldwide bigger, better and more popular than *#Weinstein*, *#DonaldTrump* or *#StormBrian*.

Others in her close knit team will be sorry to be told Streeter'll not have to rot in jail for the rest of her life. How very few ever do? She knows they will all agree she has to be punished, but many Inga is fully aware of, will have some thoughts for her and how she has also suffered over the years and is suffering right now from the c-word.

They may not say it to her face, but Inga knew people will ask who it was who cast the first stone?

There'll be a lot of talk of her human rights no doubt. What about Mindi Brookes and Judy Green just for starters, what about their human rights, and those of their families?

Some of her supporters and there will be plenty that's for sure, will be happy she'll not have to fork out for much of a bill for all the legal work. Streeter will not pay back a penny of the taxpayers hard earned cash spent over the years footing the bill in the vain search for her. Nor will she be responsible for coming up with compensation for the time Borowiak stagnated in a cell for donkey's years. What about *his* human rights?

Sat with her slender hands steepled Inga's thoughts were of a mature woman who started off by making the man in her life suffer by being incarcerated for no good reason. The very same woman who then went on to hand out dying like it was going out of fashion.

Inga glanced out into her incident room without making it obvious, aware as ever it was her role in life to ensure perpetrators such as Streeter are put away for a very long time.

Something she was aware would not happen this time round. First serial killer she could include on her service CV, but the one who'll never languish in a cell.

27

'I know this is not going to be easy, but you really do need to ignore any rumours running riot around this place. Put all your preconceived ideas out of your mind,' said Inga with her backside perched against a table top in front of her main crew.

Storm Brian had not hit Lincoln yet and in fact in typical British style the morning had been bathed in sunshine and blue sky.

Her hard working colleagues who had chased this Christine Streeter up hill and down dale now had to have it all explained. Or at least pass on what she herself had been told. The official line as it were. 'Just get everyone settled then I'll do my best with what I know.'

No matter what anyone thinks of their Swede they were all totally aware how she had cleaned some serious shit off Lincoln's streets and would continue to do so.

Those from PHU who had been attached to the main team during the early days of the enquiry had been invited to return to listen in.

'Quiet, please,' Jake ordered. 'Sit down.'

'Where shall I start?' Inga grinned nervously once all the backsides were seated. 'What I'm about to tell you is not yet for public consumption,' she said slowly and purposefully. 'That said, I have to admit I don't think I have the full story, for that you will probably have to wait for the film to come out to get all the nitty gritty.'

'What you on about?'

'Say that again.'

'Be serious,' all came out.

'How about the summer of 2006?' Inga said to bring chatter to a halt. 'It's the World Cup in Germany. Think George Bush, Iraq and Tony Blair. With all that going on this woman was planning to escape from her partner Thomasz Borowiak while his mind was elsewhere. Beaten black and blue but only where it didn't show on many an occasion when something didn't please him.'

'And she didn't think to come to us of course?' was almost a sighed aside.

'She had decided to do a runner, but more than that. Actually become somebody else entirely, and her traumatic schooldays were her inspiration, probably because the nightmare of those times were still at the forefront of her memories. Christine Streeter decided about eight months previous around Christmas time when the big present she bought him for Christmas didn't suit and he'd had a serious strop. This was never just a plan to pack a bag and walk out the door one night and take pot luck with the certainty of a very angry of Borowiak chasing after her. She planned it and probably for the first time in her life lady luck stepped in.'

'Why so long?' Sandy MacLachlan wanted to know.

'Serious planning to make absolutely sure, plus of course a distinct lack of money,' Inga replied. 'She had decided to become Susan Sawyer because she knew she was dead, and completely unbenown to Borowiak she set about creating a new identity.' She looked at Kenny, 'Stuff like that takes time when you're doing it all under cover so to speak. She applied for a National Insurance Number and then a passport using Susan Sewell's birth certificate and anything else she could lay her hands on. Probably had more false documentation, but so far I've not had the time to dig deep. Save to say whatever it was, it worked. When the passport arrived it was the key to everything I should imagine. She could open a bank account, do all sorts. Remember all this time Borowiak was still being the nasty bastard he was and probably still is and she had to keep this double life hidden.'

'Must have been a nightmare,' said Brown-Reid. 'Especially if he was some sort of control freak wanting to know what she's up to all the time, like they do.'

'Just with something like the passport,' said Ruth. 'She'd have to dash home and check the post before he could. Musta been in a hell of a state half the time.'

'All the time.'

'If I were him I'd ask t'stay inside!' said Scott. 'Whole damn world'll be after him when he gets oot.'

A hand from Inga brought peace to the room. 'Then after months of planning and saving on the quiet our Susan Sawyer or Christine Streeter's luck changed. She won the Lottery.'

Ruth stuck her hand in the air, amongst the hub-bub. 'Can I just say, it's one of the things I read about a great deal. When you decide to change your identity it's the things which appear right out of the blue to can cause you most problems. Things you'd not given any thought to.'

Inga had to wait for the chatter to die down, and took such an opportunity to drink her coffee.

'Cheque of course was in her new name. She did two things. Bought expensive wigs and bought a house up in the Yorkshire Dales. Exactly where Christine Streeter has been living with her new identity all this time. Once the initial fuss died down and Borowiak was behind bars she bought another little house up there and opened it as a holiday let. Then another, six in all and all managed for her.'

'No yacht, no Lamborghini,' Sam smirked and grinned.

'Nothing at all to attract attention. No swanky clothes, no foreign holidays I shouldn't imagine.'

'And being incognito nobody would turn up for a week's holiday and think, I recognize that woman,' Goodwin contributed.

'Hang on,' said Scott. 'This female just turns up in a village just when some woman's gone missing...'

'Who saw Christine Streeter today?' Inga butted in and three put their hands up. 'Did she look to you like the mealy mouthed little thing from school they talk about?' She pointed at Scott. 'If she looked like that in the village they'd be none the wiser I can assure you. Even the back view on the CCTV from Peterborough looks absolutely nothing like she did today.'

'Think ma'am,' said Jake. 'She must be wearing padding.'

'Could well be right. Gets home to her little cottage, takes it all off and relaxes. Good life, no more bullying, no worries. Glass of wine...lovely.' Inga took another sip.

'Why she not just stay there?' Julie wanted to know.

'Don't know of course and assume it'll all come out in the book she's written, but I think boredom set in.'

'You serious about a book?'

'A book and a film I guess, or a TV series at the very least I should imagine.' Inga then took time to drink more coffee and knew this was annoying the team trying to fathom what was going on.

'Sorry ma'am, but I don't understand.' Kenny admitted.

'All in good time,' she retorted. 'Then she made a fatal mistake, she got herself a job.'

'That'd take some doing,' said Sandy. 'What she do about references? Surely Susan Sawyer never had a job.'

'As I say, just take what I've been told,' annoyed Inga responded. 'I don't have chapter and verse on every little issue she would have faced. Maybe she bought herself into a job, I don't know.' She took a moment to smile at them all. 'How about if I tell you she also became somebody else?'

'Could have offered to work for nothing. Had a friend who knew someone.'

'Hang on, hang on,' she chided. 'Before you get carried away think on this. She bought a blonde wig and became Carly Hills, the girl who went to Canada.'

'What for?' wasn't the only comment.

'To get a job as a swimming instructor at the spa for starters.'

'She went there as a sub-contractor,' said Jake. 'Is our reckoning.'

'Then she came across our Mindi Brookes, and to cut a long story short because I don't have the full version, Mindi Brookes it would appear just happened to be on the fiddle, and decided to blame Carly Hills the new girl.' She stopped to giggle. 'What was it they called her? Business Friend or some such twaddle. Of course Carly couldn't be in trouble with the police because the moment we got involved the chances are her cover as Carly would have been blown.' Inga took a good drink of her luke warm coffee. 'Which would possibly have led to Susan Sawyer and then quite possibly to Chrissie Streeter. So she took the blame, confessed I guess, and quit almost on the spot.'

'Until,' said a grinning Jake Goodwin and two or three looked across at him.

'Until she was diagnosed with cancer,' from Inga stopped them all in their tracks. 'Year or so down the line and it gets worse and our Christine Streeter decided she wasn't going to be the loser on her own all over again, so she planned to take Elliott, Green, Nevins and particularly Brookes with her.'

'Blood tests,' said Ruth before others could follow suit.
'Exactly,' said Inga. 'Without it we'd still be up a gumtree.'
'Balance of her mind would have been disturbed.'
'Probably right,' the boss responded. 'Killed Elliott and Green. Then Mindi Brookes of course who she had worked with, but she couldn't find Helen Nevins. Time had begun to run out big time. Decided to come clean as it were, to leave a calling card. Wetting the bed was her returning to society, then she persuaded Hope Parkes to allow her to use her kitchen for an hour or two.'

'Why?' swarthy Raza asked before anybody else could pose the same question.

'Her idea of fun, rather than just sitting in her cottage up there waiting to die or walking into a cop shop and handing herself in, she did it all I think to take her mind of what lay ahead. Hope Parkes and her husband have been saving like mad to buy their house, but like so many struggle to get the deposit together. Christine Streeter aka Susan Sawyer owns the house and in exchange for a bit of fun with you Raza, she has given them the deposit in payment.'

'We never asked her if she knew Susan Sewell,' said Ruth.

'Exactly,' said the DI. 'It was no good asking her if she knew Angela Wilcox or Christine Streeter, as Hope Parkes didn't know anybody by that name. All along she was telling the truth.'

'And the business at the hotel was…'

'Just a joke,' a grinning Inga responded to Julie. 'Four of you met the same woman, four of you met Christine Streeter but you didn't know you had.'

'And now?' Sandy wanted to know and was not the only one. 'Twitter's gone berserk!'

'In court this morning as you know, be remanded, but it'll never come to court. Christine Streeter has three months max.'

'What was that bit about a film?' Brown-Reid asked after a period of thought and reflection.

'Just a minute,' said Inga to a subdued team. 'She's not going to prison, she's going straight to a special hospice the government uses.' She shook her head. 'Don't ask. I've no idea where it is, didn't know it even existed.'

'And the film?'

'Her solicitor has been handed the media rights to her story. Book, television, film, you name it, the whole caboodle is my guess.'

'A get out of jail card, via Netflix!'

'Wonder which way round it'll all be? Fact becoming fiction or the other way?'

'Some of the stupid fictional depictions actually turn up as fact somewhere down the line. Be interesting to see which way she goes with her version.'

'Like concrete shoes,' said Jake and Inga spun her head to look at him seeking an explanation with a look he recognized. 'How many times have mobsters and the mafia in novels been dropped into the sea in concrete shoes?'

'Easy way out for writers.'

'Some poor soul actually turned up like that,' said Sandy to take the wind out of Jake's sail.

'What I was about to say,' said an exasperated DS. 'Could well be the first time a bit of fiction has turned up as fact a year or so back. Just used to be legend of course but the yanks found a body of this scrote with his feet in blocks of cement.'

'Wonder how many more are on the sea bed.'

'Will be interesting to see how madam plays it.'

'All just shows anything's possible these days.'

'One thing's for sure, she'll be dead famous.' There was a combined noisy sucking in of breaths. 'Good title for her book!'

28

'Trust me to miss one as brilliant as that!' said DC Nicky Scoley as she smiled sardonically at her ex-boss. 'You'll never beat that will you? Go to work and get bitten by a rattlesnake.'

'Not surprised it's the one from this case. All been so bizarre, right from day one.' Inga looked all around one of their favourite coffee houses. 'Should probably be head down dealing with the wash-up right now, but there's been so much going on over the past couple of weeks.' She sipped her drink. 'I needed this.'

Inga just trying to get her breath back from a tortuous weekend she'll probably never forget. Even getting into the staff car park first thing had been easier said than done with kamikaze journalists and TV crews jostling in front of her MG.

'Her blood was finally your breakthrough you say?'

'When she disappeared back in 2006 she'd never had her blood taken so she didn't know and her parents didn't know it was rare. Only when we went through all the forensics from back then did we discover.' Inga shrugged and grinned. 'From there it was easy after all the cancer tests and treatment.'

Both aware as ever for the need to keep their voices down, as butterscotch blonde Nicky changed tack. 'Like we've said before, you just never know. The journey we go on from the initial call-out, if we knew what lay ahead we'd never believe it.' Nicky dipped her biscotti biscuit in her cappuccino.

Inga chuckled. 'I still think getting up on Monday morning knowing you're going to spend the day pretending to be somebody else runs the rattlesnake very close.'

'Couple of cases down the line and something else will beat this one into a cocked hat.'

'People seem surprised she got away with it so long.'

Inga Larsson had kept in touch with Nicky Scoley a former member of her team. It had been a long time since the pair had enjoyed a Monday morning Fika together. Swedish for coffee, cake and a chat. Nicky was now well settled down in Cambridge working on totally different aspects of criminal law. Her parents of course still lived in the city and it was an ideal opportunity for the pair to catch up on all their news.

'Not now we've got most of the story. First cold case I've solved at the same time as a hot one.' Inga grinned. 'Not that I actually solved it in the end.'

'Glad I wasn't here for it. Would have driven me up the wall.' She paused to sip some chocolate covered froth at the top of her cappuccino.

'Must admit I was amazed you can do things like getting a false National Insurance Number so easily. Even with the internet thought it'd still be some sleaze down a back alley.'

'Some children grow up under the radar, they never visit a doctor, don't go to school. People don't ask about them so why would they ask about a woman moving into a cottage down the end of a lane like she did?' Nicky saw Inga look at her. 'One of the things I've been working on recently. Folk who don't exist.'

'Lot of it of course is to do with home education. That really worries me.'

'Horror stories coming out all of a sudden, almost as if people have got a down on it.'

'Actually the best place to hide is in a teeming big city, where most people don't even know who their next door neighbours are.'

Nicky who having grown her thick hair slightly longer since her days with MIT, was back to her cappuccino, before she responded. 'Thousands go missing every year, and they can't all be dead. I wonder just how many of them have taken on a new identity like your woman did.'

'Just look to your left,' Inga suggested and Nicky glanced momentarily. 'The guy there reading the paper. There is absolutely nothing unusual about him, he's casually dressed but nothing outlandish and I wouldn't assume they're his work clothes, but what is he doing in here having a coffee at this time of the morning? Why isn't he at work?'

'Could be anybody. He could well be a young lad who went missing from home in Surrey fifteen years ago, and his family are still absolutely desperate for news.'

'Just on a day off.'

'Worked at the weekend.'

'Been to the hospital for an appointment, or doctors.'

'Could be absolutely anybody,' Nicky offered. 'But he could be wanted, might well be a male version of your mystery woman. Possible somebody we're after,' she offered before another sip.

Inga had stopped putting a piece of her raspberry and almond bake in her mouth to watch a woman a few tables away. 'Of course,' she admitted. 'Woman over there eating a toasted sandwich wearing gloves reminds me. Streeter was making a pie at the house in Sheffield. Raza went on and on about. Watched her wearing Marigolds to make pastry.' She snorted out a breath. 'Fingerprints. That was to stop her leaving fingerprints.'

'Every trick in the book sounds to me.'

'How many coppers, how much time, how much money has been spent over the years looking for her? And all the time she was living up there in a cottage quite content we assume. Just like him over there, not in hiding, there for all to see.'

'What's that Swedish saying of yours about liars?'

'A liar will only be trusted once.'

'And how many times was she trusted?' made them both giggle.

'But we don't see, do we? Don't see what's staring us in the face sometimes.' Nicky insisted. 'We walk along head down. Do we look up at buildings, notice the fine architecture quite often? No of course we don't, so is it little wonder she was just swanning about and nobody noticed.'

'He could be wanted for murder,' Inga suggested with a nod in the direction of the dark haired newspaper reader. With that Nicky took another look and was smiling when she turned back. 'When he went missing he could have worn glasses, now he could easy have contact lenses, makes a lot of difference.'

'Woman to his right wearing dark glasses. What's that all about on a dull dark October morning? Who or what is she hiding from?'

'Just shows how easy it all is, and how many there are.'

'Talking of dressing up, see all the Halloween nonsense is everywhere again,' said Inga spotting a poster.

'Not your scene if I remember right?'

'There's no Halloween tradition in Sweden,' Inga confirmed to her colleague. 'Certainly nothing when I was growing up. Just forced on us by America, and we don't have trick-or-treat and certainly no specific sweets or snacks.'

'At home we pretty much ignore it too, but at least we have Guy Fawkes.'

'Since we've had the web, getting a false passport and other stuff has become dead easy. Interesting though. She never applied for a passport, or at least not in her real name or the Carly one she borrowed.' Inga finally took the chance to eat a piece more delicious cake. 'Be a bit too tricky. A passport. Too invasive?'

'There are so many pitfalls down the line,' said Nicky Scoley. 'Maybe that's the one people fall foul of. But you have to wonder when do you realize you have become the person?' She glanced at the man with the paper again. 'When did he realized he really was Joe Soap no longer? Had become a new person?' She waited for Inga to take a sip of her drink. 'Take a while I bet.'

'Then right out of the blue up pops someone like Mindi Brookes,' Inga sighed. 'Urgh,' she grimaced. 'The name really grates on me.'

'Bet you're not the only one.'

'Just imagine you've accomplished all you've set your heart on, you have built a new life as a new person free from all the bad stuff and suddenly this Mindi bitch came into her life.'

'Bet when the film comes out it'll just be a boring bit.'

'I'm more worried about how they'll depict the police!'

'Tell me I'm wrong but wasn't there a programme at one time something along the lines of killing made me famous?'

'*Murder Made Me Famous*, I think it was or something like that.'

'This'll certainly make her famous,' Nicky chuckled.

'Just goes to show what twaddle these celebrities come out with saying they can't step outside their front door without being hounded by the media. She was more newsworthy than they'll ever be and was walking about for donkey's years, and nobody spotted her.'

'On the subject of stepping out of her door, is her cottage really nice?' Nicky asked.

'It's really lovely, super location on the moors, very quiet but it's been well updated. Love a look round to be honest. Day we went was not the best, all wet and chilly.'

'It'll be coming on the market.'

'Don't tempt me!'

'All set for the big day then?' Nicky queried.

'Not been easy,' Inga admitted. 'Organizing a Bröllop in Stockholm from here.'

'A what?'

'Bröllop, a Swedish wedding.'

'I can't wait,' Nicky admitted. 'Be interesting to see a wedding in another country.'

'Think I've managed to miss all the pitfalls.'

'Such as?'

'Being told for months on end how the best wedding ideas can be found on social media.'

'Smoasting seems to be the crutch for everything these days,' Nicky saw the look on her boss's face. 'Social media boasting.'

Inga sneered. 'Time you found yourself a husband young lady.'

'Boyfriend would be a start,' she laughed at.

Inga glanced across at a woman who had caught her eye. 'Did you see that?' she asked. 'That one in the stripes, she just pulled out the neck of her top and sneezed inside it.' As Nicky turned her head. 'She's doing it again.'

'What's she up to?' the DS gasped.

'That's four times. Oh no…God I thought she was about to wipe her nose on it.'

'I've never seen the like.'

'Look around us,' said an indignant Inga. 'How nice do most of these people look, decent and well behaved of all ages, know how to eat and drink properly. Kids behaving themselves, not running amok except for a couple near the door,' she just sighed and shook her head, then drained the dregs of her drink.

'Do people like her not realize they're out of kilter with society, how come they never realize decent people don't behave in such a way, ever?' Nicky saw the woman wipe her nose with the back of her hand and silently sniggered at the look on Inga's face. 'We've got to stop this, pulling people to bits over coffee.'

'Not all the time the world is full of the despicable like her we're not.'

'Has there ever been a crime cluster pattern based on Lincoln before do we know?' Nicky posed.

Inga grimaced and considered. 'One victim died down your way in Peterborough remember, so it'll be difficult to claim.'

'Hemlock woman.'

29

It had been good catching up with young Nicky again, up in the city visiting her parents for the weekend. Now back at her desk in Lincoln Central Inga Larsson could tell by the look on her colleague's face and her gestures signaled what she was being told was very interesting.

'They didn't waste much time,' Ruth said when the call finished and she slipped her phone away 'Sandy, passing on a bit of gossip he thought you'd be interested in.' Ruth smiled as she hesitated. 'The Brookes' have given Aaron Kempshall notice to quit.'

'What d'you mean notice to quit?'

'Apparently the house is owned by some distant uncle and they want him out.'

'They?'

'Think the oaf Richard Brookes could be a nasty piece of work, certainly not the nicest person I've had the pleasure of talking to recently.'

'Thought we established early on that Mindi didn't leave a will.'

'Guess she was renting off this uncle or whatever, p'raps he's said he wants Kempshall out and if this uncle lives miles away they're doing his dirty work for him.'

'Something I realized after I'd spoken to them,' Ruth admitted. 'At no time was Kempshall mentioned. He of the roll-top bidet and other silliness.'

'If this was Kathleen Streeter I could understand it,' said Inga. 'Her being all terribly religious. Be her getting shot of the nasty man who was living in sin with her daughter,' she sniggered. 'Before he's had a chance to move someone else in.'

'Their problem would be having a united front. Her old man'd be too busy fighting the Battle of Passchendaele or some other one that's got an anniversary next week or next month.'

'Not the nicest person I've come across,' said Inga. 'That Aaron Kempshall. Doing the dirty on Mindi with that hussy down in...'

'Hussy? That's not very Swedish.'

'Heard it off one of you, just like the sound of it,' she admitted with a snigger. 'He might have been doing the dirty but surely losing her under those circumstances was bad enough without them chucking him out as well. Know what I meant to ask. Was there really no horrible perfume pong from Streeter when you met her?'

'Not that I noticed,' said Ruth. 'Well made up, all plucked eyebrow nonsense, quite a bit over the top as people like her do at times.' She chuckled. 'Truth is she was probably hiding the zits which is what it's normally all about.'

'Hiding the ravages of cancer probably.'

Ruth sucked in noisily. 'Didn't think of that.'

'Here's a good question for you,' said Inga seriously. 'What will happen to Streeter's body when she dies?' Before Ruth could comment she carried on. 'Bear in mind when she dies she'll still be innocent?'

'That's a good question. Must have happened before, surely.' Ruth shrugged.

'Talking about property,' said Inga with a change of subject as her earlier chat with Nicky Scoley came to mind. 'Tell you what I thought of the other day I've been meaning to mention about what people have to deal with when they go into work. Choosing paint colours.'

'How d'you mean?'

It was what she and Nicky had done over a period. Pick holes in people over coffee or talk about the odd jobs people do for a living. Inga was not too proud to admit she had missed her chats with Nicky. 'Adam and I were looking for paint a while back,' she said as she pulled her notebook from her bag. 'Came across names like Thread Needle, Churlish Green and India Yellow,' she stopped to look up at her colleague. 'Based apparently on a cow's urine after eating mango leaves.'

'Be serious!'

'Daft names like Nancy's Blushes and Elephant's Breath. What somebody does when they get to work, choose ridiculous names for paint.'

Inga's phone rumbled on her desk. 'Yes Jake,' she said and listened intently and Ruth saw her eyes widen, watched her look all about her probably to check who was close by. 'Of course,' she eventually said softly. 'And I asked the question too,' she said. 'Payback time...yes...you're right. Thanks my man...you be long?'

Inga turned off the call. Slid her phone back onto her desk and sat back with her eyes closed leaning forward across her desk. 'Our murder victim was cloning clients' credit card details and helping herself to goods on the net. Turns out she was living with a guy who was some sort of business consultant with particular emphasis on software. Can't remember what Jake said but it was one of these odd ball jobs that don't make any sense. Process something or other which means in truth he was a crook.' Inga just peered out into the almost empty incident room 'A business friend as they stupidly call them at that spa place found out because a client she knew really well, had money withdrawn.' She stopped to snigger to herself. 'Jake's got all the details. She was running the cards through a skimmer apparently, so the story goes. This friend at the spa reported her, but our victim twisted it round and threatened our missing person with the police.' She smiled. 'Was that a big mistake, or was that a big mistake?' she smirked. 'Police is the one thing the colleague wanted nowhere near her, asking questions, taking fingerprints, DNA,' she said slowly.

'You're joking!' Ruth said too loudly.

'Yep,' said Inga, sat there nodding and then whispered very quietly. 'That's why she got a good stabbing is Jake's guess, and I reckon he may well be right.'

'Well blow me down.' Ruth stood there with her mouth partially open. 'You mean?'

Inga nodded and leant in close enough to whisper. 'Hills was the business friend, and ironically she ran the spa's expensive learn to swim in a week scheme.'

'When you know the answers all the pieces fall into line. They had a swimming pool at Forest School, so they could all swim. Do a course on teaching and she was well away. Probably got a few freebies at the spa too I bet.'

'Not that far surely from where she has her cottage.'

'Of course.'

Inga paused to think. 'From what Jake can gather from that Laurence we met at the spa hotel, he reckons it was just something to fill her time, not a full time job, probably as and when. Every few weeks do a week of swimming crash courses.'

'Nearly blew her whole world apart. North Yorkshire cops up there would have got a shock when they suddenly found who they were dealing with.'

'And when the bad times hit her, she decided some people had to pay the price, and our Mindi was one of them. Hoisted by her own petard, so to speak.'

'That close,' said Ruth clicking her fingers. 'To bringing her house of cards tumbling down. You can guarantee they'll really make something of that in the film.'

'Spa might even get some good publicity if they film up there.'

'Weren't you saying this learning to swim business is a bit pricey?' asked Ruth.

Inga smiled back at her. 'You can say that again,' she hesitated. '£1499.'

Ruth gasped. 'But you get silly food I bet.'

'What's wrong with Tofu Casserole? Just the sort of thing we have for brunch most Saturdays!' she kidded. 'Double room, bed and a lettuce leaf breakfast is £389 a night, so five nights plus the swimming at that price is a good deal. Laurence Haffenden said they have thirty in a session, two classes of fifteen running at a time.'

'That's…'

'I know,' Inga jumped in. 'Forty five grand, with evening meal and extra treatments on top.'

'We're in the wrong business.'

'But at least we've not come across a rattlesnake.'

'Not yet we haven't!'

ACKNOWLEDGMENTS

This of course is a work of complete fiction. Yellowbellies will recognize some of the places but others have simply never existed. Characters of course including all the police are figments of my imagination.

Even so it is obvious some readers are likely to conclude that they are from the real Lincolnshire Police. Please understand that whilst they have very kindly dealt with my queries from time to time neither the organization itself nor their officers have any affiliation with this book.

There is no Lincoln County Police nor is there a Lincoln Central where my team are based. One of the advantages of creating my own police force is that whilst I follow systems as much as I can, I am able to get away with concentrating on the story rather than become bogged down in the minutiae of police procedures.

Any mistakes are all my own work and I'll claim they are made in the interests of the story.

People frequently ask where I get some of the silliness in my books from. A great deal of what you have read has been drawn from hours of research and life experiences, talking to, listening to and just watching the absurd behaviour of real people mixed in with products of my imagination.

Once again my gratitude goes to all those who gave their time and of themselves to assist with research for *In Plain Sight*. Plus of course the many I have observed from afar or overheard

To discover what Inga Larsson and her team become involved in next, read on…

PREVIEW

Easter Monday
2nd April 2018

PC Gemma Harker knew from eight years' experience as a Response Officer how working nights brings out the ugly low-life scrotes and feral plebs getting up to all sorts of illegal and idiotic antics. Boozed-up domestics, fights in and outside lowlife pubs, RTAs and drunk and/or drugged-up drivers. All going on when the world has turned dark and the roads are at their quietest.

Unfortunately, every six weeks she's stuck on nights and her Mikey is on days and life in the car at night can so easily become hour after long hour of sheer tedium.

Fortunately this week was not the norm. Mikey would normally be off to work on his fold-up bike before seven on a Monday morning just as her shift grinds to a halt. This however was good news day, Easter Monday meant he'd be at home when she got there. Still tucked-up in bed if she knew the blighter.

Not the sort to think to get up early, have the kettle on with toaster and poacher ready for action, but then you can't have everything. Actually slipping in beside him might not be a bad idea.

That night with her crew, the younger less experienced PC Hugh Atkinson, they had run up and down the west side of Lincoln on the A46, circuits around the city then back out to the by-pass and down to the roundabout at Swinderby just north of Newark and back three times already. Been pretty boring up to that point, nothing really untoward so far with pubs closed and clubs most certainly not the roaring success they once were. The radio had been ominously quiet except for chatter not aimed at them and that one shout they'd taken on to relieve the boredom.

It was time for a short break which sometimes but not always, works to their advantage. Parked up in a lay-by, lights off opposite the Bentley Hotel just over the roundabout at Pennells heading north.

Sometimes shifts become tediously monotonous with just bits and bobs of criminal damage, minor traffic accidents and drunks acting as if they are on a loop with her having to zip from one to another and sometimes back again. Variety they say is the spice of life and sat there she could certainly do with a bit of spicing up as Hugh beside her chomped another lump of Snickers in his mouth, Gemma did two things. Sat there wondering about his waistline in years to come with all that sugar and the events of the shift so far.

Gemma sat there in the warm just hoping and praying some dork would come round the roundabout behind her on two wheels at stupid speed, step on the gas and shoot off up the road towards the Whisby turn-off. Give her all the excuse she needs and provide a chance for a spot of fun with her "Good evening Mr Hamilton" routine and with any luck there might be a bonus or two as there quite often is.

Smell cannabis when the shed on wheels door is opened, find no insurance for the heap on ANPR with a bit of luck and best of the lot get a good whiff of alcohol on the dope's bad breath. Wipe his tongue, have blow in the tube and another cretin would be off the streets.

Easter Monday she thought and smiled to herself sat there in the dark waiting. Mikey'll be on a day off, so they could go looking at that new furniture when she finishes her shift. He had no idea that's what she had planned, but he'd know soon enough. Idling the time away collecting her thoughts thinking about stuff she needed to do. Always acres of stuff to do.

'Oscar Papa Two.'

Gemma had to answer with Hugh's mouth full of Snickers he was still chomping away at.

'Oscar Papa Two.'

'Oscar Papa Two we have a Grade One report of an incident at Skellingthorpe roundabout. Can you respond?' Gemma had already started the BMW 3 Series as a reaction.

'We can attend from the Bentley. This an RTA?' Gemma responded as she glanced in her empty mirrors and pulled out.

'*Van driver phoned in to report a tramp claiming he's found a body. Grade One.*'

'On our way,' she almost chuckled. 'Where exactly?' Gemma tried so hard to visualize the scenario in her mind as she switched on the blues. Probably not really necessary but it always gave her a bit of a thrill even after all these years.

'*Skellingthorpe roundabout.*'

Gemma just glanced at Hugh for affirmation she wasn't about to ask a stupid question. 'Which road off?'

'*On...the roundabout,*' was said slowly and precisely. Gemma waved her hand at Hugh for him to take over the link to Control and he took down the details of the van driver who had phoned in with the info. She was top side of 70 already belting past the old gravel pits and the little roundabout at Siemens was coming up fast.

'Are you saying this body is actually on the roundabout? Driver, car shot onto it, or been hit by? Which you saying?'

'*All we have,*' said the woman on Control. '*Is this van driver, stopped by a tramp at the roundabout saying a body'd been found.*'

They screamed over the Whisby roundabout and headed up the short stretch to Damons. Over that in two shakes of a lamb's tale and Gemma knew the road so well she could floor it through the woods as the road curved round. The money-can't-buy adrenaline rush was soon over as she slowed for the roundabout ahead.

In her headlights was this scruffy old geezer with a bloody hat on waving his arms in the air. Gemma slowed and drove the whole way round the round then pulled up on the grass verge close to the turn off left to the village. They both got out of the BMW but left all the lights on, the hazards and blues. In addition to her too tight black top, the issue black trousers and boots, she had her stab vest and a yellow hi-viz she was slipping into as they waited for a car to pass with the driver gawping and trotted quickly onto the roundabout to the dishevelled old fella stood on the block paved area before all the mass of trees and bushes start.

'Right,' said Gemma. 'What's this all about then, sir?' she asked this ridiculous looking scruff bag stood there with a black balaclava and a trilby perched on his head.

'Good evening, young lady,' he said and lifted his hat. Gemma had to work really hard to hide her snigger. 'On the lookout for somewhere to get my head down and came across this big bag,' he said pointing back into the dark of the bushes, as a car screamed round past them blaring out music too loud, Gemma would chase if she wasn't intrigued by the old man himself and his story. He was well spoken which was a real surprise. This'd certainly be one to tell Mikey about. 'There's somebody already in it.' He smiled at her. 'Sorry miss, but he's dead.'

'In there?' Gemma asked and pointed into the undergrowth. 'In the bag?'

'Most certainly, my dear.'

'This an April fool?' she whispered to Hugh as they moved away. 'This Sarge taking the piss? We been set up?'

'Bit late if it is, that was yesterday,' he retorted as he glanced over at the tramp.

'He looks like somebody dressed up, don't you think?'

'That's what I was thinking, but who?'

'How should I know?'

TISSUE OF LIES
Available early in 2019

Seaside Snatch
ISBN: 978-1-291-75214-4
By Cary Smith

Lincolnshire Murder Mystery 2

Set in Skegness in 2012

If you were a childless couple absolutely desperate for a family of your very own and were offered a little blonde girl for £15,000 with no questions asked, what would you do?

That's the dilemma facing DCI Luke Stevens who also knows how once that little girl reaches puberty, she will be snatched back for the sex trade.

As desperate couples have been discovering to their utter dismay there is absolutely nothing they can do, nobody they can turn to.

Number 5 on Amazon Kindle British Detectives Bestsellers list.

'*A real pick-me-up but never an easy put down*'

'*Refreshing*'

Available in Paperback and on Kindle from Amazon.

Printed in Great Britain
by Amazon